HACKER
in Love

USA Today and International Bestselling Author
Lauren Rowe

D1452480

Published by SoCoRo Publishing

Cover design © Letitia Hasser, RBA Designs

PLAYLIST

"Birdhouse in Your Soul"—They Might Be Giants

1

HANNAH

"Hi, Hannah Banana Montana Milliken!" Kat Morgan says brightly, answering my call.

Kat's my co-worker turned bestie who's been MIA from our Seattle office this past week while slaving away on a new VIP client account in Las Vegas. Or at least, that's what our hawk-eyed boss thinks Kat's been doing. *Snicker.*

In reality, my blonde bombshell of a bestie has been playing hooky with a young, hot billionaire—a handsome playboy who took one look at Kat's gorgeous vivacity and apparently decided, *"I want to play with her."* Lucky for Josh Faraday, he was exactly Kat's type—hot, funny, and cocky as hell. And so, the glittering pair jetted off to the Neon Capital of the World for a couple days of carefree fun.

After a few days, though, when Kat informed her billionaire fling she had to return to Seattle or risk getting shitcanned, he picked up the phone and "hired" Kat for an "urgent PR job" in Las Vegas—all expenses paid and at Kat's premium rate—thereby ensuring the continuation of their fun without the possibility of Kat suffering any adverse employment consequences.

I've been picking up the slack on Kat's real accounts in her absence, but I'm not salty about it, since Kat's done countless favors for me since joining the firm almost two years ago. Frankly, I'm relieved to finally get the chance to repay her. Plus, the chances are nil I'll ever get to enjoy a scorching-hot fling with a young, hot billionaire, so I've thoroughly enjoyed living vicariously through my party-girl bestie this past week.

"Hey there, Kitty Kat," I say, pressing my phone against my ear. "Sorry to bother you, but I've run into a snag on the barbeque account." I explain the issue, and, not surprisingly, Kat offers a creative suggestion I hadn't contemplated, which we then build upon together to reach a kick-ass solution for our client.

When the work portion of our conversation is done, I lower my voice and ask, "So, are you still having a blast with Mr. Faraday?" I've googled the hell out of one Joshua William Faraday of Faraday & Sons, and it's not hard to see why Kat is currently feeling infatuated with him. Dark hair. Blazing blue eyes. An insanely fit body paired with a cocky grin. With all that going for him, Josh would be Kat's exact type even before adding in his insane wealth—but, of course, the guy being filthy rich and wildly successful on top of everything else certainly doesn't hurt.

"Yeah, I am, as a matter of fact," Kat replies calmly.

I wait, but she doesn't elaborate. It's so unlike my loose lipped, vivacious friend to answer with such calm brevity, it can only mean one thing. I whisper, "He's there and can overhear you?"

"Actually, yeah, he is," Kat replies evenly. But when she adds a little "gah!" to the end of her sentence, I know exactly what she's trying to tell me: *She finally gave in to her white-hot lust and banged the billionaire.*

When we spoke a few days ago, Kat still hadn't slept with Josh, despite her extreme desire to do so, because, she said, he'd surely lose interest on a bullet train if she jumped into bed with him too quickly. During that phone call, Kat explained, "Someone needs to teach that gorgeous, arrogant man he can't have whatever and whomever he wants with a snap of his fancy fingers—*and that someone is going to be me.*" At the time, Kat conceded it would take superhuman willpower on her part to resist Josh for much longer. But, she insisted, she was up to the challenge —determined to abstain for the higher purpose of keeping Josh's attention for as long as possible.

"You had sex with Josh?" I whisper, even though Kat's little "gah!" pretty much confirmed as much.

Kat giggles. "*Yessssssss.*"

I squeal, a bit too loudly for my small cubicle, and then glance toward the hallway, praying I haven't unwittingly attracted our strict boss's attention. Rebecca is a likeable woman outside of the office, but when we're on the clock, she runs a tight ship and doesn't suffer a modicum of bullshit. When it's clear our boss isn't nearby, I return excitedly to my call with Kat. "And was the sex a five-alarm fire, like you predicted?"

"*More,*" Kat breathes, elongating the vowel sound in a way that sounds vaguely orgasmic.

"Katherine Morgan!" I whisper-shout as my cheeks bloom to crimson. "Leave some cookies for the rest of the class!" As Kat cackles with glee, I add, "Please, tell me the hot billionaire has a hot friend for me." It's my usual joke—other than the billionaire part—the joke I always make when Kat regales me with spicy stories about her dating life. Thanks to almost two years' worth of daily lunches, Kat knows I adore hearing every detail of her dating adventures, especially given my own two-year dating drought.

In reality, despite my silly joke, I don't actually think a friend of Kat's billionaire would be a good fit for me. I've got fairly high self-esteem, as a general matter, but I've been in enough bars with the supernaturally gorgeous and extroverted Katherine Morgan to know the men who hit on her aren't even the same species as those who hit on me. And since birds of a feather flock together—since Kat's billionaire is a young mogul who could get literally any woman he wants—I have to assume any friend of Josh's would also want a bombshell type like Kat, rather than a sarcastic, bespectacled, goofy, girl-next-door type like me.

To be clear, I'm perfectly happy *not* attracting the same kinds of men Kat does. Given Kat's looks and confidence, only the cockiest of men ever have the juice to hit on her, and cocky men aren't my jam. I like nerds. Dorks. Shy, humble, brainiac types with subtle, quiet confidence. Of course, I want a man to like himself and think he's got lots to offer, but I don't want him thinking he's God's gift to women, either.

Also, I get the sense Kat's billionaire is a "bro-ski" type, a former frat boy, and that's the polar opposite of my type. I love my curves and I'm done with societal brainwashing that says I have to be as skinny as a rail to be beautiful. Fuck that. That said, I'm not immune to getting my feelings hurt from a mean-spirited comment about my appearance, and it seems like bro-ski types are the ones who always say the meanest stuff to me, especially when they've been drinking. I tried to avoid frat-boy/bro-ski types even before Angus came along and deftly shattered my self-confidence, but now that I've picked up the pieces and moved light years beyond that dark period of my life, avoiding his type has become an unbreakable rule.

"Funny you should ask that, Banana," Kat says, replying to my joke about her hot billionaire having a hot friend. "He does. And he's the coolest guy you'll ever meet. Actually, he's a fucking genius."

My lips part in surprise. I've made that same joke multiple times—whenever Kat's been telling me about her latest fling—and this is the first time Kat's replied in the affirmative.

"Kitty, I was *joking*."

"As a matter of fact," Kat continues, ignoring my comment, "his friend is here right now, and I think he'd *really* like you."

"Kat, no," I blurt as my heart rate spikes. "I'd want to ask some questions about the guy before you even think about—"

"Henn!" Kat calls out on her end of the line. "My adorable and funny friend, Hannah Milliken, wants very much to say hello to you!"

Holy crap. This is definitely a case of "careful what you wish for." Kat knows how picky I am when it comes to dating. Hence, the reason I've basically given up on it. Just because the billionaire has a friend, and the friend happens to be in the same room as Kat during this call, doesn't mean I'd actually *like* the guy well enough to want to be set up with him.

"To *me*?" a male voice says in the background on Kat's end of the call. I hold my breath, hoping to hear Kat's response. But no dice. Suddenly, Kat's end of the line goes silent in a way that suggests she's pressed the mute button.

Crap. I'm the worst at flirting, especially in situations like this, when I've been blindsided and haven't had the chance to google and gather information in advance. It pains me to think of all the weird, old-fashioned things I've involuntarily blurted—stuff old ladies would say—during what's supposed to be a flirty, fun conversation.

Kat's still not coming back.

Why?

What, exactly, doesn't she want me to overhear?

God, I hope she's not hard selling this guy too much, or I won't be able live up to the hype.

"Hello, Hannah Milliken," a male voice says, causing me to physically jolt in surprise. "I'm Peter Hennessey, but everyone just calls me Henn."

Oh my gosh. His voice is cute. Earnest. Sweet. Confident, but not overly so. I clear my throat. "Hi there, Henn. I hope Kat didn't threaten you with bodily harm if you refused to talk to me." I snort at my own joke. *Shoot. Don't do that, Hannah.*

"No, no, I'm glad to talk to you."

Sweet Sassy Molassey. Is it possible to swoon over nothing but a guy's voice? I think that's what's happening to me right now. Henn seems friendly and sincere. Warm and approachable. Or, heck, maybe it's been so long since I've actually *talked* to a potential date, as opposed to trading pointless, futile messages on dating apps, I'm overreacting to the sound of an actual human voice.

"I'm glad to talk to you, too," I say. "Although I feel like I should clarify I was joking when I asked Kat if Josh has a friend. I overheard her making it sound like it was my idea to talk to you, like I demanded to talk to you, but my question was purely rhetorical, I assure you." Again, I snort. *Shoot.*

"Yeah, she did kinda make it sound like your idea, actually," Henn says, chuckling.

My heart rate has increased. "Be warned: Kat fancies herself an expert matchmaker. Last year, I watched in awe as she brazenly *Parent Trapped* two of our co-workers. She told each of them the other had confessed to having a massive crush, but it was all dastardly lies. Although in Kat's defense, we wound up attending the wedding of those two co-workers a couple months ago, so I suppose one could argue the successful outcome of her meddling justified her nefarious tactics."

Fucking hell. Please, someone muzzle me. Not only did I ramble for far too long from nerves, not only did I turn into a bit of an octogenarian during said rambling, I think I also just now implied I'm hoping Kat's machinations in our case will lead to the same outcome as with those two co-workers—aka a freaking *wedding*. This time, for Henn and me. *Santa Maria Shriver!*

"Yeah, Kat's a sneaky one, for sure," Henn says. Strangely enough, he sounds calm. Amused. Sweet. Not the least bit like he's looking for an immediate exit strategy.

But still, just in case I'm misreading his voice and he's actually freaked out by the bizarre implication that I'm hoping this conversation will eventually lead to our nuptials, I quickly change the subject. "So, um, what are you doing in Vegas?"

"Um, you know . . . just . . . working."

That response causes a whole bunch more questions to pop into my head. From what Kat has told me, Josh and Kat have been partying in Vegas with Josh's twin brother, Jonas, and Kat's best friend since college, Sarah, who's dating Jonas. Hence Kat's introduction to Josh in the first place. So, when did Henn enter the picture? Did he come to Vegas for work and happen to bump into his good friend, Josh, during Josh's double date, or did the foursome invite Henn to meet them in Sin City in the first place and he's been doing work remotely while there? No, Hannah. All those questions are too detailed and specific to ask Henn now, during what's supposed to be a flirtatious first chat. This is meant to be an ice breaker, not an interrogation. "Oh yeah?" I say. "What do you do for work?"

"I'm a computer specialist. A freelance programmer."

Well, that reply only makes me want to ask even more questions. Based on my research, Josh Faraday runs some kind of investment conglomerate with his brother and uncle, so it stands to reason Henn would run in the same lofty circles as his good friend. Is Henn being modest with the description of his work and he's actually a tech mogul who's worth eighty kajillion dollars?

"Cool," I say, once again deciding now is not the time to interrogate the guy. Surely, Kat will give me the skinny about Henn later on. I ask, "Where do you live?"

"Um, LA, New York, Toronto, Denver. I go wherever the job takes me. I can work from anywhere, so I travel a lot. But I mostly live in LA in a crappy-ass apartment."

I crinkle my brow, feeling slightly perplexed. Henn, who's friends with a literal billionaire, lives in a crappy-ass apartment? I guess I can scratch "tech mogul" off my bingo card . . . Unless, of course, he's one of those eccentric billionaires who hit pay-dirt with some big idea out of college and then didn't bother to change his lifestyle thereafter?

Oh! Maybe Henn works for Josh! Maybe Henn is in Las Vegas with Josh, his *boss*, which means Henn isn't a mogul at all. In fact, maybe Henn purposefully mentioned his crappy-ass apartment, so I'd know, right off the bat, he's a normal, working stiff like me, despite his close connection to insane wealth. Honestly, the thought calms me. If Henn is a normal dude, then I can more easily be my normal self around him and not worry I'm too ordinary or boring for him.

"Where do you live?" Henn asks.

I smile. If I'm not mistaken, that was the first time Henn has asked a question, which suggests he's not dying to get off the phone. "Seattle. I was born and raised here."

"Oh, yeah, duh. Kat said she works with you."

Henn sounds a tad nervous now. Another good sign, I think.

"Have you been to Seattle?" I ask.

"Yeah, sure, I get up there sometimes. I love it there. Good salmon."

"Yeah, we have fantastic salmon. I love salmon. I could eat it every day and never get sick of it."

"Me, too."

Well, damn. That was the easiest back-and-forth we've had yet. "Well, if you like salmon, the next time you're in my neck of the woods, let me know and I'll take you to a restaurant that has the best salmon in Seattle. Nay, maybe even the entire Pacific Northwest, if not the world. I'll take you there and we'll feast on salmon to our stomachs' delight."

Oh, God.

No.

What the heck am I saying? I just asked the man out on a date, sight unseen, within the first five minutes of our first conversation. And not only that, I've once again morphed into an old lady while doing it. Did I really say 'nay' and 'to our stomach's delight'? *Son of a biscuit-eating bulldog.*

"*Indubitably!*" Henn says enthusiastically, his ebullient tone making it clear he's not only *not* put off by the emergence of my inner Golden Girl, he's excited by my invitation.

"Oh, what a lovely time we'll have!" I sing out like a dork. And then palm my forehead. Clear my throat. "Assuming it happens. Which is my hope."

"Yeah, I hope so, too. Thanks."

I need to press eject. Pull the cord on my parachute. Get the fuck off this call and talk to Kat and find out if I blew it. Could Henn possibly be as genuinely enthusiastic as he sounds? "No, thank *you*," I reply, though I'm not sure what we're thanking each other for. "I've enjoyed chatting with you."

"Same here."

Warmth spreads into my core. Based on his tone, I'd bet anything Henn is smiling broadly on his end of the phone call, the same as me. Shoot. I wish I knew what he looks like when he smiles.

Suddenly, I hear my boss's voice nearby. "I have to go," I whisper. "I'm at work and my boss is closing in. She doesn't like us making personal calls during the workday."

"Oh, okay, bye. It was great to talk to you."

"To you, too. Would you mind putting Kat back on? I'll pretend I'm talking shop with her."

"About the extremely important work she's doing in Vegas for her outrageously demanding client?" Henn chuckles. "Yep. Bye for now, Hannah."

Butterflies release into my belly. "Bye for now, Henn."

There's a shuffling sound followed by Kat's bubbly voice.

"Hey, baby! Isn't he the cutest?"

I whisper, "Rebecca is in the hallway. Not sure if she's coming here or not. Hang on." I listen for our boss's voice again and quickly surmise she's at least two cubicles away and staying put for now. "Okay, we're good for now. Yes! He's the cutest! So sweet and earnest."

"I know, right?"

"Can you show me what he looks like?"

"Sure, I'll send you a picture."

A few seconds later, my phone beeps, and when I look down, I'm pleasantly surprised. Peter Hennessey is a goateed hipster-nerd type. He's got dark hair and eyes, kissable lips, and an adorable, smirky smile that simultaneously conveys sweetness and snark. In other words, he's *exactly* my type.

"He's hot!" I whisper-shout.

Kat giggles. "Yup. And word on the street is he's a *phenomenal* kisser, too."

My eyebrows ride up. How on earth would Kat know that? Is she friends with Henn's ex? If so, yeesh. That could get messy. "Word on *what* street?"

"I'll tell you when he's not here. I have to run. Talk later?"

"Absolutely. Tell Henn I saw his photo and think he's super cute! No, wait, don't tell him that. I don't want to seem too eager. Only tell him that if he sees *my* photo and thinks I'm cute. Have you already shown him my photo?"

Kat laughs at my rambling. "No, but I will soon. Gotta go, honey. Talk soon."

"Bye, girl." I'm about to lower the phone from my ear when my boss appears at the entrance to my cubicle. She points at her watch, like I'm running late for something. And that's when I remember—fuck!—my meeting with the barbeque client was at ten. I calmly hold up an index finger to my boss and speak into my dead phone. "Great brainstorming session, Kat. I think the client will love everything we came up with. You, too. Thanks." I pretend to disconnect the call and smile at Rebecca. "Is the client here?"

She scowls. "They've been waiting in the conference room for almost five minutes."

Fuck my life. Rebecca hates tardiness. "Sorry about that." I rise from my chair. "Hopefully, all will be forgiven when the client hears the brilliant ideas Kat and I just cooked up for them."

2

HANNAH

"Why don't you kick things off for us," my boss, Rebecca, says. Thankfully, she's looking at my co-worker, Helena, not at me. *Phew.* I'm usually well prepared for our weekly team meetings, but I'm not myself today, thanks to the distractibility I've been suffering from since speaking with Henn yesterday. I know I only talked to the man for mere minutes, and we didn't talk about anything deep. Also, Henn said he lives mostly in LA, so there's no logical point in meeting him, really. But the thing is I felt a stronger glimmer of a spark with Henn in those few minutes than I've felt with anyone in a long time—which is why I spent last night researching Peter Hennessey, instead of preparing for today's team meeting.

I didn't learn much about Henn during my online sleuthing, unfortunately. There are lots of Peter Hennesseys in the world. In the end, the only things I found out were the following: a) Henn attended UCLA, along with Kat's billionaire, where he and Josh were both members of the same fraternity. The fraternity thing surprised me a bit, since Henn didn't give off typical frat-boy vibes during our phone call, and I can't imagine Josh Faraday belonging to a nerd-fraternity. But whatever, I've decided to withhold judgment on that. b) I found out Henn is around thirty years old, based on his college graduation date; and c) he owns a company called Your Nerd for Hire that apparently offers programming and IT support.

That's it. Everything I know.

As far as I can tell, Henn isn't on social media. At least, not that I saw, but I guess it's possible he's got some weird online handle I couldn't find. I think Henn's absence on social media is the reason he's not in any of Josh's Instagram photos. In fact, the photo Kat sent me of Henn, which she obviously snapped on the spot in her hotel room, is the only one I've ever seen.

Speaking of Kat, I haven't heard back from her yet, and I can't help thinking that's a bad sign. Surely, Kat immediately showed Henn my photo after our call. So, why hasn't she texted me his reaction? It must be bad news. Either that, or what I look like is irrelevant because I turned Henn off so completely during our short conversation by asking him out to dinner in Seattle and/or sounding like an octogenarian while doing it.

"And that's all I've got," my co-worker, Helena, says. "I'd love to get everyone's feedback."

As the group around me at the table begins offering their observations and suggestions, my phone buzzes on the table. It's a text from Kat!

> Kat: GREAT NEWS! Call me ASAP!

"Excuse me," I murmur, rising from my chair. With all eyes on me, I hold up my phone by way of explanation. "Kat has an urgent question regarding the Vegas account." It's a foolproof excuse. Our boss hasn't stopped gushing about Kat's lucrative new account this whole week.

I race out of the conference room and into an empty one across the hallway, where I place a call to Kat.

"Bananaaaaa!" Kat shrieks in greeting. "Pack your bags, girl. You're coming to Vegas!"

"What? When?"

"This afternoon. We're going on a double date tonight."

I gasp. "You showed my photo to Henn and he liked it?"

"I did and he did. In fact, his eyeballs telescoped out of his head like he was in a cartoon." Kat makes a silly sound that's apparently meant to conjure the image. "Now, go home and pack a bag. Your flight leaves at three."

My blood feels like it's quickening inside my veins, even as my heart is sinking into my toes. "I don't have any vacations days or PTO banked, and with you out of the office, I'm swamped. Not that I mind."

"None of that matters because Josh is going to hire you to assist me with the big job I'm doing here. In fact, we've both realized this job is way too big for one person to handle, even someone as brilliant as me." She snickers. "Josh wants to hire you at a premium rate with all expenses paid, same as me."

I slide into a chair, feeling dizzy. "I don't know if I can let Josh do that for me. I get why he'd pull out all the stops to keep *you* in Vegas. But why do it for me?"

Kat giggles. "Because you're yet another gift from Josh to me, silly. If it helps you to say yes, think of yourself wrapped in paper and tied with a bow."

I bite my lip. "Las Vegas has always been on my bucket list, and I'd love to see it with you . . ."

"It's settled, then. Hang up and tell Rebecca I need your help this whole week and the client will be calling any minute to—"

"I'd be in Vegas for a *week*?"

"Oh, I thought I'd mentioned that. Yes. Josh and Henn both have to fly out tomorrow morning, unfortunately, so Josh wants us to enjoy a little girls' trip on him this whole week."

"Holy crap."

"Isn't he amazing?" Kat tells me that Josh insists we paint Vegas red, on him. Spa appointments, fancy dinners, shows—he wants us to do all of it on his generous dime.

"I should offer to pay for some of that stuff," I say. "This is way too much to accept from him."

Kat scoffs. "Why don't I let Josh explain everything to you?"

"No, wait!"

Kat's not listening. In fact, she's already speaking to someone on her end of the call.

All of a sudden, a sexy male voice says, "Hello, Hannah Banana. This is Josh Faraday."

My heart stops. "Oh. Hi, Mr. Faraday."

"Call me Josh. Answer me this: do you want to come to Las Vegas and spend the week with Kat? That's the only thing that matters. If you don't, then we'll respect your wishes. If you do, then I respectfully request you let me spend whatever I wish on a gift for Kat."

"Oh, uh. Wow. Yes, I'd love to be your gift to Kat."

He chuckles. "Perfect. I'll see you in a few hours. Bye now."

Holy hell. No wonder Kat is obsessed with this man. He's sexy as hell. I babble my effusive thanks to Josh, but another male voice cuts me off.

"Hannah? It's Henn. Hi."

"Oh. Hi, Henn." My cheeks flash with heat. The contrast between Josh's commanding tone and Henn's earnest, tentative one couldn't be starker. "How are you?"

"I'm great. You?"

"Great. Shocked. Excited."

"Yeah, it sounds like we're going to be meeting each other tonight."

"That's what I've been told. Is that okay with you?"

"It's amazing. I'm embarrassed I wasn't the one to invite you, though. Josh, Kat, and I are sitting in a bar at the moment. We were talking about flying you here for a double date, and I said, 'Hell yeah, let's do it!' I went to the bathroom, thinking I'd be the one to call you when I got out, but I guess Kat took matters into her own hands. I'm sorry."

"Oh, please don't apologize. It's sweet of you to even think this way, but I took it as Kat fixing us up, which seems totally normal to me."

"Yeah, that's my point." Henn clears his throat. "I'm saying Kat doesn't need to fix us up, because I'd like to ask you out myself. Let me do that now." He adopts a more formal tone. "Hello, Hannah. I'd love to feast to my stomach's delight with you tonight in Las Vegas, if you're available and interested. Would you like to come out here and dine with me . . . and Josh and Kat?"

I giggle. "Yes, Henn, I'd love to. Thank you."

"Awesome. I can't wait to meet you."

My entire face feels hot, not only my cheeks. "Same here."

"Sorry if I was tongue-tied yesterday," Henn says. "I'm not the best at conversing with a beautiful woman. My brain kind of freezes."

Henn called me beautiful.

Henn called me beautiful.

"No, I'm the one who turned into a Golden Girl when we spoke. That's what happens to me when I talk to a . . . handsome man."

There. I did it. It took every ounce of my courage, but I managed to return Henn's compliment and confirm my interest in him without stammering or choking.

"You didn't sound like a Golden Girl to me," he says. "But if you did, I guess that's my thing. I honestly really like the way you talk. It's unique and fun. Indubitably."

There's a pregnant pause, during which I can only hope his smile is even half as big as mine.

"Thank you. I really like the way you talk, too. I'm looking forward to talking to you in person tonight."

"Awesome. Can't wait."

I clear my throat. "I guess I should go. I don't have much time to race home and pack before my flight."

"Oh, yeah. See you soon, Hannah."

Kat's voice says something in the background and Henn replies, "*Okay*, ya lunatic." To me, he says, "Kat's jumping up and down like the floor is lava, demanding to speak to you before I hang up. I'll see you soon, Hannah."

"See you soon, Henn."

There's a slight pause and then Kat's voice shrieking, "We're all set! While you were talking to Henn, Josh called Rebecca and she's *thrilled* to add you to the Vegas account."

"Am I on speaker phone?" When Kat confirms I'm not, I whisper-shout, "Henn is so sweet and swoony! Kitty, he made a point of asking me out *himself*! I'm floating on air right now!"

Kat snickers. "By the looks of him, he's feeling the same way. That boy is currently sparkling like a vampire in the sun."

"Can he overhear you?"

"Nope. We're at a noisy bar and I'm clear on the other side of the room. Banana, he's blushing and smiling from ear to ear. He looks like a schoolboy with a crush."

"Aw, how sweet."

"Your chemistry is going to be through the roof in person. Mark my words."

"*Stop.* I don't want to get my expectations too high."

"Silly girl. I'm telling you this is a match made in heaven."

"Stop. Seriously."

"Fine. Text me when you land. I'll be waiting for you at the curb."

"Thank you!" My phone buzzes and I look down. "Rebecca just texted me to come back to the conference room for some great news."

Kat bursts into gleeful laughter. "Woohoo! Call me on your drive home to tell me everything she said. Roger?"

After almost two years of friendship with Kat, I'm well aware of the response I'm required to give to that question. "Rabbit!" I shriek happily. "I'll call you as soon as I get into my car!"

———

"What did you mean when you said word on the street is that Henn is a good kisser?" I ask. As promised, I've called Kat from my car during my drive home to pack. "Do you know Henn's ex?"

Kat snorts. "No, I gathered that intel by kissing Henn myself." Kat laughs when I gasp. "Don't worry, it was right in front of Josh and nothing too hot and heavy. All in the name of research." Kat tells me the full story, which in a nutshell is that Josh, Henn, and Kat were hanging out and drinking cocktails the other night, when Henn admitted he's not confident with his flirting game. In response to that humble admission, Josh and Kat started giving Henn advice, including the gem Josh bestowed about the importance of a first kiss. Well, one thing led to another, apparently, and Josh wound up urging Kat to kiss Henn for instructional purposes. "And to my shock," Kat says, "when I kissed him, I found out Henn didn't need a single pointer from me or Josh or anyone else. That nerd can kiss."

"Oh my gosh," I murmur.

"If you get the chance to kiss him tonight, then go for it," Kat says. "You won't be disappointed."

My heart is beating wildly. "Did Henn kiss you with tongue?"

"A lil bit. Just enough to give me a little zing where it counts, if you know what I mean."

I laugh. "Christ on a cracker, girl. It's been forever since I've been kissed and even longer since I've been kissed well. I'm feeling extra-*sensitive* these days, if you know what I mean, so this bit of intel is wreaking havoc with me."

Kat giggles with glee. "Good. That's why I told you. Because I know how shy you can be at first, and I want you to give yourself permission not to hold back tonight."

"If you mean I should jump into bed with Henn, then, please, let's not get ahead of ourselves. No judgement of you or anyone else who likes jumping to the physical stuff quickly, but I've never done that and I don't think I could. It normally takes me a while to feel like I can trust someone with my body. Would I love to be kissed well tonight? Hell yes. But that's as far as I can imagine."

"Well, if that's what you want, then I'm confident Henn will deliver for you. I mean, assuming the date goes well and you're both feeling it. No rush on anything, Banana."

"Thank you. If there's one thing I know about dating, it's that it can be unpredictable. So many times, a guy who seemed super promising turns out to be a total dud. Other times, a guy I'm really attracted to decides I'm not his cup of tea."

"Well, Henn definitely thinks you're his cup of tea. When he saw your photo yesterday, he said he's always had a big thing for brunettes with glasses."

"Really? I'm glad you told me that. I usually wear contacts on a first date."

"Not this time, babe. Wear your nerdiest, thickest glasses and he'll be entranced."

I laugh. "Roger."

"Rabbit. Oh! And wear a neckline that shows off your eye-popping twins, too. Henn's definitely not an ogler, but I think I caught him covertly checking out a woman with big boobs by the pool the other day. I'm pretty sure he's a boob man."

"Thanks for the tip. I've actually got the perfect dress in my closet.

After I bought it, I lost the nerve to wear it because the neckline is so racy. Maybe tonight's the perfect time to muster my courage."

"Absolutely."

"Heck, I might even go the extra mile and wear it with a push-up bra."

"Hell yes! You might give our poor Henny a stroke, but I'm sure he'll say it was well worth it from his hospital bed."

We both giggle.

"Okay, I've made it to my apartment building, girlie. Oh! There's a spot out front. That never happens to me."

"It's a sign," Kat declares. "Tonight, all good things will fall into your lap, exactly like that parking spot."

I turn off my ignition. "Thank you again for arranging this trip. It's a dream come true."

"For me, too. I love you, girl."

"I love you, too. I'll see you in a few hours in Vegas, baby!"

"Wahoo!"

3
HENN

"Should I change into my black shirt?" I ask.

"Relax, Henny," Josh says. "Blue looks great on you. Don't forget, you've borrowed my cologne, and I happen to know it's irresistible to women."

"Yeah, on *you*."

"Calm down. You look and smell like a million crypto coins."

With a sigh, I plop down next to my best friend on the couch. When I wordlessly hold out my hand, he places his glass of Scotch into it without hesitation or need for explanation.

It's early evening and we're in the fancy penthouse suite Josh has booked for the girls' week of fun. Any minute now, said girls will waltz through that front door, and as excited as I am about that fact, I'm also shitting bricks. My hopes are too high now. I've got something to lose if this doesn't pan out. What if Hannah sees me in person and decides whatever good impression she initially had of me was all wrong? That sort of thing has happened to me in the past and it's mortifying, if not soul-crushing. It'd be especially tough this time, when I'm feeling such a strong flicker of hope.

"Why are you so nervous?" Josh asks. "She's not royalty. She's a nice, normal person."

I shrug. "It's been so long since I've been on an actual date, let alone with someone I'm excited about who seems equally excited about me, I'm not sure I remember how to do it. You know how I get." I don't need to explain that last thing any further. Josh knows when I'm feeling overwhelmed with initial attraction, I often can't put two coherent words together for at least a few minutes.

Josh swats my leg. "Bah. Dating is like riding a bike."

"Well, I broke my arm while riding a bike once, so that's a horrible analogy."

Josh chuckles. "Stop stressing, brother. Kat and I will be there to pick up your incoherent slack, if need be, until you're ready to be your charming self."

"That could take a while. Remember when we'd invite a sorority over to the house, and I'd stand there in a corner and—"

"You're not nearly that shy anymore. Just be yourself and Hannah won't be able to resist you."

I flash Josh a snarky look. "Says the guy who instructed me, mere days ago, to 'dick it' up in order to 'bag a babe.'"

Josh rolls his eyes. "I was joking."

"No, you weren't."

"Well, either way, it was terrible advice. You heard Kat. She told you to lean into your strengths—your awesome, genuine self. It sounds like Hannah is a lot like you, so that strategy should work like a charm."

"God willing and the creek don't rise." I'm not Southern; I'm from Fresno. But I've always liked that phrase.

The sound of female laughter wafts through the closed door, causing me to abruptly jerk to standing. Two seconds later, Kat and Hannah glide into the suite on a cloud. Hannah's wearing thick, dark glasses, jeans, and a dark shirt, but she might as well be dressed in World of Warcraft cosplay, based on the way my body—my skin, my heart, my very soul—are reacting to her. *Hello, wife.*

That's the crazy thought that pops into my head at my first sight of Hannah Milliken. Obviously, I know my brain is being silly. Making a joke, which it often does in times of stress. But, wow, if I could program a wife out of code, Hannah would be my template. She's even more beautiful in person than in all the photos I've devoured of her. Yes, *photos.*

Plural. I've now scoured the internet for every photo I could possibly find of one Hannah Suzanna Milliken of Seattle and quickly surmised she's totally out of my league. Hence, my nerves at present.

As the women come to a stop in the middle of the large room, I fold and unfold my arms, feeling like they've suddenly become useless sausages attached to my torso.

Kat gestures to Hannah. "Gentlemen, this is my beloved sister from another mother, Hannah Banana Montana Milliken. Hannah, meet our generous benefactor, Josh Faraday, and the sweetest genius you'll ever meet, Peter Hennessey. Henn."

At the sound of my name, I force my legs to propel me forward toward the pair, and with each step I take, I feel the synapses inside my brain damn-near short-circuiting as my tongue thickens and twists inside my mouth.

"Hi, Henn," Hannah says brightly, her blue eyes sparkling behind her sexy glasses. "I'm so happy to meet you."

I come to a stop in front of her and try to smile. "Hi, Hunnooh. Hab-be bleet choo."

Oh, God, no. *No*. Not the gibberish thing!

I try to correct course—to tell Hannah that she looks amazing—but the only sounds that come out are a string of syllables ending with a semi-word that sounds a bit like *schmamazing*.

"Why, thank you, sir," Hannah replies smoothly, without missing a beat. "You look pretty damned *schmamazing* yourself."

My breathing halts.

Wait.

What?

How?

Chuckling, Josh arrives at my side and extends his palm to Hannah. "Hello, Banana. Glad you could make it. The PR team desperately needs your assistance."

Everyone chuckles at the inside joke, so I try to join in. But once again, my vocal cords and lingual vestibule aren't cooperating. As I try to pull myself together, Hannah hugs Josh in thanks, which makes me realize I probably should have hugged her in greeting. Fuck! Should I do it now, after she disengages from Josh? No, the moment has passed. Plus, I'm rooted to my spot, anyway, my sausage arms dangling uselessly at my sides.

"Oh, it's your first time here?" Josh says in reply to something Hannah has said. "I didn't realize that. Come check out the view." He guides the women toward floor to ceiling windows on the far side of the suite. As he passes, Josh winks at me, letting me know he's got this until I've sufficiently gathered myself.

At the windows, Josh launches into giving Hannah and Kat a guided visual tour of The Strip below, while I shuffle over and stand next to Hannah. Throughout Josh's commentary, I nod and pretend to listen, but in reality, I'm far too intoxicated by Hannah's perfume, and her pretty profile and warm and friendly vibe, to pay attention to a single word he says.

"Tell Hannah that story you told me," Kat says to Josh when my brain tunes back into the group's conversation. "You know, about that time you, Reed, and Henny celebrated Red Card Riot hitting number one?"

Kat's referring to our good buddy, Reed Rivers, who owns a wildly successful record label called River Records. As Josh proceeds to explain, when Reed's first-ever band hit number one worldwide with their debut single, Josh and I dropped whatever silly thing we were doing in LA and flew here to Vegas to celebrate with him, since this is where Reed happened to be when he got the life-changing news. That night, our celebration started at the fancy restaurant we're taking the girls to tonight and continued until *sunset*—not *sunrise*—the following day.

As the girls titter with excitement at Josh's story, he flashes me a questioning look that plainly asks, "Are you ready to join in yet?" When I subtly shake my head and knit my brows together, he quickly takes the hint and returns to the girls.

Josh says, "Reed was so fucking happy that night. At dinner, he not only ordered literally every item on the menu, just because he could, he also ordered a case of their priciest champagne for our table alone, as well as a bottle for every table in the place."

Hannah and Kat both squeal with delight. Hannah says, "I love the fact that you and Henn both flew here at the drop of a hat to celebrate with your good friend. Reed must have appreciated that so much."

Josh looks at me again, checking in, and when it's clear I'm still struggling, he replies, "Henn, Reed, and I have been the Three Musketeers since our freshman year at UCLA. In good times and bad, we've always stuck together." He grips my shoulder. "Isn't that right, Henny?"

"Mm hmm."

Josh squeezes my shoulder again before releasing me. "So, hey, if it sounds good to everyone, I thought after dinner we'd go dancing at Reed's club. He won't be there, unfortunately—he had to fly to London yesterday —but it's the best place on The Strip to go dancing. Plus, everyone there knows us, so we'll get our drinks fast and made with a heavy hand on the alcohol."

"Oooh, I *love* dancing!" Hannah gushes. She smiles at me. "Do you like dancing, Henn?"

Aw, fuck. *Tongue, don't fail me now.* "Yeah, I love it." Oh, wow, I think that sounded pretty normal, actually.

"Me, too!" Hannah says excitedly, like she didn't just now say she loves dancing first.

"Yeah, me, too," I echo, without realizing I'm repeating myself. When the words come out, though, when I realize I've said the same thing twice, I make a face that says, "Whoopsie."

To my relief, Hannah smiles and responds with, "Yeah, me, too!" Like it's the very first time she's saying it. Her tone isn't mocking or snarky. No, it's pure kindness. She's clearly trying to put me at ease. Letting me know we're the same.

"Really? Me, too!" I say, yet again like it's the first time. And this time, we both crack up at our silly, circular conversation.

Hallelujah. I think we just took a gigantic step forward in terms of comfort level. Or, at least, I did. I flash Hannah a huge smile, and when she returns the gesture, I feel like my heart physically skips a beat. Man, I could drown in those baby blues and smile as I go down. Yes, my rational brain knows I'm projecting my fantasies onto Hannah, since I don't actually know her yet. But my heart, skin, and soul aren't operating rationally. They're all reacting to what they're *feeling*—an attraction that's wreaking palpable havoc with my cardiovascular system.

I take a deep breath and decide to go for it. "Honestly, I think maybe I like dancing *too* much. As you'll probably find out later tonight, the song 'Gettin' Jiggy with It' was basically written for and about me. And not in a good way."

Hannah's glorious smile could light up a pitch-black sky. She says, "Well, lucky for me, I love that song."

"You're sweet to say that, but nobody genuinely loves that song."

"I really do. In fact, I pride myself on gettin' jiggy with it on every dance floor that's lucky enough to be graced with my presence." She snorts. "You know that saying, 'Dance like no one is watching?' Well, that's me. Except that people *are* watching. Usually, with their mouths hanging open at the weirdo who's dancing like nobody's watching."

Oh, my heart. She's fucking adorable. I say, "Bah. Who cares what anyone else thinks? Dancing is supposed to be fun. In my experience, the cooler a person is trying to be, the less fun they're having."

"Agreed!" Hannah says. "That's true in all aspects of life, don't you think? Not only with respect to dancing."

"Absolutely."

Josh says, "Hannah, I feel like I should warn you: Ever since college, our friend group's mission in life is getting Henn drunk and watching him turn into a certifiable maniac on the dance floor. Please, don't think he's understating his exuberance."

"Yeah, I can get pretty ridiculous," I admit, laughing. "I promise I won't be offended if you flee to a far corner of the dance floor and pretend not to know me when I really get going."

Hannah's face is a vision of pure excitement. "Are you kidding me? No matter how crazy you get, I'll be right next to you, egging you on and trying to keep up. Dancing is a whole lot cheaper than therapy, I always say."

"That's a true statement. Although I'm a huge fan of therapy."

Hannah gasps. "Me, too! I'm so glad you felt comfortable saying that, Henn. So many people act like going to therapy is something to hide."

I shrug. "If you ask me, it only makes a person *more* attractive when I find out they're actively working on themselves."

"Me, too! Who wouldn't want to be the best person they can be?"

"Self-awareness and introspection are turn-ons."

"Yes! I couldn't agree more."

We share another huge smile as a swarm of butterflies wreaks havoc inside my belly.

Kat snickers. "Damn, I'm so sorry, guys. I was so sure you'd hit it off. I was a fool."

We all laugh.

Josh says, "Looks like there's not going to be much small talk between you two."

Hannah flashes me a shy smile. "Apparently not. That's a good thing, in my opinion, since I believe small talk is what happens when two people don't feel safe enough to be their true selves."

My heart is thundering. "Well said. Did you make that up?"

"I think so."

"Either way, it's a gem." Hot damn. I couldn't have imagined my first meeting with Hannah going *this* well. This is off the charts. Like nothing I've experienced before. Did Kat hire this girl from an acting agency? Did Kat build her out of AI? Seriously, how the hell is Hannah so fucking perfect?

"*Told you so*," Kat stage-whispers to Josh, loud enough for all of us to hear. Even if we hadn't caught Kat's words, though, her self-satisfied grin would have conveyed the same message clearly enough.

"I bow to your greatness, Madame Matchmaker," Josh replies. "Unless, of course, you don't realize it's now time to butt out and let these two highly intelligent adults figure things out for themselves."

Kat rolls her eyes. "Of course, I realize that. An expert matchmaker always knows when to take her foot off the gas, Joshua. How dare you imply otherwise." With a giggle, she kisses Josh on the cheek. "Will you and Henny whip up some pre-dinner cocktails while Banana and I get ready for our big night out?"

"You've got it."

I ask, "What's your drink of choice, Hannah?"

"Do you happen to have any champagne? I feel inspired by that story about Reed."

"If we don't have any here, I'll call down to get some," I reply.

Hannah says she wouldn't want to be a bother—that she'll drink whatever's already there. I tell her she wouldn't be a bother. We all want her to have the time of her life while she's here. But the entire exchange is immediately rendered moot when I reach the bar and discover a bottle of bubbly in the minifridge. As I hold it up triumphantly, I say, "Your wish is my command, Hannah."

"Aw, thank you. Oh, wow. I've always wanted to try that one."

I look at the label and discover it's an extremely pricey bottle. That's not a surprise, given that Josh is the one who stocked the bar.

"So have I," I say. "We'll try it together."

"Awesome. Thank you." She grabs the handle of her rolling suitcase, her face positively glowing with excitement. "We'll be quick."

"Take your time," I say. "Not that you need it. You're already dressed to kill, if you ask me."

Hannah looks down at her casual attire and laughs. "To *kill*? Maybe to maim, at most." She gestures to the suitcase. "I've packed my killing duds in there."

"Can't wait to see them."

We share a wide smile before Kat and Hannah disappear into a bedroom.

"Holy fuck, fuck, *fuck*," I whisper to Josh, still gazing at the closed door.

Josh chuckles. "That was fast."

"Huh?"

"You're already a goner. Imagining wedding bells and a minivan filled with kids, I'm assuming."

I peel my eyes off the closed door and scowl at him. "It's way too soon to say that. Yes, I'm highly attracted to her. Do I feel an amazing first spark? Yes. Am I excited to see if that spark could turn into something more? Yes. A bonfire, even? Yes. But it's way too soon for me to say I'm a goner or thinking about any kind of future with her. I don't even know her yet."

Josh flashes me a dry look that tells me he doesn't believe me.

"Yes, I think she's amazing," I concede. "And I'm incredibly excited. But I'm not getting ahead of myself."

Josh laughs. "If you say so." I understand his skepticism. I've always worn my heart on my sleeve. It's in my DNA. And I've also always been a one-woman kind of guy, even back in college. While Reed and Josh were juggling multiple women at a time and getting hives at the very thought of committing to any one of them, a girlfriend is all I ever wanted. A serious relationship. A possible future wife. Someone to love who'd love me back with the same depth and intensity of feeling. Frankly, it boggles my mind that anyone—man or woman—*wouldn't* want all that.

We head over to the bar in the corner of the large suite and set about mixing and pouring beverages.

"How are you feeling about you and Kat?" I ask. "Things seem to be going well."

"Very well."

I study my friend's body language for a long beat as he mixes a martini. As well as I know Josh, I generally can't decipher his feelings when it comes to women he's dating. That's been especially true during these few days I've spent with him and Kat. Yes, it's obvious he's mesmerized and enchanted with her in a way I've never seen before. On the other hand, however, it's also obvious a huge part of their attraction is physical, so I can't be sure if he's in a hormone-induced haze or feeling something a bit deeper than that.

"Are you planning to continue dating her after Vegas?" I ask.

"We've already talked about her visiting me in LA in the near future."

"Oh, wow, that's cool. Sounds like things are getting pretty serious, then. At least, by your standards."

Josh shakes his head. "Serious, it's not. Fun? Fuck yes. In fact, she's the most fun I've ever had."

"Oh. That's great."

I'm surprised, and maybe even a little bit disheartened by that response. I know that's historically been Josh's mindset with women— he's in it for fun and nothing else—but I thought I was seeing something deeper developing between him and Kat this week. Frankly, if Josh is only interested in something fun with a woman of Kat's caliber, then I think maybe that answers the age-old question I've been wondering since college: Is Josh even capable of falling in love? I know he's capable of love itself, based on the depth of his feelings for his brother, Reed, and me. But can he let down his guard enough in a romantic setting to let a woman burrow underneath his thick armor?

For some time now, I've accepted that Reed will never fall in love or get married or have kids. But even so, I'm positive he'll be genuinely happy forever that way. Reed loves his work, his friends, his little sister, and his lifestyle, which includes fucking beautiful women all over the world. But Joshua? Yes, he's known as a playboy, but I've always thought the right woman—a woman who understands his surprising complexity— might help him discover a secret craving for emotional security—maybe even a family of his own—that's been buried deep inside him since his tumultuous childhood. At least, that's this armchair psychologist's hunch. But, hey, maybe I'm wrong. If he's not even tempted to jump into something serious with Kat, then maybe he's literally not capable of serious. Because, for fuck's sake, from what I've seen, I can already tell there's not going to be another woman on Planet Earth who'll understand Josh Faraday better than Kat Morgan.

Four drinks in hand, Josh and I head to the couch, where we sit and wait for the women to reappear, all shiny and new in whatever change of clothes and makeup. When the pair finally emerges, the sight of Hannah would wobble my knees if I were standing. As it is, the sight of her makes me feel like I've been hit by a thunderbolt.

Hello, wife.

There it is again. Popping into my head, unbidden—only even louder this time.

"*Wow,*" I murmur, rising from the couch. Hannah was gorgeous in her jeans earlier, but her appearance now is jaw-dropping. Her blue, sparkly dress not only brings out the deep azure of her big eyes, it also shows off some spectacular cleavage that wasn't nearly as pronounced earlier when she was wearing a T-shirt. Jesus lord almighty. My jaw is practically dragging on the floor at the sight of Hannah's curves. She's glorious. Stunning. *A walking fantasy*. As the girls stride toward us, I lean into Josh and whisper, "Okay, yeah, it happened. I'm now officially a goner."

4

HENN

"I love karaoke, too!" Hannah gushes in response to me saying the same thing. She adds, "But I typically need some liquid courage to do it."

We're at dinner with Josh and Kat at the fancy restaurant chosen by Mr. Faraday. Specifically, we're sitting at a sleek corner table in elegant lighting as an army of waiters quickly refills every sip of fifteen-dollar water and tends to our every desire. We've already downed several rounds of craft cocktails and a full spread of intricate appetizers, and now we're in the midst of our respective main courses, all of which looked like works of art upon delivery to the table.

Throughout our long meal, our foursome has chatted as a group quite a bit. But whenever Josh and Kat have branched off to whisper intimately like they're doing now, Hannah and I have leaned in and done the same. By now, we've covered quite a bit of first-date conversational ground: hometowns, family, schooling, the basics of religion and politics, and hobbies. Early on, Hannah asked me about my job as a computer programmer, and I said what I always say: "I'm in cybersecurity."

When Hannah asked me what work I've been doing in Vegas, I told her, honestly, that Josh and his brother, Jonas, hired me for a job and we decided to mix business and pleasure by talking about the specifics here in person. I mean, obviously, there's a shit-ton more to that story, but the basics of what I said to Hannah weren't entirely false.

After that, Hannah asked me a follow-up question about my so-called career in cybersecurity, so I answered briefly and quickly redirected the conversation by asking Hannah about *her* job. My momma taught me the trick to being a good conversationalist is simply turning all questions around, and the trick has never failed me. In this case, Hannah responded to my questions by giving me an overview of the PR campaigns she works on for barbeque chains and dog groomers and such. But after only a brief synopsis of her work, Hannah said, "Honestly, my work isn't a particularly exciting topic. Let's talk about our hobbies, instead." And that's what we've been doing ever since, quickly discovering a shared love of all kinds of things, including our current topic: karaoke.

"I'll only do karaoke when I'm semi-drunk, too," I admit. "Otherwise, I can't make my legs walk onstage."

"Yep, I've got to be tipsy, at the very least."

"Once I get up there, though, I always have a blast, especially if the crowd is really into it."

Hannah nods effusively. "There's nothing better than a rowdy audience egging me on. I turn into the biggest, cringiest ham."

I laugh. "That's something I'd love to see."

"Careful what you wish for, Henny. There's a fine line between fun and cute and 'oh my god, someone pull her off the stage before she totally embarrasses herself.'"

Henny. Josh and Kat have used that nickname for me several times tonight, but it's the first time Hannah's used it. I have to think that's a good sign. Hopefully, it means she's feeling comfortable with me—and *not* that I've unwittingly crossed over into her friend zone.

"You know what I can't stand?" I ask. "People who go up there and sing in all seriousness. Like, you know, they actually try to impress the audience with their golden pipes. Now *that's* cringey."

"Ugh. I hate that. It's like, 'Babe, this isn't your audition for *The Voice*. We're here to laugh and sing along with you.'"

"Exactly. Thank God we agree on that, Banana, because that's a relationship dealbreaker for me. Even more so than differing views on politics and religion."

"Well, that's a relief," she says, wiping her brow. "Crisis averted."

I can't help smiling broadly. I know we're being playful and sarcastic here, but even so, the implication that *not* qualifying to be in a relationship with me would be a crisis is making my heart rate spike. Hot damn, this is the best first date of my life, and it's not even close to finished yet. "Actually, if you turned out to be a serious karaoke-ist, then I'd probably have given you a mulligan," I confess. "Dealbreakers can be fluid when the person in question is a catch-and-a-half."

Hannah bats her eyelashes. "Thank you. Back at you."

We smile like goofs at each other before sipping our drinks and smiling again.

"So, what's your go-to karaoke song?" she asks.

"Anything that gets the crowd singing along, so I'm not up there singing alone."

"I'm so glad to hear that. If a person picks a song with zero singalong potential, they're basically a psychopath. That's *my* dealbreaker for a relationship."

"Wow. Crisis averted." Again, we share a huge smile. I ask, "What about you? What's your go-to?"

Hannah deadpans, "Anything by Mariah Carey that's impossible for anyone else to sing along to."

Of course, I burst out laughing. Holy hell. Hannah is hilarious. It's not only what she says, but how she says it. Her delivery is always pitch perfect—dry and deadpanned. She's got exactly my sense of humor.

"Actually, I don't have a go-to," Hannah adds. "I like flipping through the book of songs each time and letting the spirit move me."

I gasp dramatically. "*Respect*. It's a rare gunslinger who's willing to play Karaoke Roulette."

Hannah laughs. "I've crashed and burned doing it that way. Sometimes, I reach the chorus and realize, 'Oh fuckity, I can't come close to reaching that note. But you know what I do then? Come here."

She motions for me to lean in closer, like she's going to tell me a huge secret, and when I do, the sight of her cleavage and scent of her perfume send arousal rocketing through me.

Once I'm leaning close, Hannah mimes holding out her microphone to the crowd before fake-bellowing, "Let me hear it!"

I lean back, chuckling. "Genius."

Hannah winks. "Everyone's got a superpower. That's mine."

I can't help smirking at that. That's how I've always thought of my hacking skills—as my superpower. Too bad I can't tell Hannah that, since her comment would be a perfect segue. Unfortunately, however, what I do for a living isn't the kind of thing I'd ever tell anyone lightly, especially not on a first date. Or a tenth, for that matter. As a matter of fact, I've never told anyone I'm dating the full truth about my superpowers. I suppose my future wife will know everything one day. That seems like a given. But short of that kind of commitment and trust, I can't fathom voluntarily making myself that vulnerable. Not to mention, I wouldn't want to scare off a potential wife by saying too much before she's gotten to know me thoroughly and would therefore believe me when I tell her, truthfully, that I'm deeply committed to a certain brand of ethical hacking, even if what I do to get there isn't always technically legal.

"Do you want to talk top ten lists for movies?" Hannah asks.

"Hell yeah. Of all-time or by genre?"

"All-time."

"Hmm." I pause. "Okay, in no particular order, I'd say *Groundhog Day, Eternal Sunshine of the Spotless Mind, Fight Club, The Lobster.*"

Hannah bops in her chair. "Those are all on my list, too!"

"No way. *The Lobster* is on your top ten list?"

"Absolutely. It's a masterpiece."

I'm blown away. I've never met a woman who's seen that film, let alone loved it like I do. "Isn't it incredible?"

Hannah nods and bites her lip. "Maybe we can watch it together some time, even if we're watching on our respective laptops in different cities."

My heart leaps. "It's a date. Or I could come to Seattle, and we could watch it after the salmon dinner you promised me."

She blushes. "That sounds great."

My heart rate spikes. "I'm flying to DC tomorrow for a job. I'm not sure how long it'll take. A week or two, at most. Would it be good timing for me to come to Seattle after that?"

"It would be perfect timing."

"Okay. Awesome. It's a date."

"It's a date."

"Cool. A date."

We sip our drinks, but I'm barely able to get the liquid into my mouth through my wide, goofy grin.

Hannah puts down her glass. "*Grease.* Where does it rank for you? Top ten? Top twenty?"

"Oh, top ten, for sure. For sentimental reasons. It's one of my mother's all-time favorites, so I've watched it with her a thousand times."

"My sister and I watch it every year with our mom on her birthday! At this point, we've seen it so many times, we treat it like a speak- and sing-along extravaganza!"

"I'd pay to see that."

"No need. We'll do it together when you come to Seattle."

"Awesome. Sounds like we're going to be busy."

"You might want to plan on staying in Seattle at least a few nights, since we're going to have so much on our itinerary."

"Frankly, I think we'd be doing ourselves a grave disservice if I didn't plan to stay for a full week and take you out every night." Shit. Was that too much, too fast?

"Perfect!" Hannah sings out, and I sigh with relief that I haven't fucked things up by being overly excited.

"True story," I say, resting a forearm onto the table, "*Grease* is the movie that helped me learn to dance before my first school dance in seventh grade."

"Aw. Was that your first date?"

"Fuck no. My first date was in college. I was a late bloomer."

"Me, too!"

"No way."

"Oh, Henny. I was so shy in high school."

"Same here."

"But continue."

"It was one of those everyone-come-to-the-gym-and-dance-together kinds of things. And I was so excited to go. But I'd never danced in public before, only in my bedroom. And when I went on YouTube to learn, everything was too complicated for me. So, my mom suggested I dance like they do in *Grease*, because I'd known that choreography basically my whole life. So, that's what I did."

Hannah is dying of laughter. "Please, tell me it all worked out for you, and this isn't the story of the time you got horrifically bullied at a school dance."

"Who could possibly bully a kid who's Greased Lightning? That was the night I discovered I'm a dancing *god.*"

Hannah squeals with glee.

"Or maybe it's my villain origin story," I add. "Because that's when I became addicted to making people cheer for me on dance floors. It was in that moment Henn the Dancing Maniac was born."

"Hannah the Dancing Maniac can't wait to join him."

We clink glasses and take hearty sips.

Hannah peeks at Josh and Kat, and when it's clear they're still in their own little world, she returns to me. "So, tell me. Have you seen *Pride & Prejudice*? Not the BBC miniseries from the nineties. The movie from the 2000s with—"

"Kiera Knightly and Matthew MacFayden. Yes, of course, I've seen it. Many times. I love it."

"No way."

"It's probably number ten on my overall list, but it's number one on my Love Stories and Rom Coms List, thanks to Mr. Darcy's hand-flex. You know when—"

"Mr. Darcy flexes his hand—"

"After guiding—"

"Miss Elizabeth into her carriage! That's iconic!"

"It's only one of the most sensual moments ever captured—"

"In the history of cinema!"

"Agreed!"

The energy between us is fire. In fact, the shock and excitement that's practically ricocheting off our bodies couldn't be more palpable if we'd just discovered we were married in a past life. Suddenly, though, skepticism visibly washes over Hannah's pretty face.

"What's wrong?" I ask.

Hannah snickers and waggles her index finger at me. "Ha! You and Kat *almost* got me."

5
HANNAH

Henn looks deeply confused, so I flash him a knowing side-eye and say, "Kat told you all about the hand-flex in *Pride & Prejudice*, didn't she? She told you I'd lose my shit if you mentioned that scene?"

Henn pulls a face like that's patently ridiculous. "Kat didn't say a word about *Pride & Prejudice* to me. I genuinely love that movie."

I waggle my index finger at him. "Don't you dare lie to me, Peter Hennessey. Kat knows I'm obsessed with Mr. Darcy's hand-flex. It's my version of porn."

Henn chuckles. "A) that's good to know, and B) I swear on my love for my momma—and I *really* love my momma—that Kat didn't utter nary a word to me about *Pride & Prejudice* or Mr. Darcy's hand-flex. I've seen that movie, like, five times with my mother and a couple more times on my own. If I'm scrolling and it happens to pop up on my suggested list, I can't resist watching it again."

The sincerity on Henn's face is undeniable. But since I'm in the mood to playfully torture him, I call across the table, "Kitty, excuse me." Kat peels her gaze off Josh and onto me. "Did you or did you not arm Henn with the top-secret code to the steel safe of my heart and libido? Namely, telling him about my obsession with *Pride & Prejudice* and Mr. Darcy's hand-flex?"

"I did not."

"Would you swear to that fact? And if so, would you swear to it on your love for your momma?"

"I would. Also, on my love for my daddy and all four of my brothers. Even Peen."

"Thank you. I'll accept all that love as collateral *except* in regard to your love of Peen, considering how often you gripe about him."

"Fair enough."

Henn chuckles and addresses Kat. "Your love of *peen*?"

"That's what my family calls my brother, Keane. He's Keane the Peen. Peenie Weenie. Peen Star. And trust me, the nickname fits." Kat rolls her eyes. "That boy can be the biggest fucking peen."

We all laugh and launch into asking Kat an avalanche of questions about her peentastic brother. How did he first acquire such a silly nickname? What makes him such a peen? And Kat cracks us up with story after story, concluding with the comment, "My big brother, Colby, always says Keane isn't our family's *black* sheep; he's our *neon* sheep."

We all laugh again and ask several more questions, but when that particular topic wanes, and Josh and Kat slide into another one-on-one conversation, Henn and I do the same.

Henn asks, "Why were you so sure I was scamming you about *Pride & Prejudice*? It's a great movie."

"I've never dated anyone who'd ever think of a romance as a great movie. Especially one that's a period piece, too."

Henn rolls his eyes. "Fools, every last one of them."

"Welcome to my dating history. A parade of fools."

"Yeah, it's rough out there."

I sigh dramatically and place my hand on my heart. "Sir, that's what happens when a lady is *twenty-seven*." It's a reference to *Pride & Prejudice*—to a famous scene in the movie that's become a viral internet meme. Namely, Lizzie's best friend, Charlotte, logically explains her rationale for marrying the dweeby, repellant Mr. Collins by saying she's twenty-seven years old with no money or prospects.

Henn fake-gasps. "Oh dear. You're *unmarried* and *twenty-seven*?"

Oh my gosh. Henn gets the reference! "I sure am," I lament dramatically. And then, because I'm a total dork, I can't resist launching word-for-word into Charlotte's famous speech while mimicking the actress's tone, accent, and inflection. When I finish my short performance, Henn applauds and laughs while I take a bow in my chair. "I can do Emma Stone's maybe-I'm-not-good-enough monologue from *Lala Land*, too," I say proudly. "Including getting tears in my eyes at the exact right moment."

Henn looks sheepish. "I've only seen that movie once and it was years ago, so I don't remember that monologue. I'm sure you kill it, though."

I gasp in mock horror. "*How dare you, sir. Lala Land* is second on my all-time favorites list after *Pride & Prejudice.*"

Henn looks genuinely stunned. "Wow. We've finally discovered something that proves we're not, in fact, the same person in male and female forms. I liked *Lala Land,* but not enough to want to see it again."

My jaw hangs open. "Sir, that movie is a perfect masterpiece and you've offended me to my very bone."

Henn snort-laughs. "I didn't say I hated it. I said I liked it. That's a compliment."

"No, it's a goddamned slur when talking about a masterpiece."

I'm loving this banter with Henn. So many times on first dates, my attempts at humor are met with dead, awkward silences. Or worse, my date looks at me like I've got horns in my head. But with Henn, every joke lands. And not only that, he gives as good as he gets.

"Please accept my profuse apology," Henn says.

"No, because it's not sincere."

"True."

"Is there a movie you'd consider a perfect masterpiece?" I ask.

Henn considers for a beat. "*Interstellar*, maybe?"

"Ooooh, that's a great movie. I'm a sucker for anything outer space."

"Same."

"I saw the best documentary about UFOs the other day. So good. You should watch it." I tell him the title.

"Do you watch a lot of documentaries?" he asks.

"I'm *obsessed* with them, thanks to my sister, Maddy. She wants to be a documentary filmmaker after graduation from college."

"Where does she go?"

"U Dub. She's in her second year there, but she's hoping to transfer to UCLA's film school in the fall."

Henn gasps. "You know Josh and I went to UCLA together, right?" Without waiting for my reply, Henn waves at Josh across the table. "Joshua! Do we know anyone in the admissions office at UCLA? Hannah's little sister wants to transfer to the film school in the fall."

Oh my gosh. I didn't mention that to Henn to prompt him to try to help Maddy get in. In fact, it didn't even occur to me he could do that.

"I don't know anyone," Josh says, "but Reed gets invited to sit on career day panels for the business and music schools all the time. Maybe he knows someone who knows someone."

"Cool. I'll ask him." Henn returns to me with a wink. "If anyone could help your sister, it's Reed Rivers. That dude knows *everyone*. And weirdly, everyone owes him a favor. Has Maddy already submitted her application?"

My head is spinning. Could Reed really help Maddy make her dreams come true? I'm floored at the mere thought of it. "Uh, no. She's still got several months before the deadline. She recently submitted her first full-length documentary to a bunch of film festivals. She's hoping to win some big awards on it to include in her application."

"Good thinking."

My head is still spinning. "Henn, listen," I blurt. "I can't let you ask Reed Rivers of all people to help my little sister get into UCLA. He doesn't even know her. I mean, she's brilliant, but he doesn't know that."

"Reed couldn't get her in. All he could do is make sure someone takes a good, long look at her application. And don't worry, he'd think of it as doing *me* a favor, which he wouldn't mind doing at all. Josh, Reed, and I have always done favors for each other. That's how we roll."

Henn asks me about Maddy's documentary, and I tell him the film is called *Shoot Like a Girl* and that it's about the male and female basketball teams at her school, the University of Washington. "I saw the final cut of the film last week," I say, "and it blew me away. And not because Maddy is my sister, but because the film is objectively riveting."

"I'd love to see it."

My heart leaps. "Oh. Wow. Well, Maddy's having her world premiere at a little film festival on-campus in a couple weeks. Maybe the timing will work out for you to see it then during your visit to Seattle."

Henn grins. "I hope so. I'll do everything I can to make it."

My heart is beating wildly now. "Fair warning, I'm sure my mother will be there. So, if it'd be too much to meet my mother *and* sister during our first week of dates, I'd totally understand."

"Are you kidding? I want to meet your whole family. Bring 'em on."

Whoa. My chest heaves. Isn't this the part where he's supposed to act skittish and freaked out? The part where he's supposed to noticeably pull back? "Okay. Cool. My mom and sister are basically my whole family in Seattle. My father's not in the picture and my grandfather lives in Arizona." I shift in my seat, feeling a bit disoriented. This man is emotionally available, communicative, funny, sexy, and smart—*and* he's making his interest in me clear as a bell. What am I missing? Where are the red flags? Is the fact that there's not a single red flag a red flag?

I clear my throat. "I feel like I should mention I don't have any vacation days stored up at work. I'll have to work every day while you're in Seattle. But I'd love to go out any evening you're there."

"I'll take every evening you're willing to give me."

What the fuck? He's supposed to say something vague like, "Yeah, I've got a few moving parts myself, so I'll let you know when I'm available."

I drag my fingertip around the rim of my wine glass, feeling a bit disoriented by Henn's flagrant pursuit of me. "I could come up with a few ideas for dates in Seattle, if you'd like."

"Awesome. I'll come up with some ideas, too. Maybe even some surprises, if you like that sort of thing."

"Oh, I *love* surprises. There are so few in life. Good ones, anyway."

"Then surprised you shall be, my dear. Actually, you know what? Other than dinner at that salmon place and Maddy's film festival, how about you leave the rest of our itinerary to me?"

My heart is hammering. What species of man is this? Henn seems too good to be true. Is he going to come on strong tonight and then ghost me after leaving for DC tomorrow? It honestly wouldn't surprise me, based on my dating history.

"Okay, yes, thank you," I manage to squeak out. "If you get stuck for ideas, though, let me know. It's my hometown, after all, so I'd be happy to—"

"No, no. It's Josh's hometown, too, remember? If I get stuck, I'll ask him for suggestions." Henn chuckles at my gaping expression. "You said you like surprises. Well, as luck would have it, I love *giving* them. Especially to someone as amazing as you."

He's rendered me speechless. What the fuck is this? I've never experienced it before. What's happening?

"Here we are," our waiter says, appearing out of nowhere with two helpers. Apparently, Josh has ordered a slew of after-dinner liqueurs to be poured for all of us.

"I thought we'd have ourselves a little tasting," Josh explains.

And off we go. Liquids are poured into crystal glasses, and foofy explanations are provided by our waiter. With each new offering, our four-some engages in energetic conversation about our various opinions, until finally, after the last liquid has been served and tasted and the wait staff begins clearing the table yet again, Josh and Kat slide into another inti-mate conversation. Which means Henn and I do the same.

"What'd you think of that last one?" Henn whispers conspiratorially.

I grimace. "Honestly, it tasted like rubbing alcohol with a splash of honey to me."

Henn chuckles. "I thought the same thing. I guess this means I can scratch liqueur tasting off my list of potential activities for us in Seattle."

I giggle. "I'm grateful for the experience tonight, but I don't think I'm in any danger of becoming addicted to liqueur. I've got plenty of other guilty pleasures."

Henn waggles his eyebrows. "Oooh. Tell me more."

"Sorry, my guilty pleasures aren't all that exciting. Books. Tickets to live shows—both music and comedians. Oh, and makeup and skincare stuff. I can't resist outrageously priced, beautifully packaged bottles of goop that smell amazing. That's about it."

"What's a recent show you went to that was particularly memorable?"

I list off several shows. "Oh, and I saw this amazing band that's always been a favorite of my mother's. We went as her birthday present, and they were so amazing live. They Might Be Giants."

"I love TMBG! My dad introduced me to them."

"No way."

"'Birdhouse in Your Soul' is a masterpiece."

"It is! When I heard them do it at the concert, it instantly became one of my all-time favorites."

"Mine, too."

"Nobody ever knows that song."

"My dad played it all the time. As a kid, I loved hearing a song about a glowing, birdie nightlight because I was terrified of the dark."

"Me, too."

"And then, as I got older, I realized, whoa, the song is actually a love song. The little birdie nightlight was looking for his birdhouse—his soulmate." Henn shrugs. "Or at least, that's how I interpret the song now as an adult."

I can barely breathe. "Me, too," I whisper, my heart clanging. "That's what I said to my mother and sister after the concert. My sister totally agreed with me, but my mother told me I was reading way too much into the lyrics."

"*What*? It's all right there, for fuck's sake! The birdie wants the listener to build a birdhouse in their *soul*. What else could that mean, if not a reference to soulmates?"

"I couldn't agree more. It's all right there, for fuck's sake."

"For fuck's sake."

Well, this settles it. This man was created in a factory, especially for me. No man I've ever dated has ever heard of They Might Be Giants or their quirky little New Wave bop from the nineties, let alone understood its deeper meaning and loved it. How is this man real and not a figment of my fantasies?

I take a sip of wine. "So, what are your guilty pleasures, Henn?"

"Anything computer- or tech-related. Gadgets. Accessories. Upgrades. I'm totally addicted. Also, travel."

"Gah. I'm jealous. I've never been outside of the States, except to Canada. Have you gone to lots of cool places?"

Henn nods. "I love scrolling through websites that offer cheap flights to faraway places and then dropping everything on a dime when I find a smoking-hot deal."

"That sounds amazing. Do you travel by yourself?"

"Mostly. If not, then I'm usually with Josh and/or Reed. Why not, right? I can stare at a computer screen in Morocco or Bali as easily as I can do it in my shitty-ass apartment in LA."

"God, I wish I had a job like that. I've been saving for a trip forever, but my salary is shit and vacation days are hard to come by."

"You can't work remotely?"

I shake my head.

Henn grimaces. "Sounds like you need a new job."

"I know. I'm actively looking." I glance at Kat across the table. She's still mesmerized by Josh. "Please, don't tell Kat I said that. Leaving her would break my heart. I'd only do it if the job were literally my dream job."

"What would your dream job look like?"

"I'm not sure, exactly. For sure, I'd be able to work remotely sometimes. And maybe it'd require some travel?"

Henn asks a few more questions, and ultimately suggests I might consider working in the PR department of a movie studio. He explains his thinking, and I can't deny he's onto something there.

"That's a fantastic idea. Thank you. I'll definitely pursue something like that if Maddy gets into UCLA. If she moves to LA, I think that'd be my sign to finally bite the bullet and leave my hometown, too."

"You and your sister are really close, huh?"

"We're best friends. Always have been. But it's more than that these days. A couple years ago, Maddy was in a horrible car accident. Her injuries were so extensive, she had to drop out of U Dub for a full year to recover. Ever since, I've been extra protective of her."

"Understandably. Is she okay now?"

"Physically, yes. The injury that hasn't completely healed is her grief. Her boyfriend, Justin, died in the crash."

"Oh my god. I'm so sorry."

I sigh. "Poor Maddy adored that boy. He brought out her goofy, silly side. Made her feel safe to let it all hang out. Ever since he died, she's not nearly as carefree and goofy. Not even with me."

"Aw, poor Maddy. That's so hard." Henn is looking at me with deep sympathy in his dark eyes. "No wonder you want to live in the same city as her." Henn grabs my hand on the table and squeezes it, and my entire body electrifies at his touch. "Tell me something, Banana. If you had a teleportation machine that could take you anywhere in the world right now, where would you set the dial?"

I don't hesitate. "Paris. I've always wanted to go, ever since I took French in high school."

"That's a great choice. Besides all the obvious tourist spots, you could also hit the jazz bar that's at the end of *Lala Land*."

"That's in Paris? I didn't know that. I'll add it to my dream board." I put an elbow onto the table when Henn releases my hand. "I take it you've been to Paris?"

"Only once. As cool and iconic as it is, it's one of the only cities that made me feel lonely being alone." Henn smiles ruefully. "They don't call it The City of Love for nothing. I decided I wouldn't come back until I found my person and could take her to Paris to canoodle with me as we walked along the Seine, like I saw so many couples doing."

My heart is stampeding. Thundering. Raging. Is this a sign from the universe? Is Henn imagining *me* becoming his person one day? Is he envisioning *me* being the woman he takes to Paris and canoodles with? I pick up my wine glass, intending to take a sip, but put it down when I realize my hand is shaking.

Our waiter appears with the check, which he hands to Josh, who in turn promptly hands over his gleaming black credit card without even looking at the total. As we await the waiter's return, Josh says, "Reed's club is only a couple blocks away down The Strip. An easy walk, at least for those of us not wearing heels. Are you ladies game, or would you prefer to take a cab?"

Kat says, "I was born in heels, baby. I'd prefer to walk off my dinner a bit before hitting the dance floor. What about you, Banana?"

"Easy peasy pumpkin squeezy," I reply.

Henn laughs. "Isn't it *lemon* squeezy?"

I furrow my brow. "But then the opposite wouldn't work."

"What's the opposite?"

"Hard scarred pumpkin shard."

Everyone laughs.

"Unless the opposite is stressed depressed lemon zest," Henn offers, and everyone laughs again.

"And just like that, my entire reality has crumbled," I tease.

The waiter arrives, the bill is settled, thanks are conveyed to Josh, and off we go outside and in the direction of the dance club, wherever that is, with Henn and me in front and Josh and Kat strolling behind.

After a few steps, Henn slides his hand in mine. And just like that, a torrent of electricity courses through me. It might seem silly for a grown woman to feel *this* giddy about holding hands with her new crush. But I can't help it. This is the best first date of my life, and it's not even close to over yet.

"Hey, let's get your photo in front of the fake Eiffel Tower for your dream board," Henn says. When I look to where he's pointing, there's a replica Eiffel Tower in the near distance that's apparently attached to one of the hotel/casinos on The Strip. It's smaller than the real deal in Paris, I'd assume. And its location near the neon-lit sidewalk is nothing like the elegant setting of the real thing I've seen in photos. But since its structure is a perfect copy of the real McCoy, and it's as close as I've ever come to Paris, I quickly agree a photo is a splendid idea.

Henn and I stop walking to take the shot, which prompts Josh and Kat to stop, too. Henn explains to our companions he's taking a photo of me in front of the Eiffel Tower for my dream board—which he quickly does—but before we resume our journey, Kat enlists a passerby to snap a few shots of our foursome for posterity. "We need a memento of this amazing double date!" Kat chirps.

We pose for the stranger, who kindly snaps away and then hands Kat's phone back to her.

"I took a whole bunch," our kind photographer says. "I think I got the whole Tower in the background in most of them."

"Thank you so much," Kat replies and the rest of us echo, before we all resume our languid stroll toward Reed's dance club, only this time with Kat and me walking in front of the boys as we swipe through the photo shoot together.

"Aw, she framed the Tower perfectly," Kat says, looking at the first of many group photos taken. "You never know what you're going to get with a random stranger as your photographer, but she nailed it." Kat gasps. "Oh my gosh. Look at this one, Banana."

Kat hands me her phone and I gasp the same way she did. The photo is the same as the others in terms of posing and framing, but in this one, Henn isn't looking directly at the camera, along with the rest of us. Nope, this time, he's gazing directly at me—and with such intensity, if I saw this shot and didn't know the situation, I'd assume the handsome man with the wavy dark hair and goatee was gazing adoringly at the great love of his life.

6

HENN

"Go Henny! Go Henny!"

That's what Hannah is chanting with enthusiasm at me as I boogie on down the corridor like my very life depends on it. It's almost four in the morning now, and we're still going strong as we dance, shimmy, and shake our booties down our hotel's long hallway toward the sprawling suite Hannah is sharing with Kat this week. When we parted ways with Josh and Kat in the lobby, Hannah took the words right out of my mouth by asking me to walk her to her room.

"You can take Peter Hennessey out of the dance club," Hannah bellows, "but you can't take the dance floor out of his soul, babyyyyy!"

"That's right, babyyyyy! Your turn now!" I fling my arm toward my partner in crime. "Take it away, Bananaaaaaa!"

Hannah doesn't hesitate. With the same intensity she had on the dance floor earlier, she gyrates and shimmies in a manner that's simultaneously hilarious and hot as fuck.

"You think you can handle *this*?" Hannah says playfully with a shake of her incredible chest.

"I'd certainly like to try," I reply, as my dick thickens in my pants.

Hannah bounds a few yards ahead of me, bends over with her palms on her knees, and twerks her round ass at me rapidly like she's a backup dancer for Cardi B. She's making an exaggerated "O" face as she twerks, I can't help noticing, and the effect on my hardening dick is swift and undeniable. It's at full mast now, the same way it was so many times during our dancing tonight. At one point, we pretended to be dancing gorillas. At another, "insecure cool kids on cocaine." We danced every bit of choreography we could remember from *Grease.* And then begged the DJ to play "Thriller," at which point we slayed the famous dance from the music video, although we both confessed later we actually learned it from *Thirteen Going on Thirty.* Bottom line, Hannah and I were two of a kind on that dance floor tonight—and I've never felt more attracted to anyone in my life.

"Join me, Danny!" Hannah shouts.

It takes me a second, but I realize she's doing the "cowgirl with a lasso" move from the school dance scene in *Grease.* "I've got you, Sandy!" I call out as I join her lasso-twirling choreography in time.

Hannah stops in front of a door and dissolves into laughter, so I stop and laugh with her.

"This is me," she says, gesturing to the door.

"Cool," I say lamely, as the importance of the moment dawns upon me. Should I kiss her now? All signs point to yes, I think . . . but what if I'm misreading the signs?

Our laughter has faded now. Unmistakable electricity is coursing between us. Hannah drags her teeth over her lower lip and then licks it, her blue eyes locked with mine. I can be shockingly stupid when it comes to reading signals early on, but, yeah, I'm pretty fucking sure Hannah's body language is screaming, *Kiss me, kiss me, kiss me.*

My heart thundering, I step forward, touch the side of Hannah's neck, and slowly bring my lips to hers, and, thankfully, she quickly closes the gap and presses her mouth against mine. Oh, thank God. I slide my arm around her waist and bring her closer as I introduce my tongue to hers, at which point—forget about proverbial fireworks going off—a veritable nuclear bomb explodes inside me. In fact, every drop of arousal and chemistry I've been feeling all night long converges inside me and turns into a detonation, the likes of which I've never felt before.

I press myself into Hannah's body and deepen the kiss, and she unequivocally matches my fervor. My body quaking with white-hot desire,

I press my hard bulge into Hannah's pelvis, letting her know she's driving me fucking wild, and she grips the back of my hair at the nape of my neck and devours my lips with even more enthusiasm.

Ravenously, I back her against the door and gently grip her hips, feeling physically dizzy with lust. I read somewhere that the dopamine hit released inside the brain during a fantastic first kiss lights up the same on a CT scan as a hit of heroin. I've never tried heroin, but I've had quite a few first kisses in my thirty years and none of them seemed like proof of that statement. But now, as I kiss Hannah for the first time, I know the comparison to heroin must be true. Surely, if scientists were to hook up my brain to a scanner in this moment, it'd be lit up like the Fourth of July.

"Wooh!" Hannah whispers, her fists still entwined in the back of my hair. She nuzzles her nose with mine. "Kat told me you're a fantastic kisser, but she vastly undersold your talents."

I feel my cheeks flush. *Kat told Hannah about our kiss?*

Hannah chuckles at whatever embarrassment she's seeing on my face. "No worries. Kat told me it was all harmless fun—all in the name of research." She winks. "She warned me one kiss from Peter Hennessey, and I'd want more. A lot more. *And I do.*" Her chest heaves. "On that note, would you like to come inside and ride my Slip 'n' Slide, Henny?"

As aroused as I am, I can't help chuckling at Hannah's word choice. "More than I want to take my next breath, Milly."

"I was hoping you'd say that." Breathing hard, Hannah digs into her little purse for her keycard, while I shove my hands into my pockets and tell myself not to succumb to the urge to do a happy dance. Luckily, Josh covertly shoved a couple condoms at me earlier tonight in the club—the ones I'm feeling in my pocket now—"Just in case!" he said—or I'd have to ruin the vibe by sprinting down to the gift shop in the lobby. *Thank you, Joshua.*

"Aha!" Hannah says, holding up her keycard with a waggle of her eyebrows.

A moment later, the door is closing behind us and we're kissing passionately in the middle of the hotel suite. After a bit, we begin kissing and groping our way toward the bedroom. When we get there, Hannah instantly begins vigorously ripping off her clothes, much to my delight. When she's stripped down to her black bra and panties, I exhale audibly at the sight of her. She's voluptuous in every way. Soft. Curvy. Round. *Perfect.*

I ramble excitedly, if not coherently, about her sexy perfection, making Hannah coo like a turtledove.

"Thank you," she says, even though I'm not sure I've uttered anything but well-meaning gibberish. She motions. "Your turn, please."

Trembling with excitement, I peel off my clothes—everything but my underwear, since Hannah's still wearing hers—and throw them emphatically across the room like they've offended me. For a long moment, we drink each other in, both our chests rising and falling harshly, until Hannah reaches into the valley of her sumptuous cleavage and unclasps her bra from a location I didn't know clasps existed. When the bra falls away, her mouthwatering breasts spring free of their bondage and wobble slightly before settling in, her nipples two luscious pink peaks.

"You're the hottest human I've ever seen in my life," I murmur.

With a wicked smile, Hannah wordlessly slides off her underwear, provoking me to do the same. And when we're both naked, I fold her into my arms for another kiss, this time with the tip of my hard cock nudging against her soft belly. As we kiss, Hannah quakes in my arms like a volcano preparing to erupt. So, I take that as my cue to reach between her legs and gently stroke her. To my thrill, she gasps and purrs at the sensation, goading me on.

I lead her to the bed and lay her down. And then lie beside her, kiss her deeply, and resume stroking her. When she widens her legs and lets out a soft moan, I slide my fingers inside her and discover she's soaking wet.

Groaning with arousal, I bring my wet fingers to her clit, and find it swollen and hard to my touch. For a while, I languidly slide my fingers from her wetness to her clit, before zeroing in on her bull's-eye and working it in earnest. As I work between her legs with my fingers, my mouth migrates to her breasts, the tits that have made my mouth water all night long, and Hannah responds by stroking my hard dick. She swirls the pre-cum on my tip with her fingertip before spreading it all the way down my shaft.

"Oh, god," I blurt. "If you keep doing that, I'm not going to last much longer." My breathing ragged, I gently touch her hand, signaling her to stop stroking me. "This is all about you," I whisper. "Let me make you come."

"It sometimes takes me a long time," she whispers. "I won't ever fake it. So, if I'm taking too long—"

"There's no such thing as too long. It's the journey, not the destination. I've been wanting to do this to you all night."

Hannah's body softens. She settles back, her hands at her sides, letting me return to my prior work. With enthusiasm, I lick and suck her glorious nipples and breasts, while stroking and caressing between her legs. I'm getting her as wet as I can before finally heading downtown.

When I've got her breathing hard and quaking with arousal, I pull her legs open, crawl into position, slide two fingers inside her, and start working her clit voraciously with my lips and tongue. As Hannah groans and undulates, I stay the course firmly, methodically, coaxing her to the edge. And, suddenly, she begins shrieking and barking orders.

"Don't stop!" she yells. "Please, don't stop or change it!"

I moan my enthusiastic reply, since I've currently got a mouth full of delicious pussy. After a bit, Hannah begins growling. Gripping my hair and ears. Writhing frantically and whimpering. Clearly, she's on the bitter cusp of an incredible orgasm. Is something holding her back? Does she need a push?

As my mouth continues its hungry work and my fingers continue stroking inside her, I press my thumb firmly against her anus, and holy fuck, it works! Not ten seconds later, Hannah comes completely undone. She ripples beneath my thumb while her vaginal muscles clench and unclench sharply against my fingers inside her. Best of all? Her screams of ecstasy are echoing off the walls of the room.

My entire body on fire, I grab a condom out of my pocket on the floor —thanks again, Joshua!—and then leap onto the bed and over Hannah's sweaty body. After kissing her deeply, I raise her arms above her head, lodge my tip at her entrance, and sink myself slowly inside her, as deep as my cock will go.

As Hannah moans and clutches my bare ass, I choke out, "You feel so fucking good."

"So good," she echoes in a whisper.

She hikes her thighs up around my hips and grabs my ass, goading me on, as I rock in and out of her—and soon, we're moving as one. In perfect synch. Gyrating together to maximize our mutual pleasure, until we're fucking in a goddamned frenzy of animalistic passion.

I kiss her voraciously as I continue fucking her, and she grips my back and moans into my mouth. We're spiraling higher and higher. Together. Fucking with abandon. Letting loose. Until, finally, when I'm on the bitter cusp of losing it myself, Hannah digs her nails into my back, arches her back underneath me, and comes with me buried balls deep inside her.

"Oh, fuck," I grit out. This is the closest thing to pure ecstasy I've felt in my life. I feel like I'm being electrocuted by pleasure. My eyes roll back. My skin bursts into flames. And then . . . I feel nothing but *bliss.* An eruption of rapture that sends stars dancing and swirling before my eyes.

I growl through my colossal release, while Hannah shrieks with pleasure beneath me through hers. Finally, I collapse on top of her, my breathing labored and my vision blurred.

We lie motionless for a long moment. Until, finally, Hannah deadpans, "Well, that was barely tolerable."

I burst out laughing. "Indubitably."

"But, hey," she says. "I guess having barely tolerable sex with you was better than lying here and doing nothing."

"Ditto." I kiss her cheek, roll off her, and head to the bathroom, where I dispose of the condom and do my thing. When I return to the bedroom, the sight of Hannah's naked body in the moonlight hits me like a thunderbolt. With an exaggerated growl, I leap onto the bed like a puma, scoop her into my arms, and ravish her neck, making her squeal. But when I'm done being a weirdo, I stroke her cheek and say, "All jokes aside, sex with you is something new. Supernatural. *Wow.*"

"Oh, shit. You were *joking* when you agreed it was barely tolerable? Well, this is awkward." When I laugh, Hannah does, too, before nuzzling my nose and whispering, "It was supernatural for me, too. As far as I'm concerned, your new nickname is Peter the Great. My flabber was most definitely gasted, sir."

"Not only was my flabber gasted, my awe was struck."

"It was?"

"Also, my gob was smacked."

"It was?"

"*Hard.* In fact, it's safe to say my gob was *pummeled.*"

"Whoa, you were gob-*pummeled*?" Hannah teases.

"Still am. If I'm being honest, lying here with you now, my gob has been beaten to a goddamned bloody pulp."

She grimaces.

"Too much?"

"Kinda gruesome."

I chuckle. "Yeah, okay, we'll leave it at me being gob-pummeled, then."

"I concur. I'm gob-pummeled, too. Like crazy." With that, she slides out of bed and heads to the bathroom. And the minute she's gone, I grab my phone off the nightstand and tap out a text to my two best friends in our long-running group chat.

> Me: Thank you, Joshua, for those "just in case" condoms! Thank you, Reed, for that video link you sent me last month about making women come without fail. And thank you, Baby Jesus, for finally sending me the woman of my dreams AND making her want to have sex with me AND making her want to see me again in Seattle for a whole fucking week! Thanks to all of your contributions, I can now confidently report I've found my future wife. The only question is how long I should wait before letting her in on that lil secret?

Not surprisingly, Josh replies immediately. Surely, he's lying in bed after doing with Kat what I just did with Hannah.

> Josh: Jesus, Peter. Don't say that to her before leaving for the airport, even in jest. Promise me. And don't tell her when you visit her in Seattle, either. Wait at least a fucking month.

To my surprise, Reed pops into the chat before I've replied to Josh. It's not like Reed to reply quickly in our group conversations. But I think he's in London for a meeting today, so maybe we caught him conveniently during a taxi ride or something.

> Reed: Is this the girl who flew to Vegas to have dinner with you, Peter?

> Me: The one and only. Hannah.

> Josh: Dude, they were like Phineas and Ferb all night. I never would have believed there could be a female version of Henn in this world. But there she was.

> Me: No wonder I think she's so hot.

> Reed: Good for you, Pietro. You deserve it. Gotta run. Just wanted to say a quick congrats and let you know I agree with Josh. No declarations of love or talk of the future for at least a couple months, brother. No need to say every damned thing you're thinking or feeling at first.

> Me: Oh, is that what you two always do? You wait a couple months before saying "I love you and can't wait to marry you one day"?

It's a joke. Neither of my best friends has any desire to get married. Ever. In fact, to the best of my knowledge, neither of them has even said "I love you" to any woman they've ever dated.

Josh clicks the "thumbs down" reaction to my text, and Reed sends me a middle finger emoji, so I reply with a winking emoji and return my phone to the nightstand. A moment later, Hannah returns from the bathroom, looking like a walking dream.

Hello, wife, my brain supplies. Only this time, it's a veritable scream inside my head. *She's The One.* I know it, just this fast. Obviously, I'm going to wait a reasonable amount of time to tell her so. Obviously, I'm not going to say or do anything to scare her away or make her think I'm nothing but a skeevy love-bomber who's in love with love. But I already know I couldn't find a better match for me in a thousand lifetimes. How could I? For fuck's sake, the woman danced like a gorilla with me tonight and then fucked me like a goddess. Plus, she makes me laugh like nobody else. And she's sweet as hell, too. What more could a guy want?

"Did you miss me?" Hannah asks as she slips into bed next to me.

"*Painfully.*"

"Aw, poor baby." With a snicker, Hannah reaches underneath the covers and discovers I'm not quite ready to roll again. She glances at the clock on the nightstand. "How much time do we have before you need to leave for the airport?"

"I have to leave no later than seven."

"Plenty of time."

"And yet, not nearly enough." With a smile, I take her hand and kiss the top of it—and then make a big show of flexing my hand after releasing hers—a la Mr. Darcy.

"Gah! I warned you that's my porn!" she says, before pushing me onto my back and attacking me with kisses. After a bit, her hungry mouth makes its way to my cock, which she takes into her mouth with gusto. Thankfully, my body soon rises to the occasion, and when it does, Hannah hoarsely whispers, "Get a condom." Glory be, the minute it's in place, she eagerly climbs on top of me and rides me like a cowgirl on speed.

As Hannah moves with abandon, I caress the curve of her hips and marvel that I didn't even know Hannah yesterday, and yet today I feel addicted to her. With each touch of my fingers on Hannah's soft skin, each gyration of our bodies, I feel my soul setting its course. My heart yearning. My brain cracking a code. I don't currently know what I need to do to sweep this girl off her feet. All I know is whatever it is, I'm gonna fucking do it.

7
HANNAH

I straighten the striped hotel towel covering my lounge chair before settling myself on top of it, while Kat does the same on the lounger next to mine. We're both dripping wet, having just emerged from a lovely dip in the hotel's swimming pool. As two native Seattleites accustomed to interminable gray skies and rain, Kat and I are both reveling in the scorching heat of Las Vegas.

"My body is loving all this natural Vitamin D," I murmur, settling into optimal sunbathing position.

"Girl, I can't imagine your body needs another drop of Vitamin D, given all the infusions Henn gave you last night," Kat shoots back with a snicker. When my bestie returned to our suite this morning, following her overnight escapades with Josh, we told each other every salacious detail about our respective nights. It was so much freaking fun. I'm used to hearing all about Kat's dating adventures, but this was the first time I was able to contribute to the conversation beyond "oohing" and "aahing" over Kat's storytelling.

"Can you blame me for wanting multiple infusions from Henn?" I quip playfully. "Before last night, I was so Vitamin D deprived, I'm surprised I didn't get rickets."

Kat guffaws. "Isn't scurvy the thing you get when you don't get enough Vitamin D?"

I shrug. "Either way, I can't wait to get more D when Henn comes to Seattle."

"You mean when Henn comes *in* Seattle."

We laugh hysterically. We've both had a couple fruity drinks already, even though it's only lunchtime, so I guess we're both feeling even more loose-lipped and easily amused than usual.

"I can't wait to come in LA when I visit Josh," Kat says.

"Oh, are you going there for sure?"

"He's flying me down when he gets back from New York." Kat lets out a long, pained sigh that reminds me of a hound dog lying on a porch awaiting her owner. It's a surprising thing, coming from Kat Morgan. Usually, Kat's the power player in every short-lived romance she deigns to enter—the one doling out pieces of her heart, if any, at her own pace. The one dropping breadcrumbs for the poor guy to follow and slurp up hungrily. But with Josh Faraday, it's clear *he's* the one calling the shots. And the effect on Kat is plain: the poor girl is downright lovesick.

"You're falling hard, huh?" I ask, even though her answer is a foregone conclusion.

"Too hard for my own good, I'm afraid. I can't see how this isn't going to end badly for me."

"Aw, honey. Josh is falling hard for you, too. Anyone could see that at dinner last night."

Kat shakes her head. "Josh likes me and thinks I'm fun. And, yes, he *loves* having sex with me. But he's never once looked at me the way Henn looked at you in front of the fake Eiffel Tower last night—and that was *before* you and Henn had danced like gorillas or had amazing sex, twice. I can only imagine how smitten Henn must be feeling today."

I blush. "Did I tell you we both admitted we're feeling gob-pummeled last night?"

Kat laughs. "*What?*"

I explain the origin of the silly phrase and giggle as Kat's face melts with glee.

"You two are so cute," Kat says. "Did I tell you Josh said you and Henn are like Phineas and Ferb?"

I laugh. "No, you didn't. I love it. We'll have to pick a much more glamorous duo for you and Mr. Faraday. Bonnie and Clyde, perhaps?" Kat looks lost in thought, so I add, "Kitty, I think you're not seeing what I'm seeing, when it comes to Josh. During dinner, he looked at you several times the way Henn looked at me in front of the fake Eiffel Tower. Every time you were telling a story, in fact."

"Really?"

"It was like he was gazing at a masterpiece at The Louvre."

Kat looks elated, but she bites the inside of her cheek to keep herself in check. "Or maybe he was simply looking at his current favorite sex toy." She looks around briefly to make sure nobody's about to walk by. "This is confidential," she whispers, "but when I visit Josh in LA, we're going to act out all my sexual fantasies. Some of them are pretty elaborate, so that's not a small thing for him to agree to do."

I blink several times. "Sorry, I'm having trouble computing the words all and elaborate in the same sentence as sexual fantasies. Please explain further."

Kat giggles and launches into describing a few of her top fantasies to me, all of which blow me away with their creativity.

"Wow, you've got quite the sexual imagination," I say with a chuckle.

"Don't we all," she murmurs.

"Actually, no. I don't think I've ever had a single sexual fantasy, other than getting to have sex with someone I'm wildly attracted to who knows what he's doing and enthusiastically wants to have sex with me. But since I got to fulfill that fantasy last night, I don't have anything else on my list now." I make a checkmark in the air, like I'm crossing the fantasy off my list.

"I can't imagine ever running out of fantasies," Kat says. "Once I get one checked off, another one immediately pops into my head to replace it."

"Wow."

"The best part is Josh is all-in. I told him about my top fantasies, and how they have to happen *to* me to be effective—you know, like, I can't plan them or be in charge in any way, or else they won't work because I won't be able to lose myself completely—and Josh was like, 'Leave it all to me, babe. I've got this.'"

"That's pretty hot."

Kat winks. "That's Joshua William Faraday, bitch."

We hoot with laughter.

"Sounds like Josh is the perfect man for you," I say. But it's a mistake. The minute the words leave my mouth, Kat looks lovesick again. Quickly, I add, "Listen, honey, don't put too much stock in that Eiffel Tower photo of Henn and me. As sweet as Henn's expression was in that shot, it doesn't mean anything because he doesn't know me yet. It sounds to me like you and Josh are creating something really special—your own brand of magic."

"I hope we are. But he's so damned hard to read. My biggest fear is that it's only about sex for him. I'm loving the sex, don't get me wrong. But I want more, you know?"

"I get it. All I'm saying is last night was like a fairytale for Henn and me, so don't compare yourself to us. If Henn is still looking at me like I walk on water six months from now, *after* he's gotten to know the full panoply of my annoying habits, flaws, and crippling insecurities, then, okay, you can look at that photo and think, 'Couples goals!' Until then, chalk that look up to Henn being buzzed, horny, and highly impressed with my plunging neckline."

Kat scoffs. "Henn wasn't staring at your amazing tits in that moment, babe. He was staring into your beautiful soul."

I snort. "You can see my soul in my tits?"

Kat laughs. "Hannah, you know full well Henn likes you for you."

I blush. "Yes, I do."

"But, yes, he *also* likes your tits. *A lot.*"

Again, we both laugh. Before the conversation resumes, Kat's phone rings.

"Hey, Rockstar!" Kat says brightly, which means the caller must be the youngest of the four Morgan brothers, Dax. "Yeah, I'm still in Vegas—currently, lying by the pool with my bestie and a fruity drink. No, my *work* bestie, Hannah Banana Montana Milliken. She came for a double date and stayed for a girls' trip. Mm hmm. So, tell me the latest."

As Kat dives into her phone call, I begrudgingly decide to check my work emails. But quickly, I'm diverted by an unexpected missive in my personal inbox from my all-time favorite makeup and skincare line. The subject line of the email reads: "A special offer only for you!" It's all I need to see to open the message. I can't afford to buy their wildly expensive products on my own with any regularity, so I always ask for their stuff for birthdays and Christmases.

Much to my thrill, the email says I'm among a handful of customers who've been specially selected to win a free shipment of any *five* products from their premium line, if only I'll take a brief marketing survey within the next twenty-four hours.

"Damn straight I will," I mutter, as I click on the link and then quickly begin filling out the short survey. When I reach the end of the form, another one pops up asking me to select my free gifts, all of which will be priority-shipped to the home address they already have on file for me. There's no request for my credit card or a password. Nothing whatsoever to indicate this email is a scam. So, of course, I gleefully click the "submit" button while saying a little "whoop."

"Yeah, that sounds good," Kat says on the call with her brother. "Send me links to whatever you find." She pauses for her brother to speak before responding with, "*Rabbit.* Oh, and send me details about that new bar you guys will be playing at. Maybe I'll catch your show with Ryan and Colby —unless, of course, Ry is bringing that Olivia chick with him. *Yeesh.*" She giggles. "Right? What the fuck is wrong with that man? Thinking with his dick again, obviously." Kat sighs. "Okay, Wonder Twin. You, too. Thanks for doing the legwork on this. No, I love *you* the most. Mwah, baby."

When Kat disconnects the call, I ask what's up, and she explains she and her four brothers—Colby, Ryan, Keane, and Dax—are buying a joint birthday present for their beloved mother and that her youngest brother, Dax, is taking the lead on figuring everything out.

"I usually do it," Kat explains, "but this year, I said, 'Peace out, bitches. I'm going to Vegas.'"

At my urging, Kat tells me the latest about Dax's three-man alternative-rock band, 22 Goats, including the fact that Dax and his two bandmates, Fish and Colin, have been saving money to record a full-length album in a fancy studio. Apparently, an album like that will cost at least fifteen grand. Not an easy amount to raise for three young, struggling musicians.

"But guess what?" Kat says with a mischievous twinkle in her blue eyes. "Thanks to Josh and his brother, and all the winnings they let me keep at the craps table the other night, I'm going to surprise Daxy with all the money he needs for his album, and then some."

I'm shocked. Kat is a generous person, but she's got a car payment, same as me. Also, some credit card debt, same as me. I can't believe she's lucked into fifteen grand or more and plans to give it *all* to her little brother.

"You're giving him *all* your winnings?" I ask.

"Yep. Do I have things I could pay off with that money? Sure. But those things wouldn't be life-changing for me the way an album could be for Dax and his bandmates. Dax said a high-quality album could get 22 Goats signed to an established label."

We talk a bit more about Dax and his band, and when that conversation runs its course, I tell Kat about the email I just received from the expensive makeup line.

"Check your emails," I say, since I know Kat sometimes buys this brand's products, too.

"I got it, too!" Kat announces. "Our lucky streak continues, Hannah Banana Montana Milliken!"

As Kat dives into the brief survey, a waiter appears. With his dark eyes trained on Kat, he says, "Piña colada?"

I raise my hand to attract his attention. "Piña colada here."

The man hands me the drink before passing the rum punch to Kat by default. "Your food will be out soon, ladies," he informs us. He takes a lingering look at Kat, who's still busy on her phone, and then covertly glances at my chest, which looks particularly buxom in this bathing suit, I must admit, before striding away with his tray pressed against his hip.

As the waiter disappears, Kat looks up from her phone and snorts. "He took a nice gander at your boobs. Can't say I blame him. You're a smoke show in that bikini, girl."

Kat always says stuff like that to me. She tells me I'm a smoke show. A knockout. Gorgeous. She insists men are staring at me when it's clear she's the object of their desire. And yet, I never doubt Kat's sincerity. In fact, I'm grateful for the positive reinforcement. So often, media and entertainment portray women built like Kat as the main character in the movie of life, while women built like me are relegated to sassy sidekick status. Whenever I'm with Kat, though, I always feel every bit her equal co-star.

Obviously, my blonde bombshell of a bestie can't help that she won the genetic lottery, but what she *can* help is how she chooses to react to and internalize all the unearned adulation she receives from the world. It's my theory Kat consciously decided at some point not to believe the hype. Or at least, to expand her view of beauty beyond what she sees in magazines, all of which reflect visions of herself back to her. Did Kat's mom teach her that? However she got here, it's lovely to be Kat's friend because she gleefully and sincerely shares the spotlight with everyone she loves, which thankfully includes me.

Kat turns over onto her stomach and I'm treated to a view of her bare ass cheeks.

"Good lord, woman," I say. "That suit gives new meaning to the phrase teeny weeny string bikini. Is there a thong in that ass crack somewhere?"

Kat guffaws. "You like it? Josh picked this suit out for me during a shopping spree here in Vegas. You wouldn't believe how much it cost, considering how little fabric was used."

"There's fabric? Oh yeah, I think I saw some covering your nipples and clit."

Again, Kat positively guffaws.

"Promise me something," I say. "If you ever feel the urge to spend your own hard-earned money on a designer suit like that, please don't. In that case, I'll jimmy together an exact replica for you out of nothing but dental floss and three well-placed cottonballs."

Kat cackles at my joke. "If you could also jimmy together a pair of gorgeous tits like yours to pour into said replica suit, I'd appreciate it."

"I'll place the order on Door Dash right now."

She snickers. "You and your Door Dash."

"A girl's best friend."

Kat motions to my chest area. "Did Henn have a stroke when he finally got to see those beauties, wild and free, last night?"

"He sure did. And then, he almost suffocated in them after diving in. Talk about a deep dive."

Kat hoots. "Henn kept sneaking peeks at your cleavage throughout dinner. He thought he was so subtle and clever, but it was so obvious."

"I would have been offended if he hadn't noticed them. I didn't wear that neckline and push-up bra for them to be ignored, for fuck's sake."

"Why don't you send Henn a selfie now? Give the boy a little something to stare at every night in his hotel room in DC."

"I can't text him first. I'll let him get off his flight and text me he's landed safely and *then* send him a selfie. I've got to let the boy chase me a bit."

Kat snorts. "As opposed to what you did last night?"

She's teasing me playfully, not judging me. As we both know, Kat has had more than her fair share of first-night hookups. In fact, she loves hooking up on first dates, if the guy is hot enough—as all her dates are, basically—as long as she's sure he doesn't have long-term potential. But what I did with Henn last night, including the raunchy way I invited him into my room, was a first for me, and Kat not only knows that, she's enthralled by it.

"In all seriousness," I say, "do you think I hopped into bed with Henn too quickly?"

"*What*? Of course, not. You were feeling it, and so was he, so you both went for it. Godspeed, my friends."

"Studies say sex too soon lowers the chances of a relationship becoming serious. I'm not looking for a fun hook-up. I'm looking for a boyfriend."

"Henn knows that. I personally think it's a great sign you couldn't resist inviting him to ride your Slip 'n' Slide." She snickers.

"I never should have told you that."

"And yet, you did. And now it's my favorite thing."

"If first-date sex is no big deal, then why were you so determined not to sleep with Josh too soon?"

Kat scoffs. "*Because Josh is a playboy*—a guy used to getting anything and anyone he wants at the snap of his fingers. But Henn's nothing like that. He's *humble*. Plus, he's made it abundantly clear he's into you as a person. With Josh and me, our connection is so fucking sexual, it's hard for me to figure out if that's all there is."

"Of course, that's not all there is. He's obviously totally into you."

"We shall see. In the meantime, there's no doubt we'll have a whole lot of fun."

Kat turns over onto her back again and sips her rum punch, looking contemplative, so I drink my piña colada and try to decipher the source of my pitted stomach. I think maybe I'm paranoid, thanks to my whirlwind romance with Angus two years ago that turned out to be nothing but a scam on his part. A cruel money grab. It's not that I think, even for a minute, that Henn is using me like that, but I'm not willing to trust every word out of anyone's mouth this early on, either.

"I think, out of an abundance of caution," I say, "when Henn comes to Seattle, I'll tell him I want to press the reset button on our physical relationship and slow things down. I think we both got swept up in the fantasy vibe of Vegas, but when we're back to real life, we'll benefit from taking things at a normal pace."

"I'm sure Henn will be supportive of whatever you want to do."

"It's not that I doubt Henn. It's just that I've been stupid and gullible in the past."

Kat looks sympathetic. "You're talking about that dumb jock scammer you told me about?" Kat juts her lower lip in sympathy. "Aw, honey. Don't beat yourself up about him. All women, including me, have at least one embarrassing story about some dumbass lying sack of shit who played them like a fiddle. I certainly have a story like that. Live and learn, sister."

"Yeah, but at least you didn't say yes to marrying your dumbass lying sack of shit."

"Pfft," Kat says. "I've had belches that lasted longer than your so-called engagement to that scumbag." To prove her point, she opens her mouth and lets out a loud, disgusting burp that makes me wince and guffaw in equal measure.

"It's so jarring when you do that," I say. "My brain can't process a sound that hideous coming out of something so pretty."

"That's what happens when a girl grows up with four disgusting brothers, babe; she learns to out-belch 'em all." Kat giggles with me. "Seriously, though, don't beat yourself up about saying yes when that asshole proposed to you. He was a master manipulator."

"The crazy thing is I've never even wanted to get married all that much. Yes, I want to fall in love with my soulmate and have a life partner and maybe even a kid one day. But the whole idea of marriage has never appealed to me all that much."

"Because of your parents' divorce?"

"Maybe. All I know is I've never once dreamed of myself walking down the aisle in a white dress."

"Oh, I have."

That's not news to me, but even so, Kat's Disney-like expression nonetheless touches my heart. I know Kat comes across at first blush as a wild, fun party girl, but when you get to know her, she turns out to be a diehard romantic who's awaiting her prince—a girl who genuinely believes in fairytales. Maybe that's because she grew up observing parents who've always been deeply in love. Maybe she's simply wired differently than me. Either way, I know for a fact Kat's excited to one day meet the love of her life and become his wife.

"You were in a vulnerable state," Kat says, probably reacting to the contemplative look on my face. "That fucker knew that about you and took advantage of it."

She's right. At the time, I felt totally swept away by what I thought was a fated romance. But also, and I hate to admit this, I think I also felt flattered that a guy *that* good looking was *that* into me. Supposedly. In reality, of course, the truth is that I was in bad shape mentally, thanks to the recent death of my grandmother and Maddy's horrific car accident, and Angus knew that. For me, Angus felt like a fantastical, much-needed escape from my real-life struggles. To him, I was a simple mark.

Our waiter arrives with food. As he hands Kat and me our respective meals, we order another round of drinks and then dig into our food with gusto as he walks away.

"I hope you trust your intuition when it comes to Henny," Kat says. "He's such a sweetheart."

"Oh, I do. Mostly. Nobody can be as perfect as he seemed last night. But I'd never think he's scamming me. He's just putting his best foot forward on a first date, like we all do, including me."

"Josh and Reed absolutely adore him. They also admire him. They call him a fucking genius every chance they get, and from what I've personally witnessed of Henn's amazing computer skills, that label is spot-on."

I tilt my head. "You've personally witnessed Henn's amazing computer skills? In what context?"

Kat's face reddens. "Oh. Yeah, this past week. Henn would sometimes be hard at work on his computer while our whole group happened to be there—Josh, Jonas, Sarah, and me—and we'd ask him questions, and every time he explained whatever he was doing, we were all totally blown away."

Something isn't sitting right with me. Kat won't pay attention to my computer screen long enough to learn how to perform a new function on a spreadsheet. And yet, she supposedly sat there and listened to Henn talking about his computer programming skills long enough to be blown away by them? I can't fathom it. Also, come on. Whatever cybersecurity stuff Henn briefly explained to the group couldn't possibly have been *that* impressive to merit that description. Nope. Kat has to be exaggerating—over-stating Henn's talents—because she's so invested in her match-making working out.

"What, exactly, did Henn explain to you that was so impressive?" I ask. I try to keep a straight face as I say it. Not let on I'm basically calling bullshit on her story.

"Oh. Uh. I don't remember exactly. But whatever it was, Josh and Jonas seemed really impressed by it."

I'd think her sudden backtracking humorous, if it weren't for the fact that Kat's now visibly falling apart in front of me. Her nostrils are flaring. Her cheeks blooming. Holy crap, she's even blinking rapidly. As I well know from playing drinking games with Kat that depend on bluffing and/or flat-out lying, that's all the stuff Kat does when she's not telling the complete truth. Kat always fools everyone in every game she plays . . . *except for me.* Unlike everyone else, I can *always* spot Kat's tells. And, holy fuck, I'm spotting them now.

"What are you not telling me?" I ask, all semblance of playfulness gone from my tone. I'm calling her to the carpet with my voice now. Pinning her against the wall in an interrogation room.

"Hmm?" she says meekly.

"You're not telling me the full truth about something. Spit it out."

Kat smiles, but it's her fake smile—the one she flashes at our boss, Rebecca, before turning and rolling her eyes at me. "The only thing I'm not telling you involves Josh, me, and this crazy orgasm machine called a Sybian—and I don't think you could handle the full truth about that, Banana."

She's deflecting. Hoping I'll take the bait and ask her about this newly offered topic. I admit I'm damned curious, but I can't allow myself to be distracted by Kat's usual tricks. Not when I can see deception written all over her gorgeous face. After making a mental note to google "Sybian" in the hotel room later on, I say, "Cut the crap, dude. I can tell there's something you're not telling me. Is it something about Henn?"

Kat makes a funny face and exhales. "How do you always know when I'm lying?"

"If I explain your tells to you, then you might fix them. And that wouldn't be in my interest. Is there some kind of red flag about Henn I'm not seeing? Something you haven't told me?"

"Oh, God, no. Quite the contrary. Henn is a hero." When it's clear I'm waiting for more, Kat looks around and then leans in and whispers, "Okay, fine. But this is highly confidential, okay? You can't tell a soul. Not even Maddy. Not even Henn."

My heart rate increases. "I promise."

"I mean it, Banana. Sarah told Henn and the guys about my Blabber-mouth nickname growing up, and they all made me swear I'd keep my big mouth shut about this. I'm only telling you, in confidence, so you'll feel assured that Henn is as great a guy as he seems." She pauses, apparently choosing her words carefully. "Sarah recently found out her employer was doing some shady shit, and then she got really scared because she knew *they* knew she knew. So, Jonas told Josh the situation, and Josh called Henn, and then we all came to Vegas to meet with Henn and figure out a gameplan to protect Sarah. In the end, Henn was able to hack the bastards and get some dirt on them, which we then turned over to the FBI. And now Sarah is safe and sound and happy as a clam with Jonas, and the whole saga is behind her. Thank God."

"Oh my gosh. Holy shit, Kat."

"That's why Henn went to DC this morning—because the FBI wants him to walk them through all the data we turned over to them."

"*Wow.*" I sigh with relief from the depths of my soul. "Thank you so much for telling me that. After the fiasco with Angus, I get paranoid whenever it feels like a guy might be hiding something."

"I'm sure Henn won't tell you about any of this. We're all sworn to secrecy, not only with each other, but with the FBI, too. But that won't mean Henn is hiding something from you, in a traditional sense. I promise he's everything he appears to be. In fact, like I said, he's a hero."

I put my palm onto my beating heart. "I'm swooning." My phone buzzes and I look down to find a text from the swoon-inducer himself. "Henn's ears must be ringing," I say with a chuckle. "He says he's landed in DC and couldn't stop thinking about me during the flight."

"Send him a bikini selfie and he'll keep thinking about you, all night long."

"Let's take one together. I don't want it to seem like I'm sexting him this early on."

Kat shakes her head. "Henn doesn't need a photo of me wearing dental floss, babe. Let him focus his undivided attention on your glorious tits and smile."

"Excellent point."

Kat picks up her phone. "Say, 'Slip 'n' Slide!'"

Laughing, I hold up my drink to the camera and she snaps the shot. And when the photo lands on my screen from Kat, I have to admit, it's a hot one. I forward it to Henn with the following message:

> Me: I can't stop thinking about you, too. In fact, Kat and I were just talking about you while lounging at the pool with cocktails. Cheers!

> Henn: HOLY FUCK!!! YOU'RE HOTTER THAN THE VEGAS SUN!

Henn attaches a string of emojis, including "heart eyes" and flames.

> Me: Glad you like it.

Henn: Like it? No. I'm gob-pummeled by it. I'm at the airport and had to face a wall for a minute so nobody would bump into my flagpole that's suddenly sticking out at full mast.

Me: LOL. Photo, please. Of your face. Actually, of your flagpole, too. In your pants, though.

Henn: Seriously?

Me: It didn't happen if there's no photo.

Henn: Okay. But don't show the pants one to Kat, okay? Or anyone else.

Me: I promise. Same deal on my bikini shot.

Henn: Deal.

A poorly lit selfie of Henn's face lands on my screen. There are people milling around behind him at a baggage carousel. He looks tired from his long flight. But, damn, his expression makes me laugh. Clearly, he's intending to show me the face he made when my photo landed on his screen, and it's absolutely hilarious and adorable.

Two seconds later, a photo of Henn's pants hits my screen. The crotch area. Where a discernible bulge is poking behind the fabric.

Me: SMOKING HAWT! Send me a smile now, please.

Another photo hits my screen. And there it is. The sweet, warm smile that made my heart go pitter pat throughout dinner.

Me: You've got such a lovely smile.

Henn: It's easy to smile when I think about you.

Me: You make me smile, too. I'm doing it right now, in fact.

Henn: Same. I'd give ANYTHING to be there with you to see you in that bathing suit in person. Hell, I'd give anything to see you in person in a potato sack.

Me: I can't wait to see you in Seattle.

Henn: Same. I'm already counting the days, even though I don't know how many it'll be. I've got to run to a meeting now. Have a blast with Kat and send me lots of pics of your shenanigans this week.

Me: Will do. I hope whatever job you're doing in DC goes well. Bye for now, Peter the Great. XO

Henn: Bye for now, Hannah the Beautiful. The Smoking Hot. The Funny and Smart. Thanks again for the amazing photo. I'll stare at it all week to keep me company on lonely nights. XX

When I look up from my phone, Kat is smirking wickedly at me. "There's no way in hell you're going to wait to have sex with that man when he comes to Seattle," she says. "I predict you'll pounce on him the minute he walks through your front door."

I put my phone down on a side table and scoff. "Nope. I've made my decision, and I'm going to stick to it. In fact, I'm going to ask Henn to book a hotel room, rather than inviting him to stay with me. I'll also ask my sister to be there at my apartment when Henn arrives to pick me up for our first date. See? I'm determined."

Kat downright belly laughs. "All it's going to take is one goodnight kiss and you'll be inviting him to ride your Slip 'n' Slide again."

"You want to bet a buck?" Kat and I often bet a dollar on silly things to keep our work life fun and interesting. So much so, we have this one crumpled dollar bill that's been traded back and forth between us at least a hundred times.

Kat says, "I'll bet you a *hundred* bucks you'll sleep with Henn the first night he's in Seattle."

"A *hundred* bucks?" I'm shocked. Kat and I have never bet more than a dollar on anything. "That's way too rich for my blood, sister."

"Fifty, then," Kat amends. "Why not, if you're so sure of your plan to take things slow?"

I squint sharply, making her laugh. "Okay, fine, it's a bet." I shake her hand. "*Sucker*. This is totally within my control, remember?"

Kat snorts and releases my hand. "So you think. But I'm the one who can see you, remember? You can't see yourself. And, girl, it's obvious you're bewitched and besotted by this boy." Kat and I use those two words quite a bit, thanks to our mutual love of *Pride & Prejudice*. But we normally use them to describe our respective sandwiches or some new eyeliner we've discovered. She's never once used the words to describe *me* in relation to a guy.

"It's that obvious?" I ask.

"Oh, honey." At this angle, I can see Kat closing her eyes behind her sunglasses. "The good news is you're a winner either way. If you win the bet, you'll get a cool fifty bucks and the chance to say I told you so. And if you lose, it'll be because you've realized banging Henn sounds more delicious to you than pocketing fifty bucks and getting to tell me to stuff it—and that realization, my friend, will only make the sex even hotter." Kat snickers. "*You're welcome.*"

8

HENN

I climb out of the Uber with my computers and duffel bag. I've got about an hour before my meeting at FBI headquarters a few blocks away—fuck my life—so I figure I'll use my downtime productively. I head into the coffee place I selected as my destination while standing on a curb at Dulles, and thankfully, it's pretty empty at this time of day.

I place an order at the counter for a quintuple-shot Americano and take a seat at a small table in a corner with my back against the wall. There's nobody at any of the tables nearest to me, exactly the way I like it. Also, the two surveillance cameras—both of them mounted across the room close to the ceiling—are positioned in such a way that they won't be able to capture my laptop screen or the movements of my fingers on my keyboard. *Perfect.*

It's not that I think anyone is actually watching me or tracking my physical person. Or even that anyone will go back and peruse the surveillance footage of me. But this is standard practice for me when I'm working in public because I always assume there's someone actively looking for me at all times. Or rather, for the anonymous hacker known as Bluebird—the unidentified person who's slithered into their devices and fucked them over six ways from Sunday. If not that, then I assume there's some random, two-bit hacker nearby who's trying to pilfer banking info or passwords from anyone naive enough to log into public wi-fi.

My surroundings secured, I pull out one of my three laptops and place it onto my small table, along with my coffee cup and an encrypted mobile hotspot. Before getting myself connected, however, I can't resist once again peeking at that eye-popping bikini shot of Hannah. Holy fuck. She's a goddess. Not only physically, but in every way. I've never felt this kind of insane spark with anyone. Not on a first date. Not on a fiftieth. Now that I've experienced it, I'm determined to fan the flame until it grows into a raging forest fire. Hence, the phishing link I sent to Hannah earlier today. I'm dying to see if Hannah or Kat clicked my link. But first, I'm going to force myself to do some work.

I get myself connected and log into the encrypted server I use for communications with my regular, vetted clients. I've got several new messages, including requests from attorneys who represent victims of sexual abuse. As usual, they're asking me to hack a target and scour his devices for proof he's a rapist or pedophile. There's also a message from a divorce-attorney friend of mine who represents high-net-worth clients. As usual, she wants me to track down the hidden assets of her client's soon-to-be-ex. There are plenty of private investigators who do this type of work, but nobody does it quite like me. When Bluebird's on the case, no stone goes unturned, because it's the douchebag himself who leads me to all relevant stones.

After replying to all various requests, I check on the status of a few irons in the fire. Make some adjustments to code and send a few phishing links. And when that work is done, I give myself permission to finally check my personal computer to see if Hannah and/or Kat has clicked the survey link I sent this morning.

Bingo. Well, that was easy.

I sent the link to Kat, as well as to Hannah, as a back-up measure—just in case my actual target was too savvy to fall for the oldest phishing trick in the book. I love Kat dearly and respect her intellect immensely, but she's a total shit show when it comes to tech stuff, so I knew she'd click my link without a second thought. Once I had Kat, I figured I could easily get into Hannah's devices, since both women work for the same PR firm and remotely sign onto the same server. As it's turned out, though, Kat wasn't a necessary bridge into Hannah's devices.

Okay, I'm in Hannah's phone and ready to poke around. Obviously, I'll steer clear of her personal and confidential information, stuff like her texts and emails and anything related to her finances and medical care. My overarching goal here isn't tricking or fooling Hannah into liking me. It's not presenting myself as someone I'm not—someone Hannah would like better than the actual me. I'm simply gathering intel on Hannah's niche preferences—stuff that will help me plan a week's worth of perfect dates that will sweep her off her feet. What sane person—or superhero, in my case—*wouldn't* want to do that after meeting the woman of his dreams?

When a normal person has a crush, they head to Google. Or perhaps they scour Instagram for clues and/or ask mutual friends for intel. Well, this is a hacker's equivalent of doing all that. If Superman wanted to get Lois Lane the perfect gift, he'd use his X-ray vision to peek into Lois' bedroom closet to check out what brand of dresses or shoes she likes best, and nobody would call him a creep for doing it. They'd call him romantic. *Thoughtful.* Clearly, it'd be a different story if Superman used his X-ray vision to covertly peep at Lois while she was in the shower. But that's not at all what I'm doing here, even metaphorically.

Okay, this is something Hannah didn't tell me last night: she's a sucker for buying pretty necklaces off social media ads. I could have guessed that, I suppose, since she was wearing a pretty necklace at dinner last night. *Note to self: give Hannah a necklace as a gift at some point down the line.*

Moving on.

It looks like Hannah's a bit of a gamer. She loves World of Warcraft, just like me. But she already told me that at dinner. Some other interests, based on what I'm seeing, include reading, movies, documentaries, cooking, baking, and keeping up with trash TV and celebrity gossip. But none of that is new information.

Ah, here's something that might be mildly helpful to me in terms of planning future dates or gifts. There are several digital punch cards in the wallet on Hannah's phone. One, from a crepes place near Pike's Place and another from a bakery by the University of Washington. Definitely something to keep in mind, but certainly not enough to sweep her off her feet.

I click into a florist app and discover Hannah's an avid purchaser of floral bouquets. Not for herself, however. She frequently sends bouquets to friends and family—for the usual special occasions and also in celebration of personal milestones and small victories. I already knew Hannah was a sweetheart, but this is only further proof of that fact.

I scroll through Hannah's past flower orders to get a read on her preferred aesthetic. Looks like she prefers colorful, bright bouquets filled with big, bold blooms, as opposed to delicate, elegant ones in whites or pastels. That certainly jibes with Hannah's personality. She's a bold, bright person with nothing subtle about her. A woman who wears her heart on her sleeve, the same way I do. I really like that about Hannah, because I'm not always great at reading subtle social cues.

I leave Hannah's phone and find a florist in Vegas on my computer, where I order a bright, bold bouquet to be delivered to Hannah's hotel room tomorrow morning, along with a card that reads, "Thinking of you. Can't wait to see you in Seattle! XO Henny." The arrangement I've ordered is much bigger and far more expensive than anything Hannah has ever purchased. And rightly so. My goal isn't making her say, "Oh, how sweet!" It's making her physically swoon. While I'm thinking about flowers, I order a bouquet for my mom in Fresno with a note that says, "I love you, Mom." And then, return to snooping around Hannah's phone.

What's this? Hannah's got a porn site app loaded onto her phone. Color me curious.

No, Henn. That's out of bounds. The equivalent of using your X-ray vision to be a Peeping Tom.

Somehow, I muster the strength to ignore the porn app and move along.

Another click, and I'm exploring Hannah's order history with the world's largest online ticket vendor—but it only confirms something I already knew: Hannah is me in female form. I search to find out if any of our mutual favorites will be in Seattle in the timeframe when I'll likely be there and discover a comedian Hannah and I have both seen twice in our respective cities will be performing there in about three weeks. *Hallelujah.* This is precisely the sort of intel I was hoping to find.

I tap out an excited text to Hannah, telling her that such and such comedian—one of my all-time favorites—is coming to Seattle on such and such date. I conclude with, "If you'd like to go with me, I'll grab tickets."

Hannah replies quickly:

> **Hannah:** I LOVE HIM! I've seen him twice and he's soooo funny! Sadly, his Seattle show is already sold out. I tried to get tix mere hours after they went on sale, and they were all gone. :(Thank you for the thought, though.

> **Me:** Let me see what I can do. I've got a connection.

> **Hannah:** AAAHHH! Fingers crossed! But PLEASE don't spend too much. The resale market is insane.

> **Me:** No worries. I'm on it, pretty lady.

> **Hannah:** If you somehow score tix, PLEASE let me pay half! I don't want you spending an arm and a leg. Only a leg. Haha.

> **Me:** Your money is no good to me. But I appreciate the offer.

> **Hannah:** Thank you. Cheers!

A photo lands on my phone. It's Hannah and Kat, both of them wrapped in fluffy, white robes and holding champagne flutes to the camera. They're obviously at a spa, living their best life, exactly as Josh wanted. At the sight of the shot—at the obvious glee on Hannah's pretty face—my heart bursts with affection for her.

> **Me:** Love it! I'll let you know about the tix.

Hannah: Woohoo! I AM SWOONING SO HARD, Peter the Great! XOXOXO

Me: I'm having a similar reaction on my end, Milly Vanilli! XOXOXO

There's a slight pause. And then:

Hannah: Hey, btw, have you already talked to Reed about Maddy's UCLA application? After thinking about it (while sober haha), I've realized Maddy wouldn't actually want Reed to help her out. I'm positive my sister would feel like that would be an unfair advantage. Maybe even cheating.

Me: No, I haven't talked to Reed yet. I was going to do it after Maddy submits her application. But if Reed knows someone, he'd only ask them to take a closer look at her application. She'd still have to get in on her own merits.

Hannah: I'm positive Maddy wouldn't see it that way. I really appreciate the offer, but this pit in my stomach tells me not to let you do it. As much as I'm dying to help make her dreams come true, I can't do that at any cost. I'd feel better crossing my fingers and toes for her while letting the process run its course naturally.

Me: I can respect that. I'll keep my fingers and toes crossed for her, too.

Hannah: Thank you so much.

Welp. Add this to the long list of reasons Hannah Milliken impresses the hell out of me. I was more than happy to ask Reed to help Maddy out, and honestly didn't think twice about Hannah accepting my offer last night. But now that she's made this about-face, I can't deny I'm even more attracted to her. Talk about a stark one-eighty from the longtime acquaintances and fraternity brothers who hit me up for self-serving favors to this day, simply because, at some point in our distant past, I did some small favor for them.

Okay, back to those tickets.

I head to a secret back door to the ticket seller's system; one I created eons ago that has never failed me. Fun fact: Even when a show has been advertised as "sold out," there's always a block of tickets still available— seats held back for VIPs or insiders. The best part is there's never any rhyme or reason regarding the number of tickets held back, which means a guy like me can slip in undetected, grab a couple seats from the slush fund, code them in the system as properly issued, and nobody is ever the wiser.

> Me: I scored two tix!

Hannah doesn't reply immediately, so it's back to exploring her phone I go.

I check out her Pinterest account and peruse her boards—both the ones she's posted and those she's kept private. *Aw.* One of Hannah's unposted boards is entitled "Dream Board." At dinner, she referenced having one, but I thought she was being figurative.

She's got an image of a kickass career woman on her board. Scenes of faraway travel destinations, including iconic shots of Paris. And last but not least, there's a cute little family—a man whose head has been replaced by a question mark, a woman whose face has been replaced by Hannah's, and a little baby. *Oh, my heart.* If this family represents Hannah's dream, then we really are a perfect match. I'd give up all the money in the world, all the answers to all the secrets of the universe—hell, I'd even give up my superpower—to have the kind of unbreakable love my parents had. And then, on top of that, to create a whole other person out of that love. Damn. Even thinking about doing that gives me goosebumps.

My phone pings with an incoming text, drawing me out of my daydreams. Fuck. It's one of my old fraternity brothers, Alonso. Or, as I've always called him, Asshat. To this day, he relies on our supposed "brotherhood" a decade ago to seek favors from me, despite the fact that I haven't said yes to any of his requests since college.

> Alonso: Yo, Henn. I need a favor, brother. I'm up for a huge promotion at work and a little birdie in HR told me it's between me and a guy from the outside. I'm hoping you'll dig up some dirt on the outside guy for me—anything I can use to kick him out of the running for the job.

Dick. If Alonso knew me at all, he'd know I only do favors for my tightest inner circle and he's not in it. Also, that the favors I do for said inner circle bear zero resemblance to this type of self-serving bullshit. For all I know, the other guy might be more deserving of the promotion, so why would I ruin that guy's chances, simply because Alonso and I happened to be in the same fraternity years ago? Also, is it too much to expect an actual "Hello, Henn, how are you?" from a "brother" texting me out of nowhere for a favor? Fuck him.

> Me: Hey, Alonso. Can't help you. Good luck with the promotion. May the best man win.

As I'm pressing send on my text, my phone buzzes with an incoming reply from Hannah about the tickets.

Hannah: I'm screaming, crying, throwing up, swooning! THANK YOUUUUU!

Me: My pleasure.

Hannah: I hope you didn't spend too much.

Me: Nope. Like I said, I have a connection.

Hannah: Now, that's a great friend to have! Tell him or her thank you from meeeee!

Me: I will.

Thank you, self.
You're welcome, self. Anything for you.

Hannah: They just called our names for massages. Talk soon! Mwah! XOXO

Me: Have fun! XOXO

I pop out of my conversation with Hannah and into her phone, where my gaze is immediately drawn to that porn app again. Fuck it. That sucker is calling to me like a siren.

Once I'm in the app, I head straight to Hannah's "recently watched" videos—although recently seems to be a relative term in this case, since Hannah apparently hasn't viewed anything in months. It's possible she's been watching porn elsewhere, I suppose, but I have a hunch her lackluster activity on this app means Hannah's not all that into porn in general. Perhaps, when Hannah said Mr. Darcy's hand-flex is her version of porn, she was being literal.

I skim the thumbnails of her recently watched queue, hoping something might help me make Hannah's dirtiest fantasies come true when I visit her in Seattle. But it's clear this idea is a dead end. Hannah's two most recently watched videos feature dudes voraciously eating pussy, which I already do, and hopefully much better than that.

The video right before the pussy-eaters features two dudes going at it. Again, not helpful. It's not that I have anything against two dudes having sex, of course. Love is love. Or lust. Whatever. But I'm not willing to have sex with another man, not even as a gift to Hannah. Looks like there's going to be a whole lot of pussy-eating and hand-flexing in my near future. No complaints from me on either score.

Okay, that's it for Hannah's phone.

Onto her laptop.

It takes me a minute to get in, but when I do, I quickly realize almost everything duplicates what I've already perused on her phone. Either that, or it's off-limits to me, according to my personal code of ethics. But what's this? There's a folder on Hannah's desktop entitled, "The Asshole." That's definitely something new.

Inside, there's a PDF file and a subfolder entitled "Attorney." I click on the PDF and find it's a legal form from the State of Washington, King County, entitled "Petition of Protection Order" that's dated about two and a half years ago. Hannah's name has been filled in as Petitioner, while "Greg Smith aka Angus Wellborn" is identified as Respondent.

In the body of the form, there are several possible boxes to check. According to the ones marked by Hannah, she was seeking protection from an "intimate partner" who'd committed "unlawful harassment" in the form of a "single act/threat of violence, including a malicious and intentional threat causing substantial emotional distress." In the space provided for a brief explanation, Hannah typed in the following:

"My supposed ex-boyfriend of two months, whom I knew as Angus Wellborn but later found out is Greg Smith, is a con artist/scammer who preys on vulnerable women for financial gain. Angus pursued me enthusiastically on a dating app during a vulnerable time in my life and pretended to fall head over heels in love with me, even going so far as to propose to me. By doing so, he quickly charmed me out of half the small

inheritance I'd recently received from my late grandmother. Also, unbeknownst to me at the time, Angus stole my confidential information and used it to take out a loan and several credit cards in my name.

"Before I realized what he was up to, I glimpsed a long list of names and numbers on his laptop screen, when he didn't realize I'd entered the room. The formatting of the numbers looked like social security and credit card numbers to me. I was so freaked out, I quickly left the room and peeked in his wallet to see what credit cards were in there, and that's when I found out his real name. At that point, I was so freaked out, I pretended to leave for the store and never came back. When I got home, I did some research and discovered there'd been tons of new financial activity under my name, none of it initiated by me and all of it in the two months since Angus had come into my life. Needless to say, I was heartbroken, humiliated, and furious.

"When I confronted Angus, I did it over the phone. That turned out to be a lucky thing, because he morphed into a totally different person during that confrontation. He screamed and threatened to come after me and 'shut me up forever' if I told the police anything about what I'd seen. I should mention he's a large, strong, athletic man who works as a personal trainer, so I didn't doubt he could make good on his threats.

"After several sleepless nights, I eventually decided to do the right thing and go to the police to report everything, if only to stop him from doing the same thing to the next woman, but they told me it was a 'he said/she said' situation, since I didn't think to document what I'd seen before running out. I did show them the loans and credit cards that had been taken out in my name, but they said there was zero proof it was Angus who did all that. It's now been a week since I went to the police and nobody has contacted me as part of an investigation, so I don't think they're doing anything. But now I'm terrified Angus will somehow find out I went to the police and come after me or my loved ones. I'm doing what I can to feel safe: looking for a new job and apartment and also shopping at a new grocery store. But I'd feel safer knowing he's not legally allowed to come near me, ever again. Please help me."

. . .

I close my eyes and try to contain the firestorm swirling inside me. The thumping urge inside my veins to destroy this terrorizer of Hannah and menace to society. Did the police ever bother to investigate him? Did Hannah get her requested protective order? I scroll down and note the space at the bottom of the form for Hannah's signature is empty. Also, there's no signature or stamp by the court in issuance of an order. Is there a fully signed version of this form and protective order on file somewhere, or is this unsigned draft as far as Hannah got in the process?

I click on the subfolder labeled "Attorney." Inside, there's a series of emails between Hannah and an attorney from a Seattle-based legal aid organization. Hannah's initial email is a "To Whom It May Concern" missive that requests someone please look over the paperwork she's filled out and is planning to file, in order to confirm she did everything right. The attorney who replied asks some questions about Hannah's vulnerable state upon meeting Angus, which prompts Hannah to write: "In the month prior, my beloved grandmother died, and my sister was in a horrible car crash. In retrospect, I think Angus targeted me specifically because I'd posted a tribute to my grandmother on Instagram. I think he hoped, correctly, that she'd left me some money."

The attorney asks Hannah if any of Greg Smith's threats were made in writing.

"No," Hannah replies. "All threats were made during a phone call. He did send me some horrible emails after that, though. Will these help me?" She attaches them to her reply:

All you had to do was look at me and then at yourself in a mirror to know I wasn't actually into you. I'm a personal trainer, dumbass, and you look like you've never been inside a fucking gym. If you were too delusional and stupid to figure me out, then that's on you.

If you want to blame someone, then blame yourself for being stupid enough to think you could actually pull a guy like me. A little advice? Stop baking cookies and eat a fucking carrot, bitch. You got what you deserved.

. . .

I can't breathe. Can't think straight. I feel murderous rage coursing through me in a way I've never experienced before. I look around the coffee place, feeling like smoke is physically billowing out my ears. I don't know where Greg Smith exists in this world at this moment, but when I find out, I'm going to fucking destroy him.

After several deep breaths and a long chug of my coffee, I return to Hannah's communications with the attorney. "Those texts are absolutely despicable," the attorney writes. "But, unfortunately, they're not action-able in a legal sense. Mean words alone aren't grounds for a protective order." After a bit more back and forth, the attorney ultimately advises Hannah *not* to file her legal form yet, if ever. The attorney explains, "Since he seems to be out of your life for good, and it's also highly unlikely the police will pursue him, I think you'll actually be safer if you don't poke the bear, so to speak. Let him move onto his next target and forget you exist. If he contacts you again and/or threatens you in any fashion, then file this paperwork immediately." She gives Hannah a few pointers for things to add to her form and wishes her luck. And that's that. Apparently, Hannah never filed the form or contacted the attorney again.

My heart pounding, I click out of Hannah's laptop and immediately dive head-first into searching the fucker's two names. Not surprisingly, given that Hannah filled out this form over two years ago, he's no longer at the address listed on the form. Also, the email he used to send those heinous messages to Hannah is no longer active. My "penile enlargement" spam message bounces right back.

Thankfully, I have his date of birth from the form, so I use that to collect some basic information. But, still, I can't find a current address or any social media accounts under either of the two names supplied by Hannah, since he's had no arrests or criminal record. Which means he's still out there, terrorizing other women. Probably under a new set of names.

An alarm goes off on my phone, telling me it's time to drag my ass to my meeting with the feds. With a deep sigh, I grab a screen shot of every-thing in Hannah's "The Asshole" folder, since I'm never going to enter Hannah's devices again but might need to refer back to this information when researching later. As my second alarm goes off, telling me I'm now running late, I quickly pack up my shit, throw my empty coffee cup into my computer bag to toss later, at another location, since I never leave my DNA in public places where I've been sitting a long time, and then, off I go to the one place I never would have guessed I'd willingly go in a million years: The FBI's headquarters down the street.

9
HENN

Twelve days later

"Welcome to Seattle," my Uber driver says, as he pulls away from the arrivals curb at Sea-Tac. "Coming home?"

"Visiting."

"How was your flight?"

"Easy. I came in from LA."

"I hope you brought some California sunshine with you. It's been pouring all week. Only cleared up an hour ago."

"Sorry, weather patterns are one of two things I can't control with my superpowers."

He chuckles. "What's the other?"

"I'm like the genie in *Aladdin*. Unfortunately, I can't make someone fall in love with me or anyone else."

"Damn. You mean you've gotta wine and dine her—or him, whatever floats your boat—like the rest of us mere mortals?"

"That's why I'm here in Seattle, as a matter of fact. To wine and dine someone the old-fashioned way."

"Good for you. Hope it works out."

"Thanks. Me, too."

I look out the car window and smirk to myself. I love having conversations like this with perfect strangers about my superpowers—the kind where I'm being dead-ass serious, but the other person assumes I'm joking around. I guess it helps keep me sane to vaguely confess my secrets out loud, even if only as a joke.

One of the phones in my computer bag buzzes on the car seat next to me, and when I locate the source of the sound, it's the phone the feds gave me on my last day in DC three days ago, right before I left for LA. They said they wanted a secure means of contacting me again, in case they had any follow-up questions about the job I did for them or maybe wanted to hire me for a new job. That's when I knew the jig was up— that I hadn't fooled them into thinking I'm nothing but a mediocre hacker who'd gotten lucky with the data and funds I'd recovered in Vegas.

When I look at the message, I grimace.

> We've got a time-sensitive opportunity for you.
> Sign into the secured server for details.

Fuck me.

"Is this the place?" the driver asks.

I look up from the phone to find him gesturing toward the random diner I selected as my destination.

"Yep. This is it."

"Are you meeting your sweetheart here?"

"I am."

"Good luck."

"Thanks."

I stuff the phone back into my computer bag as the car stops in front of the restaurant, and then generously tip the driver, exit the car with my bags, and stride toward the front door. When the car is out of sight, however, I turn and walk two blocks up the street to a used car lot, where I wander around for a bit in search of the cheapest piece of shit I can find.

Bingo.

When I find a vehicle that fits my purposes—a rusted jalopy with almost two hundred thousand miles on it and a price tag of less than a thousand bucks—I head into the sales office and purchase it. It's the same thing I've done multiple times during the last few weeks. During a stopover in Dallas on my way to DC. Twice during my stay in DC. During my stopover in Chicago three days ago on my way home to LA. And then, of course, twice in LA over the past three days.

This time in Seattle, like all prior times, I pay cash for the vehicle, show the sales dude a fake ID for the official transfer and registration paperwork, and then drive my new piece-of-shit ride off the lot and straight to the nearby airport, where I park in a red zone and quickly stride away. Only this time, unlike all other times, I don't catch an Uber to my next destination, but instead, catch a shuttle to the airport's nearby rental car facility. After some pleasant small talk with the man behind the counter, I get the keys to the luxury car I've reserved under my real name and head to my hotel in downtown Seattle.

In my room, I unpack and then lie on my bed with two computers. After answering a few work messages, I check the progress of some irons in the fire and make some necessary code adjustments. The usual shit. When that's done, I continue looking for the asshole who deserves to experience all the pain the online world has to offer. But unfortunately, the fucker is still eluding me.

Frustrated, I grab one of my phones and message a buddy of mine from my Bluebird handle:

> Me: Yo, Demon Spawn. Hit me back if you're available for a job.

While I await a reply, I check my texts and discover a message from my mother. She's asking me to call her when I get a chance.

"Hello, my love!" Mom says in greeting when she picks up my call.

"Is everything okay?"

"It's wonderful. How are you, Peter?"

I exhale with relief. Ever since my dad died two years ago, I've been deeply worried about my mother's mental health. The two were joined at the hip during their long marriage, and I can't fathom the pain and loneliness she feels every night looking at Dad's empty pillow. Lately, it seems like she's been turning a corner in her grief. Laughing more easily, almost like she always used to. But it's clear the grief is still there, weighing heavily on her heart, and I don't know how to help her, other than checking in regularly.

"I'm good. I just got to Seattle for work." I've made the mistake in the past of telling my mother I'm dating someone, early on, and I'll never do it again. The woman wants a grandchild more than anything, so telling her I'm dating someone only invites harassment about how it's going—and then, eventual disappointment when things don't work out as hoped.

"You're always so busy with work."

"Yep, the cybersecurity biz is booming these days. Business is so good, in fact, I've been thinking about buying myself a place. A condo, maybe." I'd never tell my mother this, but the truth is I can't figure out what else to do with the cool million bucks Jonas negotiated with the feds as my share of our finder's fee.

"A condo in Fresno would be much cheaper than one in LA," Mom says coyly.

"Let go of the dream, Mom. I'm never moving back to Fresno."

"Pfft."

"If I buy something outside of LA, it'll be in Seattle."

"*Oh*? Have you met someone there?"

Damn. The woman can sniff out a new girlfriend quicker than a cadaver dog looking for a corpse. Luckily, I've got a cover story. One that happens to be true. "No, Josh is moving back to Seattle in a couple months. He and his brother, Jonas, are starting a new Seattle-based business. A national chain of rock-climbing gyms with its headquarters here."

"How wonderful. Tell Josh I said congratulations. And how's the third musketeer doing these days?"

"Reed is being Reed. He's been expanding his roster with lots of new artists. Globetrotting. And, of course, exploding every ovary in every room he enters. Probably, half the nut sacks, too."

"*Peter.*"

I laugh at Mom's shocked reaction, and she snorts in reply. Mom often pretends to clutch her non-existent pearls when I say something particularly outrageous, but she knows full well I grew up watching my father endlessly crack her up, oftentimes with jokes far dirtier than that one.

"I saw a little write-up about Reed in *Rock 'n' Roll* magazine," Mom says. "They called him The Man with the Midas Touch."

I chuckle. "Yeah, I saw that."

"Did Reed like being called that?"

"He didn't say so, but I'm sure he did. Surely, it'll add to his mystique, which in turn will help his brand, which in turn will make him even more money. Plus, it'll help attract even more women. Not that he needs any help with that."

"Is he still dating a different supermodel or actress every week?"

"Nope. He's up to two or three a week now."

Mom tuts. "Such a cad."

"There are lots of women who find cads *extremely* attractive, Mom, so he's got little to no incentive to change his ways."

"It's a tale as old as time. Young women always want to tame the bad boy. I know I did."

I scoff. "When did you ever want to tame a single bad boy? You dated the nicest human who ever lived since high school."

"Yes, and your father was quite the bad boy back then."

I cackle.

"He was!" Mom insists. "Your father was never worried about getting into trouble like the rest of us. He was funny and irreverent. That's why every girl wanted him."

"But he only had eyes for you."

"That's right." Her voice is dripping with pride and love. *And pain.* Aw, Mom. I can't imagine this "bad boy" story of hers is remotely accurate, considering what I know about my sweet, doting father. That man didn't have a bad or mean bone in his body. But I'd never challenge my mother's happy memories of my late father, no matter how skewed they might be. That's all the woman's got left of her knight in shining armor these days, after all. Her happy memories.

"Fresno is a great place to raise a family," Mom says, out of the blue.

"Well, since I don't have a family, that's not a concern of mine."

"It might be one day. I hope and pray?"

"I don't know if they taught you this in school, but hopes and prayers aren't where babies come from, Mom."

"Oh, hush."

I laugh. "If you want to live in the same city as me so badly, then move to LA. I keep telling you I've got enough money saved up to—"

"No, no. I have no desire to move to LA when Nora and all my friends, and my garden, and my book club, and my favorite aqua aerobics instructor, and all my students, are here."

My heart pangs. Mom didn't say it, but I know the top item on that list —the list of things keeping her in Fresno—is the dream home she shared with my father, where she still sees visions of him in every nook and cranny.

"Okay, Momma. I've got to get some work done. Do you need anything, big or small?"

"Nope. Thank you again for those flowers. That was so sweet."

"You're very welcome. Those weren't your birthday present, you know. I'll send another bouquet for that."

"Or you could bring it in person. Nora and some friends are coming over for dinner and cake. I'd love for you to come, too."

"It's a date."

"Really? Yay! I can't wait to see you!"

"Same here. Love you, Momma. See you then."

She squeals with glee. "I love you so much, sweetie. Don't work too hard! Touch some grass! Feel the sun on your face!"

"I will. Bye now."

We say our goodbyes and end the call, and it's back to work I go. I check my messages and discover I've received a reply from my hacker buddy. *Hallelujah.*

Demon Spawn: Greetings. What can I do for you?

Me: Greetings. Are you still living in your van?

Demon Spawn: Yes, sir. I'm on an endless road to nowhere and everywhere, all at once.

Me: Sounds fun. Can I give you some paid destinations?

Demon Spawn: Anything for you, Bluebird. What's up?

I send him (or her?) every piece of data I've gathered on Greg Smith aka Angus Wellborn and ask him to locate him and get physical eyes on him, whether at his mother's address outside of Dallas, or at whatever address he can figure out from his own research.

Me: Unfortunately, I haven't had much time to invest in the project myself. So far, I'm running into dead ends, probably because his name is so fucking common.

Demon Spawn: Gotcha. If I get eyes on him, are you thinking a drive-by scan or over the shoulder password peek, or something more elaborate than that?

Me: He's not a pro, from what I can tell, so maybe we'll get lucky, and he'll use public Wi-Fi or unsecured Bluetooth. Do whatever it takes, though. This one's top priority.

Demon Spawn: Got it. I'll get on it right away.

Me: Thanks. Also, while you're driving around, I've got another project for you. I'll pay you to do it in every major city you drive through.

I send him the information, and he asks my timing on both projects.

> Me: ASAP on finding and breaching him. No timing on the second thing. Just keep at it in every new city until I tell you to stop. I've got no upward limit on my budget. I'll pay you each and every time, no questions asked.

> Demon Spawn: Damn, I feel like I've won the lottery. Thanks! I'll be in touch.

I close my laptop and head into the bathroom, where I hop into the shower in anticipation of my date with Hannah. As hot water pelts me, I press my palms against the tile wall and consciously try to force the primal rage coursing through me. I'm not a violent man, by nature. But thinking about this fucker, and what he did to Hannah, what he *said* to her, Jesus Christ, it all makes me want to commit a grisly murder.

It takes a while, but after a bit, I'm able to calm myself down and feel like myself again. I get out of the shower, shave, and wrangle my unruly hair. I dress in one of the snappy new outfits I bought—with Josh's help via FaceTime—for my big week in Seattle. And, finally, after checking my visage in the full-length mirror and deciding this is as good as it gets, I grab the bouquet of flowers I bought at the airport, send Hannah a text regarding my ETA, and stride out the door with a spring in my step and a massive smile of anticipation on my face.

10

HENN

Hello, wife.

When I see Hannah's gorgeous face in her doorframe—when I take in her dazzling smile and big blue eyes behind thick-framed glasses—those are the words my brain supplies. I thought I remembered the power of Hannah's magnetism, the electricity I felt in her presence. I thought I'd be ready to pick up where we left off by the end of our time together in Vegas. And yet, here I am at her doorstep in Seattle feeling every bit as tongue-tied and awestruck as I did when Hannah first entered that hotel suite with Kat. My flabber is once again firmly gasted. My gob, soundly pummeled.

"*Henny!*" Hannah shrieks, before launching herself toward me like a missile.

Reflexively, I open my arms to receive Hannah's hurtling frame, and just like that, our bodies crash and cleave together like they were designed to do it. As Hannah presses her body into mine, I nuzzle my nose into her dark hair and inhale the scent of her shampoo. "All's right in the world," I murmur. Or at least, that's what I've meant to say. Who knows what garbled syllables actually came out of my mouth.

"It sure is," Hannah whispers back, proving, yet again, she speaks fluent Nervous Henn better than anyone I've ever met. "Oh, Henny," she says, "I've missed you so much."

"I've missed you, too," I manage to say.

There's an intoxicating scent emanating from the crook of Hannah's neck. A touch of perfume? I follow the aroma and softly kiss the epicenter of its source, and the effect on Hannah is immediate and plain. In fact, the moment my lips make contact with Hannah's flesh, she wobbles in my arms and lets out a soft exhale of pleasure that sends tingles skating across my skin and straight into my dick. Feeling emboldened, I trail several soft, slow kisses up the full length of her neck, all the way to her cheek, and then to her ear, which is where I whisper, "You're a fucking knockout."

In response, Hannah grabs my cheeks with both hands and plants a kiss on my lips that causes my tingling dick to thicken. Our kiss is sheer bliss, the same way it was in Vegas. Even better, actually, now that we've had so long to anticipate and yearn.

"I've been dreaming of getting another amazing kiss from Peter the Great," Hannah says softly. "*Wowzers.*"

"Speaking of *wowzers* . . ." I step back and look Hannah up and down. "There's no Superglue in the world that could keep my eyes in their sockets when you're wearing that dress. Get the crash cart for me. *Stat.*"

Hannah bats her eyelashes. "I'm glad you like it. I saw it in a window during my lunch break the other day and couldn't resist."

"Lucky for me you didn't. Look what you're doing to me, woman." I motion like I'm going to point at my crotch, but unexpectedly flex my hand, instead, and she bursts into laughter.

"Whoa. Easy on the X-rated stuff when my little sister's inside and waiting to meet you." Chuckling, Hannah grabs my hand and pulls me inside the apartment, where I discover a young brunette who strongly resembles Hannah.

"Madelyn, this is Peter Hennessey—Henny." Hannah smiles at me. "Henn, this is my little sister, Madelyn. Maddy. Madelyn the Badasselyn."

Maddy rolls her eyes playfully at that last moniker, while opening her arms to me for a hug. "It's great to meet you, Henny. I've heard wonderful things about you."

"I've heard wonderful things about you, too. I'm looking forward to seeing *Shoot Like a Girl* at your film festival on campus."

Maddy gasps and looks at her big sister with wide eyes. "You didn't tell me Henn is coming!"

"I didn't want to say anything, in case his plans changed."

My eyebrows ride up. Seriously? After all my daily texts, and all the bouquets of flowers I've sent, and all the times I've told Hannah wild horses couldn't keep me from making it to Seattle, Hannah wasn't certain I'd actually make it?

"I hope it's okay for me to come to the festival," I say. "Hannah told me your film is a documentary masterpiece and I'm a huge fan of the genre."

"I'm thrilled you're coming! My biggest fear in life is the theater being totally empty for my little world premiere, after I've spent the last year of my life working so hard on my film."

She's adorable. The kind of person, like Hannah, you'd hope would be the one to find your lost wallet, because you'd know she'd move heaven and earth to return it to you, untouched, even if it was stuffed with two thousand bucks. If Hannah hadn't expressly asked me not to ask Reed for his assistance in getting Maddy into UCLA, meeting Maddy now and beholding her sweet, genuine energy would have been enough to make me bypass Reed all together, hack into UCLA's system, and get her admitted myself. I can't imagine UCLA's system could be much more difficult to infiltrate than U Dub's, and that was easy peasy lemon squeezy. Or is it *pumpkin* squeezy, like Hannah says? Damn. Hannah's got me rethinking everything.

Hannah heads to her kitchen to put the flowers I've brought her into water, so I sit on the couch and converse with Maddy about her documentary. A few minutes later, Hannah returns and asks if I'd like a tour of her place.

"Lead the way."

There's not much to see, in terms of square footage. The place is a shoebox. But Hannah's certainly made the most of her small living space. It's warm and welcoming. Bursting with color and character.

When we reach Hannah's small bedroom, the latest bouquet I sent her is displayed proudly on her dresser. When she notices me noticing the flowers, she says, "I can't thank you enough for all the flowers you've sent me."

"It was my pleasure. Glad you liked them."

Hannah is blushing. Fidgeting. Looking flustered.

Suddenly, I'm painfully aware we're standing mere inches from her bed. What would we do right now, if Maddy weren't in the next room?

Clearing my throat, I gesture to a framed photo on Hannah's dresser. It features Hannah, Maddy, and an older woman who resembles the two sisters. "Is that your mom?" It's a weird and stupid question. Stupid because the woman looks too much like Hannah and Maddy not to be their mother, and weird because I'm asking the question with a tingling dick. But it's the only thing I could come up with in the moment, after all the blood from my brain whooshed between my legs at the thought of what we might do in Hannah's bed at some point this week.

Hannah confirms the woman in the photo is, indeed, her mother. She also tells me the photo was taken during a trip to nearby wine country. She doesn't tell me about the absence of her father in the shot. Hannah already mentioned at dinner in Vegas that her father isn't in her life and that her mother has had perpetually shitty taste in men since her parents' divorce years ago.

"Are you ready to head to the restaurant?" Hannah asks.

"Let's do it."

We say goodbye to Maddy and head out to my rental car on the street. As we walk to the car, I slide my hand in Hannah's, the same way I did in Las Vegas, and the minute our palms connect, the effect is the same as then. *Fireworks*.

I open her car door and let go of her hand, so she can take her seat . . . and as I walk around the bumper to my side of the car, I realize I'm flexing my hand in earnest. Not as a tribute to *Pride & Prejudice*. Not to be funny. But because this woman actually makes me feel like I've been physically electrified by her touch.

11

HANNAH

Henn puts down his menu and smiles at me across the table. "You're the one who's been here a bunch of times. What do you recommend?"

As if on cue, the waiter arrives bearing the wine he recommended earlier. I discuss some food options with him, as Henn looks on and expresses adorable excitement about everything we come up with.

As the waiter walks away, Henn and I launch into easy conversation. First, about the fact that our waiter looks uncannily like the *Where's Waldo?* guy sprung to life in the cutest way. And then, about the fact that Kat flew to LA to visit Josh last weekend and, apparently, things went spectacularly well for the pair.

According to what Kat's told me in confidence, she and Josh have now jumped headfirst into fulfilling each other's sexual fantasies. Also, they've agreed to be exclusive while doing so, much to Kat's delight. I think it's probable Josh has told Henn at least something about his crazy shenanigans with Kat. For all I know, Henn knows even more than I do about all that. But I'd never even hint at the stuff Kat told me, confidentially, in order to tease out whatever details Henn might know.

When our brief discussion about Josh and Kat ends, I consider asking Henn about his recent work trip to DC. Thanks to what Kat told me at the pool in Vegas, I know generally what he was doing there—but also that he's sworn to secrecy about it. Okay, but what about Henn's work, in general? What, exactly, does he do? When I asked Henn about that topic during dinner in Vegas, he said his work was far too boring to discuss. But now that I know Henn swooped in like a superhero to protect Sarah from her shady employer, and that he's skilled enough at whatever he does to be flown to DC to work with the freaking FBI, I'm thinking he was probably being humble when he said that.

"So, I googled you," I admit. "I saw your company's website: Your Nerd for Hire."

"Impressive, right?" He's being sarcastic.

"Actually, yes. I'm impressed you've got your own company, though I'm not smart enough about computers to understand exactly what services you provide." I've meant my comment as a prompt for Henn to explain his work in detail. But he doesn't take the bait.

"I googled you, too," he says. "Devoured every photo of you I could find."

Is he deflecting? Changing topics on purpose?

With a wink, I mimic his sarcastic tone from a moment ago. "Impressive, right?"

"Honestly, yes. You're definitely out there living your best life."

"I'm trying, at least. I noticed you're not online much. At least, not under a name I could find. Do you have any social media?"

Henn shakes his head. "Social media isn't my thing. For me, it's not conducive to robust mental health."

"Well, that's probably true for most."

The waiter appears with an appetizer, and we dig in.

"If I'm being honest," Henn says, "I actually consider social media the root of all evil. The downfall of civilization as we know it."

"Wow."

"We won't be around to see it, probably, but I think we're witnessing the slow slide of civilization into a dark abyss from whence we'll never return. When anthropologists two hundred years from now, if there are any, look back and track the history of our slide, they'll pinpoint the inception as the advent of social media."

"That's kind of dark."

"Is it? Oh."

"And yet, it rings true." I take a bite of food. "For me, social media is a nice way to see my friend's photos. Plus, I genuinely enjoy being bombarded with ads for stuff I don't need. Oh, and I'm addicted to random dog videos. Have you ever seen that dog who presses buttons to talk?"

Henn deadpans, "I love her like she's the child of my loins."

"Same! If getting to see that dog chit-chatting with her owner every morning brings about the end of civilization, then so be it. It was totally worth it, if you ask me."

"That's a fair point." Henn chuckles. "That dog is probably representative of our future as a society. One day, we'll all communicate solely by pressing buttons."

"Aren't we pretty damned close to there?"

Henn makes a face like I've just scored the final blow in a formal debate. With a nod, he murmurs, "Touché, *mademoiselle*."

"Isn't that what you do for a living, in essence? You press buttons to communicate?"

"By George, it is." Henn side-eyes me. "Wait. You're saying I'm basically a talking dog?"

"A cute one, though." I laugh along with him, thoroughly enjoying our easy, silly banter. After eating another bite of an appetizer, I ask, "What kinds of things are you typically working on when you're pressing all those buttons? I know you said cybersecurity is your main thing, but your website lists some other things, too—stuff I didn't understand." I smirk, feeling damned pleased with myself for so seamlessly bringing our conversation back to Henn's work—a topic we still haven't explored in much depth.

"Do you know any coding languages?"

"Yes," I reply. "I know how to use around ten percent of my iPhone's capabilities."

Henn laughs at my silly joke. "Why didn't you tell me you're an expert-level coder?"

I shrug. "What can I say, dude? I'm humble."

Henn grins and takes a sip of wine. "Besides cybersecurity, I offer services in integration, automation, template building and search engine optimization. Some other things, too. But that's the main stuff. I'd be happy to explain it all to you, in excruciating detail, if you'd like."

I can't help giggling. Henn's facial expression is tantamount to a dare. It's like he's daring me to give him permission to unleash the world's most boring monologue.

"No, I'm good," I say. "I can google all that stuff later, if I find myself dying to know."

"Suit yourself. You're missing out, though. It's wildly exciting stuff." He waggles his eyebrows, making me laugh again.

"Is your company a one-man operation, or do you have a team?"

"It's just lil ol' me, sitting alone in front of a computer screen all day, every day, drinking way too many Americanos and noticing my eyesight deteriorating in real time."

I grimace at that description. "Do you like what you do well enough to ruin your eyesight over it, hopefully?"

"I do, actually. I fucking love what I do."

"Oh, that's great to hear. Not too many people can say that. I bet you love being your own boss, too."

Henn nods. "Although the downside is I'm constantly having to run to HR—me—to report sexual harassment of me by me. So that's a bummer." Henn chuckles along with me. "Seriously, though," he continues, "I'd be a horrible employee. I'd fire myself instantly for insubordination and a total lack of accountability."

I sip my wine. "Having a boss is the absolute worst part of my job. Well, having *my* boss, anyway. She's super old school. Like, she wants to see our faces in the office until late at night, and she hawks over us like she thinks we're too stupid or lazy to do our jobs right."

"Ugh. It's basic management, dude. Make people feel valued, not belittled."

"Exactly. I wouldn't mind the job if I had a good boss. In fact, I think I'd love it."

"Maybe you should start your own PR company and work for yourself. I'd help you get a website and some SEO going."

My jaw hangs open at Henn's generosity. "You'd do that for me?"

"What good are my superpowers, if I don't use them to help the coolest person on Planet Earth make her dreams come true?"

Even as my belly is bursting with butterflies, I manage to pull off a sarcastic bit. Furrowing my brow, I deadpan, "Wait a motherfucking minute, sir. You're saying there's someone cooler than me on *another* planet?"

Henn chuckles. "My apologies. I should have said the coolest person in the universe."

"That's better. Jeez." I laugh with him. "All kidding aside, thank you so much for the offer, but I'm not sure I'm ready for self-employment."

"Sure, you are."

I bite back a huge smile and lean forward. "This is confidential, but I've actually got a possible dream job in the works, as we speak." I hold up crossed fingers. "Kat's thinking about starting her own PR company, and she asked me if I'd consider working for her, if she does."

"*For* her or *with* her? Would you be Kat's partner or employee?"

I twist my mouth. "We didn't talk specifics. Maybe I'm *assuming* I'd be her employee?"

"Aren't you Kat's boss at your current firm?"

"Technically, yes, ever since my promotion. But we've always worked together as a team. I don't care about labels and titles all that much. All I care about is making what I'm making now, or close to it, and getting to continue working with my best friend."

Henn's dark eyes noticeably sparkle. "Have I mentioned I really like you, Hannah Milliken?"

I don't know what I've said to elicit that reaction, but I'm thrilled to hear it. As heat crawls across my cheeks and a wide smile splits my face, I reply, "I really like you, too."

As we're both beaming smiles at each other, the waiter arrives with our main courses—salmon, of course—and we enthusiastically dig into our food.

"Well?" I ask.

"Fantastic," Henn confirms after his first bite. "I'm most definitely going to feast till my stomach's delight."

I roll my eyes. "I don't know where half the weird stuff I say comes from."

"I love the way you talk. Makes me feel like I'm not quite so alone in this big, bad world. In middle school, I tried to talk like everyone else for a few months, but it hurt my brain too much, so I had to stop."

"Same here. God, I tried so hard in middle school to sound like everyone else, but it was hopeless. Thankfully, I finally realized I felt happiest when letting my inner dork hang all the way out. And I haven't looked back, ever since."

Henn looks visibly blown away. "You *literally* tried talking like a normal person, or you're saying you can relate?"

"No, literally. For, like, three months in middle school. It hurt my brain, same as you."

Henn still looks stunned. "I've never met anyone who *literally,* consciously tried to talk differently as a kid, besides me."

I sip my wine. "It made me realize I've got no choice but to be me. My true, dorky self. After that, I actually categorized my species of dork. Scientifically, I mean. *Dorkus Millikeningus.*"

Henn guffaws. "Is Dorkus the genus and Millikeningus the species?"

"Correct."

"Oh my God, you're amazing. Am I the same genus as you?"

I don't hesitate. "Of course, you are. Can't you tell? We're different species, though. You're *Dorkus Hennessingus.*"

Henn throws his head back and laughs from the bottom of his soul. When he gathers himself, he says, "What about Josh and Kat?"

"They're not our same genus, obviously. They're both of the genus *Cool-kid-opholus.*"

Again, Henn belly laughs. "Species?"

"Can't you guess?"

Henn pauses. "*Faradingus* and *Morganingus*?"

"Now you get it. It's all highly scientific."

Henn grins at me for a long moment, his dark eyes blazing, before saying, "Reason number seven billion why I like you so much: you're fucking hilarious."

"You *like* that about me? Weirdo."

"Right? Who actually wants to laugh? I'm a freak."

"Seriously, though, you'd be shocked how many guys *say* they're looking for a woman with a great sense of humor, but when you ask them what that means, it turns out they want a woman who laughs at *their* jokes.

It never even occurs to them to want a woman who makes *them* laugh in return."

"Well, that's dumb. There's nothing sexier than a funny woman."

"That's not the majority view, I'm afraid."

"The majority is full of idiots, then."

"The dating pool is, anyway." I lean back and study Henn for a long moment, marveling at his emotional intelligence. I ask, "Can I ask you a serious question? You once mentioned you're in therapy. What prompted you to go?"

Henn ponders the question for a moment. "I started struggling with depression and anxiety in middle school, and my mom got me into therapy. From that age on, I've always worked pretty consciously on my mental health. In high school, I was mostly doing great. But in college, being away from home for the first time was hard on me. I felt like a friendless weirdo, until I met Josh. Luckily, he convinced me to join a fraternity with him, and then we became friends with Reed, early on. And suddenly, I was doing great again. Better than ever. So, I stopped going to therapy because I thought, 'Why pay someone to listen to me being happy?' But then, a couple years ago, my dad died, and I went back to help me process all those hard feelings."

"I'm so sorry, Henn."

"Thank you. One minute he was gardening with my mom, and the next he was gone." He snaps his fingers. "Heart attack."

"Oh my gosh. That's horrible."

He tells me a few lovely things about his father. And then, he talks about his mother's grief and how worried he's been about her. "Even though I'm doing well now," Henn says, "I've kept going to regular therapy to make sure I stay strong for my mom. Also, because I've realized my job is super stressful, and it's nice to have an outlet to talk about that."

"I'm so glad you do that for yourself."

"What about you? What's your story with therapy?"

I tell him about my parents' divorce. My mother's ultra-chaotic love life since then. The fact that I became Maddy's de facto mother, in a lot of ways, at around age ten. "Like you, I had some anxiety to deal with," I admit. "I had it under control, pretty well, until a few years ago, when, in a short period of time, my grandma died, Maddy had her accident, and my dating life became toxic. I went to therapy to deal with all that, and I've been going regularly ever since." When Henn looks concerned, I touch his hand and smile. "I'm doing great now. Don't worry about me."

Henn looks into my eyes for a long beat, and I can't help thinking he's trying to decide whether or not to say something.

"Whatever it is, you can say it."

Henn twists his mouth. "I'm really glad you're doing well. You deserve to be happy. To be treated well. To feel safe and protected."

"Thank you. You deserve all that, too."

Henn opens his mouth to speak, but before he says a word, our waiter appears to clear plates and ask if we want dessert.

"Actually, I've arranged a surprise dessert at another location," Henn says to me. "It's within walking distance." As I express excitement, Henn turns to the waiter. "Just the check, please."

"Surprises and desserts are two of my favorite things," I say, bopping happily in my chair. "Put them together, and you've concocted an atomic bomb of pure joy for me."

Henn chuckles. "Yet another reason I like you. You're easy to please."

I gleefully flutter my palms together. "So, what's the surprise dessert?"

"It's right down the street. You'll know soon enough."

I gasp. "Are you taking me to Holy Crepe?"

"Damn. How'd you guess so fast?"

"It wasn't a guess as much as a hope. I love that place."

"I've rented it out for us. The owner, Francois, is going to give us a private lesson in crepe-making."

I squeal like I've won the lottery. "I love Francois! And Holy Crepe is one of my all-time favorite dessert places in Seattle."

"That's lucky. I figured, if I can't take the girl to Paris for dessert, then I'll bring Paris to the girl."

Our waiter appears again, this time to place the bill in front of Henn, who picks it up without so much as a glance at me. Once again, I find myself swooning. So many times on first dates, even when a guy's the one who asked me out, he'll look at me when the bill arrives as if to say, "Are you going to pay your fair share?" But not Peter Hennessey. Even though he's clearly not loaded like his two best friends, he hands the waiter his credit card without so much as a glance at me, the same way Josh did at that fancy restaurant in Vegas.

"Why don't we go Dutch?" I offer, reaching for my purse.

"Absolutely not," Henn says. "Let's get something straight, Milly Vanilli. You'll never pay a dime when you're on a date with me. That's non-negotiable, so, please, don't even offer."

Oh, my heart. I think it just physically skipped a beat. "Thank you."

After getting his credit card back from the waiter, Henn stands and pulls out my chair for me—so sweet—and we proceed to walk hand in hand toward the front door of the restaurant. As we walk, I can't help internally rhapsodizing about how handsome he is. How generous and sweet. I feel all the same electricity coursing between us as I did in Las Vegas, but even more so.

When we step outside into the cold night air, I fling my arms around Henn's neck and give him a huge kiss in the middle of the sidewalk. God help me, I'm falling for this gorgeous boy. If he hadn't already paid good money to rent out Holy Crepe for a private lesson, I'd invite him back to my place now, my silly plan to slow things down physically be damned. But since he did, and I'm grateful for it, I'll take this time to get my bearings and pull myself together—to remind myself the most important thing here is giving this budding relationship the best possible chance of turning into a full-blown love affair. After one final kiss, I release Henn, wink at him, and whisper, "Come on, handsome. Let's learn how to make crepes."

12

HANNAH

When we reach the front door to my apartment, I turn around and slide my arms around Henn's neck. "Thank you for a magical night." I kiss him, and he kisses me back, and in three seconds flat, we're making out against my front door—the kind of make-out session where I've got my thigh around his hip and he's groping my ass while pressing his hardness against me. The kind where we're both shuddering and breathing hard and writhing like we're being electrocuted with primal lust. It's utterly delicious.

To my surprise, even after several minutes of heat, Henn doesn't suggest we continue our fun inside. Does he think Maddy is still inside my apartment, and this is all the sexual activity he's going to enjoy before returning to his hotel room for the night? That was my initial plan for tonight, actually. I told myself I'd press the reset button on the physical stuff this week. But now that I'm here, and Henn's desire for a long-term relationship couldn't be any clearer, I want nothing more than to drag this hottie into my bed and enjoy an enthusiastic repeat of our electrifying night in Vegas.

I break free of Henn's lips. "You want to come inside?" Henn nods effusively and opens his mouth to speak. But before he gets a word out, I add, "And by that, I mean: inside *me*?"

Henn chuckles. "Even better."

It takes a minute to find my keys in my purse, but finally, we tumble inside my place as one horny unit and immediately begin stripping off our clothes as we bumble our way, kissing, toward my bedroom. Once we make it to my bed, Henn lays down my writhing, naked body, spreads my thighs, and launches into eating me with the enthusiasm of a starving man attacking a long-awaited meal.

As Henn's lips and tongue perform their hungry work, I grip his hair between my legs, throw my head back, and moan with relief and pleasure. They say absence makes the heart grow fonder, and I can now personally attest to that fact. What they don't tell you, however, is that absence also makes The Horny grow a shit-ton hornier.

I cry out when my orgasm slams into me, and Henn groans at the sound of my pleasure. With a loud exhale of ragged, warm breath, he snatches up his pants from the floor, presumably intending to grab a condom.

"No condom needed," I gasp out. "I'm on the pill. Come over here and fuck me hard." I've never said those words out loud before, and, damn, it feels sexy as hell to say them.

Without hesitation, Henn returns to the bed and wordlessly guides me onto my hands and knees. When I'm in position, he grips my hips, slides his finger up and down my wet, aching slit several times, and finally plunges himself inside me from behind.

Holy shit.

As I grip the bedspread beneath me to keep from collapsing face-first onto my bed, Henn fucks me with so much enthusiasm, I'm surprised he's not physically splitting me in two. Henn isn't a huge man, in terms of his equipment. But he's not small, either. Which means, from this position and at this angle, I feel like my eyes are nearly popping out of my head with each beastly thrust. "Oh, God," I choke out, when my innermost muscles begin tightening sharply around Henn's cock. I'm like a spring gun getting ready to unload.

"Not yet," Henn grits out. "Not yet, baby. Hold on."

"I can't."

"I'll tell you when."

"I can't hold on."

I feel the front of Henn's body pressing against my back. I feel his fingers on my swollen, throbbing clit. Henn massages that hard bundle of nerves in circles as his hips continue gyrating, as his cock continues its confident thrusting. Circles. Thrusting. Hot breath in my ear. I'm trying hard to hang on, but it's all too much. My eyes are rolling into my head.

"I can't hang on."

"Come, beautiful," Henn whispers. "Come now, gorgeous creature."

Gorgeous creature. Holy fuck, that was hot.

Blasts of white light overtake my vision as my body releases. A delicious kind of warping twists my insides. Henn groans loudly as my orgasm rolls and squeezes against his erection inside me, until we both collapse onto my bed into a sweaty, satisfied heap.

"Oh my god," I whisper, breathing hard. "That was incredible."

After a moment to collect himself, Henn rolls off my back and lies alongside me in the bed. I'm on my belly now. He's on his side. We're both sweaty and smiling and visibly enthralled.

"Sorry, for me, it was barely tolerable," Henn says. But his smile tells a different story.

"Well, yeah, for me, too. I didn't want to hurt your feelings. But hey, at least it was worth losing fifty bucks over." I tell Henn the story of the bet I made with Kat in Las Vegas, and he hoots with glee throughout my telling. "Kat knows me better than I know myself," I admit. "She was positive I wouldn't let you drive back to your hotel tonight, and she was right."

Henn strokes my forearm. "We can take it slow throughout the rest of the week, if that's what you want to do."

I shift onto my side to match Henn's position. We're now lying nose to nose in the moonlight. "The only thing I want to do this week is the same thing we just did, in various positions, over and over again, every night. Mornings, too, before I have to go to work."

Henn grins. "I'm at your service."

I exhale, puffing out my cheeks while doing so. "I wish so much I had some PTO banked at work, so I could take a few days off while you're here. I'm sorry."

"Don't apologize. I'll work whenever you're working. This way, we'll get to see exactly what it would be like if we actually lived in the same city."

Oh, my heart. Is Henn hinting he's imagining himself moving to Seattle one day? Or is he hinting he's hoping *I* might consider making a move to LA? Either way, I feel like Henn is yet again making it clear he sees potential for this thing to blossom into a serious, long-term relationship, and I couldn't be happier about that. Maybe I'm getting ahead of myself, but I've never felt a connection like this before, so I can't help wondering how we're going to manage the long-distance nature of our relationship going forward.

Henn moves a lock of hair out of my eyes. "Thanks for paying fifty bucks to sleep with me. I'm honored."

I scoff playfully. "I was horny, dude. And you were here, so . . ."

Henn gasps. "You mean it was nothing personal? I've got a dick, and I'm here, so you figured I'd do?"

"Thank you for your service." As Henn chuckles, I scoot closer to him and brush my fingertips across his cheek. "Of course, it was personal. In fact, you're the only person in the world I'd pay fifty bucks to sleep with."

Now it's Henn's turn to scoff playfully. "Liar. Who's your celebrity crush?"

"It doesn't matter. I wouldn't pay fifty bucks to sleep with him. Twenty, tops."

"Who is it?"

I smile, suddenly realizing how much Henn reminds me of the actor I'm about to name. "Have you seen *Easy A*? He's the love interest in that one."

"Penn Badgley. *Easy A* is one of my all-time favorites."

"Mine too!" I launch into singing "Pocketful of Sunshine," a song that plays a major role in that movie, and Henn doesn't hesitate to join in, until our singing eventually dissolves into giggling.

Henn asks, "Do you have a crush on that actor in general or on his character in that movie?"

"I love him in everything, but I think I love him most when he's playing that obsessed psychopath in 'You.' Have you seen it?"

"Love it."

"I hate to admit it, but I think it's so hot that he knows who he wants and he's willing to do anything to get her."

Henn bites back a smile.

"To be clear," I add quickly, "I wouldn't want him doing all that stuff in real life. I don't condone murder or anyone throwing a rival into a cage in a basement. I'm just saying, as a concept, I appreciate a man who's willing to go the extra mile to get the girl he wants. At least, for the sake of entertainment, anyway."

"Got it. Murder and a cage for my rivals: bad. Going the extra mile to get the girl: good."

"*Very* good." I nuzzle his nose. "Speaking of which, thank you for flying to Seattle to take me out. And for all the flowers. And for the amazing dinner. And for renting out Holy Crepe and arranging a private lesson for us. Talk about going to the extra mile to get the girl."

"Oh, *that* kind of extra mile is good? *Phew*. I thought you meant you wanted me to *hack* you."

I laugh. "Hey, whatever it takes, right?"

Henn winks. "Absolutely."

I run my fingertip flirtatiously along Henn's bare shoulder. "I'm sorry I'm saying this after you've already paid for a hotel room, but would you like to stay here with me this week?"

"I'd love to. Thank you."

"Every minute I'm not at work this week, I'd love to spend with you."

"Awesome."

I drag my fingertip across his bare belly underneath the covers, along the treasure trail of soft hair leading to his penis. "Fair warning: I plan to get as much *bang* for my fifty *bucks* as I can out of you this week."

Henn chuckles. "Like I said, I'm at your service. Get your money's worth, baby."

"Oh, I will." I brush my fingertips across his dick, and it's only semi-hard. Clearly, he needs a bit more time to recharge his battery. "So, who's your celebrity crush?"

"Emma Stone."

"Liar."

"Not lying. I fell in love with her in *Superbad* and then *Easy A* sealed the deal. I love her because she's gorgeous, but also kind of a dork. Plus, she's funny and smart, too. In my book, a girl like that is the total package." He looks at me pointedly and grins, and it's plain he's nonverbally telling me he's just described *me,* every bit as much as Emma Stone.

"I think you just implied I'm your type," I say flirtatiously.

"Ma'am, there's no better example of my type than you. God used you to make the mold of my type, and then he smashed it into a million tiny pieces, so you'd never be duplicated again."

After I regain my ability to speak and breathe, I exhale a shuddering breath and whisper, "Damn, you're good."

"I meant every word."

"That's why you're so damned good."

I stroke his full length under the covers, making him tremble with arousal. And soon, it's abundantly clear I'm going to get the next bang for my fifty bucks right fucking now.

13

HENN

"This is fantastic," I say, looking up from my plate and smiling at Hannah's expectant face. "I love it."

"It's so easy to make," she says. "I frequently make it for myself on work nights."

We're sitting at Hannah's small kitchen table on our sixth night together in Seattle, and it's the first time she's cooked for me. Last night, when Hannah got home from work, I had my famous stir-fry ready for her, along with a chilled bottle of white and a fresh bouquet of flowers. Her reaction was fucking awesome. Like I'd slayed a dragon for her. In fact, she attacked me on the spot. Which meant I had to reheat the stir-fry and the texture of the veggies wasn't perfect by then. But hey, I'm not complaining. I'll take a flood of lust and passion over perfect veggies any day of the week. Before last night's stir-fry, however, we'd gone out or ordered in every dinner.

"Can I get the recipe?" I ask. "I think I'll make it for my mom when I go home for her birthday next week."

Hannah launches into an explanation of the recipe, but midway through, our phones simultaneously buzz on her kitchen table. When I glance at my screen, I've received a text from Kat in the group chat she created for herself, me, Hannah, and Josh while the girls were enjoying their week together in Vegas.

> Kat: Hello there, dahlings! Joshua surprised me by flying into Seattle two days early tonight! Woohoo! We're doing karaoke with Jonas and Sarah tomorrow night. If Henn is still in town, please join us! If not, Hannah, come on your own or bring a friend or your sister!

I look up from my phone to find Hannah jutting out her lower lip with disappointment. Clearly, she's bummed I'm leaving Seattle tomorrow and therefore won't be able to make tomorrow's karaoke night a triple date.

"I could change my flight and stay a few more days," I suggest tentatively.

Hannah's face lights up. "Really? But I thought you said you have some work to do in LA."

"I do, but I can push it back. My only hard deadline is making it to Fresno by Thursday afternoon for my mom's birthday. But I could fly straight from Seattle to Fresno to make it there on time."

"Yes!" With that, Hannah launches herself out of her chair, sits on my lap, and begins peppering my lips with a rapid-fire stream of happy kisses. As she kisses me, I wrap my arms around her and laugh, feeling overcome with the love I feel for this amazing woman. Yep, it's love. I know it for sure now. In fact, I've been so certain of my love for Hannah for the past few days, it's taken superhuman strength not to tell her so. Luckily, I'm not so far gone that I don't realize it's way too soon to say it out loud. What weirdo says "I love you" after only one full week together? But knowing I shouldn't say it doesn't mean I'm not feeling it. Or that I'm not dying to saying.

Hannah nuzzles her nose against mine. "No more wining and dining me for the rest of your stay, though. Thank you for all the amazing surprises and dates you've showered me with this week, but for the rest of your time here, we're going to do everything on the cheap. We'll have homecooked meals or cheap takeout and movie nights at home. You've already spent way too much money on me."

She's wrong about that. There's no such thing as spending too much money on Hannah Milliken, as long as she's enjoying herself. In all honesty, I can't think of anything I'd rather spend money on than bringing a smile to Hannah's face. Plus, the truth of the matter is, I haven't spent nearly as much as she thinks, since half the fun stuff I've arranged for her has been accomplished through my superpowers, rather than on the open market.

Granted, I did pay real money on a few fairly expensive meals this week. The bill at the first restaurant with great salmon wouldn't have been all that expensive, except that we ordered a hefty number of appetizers and wine. No complaints though. It was awesome.

I also legitimately rented out the crepes place that first night and also took Hannah, her mom, and sister out to an *extremely* shi-shi place to celebrate after Maddy's on-campus film festival. Oh, and the Italian restaurant before the comedy show was a pretty fancy place, too.

But I also did plenty of stuff on the cheap. One night, I picked Hannah up from work a bit early and whisked her off to Kerry Park, where we enjoyed an elaborate but not all that expensive sunset picnic I'd arranged. Another night, we ordered takeout and watched *Grease* together, since I'd been wanting to get the full speak-and-singalong experience Hannah told me about in Vegas. Another night, we ordered pizza and binge-watched *Money Heist,* a kick-ass series about a band of bank robbers and their hostages in Spain. Also, unbeknownst to Hannah, the video arcade I'd supposedly rented out one of the nights and the tickets to the comedy show didn't cost me a dime, thanks to my superpowers.

"Don't stress for a second about me spending money on you," I say. "I can't think of something I'd rather spend it on than making you smile."

Hannah blushes. "But simply being with you makes me smile. See?" She flashes me a big, goofy grin that's so over the top, it makes me laugh and kiss her.

As we're kissing, our phones simultaneously buzz again. This time, it's Josh replying in the group chat.

Josh: Henn, if you're not still in Seattle, then get your ass here on a flight ASAP. Sarah says she's going to get Jonas onstage to sing tomorrow night. I don't know if she'll succeed, but if anyone can do it, it's Sarah Fucking Cruz.

Chuckling, I tap out a reply:

Me: I'm still in Seattle. I was supposed to leave tomorrow morning, but I'll change my flight.

Josh: Good boy.

As I put down my phone, Hannah asks, "Why is it such a big deal for Jonas to sing?"

"He's an introvert, through and through. Also, kind of . . . How shall I put this? Serious? Intense? Humorless? Jonas absolutely abhors being the center of attention."

"And he's Josh's *twin*?"

"Fraternal."

"Ah."

"They're nothing alike. At least, not in any obvious ways. Josh got all their gene pool's extroversion and Jonas got all its intensity."

Our phones ping again. This time, it's Kat giving details—when and where—about tomorrow's karaoke night. As Hannah leans back into her chair and engages Kat in a text exchange, I open my airline app and change my flight. When I flash Hannah a thumbs-up, signaling I've successfully accomplished my task, Hannah concludes her conversation with Kat, and we return to our meal.

"More wine?" I ask.

"Thank you."

I pour, and we both take long sips.

"I'm so happy for Kat," Hannah says. "Josh flying into Seattle two days early to see her is no small thing." She drags her fork through the remnants of her food. "During lunch with Kat today, she said she's been counting the minutes until Josh's arrival on Saturday. I can only imagine how thrilled she was when he unexpectedly showed up tonight." Hannah bites her lip. Is she fishing for me to divulge something—anything—Josh might have told me about his feelings for Kat?

If so, it's a tall order. The truth is Josh has been pretty tight-lipped about Kat. All I know is that he flew her to LA this past weekend so they could start fulfilling each other's sexual fantasies. I do think it's a good sign he wanted to see Kat past Vegas. Also, that he flew in early to Seattle, too. But with Josh Faraday and women, you never fucking know, so I'm not sure I can accurately read the tea leaves here. Even if Josh is feeling something extraordinary with Kat, his feelings could change on a dime. Often, the minute Josh starts feeling something real, that's when he dips, so I wouldn't want to say something Hannah might pass along to Kat, which might then get Kat's hopes up too high about her future with Josh.

The silence at our small table has become awkward. Clearly, I was supposed to fill it some time ago, and I didn't.

Hannah clears her throat. "Did Josh tell you he's going to meet Kat's entire family on Saturday night?"

My jaw drops. "No, he didn't mention that. Is that for sure?"

Hannah's beaming as she nods. "Kat said he's coming to dinner at her parents' house and all her brothers will be there. She's over the moon."

"Holy fucking shit. That's huge. I can't remember Josh ever doing that before. He's incidentally met a girl's parents or siblings here and there— like, at a charity auction or gala—but doing it on purpose at a girl's parents' house is definitely a first."

Hannah is visibly giddy. "Josh must *really* think Kat is special, then."

"It sure seems like it."

Hannah bites her lower lip. "Has Josh said anything to you about what he's feeling for Kat?"

I take a sip of my wine, considering my response. I want it to be accurate, of course, but I also don't want what I say getting back to Kat and creating false expectations. "I know Josh really likes Kat," I say carefully. "I know he lights up in a way I've never seen before when he's with her."

"Oh my gosh."

"But I also know Josh is a complicated dude, especially in terms of his romantic entanglements. He's normally allergic to any kind of commitment with women. Well, with anything. Usually, he won't even commit to plans for next week."

Hannah takes a sip of wine. "Maybe he's turning over a new leaf."

"Maybe," I agree, but even as I say it, I'm not sure I buy it.

Hannah sighs. "Long distance relationships can be really hard. Or so I've heard. Seems like Josh is motivated to make it work with Kat, though."

Hmm. Is Hannah still fishing for information to pass along to her bestie, or is she hinting she's worried about how *we'll* manage a long-distance relationship? I've certainly been wondering about that very thing myself. Before I leave Seattle on Thursday morning, will Hannah agree to be my girlfriend? Will we make a firm plan to see each other again? I'm dying to talk about that stuff now, but I'm nervous to be the one to initiate those sorts of conversations, in case it's too early. I feel wholly ready to commit to Hannah now. To say "I love you" and know it's the truth. Hell, I feel ready to start planning a life together. But I'm not stupid enough to think Hannah could possibly be ready to do all that, too, after only one full week together.

I take a long sip of wine to keep my tongue from betraying me. Finally, when I feel in control of myself and certain I won't blurt "I love you, Hannah!", I put down my glass and say, "There's really no such thing as a long-distance relationship for someone like Josh. That dude hops planes like the rest of us catch taxis. Besides having an unlimited budget for commercial flights, he's also got access to his uncle's private jet."

"Wow. Can you imagine?" Her eyes widen at whatever she's seeing on my face. "*You've flown on a private jet?*"

"Yeah, several times, thanks to both Josh and Reed. Both of those guys love the finer things in life. Plus, they're both ridiculously generous with their best friends."

"Is flying private as glamorous as it looks in movies?"

I can't help noticing Hannah's blue eyes are sparkling like crazy. *Note to self: fly Hannah somewhere on a private jet one of these days.* "Yeah, it's pretty sick, not gonna lie. It definitely makes you feel like a baller. But it's not life-changing or anything. It's just another fun memory, basically."

"A bucket list item."

"Exactly. Something to check off."

Hannah smiles. "You're so humble and grounded. I really love that about you."

My heart rate spikes. *Love.* Oh my god. She said the "L" word. Granted, she didn't say "I love you." But, still, I think that's the first time she's used the word in relation to me.

"Thank you," I manage to say. "I really love the same thing about you." *I love you, I love you, I love you, Hannah Banana Montana Milliken. So much so, I'm bursting at the seams to say it.* But since I can't, I murmur "459" under my breath as a means of relieving some of the pressure and yearning building inside of me.

"Hmm?" Hannah says, tilting her head.

"Hmm?" I echo, my eyebrows raised. Damn, I thought that clever little code word wasn't audible.

"Did you say something?"

"I don't think so. If I did, I was probably thinking of some coding I did earlier today."

Hannah chuckles. "I can't imagine what it's like to be inside your brain."

"It's exhausting. I don't recommend it. So, anyway, for dessert, I've got a surprise for you—one we're going to feast on to our stomachs' delight at another location."

Hannah plunks down her fork. "*Peter Hennessey.* You've already given me way too many gifts and surprises. Tonight was supposed to be all about *me* spoiling *you.*"

"That's what you said, but I never signed onto that."

"Henny."

"I arranged tonight's surprise this morning, when I thought tonight would be our last night together for a while. You think I'd let our last night pass without some kind of romantic gesture? Please. You insult me."

Hannah bats her eyelashes. "Thank you, but I wanted you to finally get to feel the way you always make me feel. After dinner, I was going to surprise you by making *you* my dessert—with whipped cream and everything."

My eyebrows shoot up. "Now that's a fantasy I didn't know I had until now. Can we do that after my surprise for you?"

"Of course, we can. But now that we're having an actual dessert, maybe I'll massage you with some scented oils, rather than making you dessert. At least, for tonight. I'll make you dessert tomorrow night, now that you're staying."

"It's a date. Good thing I'm staying. I wouldn't have wanted to miss that."

Hannah puts her forearm on the table and smiles seductively. "Is there anything else kinda sexy you'd like to try this week, now that you're staying a bit longer? A fantasy you'd like me to fulfill for you, perhaps?"

I blink rapidly. *Whoa.* That's one hell of a sexy thing to hear from the woman you're head over heels for. Plus, the comment answers a question I've been wondering about all week. Namely, if Kat has told Hannah anything about the fantasy-fulfillment extravaganza Josh and Kat have been embarking on since her visit to LA last weekend. Josh didn't give me any details, out of respect for Kat. But he did tell me she's got a shit-ton of elaborate fantasies, and he's hell-bent on going the extra mile to fulfill all of them, no matter how much prep work or arrangements they might require. I can't imagine Hannah would ask me such a titillating question out of the blue, especially considering she had lunch with Kat today. Did Kat tell Hannah even more details than Josh has told me, and now Hannah's wondering why the fuck I don't do this or that kinky thing for her, the way Josh does for Kat?

"You've already fulfilled all my fantasies, and then some," I reply honestly. "Just by being a goddess who enthusiastically wants to have sex with me." I place my forearm onto the table and smile, matching her position. "What about you? Do you have any fantasies I could fulfill for you? Anything at all. Don't be shy now." Frankly, I've been dying to ask Hannah this very question all week. Little did I know she'd give me such a natural opening to ask it.

Hannah twists her mouth. "Well, I like watching gay porn sometimes. Would you be willing to have sex with a man while I watch?"

My stomach drops as my face drains of color. "Oh. Uh . . ."

Hannah bursts out laughing. "I'm kidding. Not about watching gay porn, to be clear. I love it. But I promise I have no desire to watch you having sex with anyone, man or woman. No desire to do a threesome, either. So, if that's your fantasy, sorry, it's not going to happen."

Both of my best friends have told me about their threesomes over the years, and I've never once been envious of them. Fascinated? Entertained by their stories? Yes and yes. But I can't say I've ever wanted it for myself. Maybe I'm a weirdo for not being into the idea. Maybe I'm boring. But my biggest fantasy has always been finding a woman who wants to be with me as much as I want to be with her, and then having lots of sex with her and nobody else till the end of time. "I don't want a three-some," I say. "I'm a one-woman kind of guy."

Hannah flashes me an adorable smile. "Why am I not surprised to hear that?"

"As far as your love of gay porn goes," I say, "I want to make clear I'm all for it. I'm a big supporter of gay people. Queer people. Love is love."

Hannah giggles. "I know that, Henny. You don't have to engage in gay sex to seduce me or prove you support gay rights."

I lean back with a smile and then circle back to the topic I'm dying to hear more about. "So, um, back to you and your fantasies. Does anything come to mind?"

Hannah shrugs. "Not really. My fantasies, if you want to call them that, are mostly things that take place outside the bedroom. Being pursued and romanced and treated with respect. Being with someone who makes me feel special and adored—someone who makes me laugh, hopefully, and then having lots of hot sex with him." She winks. "Even better if that sex costs me fifty bucks."

I return her wicked smile. "Okay, well, if you ever think of anything, big or small, normal or weird, that I could do for you, will you tell me?"

Hannah's cheeks bloom. "I will." She runs her fingertip along the rim of her wine glass and opens her mouth, like she's about to say something further. But eventually, she takes a sip of her wine and silently returns the glass to the table.

"Are you having a thought you're too shy to say out loud?" I prompt. "If so, there's no need to hold back with me. I'm all ears."

Hannah bites her lower lip, her expression confirming my hunch: she's holding back.

"It's kind of kinky," she warns.

My eyebrows ride up. I have the urge to command, "Tell me all about it, right fucking now!" But what comes out of my mouth is a calm and measured, "I'm all ears."

Hannah shifts her weight in her chair. "Have you ever heard of a machine called a Sybian?"

Welp, that confirms it. The Blabbermouth, as her brothers apparently call her, has most definitely blabbed to Hannah about whatever she's been doing with Josh. "Yeah, I've heard of it. Josh was obsessed with them in college, so I've seen quite a few YouTube videos of women riding them." I try to keep my body language relaxed. Nonchalant, even. If my face looks too excited, then Hannah might feel compelled to do something as a gift for me—something she doesn't truly want to do—and I don't want that, no matter how titillated I'm feeling about her surprising mention of the internet's favorite orgasm machine.

"I read online that you can rent a Sybian for a night," Hannah says tentatively.

"Oh yeah? I didn't know that." It's the truth. I had no idea. "Are you telling me this because you'd like me to rent one for you?"

"I'm not positive, but I'm definitely curious."

My heart is thundering. Talk about a sexy surprise. "I'd be happy to rent one for us. No pressure, though. It'd be there, if you decided to try it."

Hannah makes an adorable face like she's sticking her finger into a light socket. "I'm curious to try one . . . but I'm not, like, chomping at the bit. I can't make any promises about what I'd do, if you actually rented one."

"I wouldn't rent one, unless you wanted me to."

"I mean, I might like to have the *option* to give it a whirl. But even if I muster the courage, I'll probably not be like 'Yeehaw!' and be able to ride the thing like a rabid cowgirl—you know, like all those girls do in the videos."

Hannah's watched video*s*—plural?—of women riding Sybians? Well, color me shocked—and also damn-near hyperventilating. At least, internally. "It'd be all about you and your comfort level," I say evenly. "If you're curious enough to maybe want to try to overcome your inhibitions and try something kinky like that—and if you think it'd help, rather than hurt, to have the thing sitting in your bedroom, ready to ride, if you so choose—then I'll rent one and promise not to pressure you in any way. On the other hand, if having the machine rented would stress you out, then never mind. I'll pretend you never said the word Sybian, unless and until you mention it again. If ever."

Hannah's blushing a beet red. "Thank you. Yeah, I actually do think it'd help me to have the thing sitting in my bedroom, just in case. You'd have to promise not to set your expectations too high, even if I decided to ride it, though. I might not be able to relax enough in front of you to have a single orgasm, let alone multiples like in all those videos."

All those videos. Jesus Christ, I'm hard as a rock underneath Hannah's kitchen table. "I'd have zero expectations about it. Like I said, you could take one look at it and decide, 'Nope.' And that'd be fine." I take a sip of wine and try not to look as turned on as I feel at the thought of Hannah riding a Sybian. Back in college, Josh excitedly told me about the existence of the infamous orgasm machine, which a woman straddles and rides to hopefully achieve multiple full-body orgasms. After he told me about it, I got lost down a rabbit hole on YouTube that very night and devoured at least twenty videos of women losing their minds on the machine. But that's where my interest ended—with one night of binge-watching and jerking off. After that, I honestly forgot the thing even existed. But now, suddenly, I'm a horny college kid watching Sybian videos in my fraternity house, all over again. Thankfully, I'm now mature enough to realize my enthusiasm could very well feel coercive to Hannah, if I'm not careful, and that's the last thing I'd ever want.

Hannah exhales. "Okay. Let's do it. Will you try to rent one for me?"

"Sure thing." Thankfully, I sound far calmer than I feel.

Hannah's blue eyes are twinkling. "I'm excited to explore my sexuality with you. When I invited you to ride my Slip 'n' Slide in Vegas, that wasn't normal for me. You brought out something new in me—something wild. I'm excited to keep exploring that side of myself."

I'm physically vibrating with excitement. But somehow, I manage to say, "Consider me the Lewis to your Clark, baby." As Hannah laughs, an alarm goes off on my phone, and I quickly turn it off before announcing, "That means it's time for your latest surprise."

14

HENN

I park my car, turn off the ignition, and smile at Hannah sitting next to me. She looks gleefully expectant, I'd say—like a kid on Christmas who knows she's been a very good girl and can't wait to see what exciting present Santa has brought her.

"Sit tight, pretty lady. I'll get your carriage door for you."

"So chivalrous! But, dahling, isn't that what we pay the footman to do?"

"*Pish.* I'd never let a footman touch one of your erogenous zones."

Hannah giggles happily, the way she always does when we trade *Pride & Prejudice* jokes. Which we do frequently. Because we're dorks. Two dorks of the same genus, as a matter of fact, as the paper in my pocket attests. Speaking of which, as I walk around the back of my rental car, I slide my hand inside the front pocket of my coat to triple-check that folded piece of paper is still there. It is. Same as last time.

At Hannah's side of the car, I guide her out by the hand and do the hand-flex thing for her, as usual. And yet again, the bit kills.

"My coat is in the back," Hannah says.

"Oh. Glad you mentioned that. I almost forgot our dessert." I open the back passenger door and grab her coat, as well as a little something I stowed on the car floor, out of sight, earlier today. After hitting another used car lot and doing the whole rigamarole with it while Hannah was at work, I swung by Hannah's favorite bakery—which I know about, thanks to the digital "VIP" card on her phone—and bought six different varieties of cupcakes to surprise her with tonight.

"*Allison's* Bakery!" Hannah gasps out when she sees the pink cardboard box in my hand, its logo emblazed on its top. "The absolute best!"

"You mentioned that."

Hannah furrows her brow. "I did?"

Shit. Why'd I say that? *Come on, Peter.* It's justifiable to tell a little white lie in order to pull off a fun surprise. It's also justifiable to lie to ensure my online identity remains safe and anonymous until it's time to reveal it. But there's no justification for gaslighting the poor girl by telling her she said something she didn't.

"Actually, wait, no, I think maybe I googled and found out this bakery is highly rated."

"Oh, I'm sure it is. Their cupcakes are a little taste of heaven on earth." Hannah bats her eyelashes. "Thank you for getting them. You're always so thoughtful."

My heart thumping, I take Hannah's hand and lead her up the sidewalk for a couple blocks, since I purposefully parked far enough away from our destination to keep the mystery intact for as long as possible. After I've guided her around a dark corner, we head down a little pathway to the back service entrance of our destination, where there's no discernible signage to tip Hannah off.

"Where the heck are we going?" she whispers excitedly.

"You'll see."

"You and your surprises."

"You said you love 'em."

"I do."

We're going to have the planetarium to ourselves tonight, the same way we had that video arcade to ourselves the other night. The only hiccup this time is that I couldn't figure out how to keep the surveillance cameras off indefinitely. At least, not in the amount of time I was willing to devote to the project. That's why Hannah and I will need to skidaddle from the place by ten sharp. I think that'll work out just fine, though. Almost two hours should be plenty of time for me to show Hannah the folded piece of paper in my pocket and maybe even tell her I love her, if the timing feels right in the moment. When I thought tonight would be our last night together for a while, I planned to say it tonight for sure. No matter what. But now that we have several more nights together, my plans are more fluid. Either way, we'll gaze at the stars while enjoying Hannah's favorite brand of fancy cupcakes, and it'll be yet another happy memory of our amazing week together.

When we've reached the service entrance, I release her hand and quickly enter a six-digit code on a metal keypad, causing the door to unlock with a soft buzz.

"Hannah Banana Montana Milliken, the universe is all yours."

I hold the door open for her, and Hannah takes two tentative steps inside.

"The planetarium! Oh, Henny!" She throws her arms around my neck and peppers my face with kisses. "Are we acting out the planetarium scene from *Lala Land*? Am *I* Emma Stone tonight?"

Aw, fuck. I forgot about Hannah's obsession with *Lala Land*. We haven't gotten around to watching that one together this week, so I've still only seen it once, years ago. Fuck me. If I'd actually thought to bring Hannah somewhere to perform a re-enactment of that planetarium scene, I'd do it at The Griffith Observatory in LA—the actual filming location. I would have dressed the part, too.

Shit. My fate is sealed. It's too late to contradict her. Her face is positively beaming with excitement. "You guessed it," I say, making Hannah squeal.

"You know me better than I know myself!" Hannah says happily. "Here I thought I didn't have any fantasies, but you knew all along I'd get crazy-turned on dancing with you in a planetarium in the moonlight."

Well, well, well. That's a twist I didn't see coming when I hacked the planetarium earlier today to arrange this little surprise. "I figured it might get your motor running," I reply with a wink.

Hannah puts the cupcake box down on a ledge. "I need to run to the restroom before we get started."

I have no idea what that means. *Before we get started with what?* "Yeah, me, too," I reply.

"I'll meet you right back here, Sebastian!"

Fuck. I think that's the name of Ryan Gosling's character in *Lala Land,* but for the life of me, I can't remember Emma Stone's. Which means, all I can reply with is, "Can't wait."

We head toward the bathrooms and through our designated doors, and the second I'm alone, I pull up the planetarium scene from *Lala Land* on my phone. Well, fuck me. Hannah thinks we're going to dance around the planetarium like that? I can certainly free-style dance like a fool, but I've never had a single ballroom dancing lesson. If I'd actually meant to re-enact this scene, I certainly would have taken a lesson or two to pull it off. But even then, I wouldn't be able to defy gravity and dance on the walls and ceiling, the way the actors do in the scene. Fucking hell. Can I deliver even a semblance of this dance routine for Hannah? I don't think so, but maybe with some false confidence, I can at least deliver a *vibe.*

Luckily, there's an orchestral song playing throughout the scene, and since Hannah's seen the movie many times, she'll surely recognize it. Hopefully, when Hannah hears the song, it will transport her imagination and plop her straight into the movie, even if my clumsy feet aren't doing the trick.

I leave the bathroom and return to our designated spot, and a few minutes later, Hannah appears.

"I have an idea," she announces, as she waltzes toward me with a sly smile on her face. Thanks to the video I just watched, I recognize that comment as the line Emma Stone says to kick off the planetarium dancing scene, so I press play on the video in my hand to start playing the song from the scene.

"Oh, Henny," Hannah says on an exhale. "You're such a romantic." She whirls around gracefully on her way toward me, so I walk toward her, slowly, with my arms behind my back, the way Ryan Gosling does at the beginning of the scene.

"You look just like him!" she gushes.

"Mia." I offer her my hand and lead her the best I can in a waltz around the moonlit space—and despite my lack of genuine confidence and gracelessness, Hannah swoons and coos like a happy dove as we dance.

Occasionally, I twirl or dip Hannah. Several times, she breaks free of our embrace to do a cute little pirouette or shimmy. But mostly, we dance with our bodies close, like our hearts are beating as one. Granted, I didn't plan this moment, but I think I'm pulling it off rather well. So much so, the moment feels downright magical—the perfect set-up to finally say the three little words that have been on the tip of my tongue for days now.

"Oh, Henny," Hannah says, just before the magic words lurch out of my mouth. "*I'm so turned on.*"

Well, now.

Declarations of love can wait. Clearly, it's time for some *Lala Land* lust.

My cock tingling, I guide Hannah to a nearby bench, sit her down, and drop to my knees between her open legs. After looking up into her hungry blue eyes for a long moment, I peel down her undies, letting my fingertips skim her skin the whole way down, and then lift her skirt slowly, skimming her flesh the whole way up. My runway cleared, I begin peppering her inner thighs with soft kisses and nips and swirls of my tongue.

The effect of my efforts on Hannah is clear and instantaneous. In fact, it quickly feels like I've cranked the dial on her dimmer switch to high. With a loud moan, she runs her hand through my hair, spreads her thighs wider and tilts her pelvis toward my hungry mouth. Clearly, she's giving me full access to her every nook and cranny. Goading me on. Nonverbally begging me to devour her.

I slide my fingers inside her while getting to work, and in no time at all, Hannah is throwing her head back and coming hard against my mouth. In a frenzy of desire, I get my pants unzipped and down, my briefs along with them, and guide Hannah off the bench. When she hops into my waiting arms, I take two shuffling steps to the nearby wall, guide her down onto my straining, yearning cock, and proceed to fuck her against the wall like my life depends on it.

My bliss comes fast. I don't know if it's the fact that I know I'm fulfilling a fantasy for her. Or if it's that we're in a public place, albeit alone in it. Or maybe it's that her arousal came on so fast and strong. Whatever it is, I'm finding it impossible to hang on.

Thankfully, when my orgasm comes, Hannah digs her fingernails into my shoulders and lets loose with an explosive orgasm of her own—one that twists and warps deliciously against my cock that's currently lodged balls deep inside her.

"Oh, God," I murmur, before turning slack against her.

With a deep sigh of contentment, Hannah slides her feet onto the floor and her forehead against my shoulder. "Holy shit. Talk about Peter the Great."

I take a deep, steadying breath. "That was definitely my favorite kind of hard drive."

Hannah cackles. "I was highly impressed with the *RAM* in your hard drive, sir."

"That's thanks to you turning my floppy disk so damned hard."

She gasps. "Did we just invent a new kind of dirty talk? Dirty Talk for Dorks."

"*Cum*-puter speak."

Hannah bursts out laughing again. "You've got to trademark that."

I laugh while pulling up my pants. "I think the trademark application would be a waste of money. Surely, we're the only two dorks in the world who'd find cum-puter speak sexy." I slide my hand into my pocket, intending to pull out that little piece of folded paper, but it's not there.

Shit.

I look around in mild panic and spot it on the floor next to the bench. My last comment is the perfect segue to show her what's on that piece of paper—to tell her I love her and that I'm positive she's the only dork in the world for me. But I don't want to skitter over there like a cockroach to pick up that paper. I want to be smooth about it.

Hannah says, "Ya wanna gaze at the stars with me?"

I glance at the paper on the floor again, as beads of sweat form on my forehead. "Yeah, I suppose we should put the telescopes to good use, as long as we're here." As Hannah walks toward a nearby telescope, I quickly snatch the paper from the ground and shove it hastily into my pocket. *Phew.* That could have been a disaster for me, if Hannah had seen the scrap of paper and thrown it away. Or worse, unfolded it and looked at it.

As Hannah bends down and peers into a telescope, I finger the paper in my pocket and suddenly realize I can't show it to her yet. Really, I've got no business saying "I love you" to Hannah before I've been at least half-way honest with her about my life. At the very least, shouldn't she know the truth about how I got that code at the door before she, hopefully, says "I love you" back to me? Shouldn't Hannah know the gist of my superpowers? If I don't come clean before saying "I love you," then would I really be any different from that asshole, Greg Smith, who said whatever he had to say to gain her trust and take her money?

Hannah straightens up from the telescope. "Take a peek. It's so beautiful."

I stare at her for a long beat, before finally releasing the paper in my pocket and stepping forward to take a peek. "Oh, wow. Yeah. Beautiful."

"How long did you rent the place?"

Fuck. It's time for me to decide. Am I going to lie in response to that question or not? Am I going to start the process of divulging the gist of my secrets to Hannah now or not?

"We've got the place for another hour or so," I say. "The security cameras will turn back on at ten, and we'll need to be gone when that happens." I feel myself blushing, but I forge ahead, anyway. "I didn't actually rent this place out. Not officially." I hold my breath as Hannah's brow furrows.

She tilts her head. "We're not allowed to be here?"

"Not legitimately, no."

She gasps. "Someone who works here is making money on the side by renting the place out on the down-low?"

Aw, fuck. I'm losing my nerve. In a flash, my brain engages in a violent tug-of-war. Should I correct her or not? That narrative works pretty damned well for my purposes—it deftly reveals the illicit nature of our visit without inviting a stream of questions I don't want to answer quite yet. "You guessed it," I say on an exhale.

Whether I hacked into the planetarium or obtained access through a rogue employee making money on the side, the result is the same, right? *We're trespassing.* Committing a crime, albeit a petty one that won't hurt a soul, all in the name of having a sexy, memorable, fun adventure. If Hannah accepts this version of technical illegality as the cost of making an exciting memory, then surely her acceptance will inch me even closer to revealing more of the truth to her, one day soon. Not the whole truth, of course. Not even Josh and Reed know that. But even if I'll never tell Hannah the full, granular truth about my superpowers, I know in my gut I should at least tell her as much as Kat and Sarah know about them. The only question is *timing*, and my gut *also* tells me one week is too soon to take that leap of faith.

I swallow hard and say, "I hope you don't mind me employing some questionable, albeit harmless, tactics to make *Lala Land* come to life for you."

Hannah looks wholly unbothered. "Not at all. I think a tiny bit of breaking and entering is perfectly acceptable for a great cause."

My entire body feels electrified. "My thoughts exactly."

"Actually, now that I know we're technically trespassing here, it's like we're fulfilling yet another fantasy of mine. One I didn't even realize I had. We're Denver and Stockholm, baby!" She's referring to the show we've been binge-watching together this week—*Money Heist.* Every time we watch that show, Hannah goes on and on about her obsession with the romance of Denver and Stockholm—a bank robber with a heart of gold and his sexy, smart hostage.

Hannah steps forward and touches my cheek. "Thank you for tonight and for every date you've arranged this week. You make me feel so special."

"As you should."

She kisses me and whispers, "I'm falling so hard for you, Henny."

My heart stops. My breathing hitches. Saying you're "falling" for someone is a world apart from admitting you've already fallen. Thank God, I didn't pull out that paper and say the whole damned thing a few minutes ago. As it turns out, Josh and Reed were exactly right: I need to wait at least a month to tell her.

"I'm falling hard for you, too, Hannah."

Her blue eyes dance. "Do you want to eat some yummy cupcakes while checking out the exhibits?"

"Let's do it."

For the next thirty minutes, that's exactly what we do, until an alarm on my phone tells me it's time to get the hell out of Dodge.

"We should throw this away at another location," Hannah says, holding up the pink bakery box. "If they empty the trash cans at the end of each day, they might realize someone was here after-hours in the morning."

"Look at you! One petty crime and you're already a criminal mastermind."

She shrugs. "I listen to true crime podcasts all the time. And rule number one for getting away with murder is leave no forensic evidence behind."

"You're a genius."

"Stick with me, kid."

"You're in charge of planning all our heists, robberies, and planetarium trespasses from now on."

"Deal." The pink cupcake box in one hand, Hannah slides the other one into mine, and we walk as a criminal unit toward the back service door. The night didn't go exactly as I'd envisioned it. I never showed her the piece of paper in my pocket or told her the magic words that have been practically burning the tip of my tongue. But overall, I think it went stupendously well, regardless. In the end, I stumbled into making a hot fantasy come true for Hannah, while also dipping a tentative toe into the Pool of Truth.

Okay, new plan.

I'll tell Hannah "I love you" after I've told her some critical truths about myself. The good news is I think this little trespassing jaunt has paved the way for that moment, quite nicely. In no time at all, I predict the time will come for me to reveal a whole lot more about myself to Hannah . . . and then, to me saying the magic words and hearing them back. Which, then, hopefully, will one day lead to Hannah and me committing to face the world, together, as a team, the same way my parents always did.

15

HENN

After a quick breakfast of cereal at Hannah's kitchen table, we kiss and hug goodbye in her doorway.

"I wish I didn't have to go to work," Hannah murmurs, skimming her lips over mine.

"Now that I'm staying till Thursday, we can spend the whole weekend together doing anything you want."

"I'm so glad you're staying."

I slap her ass. "Go on, Stockholm. The sooner you get into work, the sooner you can sneak away for dinner before karaoke."

Hannah sighs. "It doesn't work that way. My boss doesn't care how early you came in, she wants to see people working late, no matter what."

"Even on a Friday night?"

"*Especially* on a Friday night."

I roll my eyes. "Babe, we've got to get you a new job."

"For shizzles. But there are too many moving parts for me to start looking in earnest. Once I know Maddy's fate at UCLA and also whether or not Kat is going to start her PR company, then I'll be able to decide which city or cities should be the focus of my job search."

My breathing halts. "Are you saying . . . if Maddy gets into UCLA, you'd seriously consider moving to LA?"

She nods. "I've always dreamed of living somewhere besides my hometown, but what's stopped me is not wanting to be away from my sister. If Maddy were to move to LA, I'd see it as a golden opportunity." She frowns. "Although . . . I guess if Kat ultimately decides she wants to start a company in Seattle with me as part of it, that'd be a wrinkle." She shrugs. "But if we get that far, maybe Kat would let me work remotely. Who knows?"

My brain is whirring and clacking—instantly making plans and devising strategies. So much so, I suddenly realize Hannah's mouth is moving, and I haven't been listening. "What was that? Sorry."

Hannah says, "I asked if six o'clock works for you to come to my office before karaoke. I want to introduce you to my friends at work, and then I thought we'd grab dinner at this cute little Thai place down the street."

"Any time works for me. I'll just be sitting here working all day."

"Great. I'll see you at six."

I lean my shoulder against Hannah's doorjamb. "How are you planning to introduce me to your work friends?"

"Whichever you'd prefer—Peter or Henn."

My smile widens. "I don't care which name you call me, as long as it's preceded by the phrase 'my boyfriend.'"

"*Oooh*." A huge smile unfurls across Hannah's face as she slides her arms around my neck. "You want to be my boyfriend, do you?"

"I do. Very much."

She kisses my cheek. "Okay then. *Poof.* You are. I'll see you at six, boyfriend."

"See you then, girlfriend."

"How exciting."

After another kiss, Hannah slides away, raises her arm into the sky like a knight raising a sword in battle, and shouts, "To the salt mines I go!"

Chuckling at her silliness, I watch her march down the length of the hallway, looking adorable in her kitten-heels-purple-blouse-black-pants work outfit, until she disappears around a corner and presumably into an elevator. When she's gone, I run my palm over my face and mumble, "Damn, I love my girlfriend." With a lovesick sigh, I amble back into her apartment, and a moment later, I'm seated at Hannah's kitchen table with two laptops.

First things first, I find a place that rents Sybians and give them a call. They're all booked through the weekend, unfortunately, but that's okay, since my new flight leaves Thursday morning. I book a machine for Wednesday, figuring I'll go out with a bang. After that, I click into my bank account to see if the money Jonas negotiated as my share of our finder's fee has finally come through. Holy fucking shit. *It has.* I'm a millionaire, baby, tax-free and legitimately earned. Holy fuck. I've never seen so many zeroes in my life—at least, not in my own bank account.

I stare at my screen for a moment, trying to decide what to do with all that dough, and finally decide to do precisely what I said to my mother the other day: buy myself a spiffy condo in LA. Or Seattle, I suppose, if Maddy doesn't get into UCLA and/or Hannah decides to stay in Seattle to work with Kat.

If I'm being honest, I'd strongly prefer for Hannah to move to LA, rather than for me to make Seattle my new home base. Even with Josh moving back to Seattle, he'll surely visit LA frequently for business reasons, and Reed still lives in LA. Plus, it's an easy drive from LA to visit my mother in Fresno—and that's a top priority for me now that Dad is gone. Also, the weather in California can't be beat, and I've realized that's not a small thing for a guy who's battled depression in the past.

My fingers feel twitchy. My brain is buzzing. I bet it'd be easy to hack into UCLA and take a look around. When I recently hacked into the University of Washington to find Sarah for Jonas, it was easy peasy lemon squeezy. Or is that pumpkin squeezy, like Hannah says? Either way, it's hard to overlook the blockbuster outcome of the simple hack I did for Jonas, all in the name of potential true love. For fuck's sake, Sarah is now living with Jonas at his house, and they're deeply, hopelessly in love. So, really, why *wouldn't* I perform a similar hack for *me* this time—to get *myself* a happy outcome like that?

No, Peter. In your case, the ends wouldn't justify the means. Hannah specifically told you Maddy wouldn't want any outside help getting into UCLA, and you need to respect her wishes, no matter how much you want Hannah to move to LA.

But what if UCLA uses a system that's similar to U Dub's? Wouldn't that be an interesting thing to know, sheerly out of professional curiosity? If that's the case, then it'd take me only minutes to get inside UCLA's system and peek around at the admissions database. Once I'm there, I wouldn't necessarily tamper with Maddy's application status. I could simply take a peek to see what's up and then leave without doing a damned thing.

And what are the odds of you doing that, Peter?

Slim to none, probably.

Exactly.

My phone beeps, saving me from my internal tug of war, and when I look down, I've got a new message on my encrypted server—a much-anticipated update from my hacker buddy, Demon Spawn.

> Demon Spawn: I think your target's made of smoke, my friend. He was spoofing that IP address you gave me, not surprisingly, and he hasn't been at mommy's house in Dallas recently. I staked it out for a while and then asked Mommy if I could deliver a package for him there, and she said her son hasn't been around in months and she didn't expect him to come by any time soon. Unfortunately, there are a shit ton of Greg Smiths in this world and I'm not seeing any activity on his known aliases. I can keep looking through Greg Smiths, as long as you want. Just wanted you to know why I don't have the guy cracked yet.

> Me: All good info. Thanks. Yeah, keep doing what you can. I'll take over the job myself whenever I have the time. In the meantime, what's the latest on the used car project?

Demon Spawn updates me on his efforts on that front, and I laugh my ass off at the long list of cities where he's purchased and ditched shitty-ass cars.

Me: Great job. Sending payment now. Keep it up until I tell you to stop.

After we've said our goodbyes, my brain immediately returns to thoughts of Hannah and my strong desire for us to live in the same city. I look at my keyboard, and my fingers instantly begin twitching again.

I think it's perfectly natural for someone like me to wonder if one university uses the same system as another I've already hacked. Wouldn't any hacker worth their salt want to find that out? Knowing if I *could* hack a certain university doesn't mean I'm necessarily going to hack it. Or that, if I do, that I'm definitely going to do a bad thing, once inside. There are plenty of online spaces I've infiltrated, just because I can, simply to have some fun looking around . . .

No, Peter. Stop.

Flapping my lips together, I force myself to dive into my actual work and forget about my thumping desire for Hannah to move to LA. But after only a few minutes, I realize my attempts to divert myself have been fruitless. My fingertips are still twitching. The buzz in my brain has become too intoxicating to ignore. *I simply can't resist.*

Okay. Here's the deal. If UCLA doesn't use the exact same template as U Dub, then I'll leave it alone. Forget about it forever. And if UCLA *does* use the same template, or maybe a similar one, then, okay . . . at that point, I'll . . . decide what to do next.

Sounds good. It's a deal.

Click, clack.

Clack, click.

Hmm.

Welp, it looks like UCLA's system isn't the exact same thing as U Dub's. Which means it's probably time for me to move along now.

Spoiler alert: I don't move along. In fact, I spend the next two hours figuring out how to get in. And when I do, I head straight to the one place I shouldn't go: the admissions database, where I quickly discern the mechanics of their internal search engine and enter the name *Madelyn Milliken.*

Nothing comes up as a search result, so I try *Maddy Milliken.* And then, some variations on Milliken with typos in them, just in case. Still nothing. Which means Maddy's application hasn't been entered into the admissions system yet.

Phew.

That was a lucky break. Like a fool, I almost did something I'd probably regret later on.

"You dodged a bullet, Peter," I whisper into the void of Hannah's tiny kitchen. "Now, log out and never go back."

A text comes through on one of my phones—the burner given to me by the FBI bigwig I worked closely with in DC. She says she has an urgent job for me—an offer I won't be able to refuse—and she wants to talk to me about it ASAP.

"Fuck me," I murmur in annoyance. I've spent my whole career trying to be undetectable to The Man. Or, I guess, in this case, to The Woman. I've worked hard to slither and slide through online spaces like a phantom, while presenting Peter Hennessey as a mediocre cybersecurity dude. And now, the fucking Deputy Director of the FBI wants to hire me for a job? Shit.

The thing is, though, I'm far too intrigued, and maybe even a bit flattered, *not* to place the call. And so, in the end, that's what I do. And when I finally talk to Deputy Director Leach, and hear her out, I discover she's exactly right: *the offer she's made me is one I simply can't refuse.*

16

HANNAH

When I see Henn sitting at a small table at the Thai place, I wave and walk toward him, and he rises to greet me. Unfortunately, I wasn't able to introduce Henn around the office as originally planned, thanks to the kerfuffle caused by Kat announcing her immediate departure this afternoon. So, Henn kindly agreed to meet me here at the restaurant, instead.

"Hey, baby." Henn kisses my cheek. "Everything okay?" When I called Henn to ask him to meet me at the Thai place, I didn't tell him what happened to change our plan, but instead told him I'd spill some big tea tonight at the restaurant.

"Everything is great," I say, settling into my chair. "Kat quit her job today, and our boss melted down." I snicker—but before I can continue my story, our waiter appears with menus and a few suggestions. We order a couple of Singhas, the most "famous" of Thai beers according to our friendly waiter, and immediately resume talking as the server leaves. I touch Henn's arm. "I wish you could have been there to see Kat's grand exit. She did it with such panache."

"Of course, she did. Panache is Kitty Kat's middle name."

"Thank God, she took me out to lunch before doing it to tell me her plans, so I wasn't blindsided in the moment. She was actually planning on giving proper notice and being professional and all that, but then our boss started acting like a total bitch, so Kat finally said, 'Take this job and shove it up your tight ass, Rebecca! I'm out!'"

Henn laughs with me. "I guess Kat's not angling for a recommendation letter for her next job, eh?"

"She doesn't need one. That's the best part. Kat told me today she's one hundred percent going to open her own PR company!"

"Oh, wow. Are you going with her?"

"Not yet. Kat's not sure she'll be able to take me on. She'll know in a month or so, after she gets everything going."

"Is that what you'd want?"

"I think so. Can you imagine how fun it'd be to create a new business with my best friend?"

"Yeah. Awesome."

Oh, Henny. It's not hard to notice the anxiety flickering across his handsome face. Plainly, he's wondering how a new job in Seattle would impact the chances of me moving to LA one of these days. Frankly, I'm wondering the same thing, especially now that I've told Maddy I'll move to LA and live with her, if she gets into UCLA. Fuck a duck, my head is spinning these days, whenever I try to imagine the foreseeable future.

"There's still a chance it won't work out with Kat," I say. "Kat told me not to quit my job yet, just in case. Plus, I've got Maddy to consider. Lots of moving parts." I'm not willing to say it yet, but Henn is rapidly becoming a major consideration for me, too. If things keep going this well between us, then it's reasonable to think one of us will need to move at some point. If Maddy gets into UCLA, that's an easy one. In fact, it'd be the best of all worlds, since I could move to the same city as my boyfriend, without pinning my relocation solely on our spanking-new relationship. But what if Maddy doesn't get in?

"If you do wind up working with Kat, do you know if you'd be her partner or employee?" Henn asks, yanking me from my thoughts.

"I don't know. Kat walked away with some big craps winnings in Vegas, so I think she's got way more money to invest in a start-up than me."

"Yeah, Josh told me he and Jonas made a killing, thanks to Kat's hot rolling streak, so they gave her a bunch of their winnings."

"Do you know how much they gave her?"

"No. But those boys bet big, so it had to be quite a bit."

"When Kat and I were in Vegas, she said she was going to give her winnings to her brother, Dax. He's in a band and they've been saving to record an album. But today at lunch, she made it sound like she's still got a bunch of cash to invest, thanks to Josh, so maybe Dax refused to accept the money from her." I shrug. "Either way, Kat's got enough money in the bank to quit her job without notice and without having another job lined up, and also to invest in a new start-up. As long as I've known her, Kat has had no savings and plenty of credit card debt, so I think it's highly possible Josh has been extremely generous with her, even beyond those craps winnings."

Henn suddenly looks uncomfortable, which makes me think I'm being too gossipy for his taste. Luckily, the beers come to save me from the awkward moment.

After we've both taken sips of the beer and agreed it's delicious, Henn asks, "So, did you and Kat talk about you possibly working remotely, if you wind up working with her?"

"We didn't talk any specifics because it might not even happen, you know?"

Henn presses his lips together before taking a long sip of his beer. If I had to guess, he's thinking about the future, as much as I am.

I touch his hand. "Let's not get ahead of ourselves, okay? For all I know, Kat might decide to make her business a one-woman show. Or maybe Maddy won't get into UCLA, and I'll decide to stay here till she graduates. The future is kind of blurry for me right now. I can't see anything too far ahead." It's the truth. I'm head over heels for Henn, but that doesn't mean I trust my feelings enough, after only one week, to uproot my entire life for him. I took a foolish, embarrassing leap of faith with Angus and quickly learned I'm a naïve idiot who's a horrible judge of character. I don't think Henn is anything like Angus—of course, not—but that doesn't mean I'm willing to jump head-first into a whirlwind romance, without a proverbial parachute, ever again.

Henn fidgets with his napkin. Takes another long sip of his beer. And then, "So, has Maddy heard anything about her application?"

"Not a thing. She logs into her dashboard twice a day to see if there's been an update. Apparently, it'll change to 'received' at some point. And then, 'under review,' at which point I'm sure my sister will start mania-cally checking her dashboard fifty times a day." I laugh, but Henn looks stiff and nervous. Am I imagining that?

The waiter appears and takes our orders. As he leaves, Henn shifts in his chair and says, "So, um, I've got some bad news. I'm really sorry, but I can't stay a few days longer, after all. I have to leave tomorrow morning for a big job."

"Oh, wow. Okay."

"I got the call today, and I really can't turn it down. I wouldn't have said yes to them, but the potential payday is huge. Biggest of my life."

"Wow. How exciting, Henn. Congratulations."

"I tried my hardest to put off the initial meeting for a week, so I could stay here with you till Thursday morning, as planned, but they said the meeting has to be this weekend. There's a big conference or summit or whatever this weekend, and lots of people they want me to meet with will all be there, all at once."

My head is teeming with thoughts. Kat told me Henn worked with the FBI in DC before coming here to Seattle, but Henn's never uttered a word about that. Is this job related to that one? The word summit seems like a governmental kind of word. Did Henn do such a good job for the FBI the last time, they've hired him again? "I'm thrilled for you," I say. "It sounds like a huge compliment they've hired you for such a big job."

"Well, I haven't been hired, exactly. I'm being given the chance to compete for a huge payday, along with some other programmers. It's highly possible I'll put in a couple weeks of hard work, round the clock, for nothing. On the flipside, though, it could wind up being the most lucra-tive couple weeks of my life."

"Sounds like it's definitely worth the gamble."

"Indubitably."

I'm dying to know how much money is at stake here. How big is a big payday to Peter Hennessey? Ten grand? Twenty? *Fifty*? I don't feel comfortable asking him or anyone else about their finances, even though I'm extremely curious. So, instead, I ask, "The job will take a couple of weeks?"

"They're actually projecting at least a month, but I'm always faster than anyone predicts. The bad news is that however long it takes me, I'll have to do it all on their system, in person. No remote work allowed. Also, whenever I'm working, I'll be required to leave all my devices at the door for security reasons, so I won't be all that communicative by day while I'm gone. Don't worry, I'm sure we'll be able to chat at night after work, but that's about it."

Okay, that definitely sounds like Henn will be working for the feds again. "How mysterious," I say coyly. "Who's the client? The CIA?" I flash him a playful side-eye. "Tell me the truth, Peter, are you a spy?" I've kept my tone flirtatious, even though I'm asking a genuine question. *Is Henn a freaking spy?*

Henn leans forward and whispers, "Yeah, I'm the American James Bond. Hope that doesn't change anything between us."

"It's actually a huge relief, because I happen to be a German operative."

"You don't say." He chuckles. "More proof we're a perfect match."

My head is spinning. What the heck is the nature of this confidential job that's requiring Henn to fly off at a moment's notice, work on-site, and give up his devices while he's there? I ask, "Are you allowed to tell me anything about the client?"

Henn shakes his head. "I had to sign a strict NDA—the strictest of my career—so I'm not at liberty to say much of anything about the client or the job."

"So mysterious."

"Not really. NDAs are standard in my industry. Most clients go to great lengths to keep their intellectual property from getting leaked or hacked. It's a monumental task to keep things contained these days."

"Sounds like a spy thriller."

"It feels that way sometimes. But I assure you, it's not."

Hmm. Do I believe him about that? I'm not sure I do. To be fair, what Henn said about NDAs being standard in his industry makes perfect sense, intellectually. But after the fiasco with Angus, my gut can't help feeling like secrets of any nature are a red flag. I know it's probably irrational paranoia, since I'm ninety-nine percent sure Henn is exactly who he seems to be—a lovely, brilliant cybersecurity specialist who's one-hundred-percent life partner material, but it's that one percent doubt that's causing my stomach to churn.

I raise my beer and force a smile. "Congrats, Henny. Here's to you completing the job and getting the payday. Either way, congrats on getting the call."

"Thanks." He clinks my beer and takes a sip. "There's an outside chance I could see you, briefly, next weekend. I told them I have to fly to Fresno for my mother's birthday on Thursday, no matter what, and they said that'd be fine, as long as I come back right away. After Fresno, I'm planning to swing by LA to take care of a few things and grab some stuff from my apartment, so maybe I could swing up to Seattle after LA to take you to dinner, and then fly back out of Seattle on a red-eye."

"I'm exhausted, just hearing you say that. Don't worry about seeing me, honey. Spend as much time as you can with your mom for her birthday, and when the job is over, and the payday is yours, we'll celebrate by spending lots of quality time together."

Henn twists his mouth. "Yeah, I guess that's probably for the best. It sucks that they've set this up as a competition. They're not assembling a collaborative team, as much as a pack of self-interested gunslingers and bounty hunters. The longer I'm away from the job, the more likely it is another programmer will swoop in and complete the project while I'm gone."

"I'd never forgive myself if you came to Seattle to take me out to dinner, and that was the difference between you getting the money or not. Please, don't worry about seeing me until the job is done."

Henn sighs with relief. "Okay. Thanks for understanding."

"Of course, I do." I put my palm on the table for Henn to take, which he does. "I'm not going anywhere. Do your best, and your girlfriend will be right here waiting for you whenever you're done."

"I'll FaceTime you every night."

"Then we'll be great. We're adults. We can do long-distance for a while. And when the job is over, we'll be together again. Maybe you can come back to Seattle and stay another week or two."

"I'd love to. Or you could come to LA."

"If I'm still at this same job, then I could only come for a weekend. Unfortunately, I don't have any vacation days stored up."

Henn looks wistful. "Sorry the Sybian rental didn't work out this time. I promise we'll do it next time."

I blush. "It's okay. I'm still not completely sure I could ride one in front of you, anyway. I'd love to try, but I think I might feel too shy, when push comes to shove."

"Like I said, it's totally up to you. No pressure."

"I'm not saying I *won't* do it. I'm just saying you shouldn't set your expectations too high. I've never even masturbated in front of anyone and riding an orgasm machine in front of you seems like a huge leap beyond my comfort zone."

Henn considers that. "Okay, well, if you want to take baby steps, instead of a huge leap—and this is totally up to you, of course—maybe we could use this time apart to get comfortable doing stuff in front of each other on FaceTime?"

I look around the small restaurant and whisper my reply. "That sounds like a great idea. But let's not make any firm promises about that and see how it goes, okay?"

"Of course. I've never had FaceTime sex myself, so I'm no expert. I hope you're not upset that I've raised the idea."

"Upset? Oh, God, no. I'm thrilled you said it. I don't want you feeling like you have to censor yourself with me, Henny. As it stands now, you seem totally perfect to me, which can't possibly be true, so I'm thinking you're probably not saying lots of things you're honestly thinking."

Henn furrows his brow. "No, not really. And as far as me being perfect, I feel like I've shown you lots of imperfections this past week. Hordes of 'em, in fact."

"I haven't noticed them, if so."

Henn looks genuinely baffled. "Seriously, I'm like a human Whack a Mole of imperfections."

I giggle. "If you say so. As far as I'm concerned, nothing you do even slightly annoys me."

"Well, I feel the same way about you. Is there stuff you're not saying or doing because you're censoring yourself?"

"Not intentionally."

Henn shrugs. "So, maybe we're both perfect."

I laugh. "That's not possible."

"I've seen no evidence to contradict my assessment of your perfection, and I'm an evidence-based person, so it must be so."

I roll my eyes. "It's only been a week, babe. I'm sure we've both been on our best behavior this week. But that's to be expected. It's only natural at the beginning of a relationship to put your best foot forward. Frankly, it'd be a red flag if we didn't at least try to do that at first."

"I really don't think I've been on my best behavior this week."

"Of course, you have. So have I. It's unavoidable."

Henn runs a fingertip along a groove in our small wooden table while biting the inside of his cheek. "I hope you know you can tell me anything, Hannah. Show me anything." He looks up. "I want you to know you're completely safe with me. I like you, exactly the way you are."

I'm floored. Where did that come from? "Thank you. I do feel safe with you."

"You can tell me anything."

"Nothing about you even remotely annoys me."

"Not only about that. About anything. Things that are maybe embarrassing to you. Or traumatic. All I'm saying is you don't have to sugarcoat anything for me. You can tell me about any experience that's shaped you into the person you are now."

I tilt my head. Henn's body language is perplexing. I feel like I'm a thief who's been unknowingly caught in surveillance footage, while Henn is a cop who's interrogating me without tell me he's already got the goods on me.

"Do you have a specific question for me?" I ask.

"No. I just want you to know you can talk to me about anything, even something that makes you feel vulnerable."

I process that for a moment and suddenly realize I'm probably feeling confused because I've never dated a man who's in therapy. A man used to talking about feelings—a man who's so damned willing to engage in direct communication. The thing is, though, as much as I sincerely appreciate Henn's attempts to open me up, that's not something I normally do very easily, despite how friendly and extroverted I come across. In truth, I don't currently feel ready to unload every vulnerable or sensitive thing I've ever thought or felt to Henn this early in our relationship.

I've already told Henn some basics about difficult times in my life—

about my parents' divorce and my sister's accident, for example. I think I mentioned my grandma's passing, too. But I don't feel the need to take Henn for a deep dive into the horrible darkness I felt after the perfect storm of my grandma dying, my sister almost dying, and a scumbag named Angus taking advantage of my rocky mental state in order to get his grubby hands on my tiny inheritance. In fact, I'd rather never talk about that shit again with anyone. Not even with my therapist. On the contrary, I'd rather forget all that stuff ever happened.

"I have a confession to make," Henn announces. "When I'm at my apartment or in a hotel room by myself, I'm not nearly as neat and clean as I've been pretending to be this week at your place."

I sigh with relief. I don't know what I thought Henn was about to confess to me, but that wasn't it. "Oh no," I say in mock horror. I point at the door. "Get the fuck out."

"Have you noticed how careful I've been to use a coaster with every drink this week?"

"I have, and I've appreciated the effort."

He snickers. "I don't even *own* a coaster at my place."

I gasp. "*No.*"

"I'm also not the best about getting my dirty clothes into the hamper. Sometimes, they live on the floor or draped over the back of a chair until laundry day on Sundays."

"You're going to need to be a whole lot more shocking than that to freak me out."

"Okay, how about this? I frequently leave little hairs in my sink after shaving. Sometimes, a blob of toothpaste, too. But why clean that shit up right away, when nobody else will see it and I don't mind?"

I lay my entwined hands on the table in front of me. "I sincerely appreciate your honesty. Thank you. Now, please, get the fuck out." When Henn laughs, I add, "All of that falls under the umbrella of trying to make a good first impression. Like I said, it'd be a red flag if you *didn't* try to do that—if you stayed at my house and acted like a total slob the whole time."

"Uh oh. The things I've described make me a total slob?"

"No. A mild slob. I do the same stuff, except for the part about the sink. I can't stand a dirty sink."

"Get the fuck out." Chuckling, he lays his arm on the table. "Have you done anything this week to make a good first impression?"

"I sure have. I'm normally a whole lot grumpier in the morning before my first cup of coffee than I've been with you. I've been downright cheerful when I open my eyes and see your handsome face, but that's not typical for me." I giggle. "Maybe that's what I'm always like when I wake up in total and complete sexual satisfaction every morning, but I didn't know that until I met you."

"I'm not normally a morning person, either. But when I open my eyes and see you, I feel instantly giddy. Like the world is my oyster."

My heart skips a beat. "That's how I feel, too."

As we trade giddy, smitten smiles, our waiter appears with our food. As he leaves, we dig in with gusto. As we eat, the conversation briefly shifts to our food, until I say, "Kat referred to us as Bert and Ernie today. Isn't that cute?"

"That depends. Which one am I?"

"She didn't say, and I don't have a preference, so you can take your pick."

"I'll be Ernie, then. He's the chill one, right?"

"So, you're saying I'm a cone-headed, high-strung crank? Get the fuck out."

Henn laughs. "You said you didn't care."

"It was a trap. Welcome to my annoying side, Peter. Careful what you wish for."

Henn hoots with laughter. "Oh my god, I love yooo-uu-rr . . . sense of humor."

Suddenly, the poor man is melting in front of me. He's red-faced. His features are contorting. What the heck is happening to poor Henny?

If I had to guess, I think his brain just now cockblocked his heart, and what his heart wanted to say got stopped by The Brain Police at the border of his lips. If I'm right about that, if Henn nearly said what I think he was going to say, then I'm glad his brain took over. We're still getting to know each other. Plus, he's going away for weeks. In my opinion, it's way too soon for us to take things to the next level now without first spending adequate time at this one.

"I love your sense of humor, too," I reply with a smile. "It's one of my favorite things about you."

His chest heaves. "Thank you."

I take a deep breath. "We should probably head to the karaoke bar now. It's about a fifteen-minute walk from here."

"Cool." Henn signals for the check, and after paying it, he rises and offers his hand to me. "Ready to sing your ass off, Bert?"

I slide my hand in his. "Ready, Ernie. Let's sing a duet with such dorky enthusiasm, we make all the cool kids in the bar cringe with second-hand embarrassment."

17

HANNAH

"*You're the One That I Want.*"

That's the song Henny and I are currently belting out onstage —with aplomb, I might add—while also acting out the famous scene from *Grease* to a tee. At least, that's what I'm trying to do. In reality, the adorable look of pure glee on Henn's face as he sings and dances and basically *becomes* Danny Zuko is making it hard for me not to giggle my way through my lyrics. But since I'm a pro, y'all, and the show must go on, I'm doing my mighty best to overcome my giggles. Well, mostly. But only by a thread.

For his part, Henn is so into the song and his character—he's a thick slice of ham on this karaoke stage!—he's got the entire bar cheering and singing along with us. Either there are zero cool kids in this bar—which I know for a fact isn't the case, since Josh, Kat, Jonas, and Sarah are sitting at our table in the back—or Henny is just so freaking cute and likeable, he's won every heart in attendance over, even the coolest ones.

When the song ends, Henn and I join hands and take a deep bow together, like we're Broadway performers at our curtain call, and then peck each other's lips and bound off stage. As we move through the crowd toward our group in the back, people high-five and compliment us. So much so, by the time Henn and I finally reach Kat, Josh, Jonas, and Sarah at our table, we've made at least twenty new best friends.

As we resume our seats, the beginning bars of "Living on a Prayer" begin. When I'm settled in my seat, I look toward the stage to find a bearded dude poised to give an enthusiastic performance. The group compliments Henn and me and banter ensues about who's the best singer in our group thus far.

"Hey, at least I'm a better singer than Jonas," Josh says, referring to his handsome, quiet twin brother sitting next to him. It's the first time I'm meeting Jonas Faraday, though I've now heard a lot about him, and I must say the rumors are true. He's gorgeous, quiet, and serious, from what I've seen. Kind of mysterious, too. Magnetic and intense. We haven't had the pleasure of hearing Jonas sing tonight, as of yet, but we're all hoping the moment will soon arrive.

To my surprise, Jonas, who's been pretty quiet up till now, joins the banter regarding Josh's singing abilities. He says, "Don't congratulate yourself on being a better singer than me. I'm literally tone deaf—hence the reason you'll never catch me doing karaoke."

I can't help noticing the group, other than Jonas and me, exchanging a covert, conspiratorial look in response to Jonas' comment. When Jonas went to the bathroom earlier, Josh told Sarah he'd pay good money to witness his brother singing onstage, and Sarah confirmed she's determined to get Jonas up there. But not as a bet, Sarah clarified. And not to embarrass Jonas, either. Sarah explained, "Frankly, I'd love to see my sweet Jonas doing literally anything he's not spectacularly good at."

"So, anyhoo," Henn says to the group. "We've already seen Josh and Kat's spectacular rendition of 'Total Eclipse of the Heart'—which was legendary, by the way—and now Banana and I have stopped the earth rotating on its axis for approximately four and a half minutes with what can only be described as sob-inducing spectacularity . . ." He looks at Jonas and Sarah. "So what are you two planning for our delight and entertainment?" He flashes an extra-big smile at Jonas. "I'll die a happy man if I get to witness you sing karaoke, big guy."

Real subtle, Henny. Jeez. In my opinion, Sarah will have a much better shot at luring Jonas up there if the rest of us don't even mention it.

There's some back and forth in the group, which results in Jonas basically swearing on a stack of bibles he'll never get up there to sing, at which point Sarah begins whispering something into his ear. As Jonas and Sarah canoodle, Kat and Josh begin doing the same thing, so I take the opportunity to lean in and chat flirtatiously with my hot boyfriend, too.

"Do you think Sarah will be able to get Jonas up there?" I ask.

"Absolutely. When Sarah Cruz sets her mind to something, it's as good as done."

I crinkle my brow. I don't doubt Sarah's tenacity, based on some of the stories Kat's told me about her hard work in law school and life in general, but how has Henn been able to discern that fact about Sarah during their brief time together in Vegas? Has Kat told Henn some of the same stories about Sarah she's told me, or does Henn have some interesting stories to tell, thanks to their shared escapades in Las Vegas?

"Yeah, Kat's mentioned that Sarah is a badass of epic proportions," I reply. "Apparently, she finished in the top ten percent of her class after her first year of law school."

"Really? Wow."

Interesting. Henn's confidence about Sarah's tenacity isn't rooted in her amazing law school performance. So, what's it based on, then—whatever Henn and Sarah did together in Las Vegas?

The bearded guy onstage gets to the finale of "Living on a Prayer," drawing our attention. When he's done singing, the crowd, including our table, applauds wildly, and three giggling women clamber onstage to begin their rendition of Wilson Phillips' "Hold On." As they begin, our cocktail waitress appears and asks if we'd like another round.

Josh, who normally takes the lead when it comes to drink orders, requests another round, as well as some shots of Patron, too, at which point, his brother, Jonas, uncharacteristically calls out, "And a couple bottles of champagne! We're celebrating tonight."

"Oh yeah?" the waitress calls back to Jonas above the din of the music. "What are we celebrating?"

"Oh, just, you know . . ." Jonas looks lovingly at Sarah. "*Life*."

Aw. They're too cute. Blabbermouth that she is, Kat has already revealed to me, in strict confidence today at lunch, that Jonas is going to propose to Sarah next week in Greece—which Kat only knows because Jonas asked her opinion of the ring he bought for Sarah—and after watching the pair for the past hour or so, I can plainly surmise Sarah's reply to Jonas's proposal will be a resounding *yes.*

Josh says, "Well, Jonas might be celebrating *life,* but I've actually got a few *specific* things I'd like to celebrate tonight." Josh raises his glass and the rest of us follow suit. "First, I want to celebrate Hannah officially joining our *Ocean's Eleven* crew. Welcome, Hannah. You fit right in."

My flabber is gasted. "Thank you," I squeak out. I push up my glasses, feeling fidgety and excited. I can't believe Josh even thought to welcome me as his first order of business—and that the whole group is now echoing Josh's sentiments with such enthusiasm.

"We all have our roles to play, Hannah," Josh continues. "So now that you're officially part of the crew, I'd like to christen you our cookie-baking Olivia Newton-John."

I giggle. "Wow. Thank you. I accept my role with humble gratitude. What's everyone else's roles?"

"Well, he's the asshole," Josh says, motioning to his brother. "Also, the comic relief, though hardly ever intentionally." He winks at his brother, who's rolling his eyes, before shifting his gaze to Sarah. "Sarah's our George Clooney—our fearless leader—and also Jonas' handler. Without Sarah, Jonas becomes very, very cranky—so I'd like to take this moment to expressly thank Sarah Cruz for coming into my brother's life. By doing so, you've made mine immeasurably better." Josh beams a huge smile at Jonas, who laughs heartily. Next, Josh flashes an adoring grin at Henn to my right. "Henn's our fucking genius, of course. I'm sure that's not news to you, Hannah. Plus, the guy's heart has a ten-terabyte storage capacity."

"Yes, I'm well aware of that," I say. I take Henn's hand and squeeze it, emphasizing my agreement with Josh's description of him. "And you and Kat? What are your roles in the crew?"

"Well, unfortunately, I'm nothing but a playboy," Josh says. "Just coasting on everyone's coattails, pretty much. I'm not particularly useful or smart. Just the eye candy of the group."

As we all crack up, Kat bats Josh's shoulder and says to me, "Don't listen to him. He's wise and powerful beyond measure."

"Oh, well that's true," Josh agrees. "Hannah, you might as well learn it now: I'm wise and powerful beyond anything your feeble mind could possibly comprehend. Let me just say, in advance of whatever pearls of wisdom I'll bestow upon you one day in the near future: *you're very welcome.*"

I giggle. "Thank you, Josh, in advance. Wow, I'm honored to be in your presence."

"As you should be. Thank you." Finally, Josh turns to Kat. "And Kat here? Well, the list is too long to say it all right now, but I'll give you the Cliff's Notes version. She's our secret weapon. The Party Girl with a Hyphen who also happens to be The Party Girl with the Heart of Gold. Plus, she's a suicide bomber, a terrorist, and, sometimes, if you really rile her up, a very stubborn cat." When Kat guffaws, Josh adds, "*And* she's got the best laugh you've ever heard, as I'm sure you already know. The girl laughs like a dude."

We all agree Kat's laugh is positively adorable and infectious, and Kat looks visibly touched.

"I have an item for the toast," Jonas says.

"Hang on, bro," Josh says, waving him off. "I'm not done with Kat." Josh looks deeply into Kat's eyes, instantly causing my heart to pound vicariously. *Whoa.* That's quite a heated look Josh is bestowing upon my beloved bestie. Kat once said she wished Josh would look at her like Henn looked at me in front of The Fake Eiffel Tower. *Well, the girl just got her wish.*

"She's loyal," Josh says reverently, his eyes still locked with Kat's. "And honest. A force of nature when she wants something. She loves her family. And her hair smells incredible."

Kat's chest heaves. Something big is happening here. *I can feel it.* And based on Kat's body language, she can feel it, too.

"There's more, but we'd be here all night," Josh says. Slowly, he leans in and kisses Kat's lips, sending zings of arousal between my legs and an arrhythmia into my heart. Good lord.

We all look away, as Josh and Kat's kiss deepens.

Jonas clears his throat. "I want to salute Sarah for making it through her first year of law school."

"Well, jeez, don't jinx me," Sarah says. "I've got to get through my exams before I'm toast-worthy."

"But you finished your classes yesterday," Jonas replies. "There's no reason not to celebrate that."

Sarah bats her eyelashes at Jonas. "Thank you." She addresses the table, to which Josh and Kat have returned their attention. "Can I add an item to the toast-list, too?" Sarah asks. "I want to toast Henn and Kat for officially becoming *mill-i-on-aires* this week. Congrats, guys."

My mouth hangs open. *What?*

My head swivels toward Henn, but he's not looking at me. Neither is Kat. Both are looking at Sarah.

Speaking to Sarah, Henn asks, "Didn't you get your finder's fee money this week, too?"

Finder's fee money . . . too? What the fuckity are they talking about? Kat hasn't said a word about this, not even during our lunch today—and that's totally out of character for her. Is this finder's fee thing the reason Kat quit her job today without notice and now feels confident enough to start her own business? That's got to be it. So, why wouldn't Kat tell me that? Henn being mum about the money isn't as weird to me. He can be pretty tight lipped about work stuff. Plus, his finances are none of my business. But Kat tells me everything.

Although . . . Back to Henn. He always makes it seem like he's a normal, paycheck-to-paycheck kind of guy. A humble dude who lives in a "crappy-ass apartment" and only travels when he finds a great deal online. He's certainly never contradicted me when I've made comments about both of us needing to hustle because we're not rich. But is that the reality? Is Henn a normal person when it comes to money, like me, or is he wealthy beyond anything he's been letting on?

"Congrats to all three of you," Josh says. "Oh, that reminds me of a biggie." He raises his drink. "To Kat. She officially took a leap of faith today and quit her job to start her own PR firm. Congrats, babe. The sky's the limit."

Josh's toast makes me realize I should congratulate Kat, too. Raising my drink to her, I say, "I'm so excited for you, even though I'll miss you terribly. Working with you has been the best part of my job."

"Well, like I said at lunch," Kat replies, "the master plan is to bring you on as soon as humanly possible, Hannah Banana Montana Milliken. As soon as I know what I'm doing, you'll be my right-hand woman."

"Cheers to that. Just call me and I'll come running, girl. Whatever you touch turns to gold, Kitty Kat—I have no doubt your new company will be golden, too."

"Thank you, honey."

The waitress returns with a new round of drinks, plus the shots and bottles of champagne the Faraday brothers ordered for us, and conversation about Kat's new PR company and what to call it consumes the table.

I can't focus on the group's discussion. I'm still too blown away—and, frankly, confused—by the revelation that Sarah, Kat, and Henn have all received a million bucks this week as some kind of finder's fee. And yet, this is the first I'm hearing about it.

What did those three *find* and for *whom*? Did the trio stumble upon some new, exciting company in Las Vegas for the Faraday brothers to invest in or purchase, so the brothers gave the trio a commission on the deal? Or did the finder's fee have something to do with whatever this group did to take down Sarah's nefarious ex-employer?

Either way, I don't understand why Henn didn't tell me he came into some big money this week. I don't need details because Henn's finances aren't my business, but it's weird I've been living with him this whole week and he didn't bother to mention a really big thing that happened to him.

Unless . . . Maybe it wasn't a big thing for him. Maybe Henn is secretly a multi-millionaire, and a million bucks is chump change to him. No, that can't be it, because Sarah specifically said Kat and Henn "became" millionaires this week. Santa Maria. My head is spinning.

"Okay, everyone, get 'em up," Josh commands, pulling me from my spiraling thoughts. He's referring to the glasses of champagne that have now been poured. When we all raise our flutes, Josh says, "To Hannah and Henn, and to Sarah for finishing her first year of law school, and to three newly minted *mill-i-on-aires*."

Okay, there it is again. Henn definitely *became* a millionaire this very week, along with Sarah and Kat . . . but he didn't even hint at that astonishing fact to me. If the situation were reversed, I can't imagine I wouldn't have blabbed *something* about my amazing windfall to Henn. Am *I* the weird one? Are people normally far more discreet than that in the face of financial windfalls? Henn did tell me during dinner at the Thai place that the last-minute job he's taken could be the biggest payday of his career, so he's not immune to talking about money with me, at least in general. But why tell me about a possible payday today and not about an actual one he got this week?

Oh my God. Henn must stand to earn *more* than a million bucks for this new job! Henn said the payday he'll be chasing will be the biggest of his career—and he said that *after* getting a million bucks as a finder's fee. No wonder he's willing to ditch my ass to chase that cash! Holy fuck! Go, Henny, go! I throw back a shot, suddenly feeling extremely dizzy.

"And last but not least," Josh is saying when I tune back in. "To Kat and her new baby." My heart stops for a split-second, until I realize with relief that Josh is referring to Kat's new PR firm, not some bun in Kat's oven she's never told me about. "YOLO, Kat," Josh says with a wink. "I'm glad you've decided to go for it. May you climb and conquer."

As we all convey our boisterous congratulations, Sarah says, "Wait! *Duh.* We've got to toast Climb & Conquer, too!" She picks up a shot of tequila and raises it. "This one we've got to do with Patrón in Joshy-Woshy's honor." When everyone has picked up a shot, Sarah continues. "To Climb & Conquer. I can't wait to watch the Faraday twins climb and conquer every peak of their dreamscape."

After everyone clinks and throws back their shots, Sarah leaps up and pulls on her man's muscled arm. "Are you ready, hunky monkey boyfriend? The alcohol has started to kick in. It's time for you to pay your debt."

There's some slight resistance from Jonas, but, ultimately, much to our table's shock and delight, he stands and lets Sarah pull him onstage.

"Well, I'll be damned," Josh murmurs. He leans in and says something to Kat that ends with, "God, he must really love that girl."

A moment later, Jonas and Sarah are onstage doing a truly terrible rendition of "I Got You Babe" by Sonny and Cher. Sarah's a pretty good singer, actually, by karaoke standards, but Jonas is so tone-deaf, the entire audience can't help rising to its collective feet and cheering him on. Of course, our table is absolutely loving it, too—although Josh isn't at the table any longer. He's now standing closer to the stage by the DJ booth, reveling in every detail of his brother's performance.

When Jonas and Sarah reach the slow finale of their song, the entire bar erupts into a raucous standing ovation. When the song is done, Jonas dips Sarah dramatically, kissing her like no one else is in the room, and she comes up red-faced and giggling.

As the trio—Jonas, Sarah, and Josh—returns to our table, two stoner dudes get onstage and start singing "American Pie." Once everyone is seated again, our group showers Jonas and Sarah with praise and questions, at which point Jonas swears that was the first and last time he'll ever sing karaoke.

Kat says, "So, Henny, how long are you in town? Do you and Hannah want to do dinner with Josh and me Sunday night before Josh heads to the airport?"

"Sorry, leaving tomorrow," Henn says. He looks at me apologetically, and I wink at him to reinforce my genuine support for his change of plans. Hot damn. Now that I know Henny is probably chasing more than a million bucks, I'm feeling even more supportive. Growing up, my mom always used to say, "Love is the most important thing, but it's just as easy to fall in love with a rich man as a poor one." I always used to tell her to stop saying that. I'd insist a man's bank account didn't matter to me, whatsoever. Well, now that I've unwittingly followed my mother's advice and fallen in love with a rich man, I must admit I'm giddy about it.

"Where are you off to next?" Josh asks, speaking to Henn.

"Munich," Henn replies, causing my jaw to practically clank onto the table. *Henn is heading to Munich tomorrow?* I could have sworn he told me he's heading back to DC. Or did I assume that detail, after hearing him say the word summit? Either way, I'm positive Henn didn't mention Munich as his destination—and I find that super weird. Is Henn so blasé about international travel it didn't occur to him to mention that exciting detail to me—a girl he knows is obsessed with the dream of international travel?

Henn glances at me while my jaw is still hanging open, and whatever he sees on my face causes a look of concern to wash over his. He shifts in his seat before addressing Kat. "But, uh, maybe you and Hannah could come visit Josh and me after my trip and we can all go out together in La La Land."

Kat looks at me for confirmation, but I'm still too befuddled by Henn's Munich revelation, on top of the million-dollar finder's fee thing, to meaningfully engage with her. All of a sudden, I feel like there might be a whole lot more to Peter Hennessey than I've realized. Am I crazy to think a guy would tell his girlfriend he's dropping everything to travel to Germany the next day? For fuck's sake, I joked that I'm a German operative at dinner, and he didn't think to mention it then? I was half-kidding at dinner when I asked Henn if he's a spy, but suddenly, that doesn't seem like such a far-fetched idea to me.

Kat is looking at me expectantly, awaiting an answer about that possible double date in LA. "Yeah, uh . . . Great," I murmur, picking up my drink. My brain is exploding. I need to shift the topic. "Hey, Kat, maybe you should think about opening Golden PR in Los Angeles instead of Seattle. Maybe you could do PR for the entertainment industry." I know Kat's been dying to talk about the future with Josh. Namely, the possibility of her moving to LA to be with him. So, why not help a sister out and raise the topic for her?

To my astonishment, Jonas jumps in to reply to my comment before Josh or Kat. And even more shockingly, what he says is unexpectedly rude. "Well, that'd be pretty stupid."

"What would be stupid?" Henn asks, instantly coming to my defense. "Sounds like a great idea to me."

I flash Henn a look of gratitude. I don't know if Henn is a spy or not. Or why he hasn't even hinted about his newfound wealth to me. All I know is he's awfully cute when he's feeling protective of me. Honestly, it feels amazing to finally have a boyfriend who doesn't hesitate to defend me.

"No, no," Jonas says with a chuckle. "I meant it'd be stupid for Kat to move to LA. What would be the point of her doing that when Josh is moving back home to Seattle in a couple months?"

My jaw drops, yet again. Well, that's a twist I didn't see coming. Kat didn't mention Josh moving back to his hometown during our lunch today! On the contrary, Kat went on and on about how hard she's finding the long-distance aspect of her relationship with Josh. Did Josh tell Kat this amazing news after my lunch with her today?

"*What?*" Kat shrieks. "*You're moving to Seattle*—for good? To *live?*"

Okay, that reaction makes clear Josh hasn't already told Kat his amazing news. I look at Josh, excited to revel in this happy surprise with him, but my stomach sinks when I see his stiff body language. His pale face. The look of barely contained panic twisting his handsome features. *Uh oh. I think Jonas just spilled some of his brother's beans.*

"Yeah," Josh says to Kat, his voice tight. "I'm moving home. Just got a place."

It's plain to see Kat isn't interpreting Josh's demeanor the same way I am. Otherwise, she wouldn't be acting this enthralled. "When?" she gasps out excitedly. "This is *awesome*. A dream come true."

"In two or three months, probably." Again, Josh's stiff energy doesn't match Kat's.

"Why didn't you tell me?" Kat says excitedly. "Did you just decide today? This is incredible news. Oh my god. I'm elated!"

Jonas looks deeply confused. To Kat, he says, "You didn't know?"

Kat's smile falls a bit. "No, he didn't mention it to me." *Boom.* She suddenly gets it. Her brow furrows. Her energy wilts. "Why didn't you mention it to me, Josh? Were you planning to surprise me?"

"Uh . . ." That's all Josh manages, before pressing his lips together into a thin line.

"How long have you known?" Kat asks. "You said you already found a place?"

Josh looks guilty as sin. "Yeah, I've known for a little while. Let's talk about it later, okay?"

"How long have you known?" Kat demands, her tone hardening. "Did you know when I said that thing about the long-distance thing being brutal? Did you know then?"

Josh looks sheepishly at the group. "Let's talk about it later, babe. Don't get all worked up about it. I was just waiting until it was for sure."

Kat visibly perks up. "Oh, it's not for sure yet? That's why you didn't tell me?"

"Well, no. Actually, it's for sure. I'm moving."

"Oh." Kat looks conflicted now. This would be the best possible news, if only Josh himself had bothered to mention it to her. "That's great," Kat says weakly. "So, you've already made plans? You've got a place?"

"Let's talk about it later. What's everyone planning to sing next?"

As Kat asks Josh another stream of questions, I lean in and whisper to Henn. "Looks like you're not the only guy who doesn't tell his girlfriend big news."

Henn grimaces. Thanks to my comment, he now knows, for sure, he didn't misinterpret the look of pure shock and hurt he saw on my face earlier. As the two guys onstage finish their song to raucous applause, Henn runs his hand through his dark hair and says, "You've got some questions for me." It's a statement, not a question.

"I sure do."

The place is noisy, what with everyone applauding the "American Pie" dudes, so I motion toward the front door, signaling we should take our conversation outside.

"Grab your coat," Henn says, rising from the table. "It's cold out there."

As we reach the front door, the karaoke host booms behind us, "And noooow, I have a very special treat for you!" Normally, I'd love to witness a "very special treat" in a karaoke bar, but at this particular moment, the only thing I want to witness is Henn giving me honest answers to several major, nagging questions.

18

HENN

"*Of.* You're right. It's chilly *con carne* out here," Hannah mumbles as we step out of the karaoke bar and into the cold Seattle night. She pulls her coat tightly around her. "Thank you for reminding me to grab my coat. *Brr.*"

"I've got you, babe." I wink, feeling oh-so clever to have referenced a karaoke duet, but Hannah doesn't smile or wink back at me. She certainly doesn't burst into singing the song, either, which I'm half expecting her to do. All of which suggests this conversation is probably going to be a rough one for me.

Fuck.

When Sarah congratulated Kat and me on becoming millionaires this past week, I was excited and relieved. In that moment, I felt certain Kat must have blabbed the basics of our *Ocean's Eleven* shenanigans to Hannah, and Sarah knew it, which therefore made Sarah feel comfortable talking about the finder's fee payments in Hannah's presence. How else to explain Sarah's comment?

Honestly, I was grateful Sarah had broken the seal that way, because it meant I could now speak freely about the topic in front of Hannah without being the one to break our solemn vow of confidentiality—one we made not only to each other, but also to the FBI. It was that chain of assumptions and deductions that led me to reply to Sarah by asking if she'd received *her* million-dollar finder's fee, too.

But then I saw the look on Hannah's face, and I knew my assumptions had been faulty. That Hannah hadn't, in fact, already known about the finder's fee situation before Sarah mentioned it. I also realized, much to my dismay, that Sarah must have assumed *I'd* already clued my girlfriend in on everything . . . which then, in turn, prompted me to realize that's probably what a normal boyfriend would have done in the same situation . . . which therefore meant I might very well have fucked up royally by keeping Hannah totally in the dark. How badly have I fucked up here? And how much can I rightly divulge to Hannah now in order to fix it?

People are smoking and milling around the bar's front entrance, so I motion down the sidewalk, and Hannah follows me to a desolate spot about a hundred feet from the bar's bustling façade. As we stop and face each other, the famous song from *The Bodyguard*, Whitney Houston's "I Will Always Love You," begins blaring, but I can barely register the tune through my blossoming anxiety.

"What's on your mind?" I force myself to ask.

Hannah crosses her arms over her chest. "Do you think it's normal Josh didn't bother to tell Kat about the new house he bought in Seattle?"

I'm shocked. That wasn't on my bingo card of things I thought Hannah would ask me. "Uh, well, in terms of Josh, yes, it's normal. It's actually very on-brand for him. For a person who's *not* a raging commitment-phobe like Josh, however, it'd probably be more than a bit weird." I furrow my brow. "That's what you wanted to come out here to talk about?"

"This topic is only the appetizer, not the main course. First of all, I wanted to get your thoughts about Josh not telling Kat—his *girlfriend*—some big, exciting news about his life. I thought your response might help me understand you better."

Ah. So, I've read her correctly. She's pissed I've kept her in the dark about the finder's fee. "I'd rather talk about you and me."

"Hang on. I'm still curious to know a bit more about Josh. Why is his silence on-brand behavior for him?"

I shrug. "Because Josh self-sabotages whenever romantic relationships get too real or intense for him."

"Do *you* self-sabotage in romantic relationships?"

"No, I've got the opposite problem, at least when it comes to you. Every time I look into your big blue eyes, I have to keep reminding myself there's no rush." Hannah is clearly unmoved by that comment, which is a bummer. I thought that was pretty smooth. "Hannah, please, tell me what's on your mind in relation to me."

Hannah twists her mouth, apparently considering her next words. "Was there a specific reason you didn't tell me at dinner earlier you're going to Munich tomorrow?"

Again, I'm floored. I wouldn't have seen that question coming if she'd given me a hundred guesses. "I didn't mention Munich at dinner?"

"No. To be fair, you didn't identify your destination. So, I assumed you were going back to DC, since you said the word summit and that sounds like a DC kind of governmental word. The thing is, what boyfriend doesn't say, 'Hey, babe, I'm going to Germany tomorrow for a month'— especially after said girlfriend has already joked she's a German operative?"

I grimace. She's got a fair point. "I'm only going to be in Germany for two or three days," I say lamely. "From there, I'm going to Fresno for my mom's birthday, like I told you, and then to LA overnight to pack and handle a few things, and then to DC, just like you thought, where I'll do the actual work for however long. So, in the end, your assumption was correct."

Again, she's unmoved. "Are you working for the government?"

Shit. This is exactly why I haven't revealed jack shit to any other woman I'm dating. Because I've always known one revelation about my work would naturally lead to lots more. I look around to make sure nobody is around and whisper, "Yes. But that's a detail I'm not supposed to reveal to anyone because of my NDA. You can't tell a soul."

"I won't. I promise." She tilts her head. "Do you even have your passport with you?"

"I do now. I didn't when the client called today, but they arranged for a messenger to get it from my apartment and bring it to me at your place."

Hannah throws up a hand in frustration. "Now see, that's exactly the kind of story I would have thought you'd tell your girlfriend over dinner."

I make a face conveying my confusion. "Why? I never talk about my work. Like I said, most of the time, I'm governed by an NDA—or if not, there's always at least an implied promise to keep my mouth shut."

Hannah exhales. "But when Josh asked where you're going, you told him right away. You didn't say, 'I can't tell you that.'"

Again, she's got a point.

She says, "It's not that I think you've been specifically hiding tomorrow's destination from me. It's more that I feel like I'm not first in line to hear your stories. Like you don't trust me as much as you trust Josh and the other people at that table tonight. I don't like that feeling, Henn. We're not acquaintances or buddies. I'm supposedly your girlfriend."

"Not supposedly. You are."

"Well, to me, a girlfriend is the person you want to share the news of your life with. Good, bad, silly news. Whatever."

I twist my mouth. "I'm sorry."

"Sorry won't fix it, if we don't figure out what's going on here." She exhales. "I don't think the Munich thing would have rubbed me so wrong if it hadn't been for the finder's fee revelation right before that."

Okay, here we go. Finally, the thing I thought we were coming out here to discuss.

"I respect and admire that you're a humble, down to earth person," Hannah says. "You're not one to brag about anything, and that's attractive to me. I also fully accept your finances are none of my business. But all that said, it was embarrassing and disheartening to find out from Sarah, and not from my boyfriend, that you'd had such an exciting thing happen to you this week. It was also humiliating to realize that everyone at the table assumed you'd already told me about your exciting thing, which made me feel like I had to play along to save face." Hannah scowls. "I *really* didn't like that, Henn—knowing you didn't trust me enough to tell me something everyone else already knew. I felt stupid and embarrassed about that."

I shift my weight. "If it makes you feel any better, we all had to sign a strict confidentiality agreement. That's probably why Kat didn't tell you about the money, either."

"Kat's not my boyfriend."

"True," I say softly.

"Speaking of Kat, it makes perfect sense now that she quit her job *today,* and without notice. I'd quit suddenly too, if I had a million bucks sitting in my bank account." She levels me with her big, blue eyes. "What was the finder's fee for? What did you three *find* to the tune of a million bucks each? And who made you sign the NDA?"

Hannah's eyes are searching. Vulnerable. Pleading with me to enlighten her—to let her in and confirm she's every bit my trusted confidante as the others. All of a sudden, I realize this is a make-or-break moment for our budding relationship. Either I trust Hannah enough to tell her the basics about what went down in Vegas, or I don't—and if not, then she's absolutely right: I can't rightly call myself her boyfriend.

I look around, making sure nobody is nearby and then whisper, "Okay, what I'm about to tell you is highly confidential, so you can't tell a soul. Not even Maddy."

Hannah nods solemnly, her blue eyes sparkling. "I swear on my life."

I look around again. "The reason Sarah felt comfortable talking about this, I think, is that it's really her secret to tell or keep—not mine. But now that she's included you in our circle of trust, I think it's fair for me to tell you the gist of what happened."

A couple walks past us on the sidewalk, so I wait a minute for them to pass before speaking again. "Sarah found out her employer—a high-end dating agency—was doing some shady shit on the down-low, and she got scared for her safety. Rightfully so, because she was physically attacked by one of their goons."

Hannah gasps. "What? When?"

"Right before Vegas. She's okay now. But of course, Jonas went ballistic and wanted to protect her at all costs. So, at Josh's request, I flew to Vegas to meet with the group—Sarah, Jonas, Josh, and Kat—and we put our heads together and figured out a way to take the motherfuckers down." I tell her the basics of what our *Ocean's Eleven* crew did and explain that my specific job was pilfering information and funds from the bad guys' online system. "Sarah put all the info into a detailed report," I explain, "which we then turned over to the FBI, along with a whole bunch of their dirty money. As part of the deal Jonas struck with the feds, we took a small cut of the funds recovered. Plus, Jonas promised I'd help them process all the information and data we'd turned over, which is why I flew to DC after Vegas."

Hannah processes that. "And they were so impressed with your work, they called you for tomorrow's job?"

I nod. "The woman I worked with the most in DC is a bigwig at the FBI—the Deputy Director. Second in command."

"Wow."

"I guess she told some bigwigs from other departments or agencies about me, and the next thing I know, I'm being flown to a big meeting in Munich tomorrow. I honestly don't even know anything about the job yet. I'll find out what they want me to do when I get there."

Hannah's eyes widen. "Do you have any guesses?"

I shrug. "I'm sure they'll want me to take a crack at an encryption of some sort. That's the only thing that would make sense, given my skill set." I bite back a smile. "I do know the payday, if I'm successful, though." I pause for dramatic effect. "Two million big ones, baby."

Hannah's eyes become two saucers. "*Dollars?*"

I nod. "With a payday like that, plus the million I got today, I could forget about buying a condo and jump straight to buying a kick-ass dream house."

"Hell yeah! Congratulations, Henny!" Hannah throws her arms around me enthusiastically, and as our lips and tongues dance and swirl, I feel like the weight of the world has been lifted off me. Granted, I haven't told Hannah chapter and verse about my work, and probably never will, but I've now told her enough to surmise the basics. For fuck's sake, who else but a world-class hacker could possibly take down a global crime syndicate by pilfering their data and stealing their illicit funds? Who else but an elite hacker would be flown to Munich by the US Government to presumably help crack an encryption?

When Hannah pulls out of our embrace, her face is flushed and her eyes sparkling. "I understand your work is confidential," she says. "But will you promise me, going forward, that I won't be the last person to know something about you? I don't mean stories from college or whatever. I mean recent stuff. Stuff all our friends would assume you've already told me about."

"The Vegas thing was a one-off. I promise." It's actually an easy promise for me to make, since I can't imagine another situation where I'd work with a group of my friends. Not to mention, I can't fathom another scenario where my friends would know details about a hacking job of mine and then congregate in the same place as Hannah to talk about it.

"Thank you," Hannah says. She runs her fingertip down the buttons of my shirt. "So, hey, do you wanna ditch this karaoke stand and go back to my place?" She bats her eyelashes. "I've never been fucked by a millionaire *spy* before, and I must admit the thought is turning me on like crazy."

I chuckle. "I'm not a spy."

"That's exactly what a spy would say."

"I swear to God."

"Not to *Steve Jobs*? Interesting."

I chuckle. "Sorry to disappoint you. I'm truly not a spy."

Hannah places her finger on my lips, playfully shushing me. "Play along, Peter. I've just discovered a hot fantasy I didn't even know I had."

I quirk an eyebrow. "Tell me more."

Hannah snickers. "I'm thinking we could try a little spy-thriller-infused role-play. Like, maybe you're James Bond and I'm a German operative named Zelda, and it's your mission to seduce and/or fuck all my top-secret information right out of me."

"Britain and Germany are allies. They share intelligence." When Hannah flashes me a look that says, "*Seriously?*", I quickly backtrack. "But who cares about that? I'm sure the two countries don't tell each other *everything.*"

"Of course, they don't."

I stick out my hand and adopt a British accent. "Hello, Zelda. The name is Bond. James Bond."

Hannah takes my hand and assumes what I think is meant to be a German accent, though it's hard to say. "It's a pleasure to meet you, Mr. Bond. You're quite zhe charmer. But not charming enough to charm zhe beeg secrets out of me."

I wink. "I'm the best of the best, my dear. I assure you, by the end of the night, you'll be telling me every last thing I want to know—right after you've screamed my name."

19

HENN

"Velcome to my lair, Mr. Bond," Hannah says, using her version of a German accent.

"Brilliant." I don't know if James Bond would reply that way in a situation such as this. Probably not. But it seems like Brits use that word as a catch-all, so I think it works well enough for our spy-thriller LARPing.

"Martini?" Hannah asks, once we've entered her tiny apartment.

"Shaken, not stirred."

"How predictable." With a flick of her dark hair, Hannah glides into her kitchen, grabs a bottle of vodka and two tall glasses, into which she pours two double shots and nothing else. After swirling the glasses around, she hands one to me and barks, "You'll take what I give you. It's a metaphor for the rest of our night togezher."

I raise an eyebrow. "I think you're underestimating me, Zelda. I'll take whatever I want, and you'll like whatever I give you."

"We'll see about that."

"Yes, we shall." I throw back my vodka as Hannah does the same. And then, I take her empty glass and place it on the counter with mine, back her ass into the counter, and kiss her deeply. "Zelda," I whisper against her lips, my hard-on nestled against her sweet spot. "What do you say we put our missions aside for the night and simply enjoy each other's bodies without ulterior motives?"

"Zhis is precisely vhat a spy would say to provoke his unvitting target into revealing top-zecret information, Mr. Bond."

"Call me James. And I assure you, I'm far too enchanted by the *blitzkrieg* of your beauty, wit, and charm to even think about manipulating you in such a devious manner. The only thing I'm aiming to provoke from you, my dear, are deep moans of pleasure."

Hannah briefly breaks character to giggle with glee. But when she regains composure, she pushes her glasses up, furrows her brow, and says, "You are undereztimating *me*, Mr. Bond. I do not recommend zhe practice."

"I'm hereby calling a truce."

"Vell, I am not."

With a wink, I take Hannah by the hand and lead her into the bedroom. Once there, I take her into my arms and kiss her deeply, until one thing leads to another and we're making out on the bed in our underwear. As our arousal ramps up, it suddenly occurs to me I should probably gather some props to make things extra spicy, or else I'm likely not going to deliver on whatever expectations Hannah's got for this role-play.

"Stay put, Zelda. I need to gather a few well-chosen implements of torture." I get out of bed. "Got any bungee cords or soft ropes in this hideaway?"

Hannah puts her hands behind her head with a smile. "The closet in the hallway. But don't be gone too long, Mr. Bond. I'm not a patient spy."

"I'll be back before you can say 'mind the gap.'"

Hannah giggles as I leave the room, and it's clear she's once again not laughing in character. No, that delightful giggle is pure, delicious Hannah Milliken.

In the hallway, I grab some bungee cords from a closet and then gallop around Hannah's apartment gathering supplies, my hard-on straining against my briefs as I go. I've never done any kind of BDSM before—not even light bondage—so I'm not sure how to do it. I'm willing to try my best, though, in order to give Hannah a spicy, fun night to remember while we're forced to be apart for who-knows-how-long.

Hey . . .

The thought occurs this role-play idea might wind up serving a higher purpose for me tonight. I've been dying to say "I love you" to Hannah all week, but I've stopped myself because, rightfully, I've known down deep it's still way too soon. But what if I can somehow coax *Hannah* to say the magic words first, through the guise of James Bond torturing the words out of her? Ha! If I can pull that trick off, then hot damn, I'll be walking on air as I board my flight to Munich tomorrow morning.

I return to Hannah's room, various props in hand, and discover she's no longer lying on the bed in her underwear the way I left her. No, she's standing at the foot of her bed, her hands on her hips, wearing nothing but sky-high heels and a smile.

I stop short inside the door, floored by the sight of her in the moonlight. Hannah's nipples are erect. Her expression wicked. Where did she get those clear, platform heels? She looks primed and ready to dance on a pole in the best possible way.

"I've had a change of zhe mind," Hannah declares in her silly German accent. She steps forward and slowly takes the bungee cords and other items out of my hands. "Get onto zhe torture platform, Mr. Bond. Ve're going to see what top-secret information *I* can fuck out of *you*."

———

I'm delirious.

Blissed out on white-hot pleasure like nothing I've experienced before.

I'm hog-tied to Hannah's bed, my naked body covered in melted ice, candle wax, and traces of Hannah's natural lubrication. It's not what I envisioned when I scurried around Hannah's apartment earlier collecting props for *my* planned torture of *her*. But I'm not complaining. Not when I'm having so much fun, and it's obvious Hannah is having the time of her fucking life.

To begin with, Hannah teased every inch of my bound body with her lips, tongue, fingers, ice, and wax, before moving on to giving me a blowjob that made my eyes roll back into my head and my heart feel like it was physically cracking my sternum.

After I lost it, Zelda called me a "bad *spion*"—I'm guessing she peeked at Google translate while I was scurrying around her apartment earlier—and then, with that particular mission accomplished, Hannah left my slack, tethered body for dead while she showered for an eternity in the adjacent bathroom. I'm not complaining about her lengthy absence, by the way. It was an extreme pleasure to lie there, bound and sexually satisfied, listening to my girlfriend singing "Auld Lang Syne" in the shower at the top of her lungs.

Upon Hannah's return, she immediately went back to work on me again, initially teasing me with some kind of soft feathery thing, and then, with her lips and tongue, until my cock miraculously became rock-hard again. When I was sufficiently at her mercy, Hannah slipped on her high heels again, straddled me, and began riding my newly hard cock like a drunken barfly riding a mechanical bull. It's what she's still doing now, with her head thrown back and her nipples as hard as stones. *And I'm fucking loving it.*

"Tell me zhe secret!" Hannah demands with a sharp twist of my nipples.

I'm out of my head. Jacked up on pleasure. Drowning in a sea of love and sexual delirium. "I'm falling for you," I murmur.

"Yes!" Hannah shouts, her movements on top of me intensifying. She twists my nipples again. This time, a touch harder. "What else?"

"I . . . I'm crazy about you."

Another twist. "*What else?*"

"I . . . I adore you."

Fucking hell. She twists my nipples again, even harder. And even though it hurts like hell, I'm suddenly and unexpectedly shattered by a massive orgasm that comes on like a hurricane. I yell Hannah's name as my release throttles me, and then twitch against my bindings like a fish on a riverbank until it subsides.

"Jesus Christ, Hannah," I murmur.

"I'm Zelda."

"Well, Zelda's a fucking sadist."

"Correct. And proud of it. Stupid Hannah wouldn't hurt a fly."

I can't help laughing. "Did either of you come?"

"No. We both got close, but no cigar."

"Untie me. I'll get you both there in record time."

Breathing hard, Hannah unties my bindings and flops onto her back, at which point I attack her breasts and nipples with my mouth while fingering her clit and G-spot.

As promised, it doesn't take long. In fact, in mere minutes, Hannah or Zelda—not sure which—arches her back and comes hard against my fingers inside her. When her release is complete, she snuggles against me and sighs like a Disney princess looking into a wishing well.

"Is that you, Hannah?" I ask.

"Yes. Zelda left through the window like a puff of smoke."

I chuckle. "Tell her thank you for me."

"I will. Are you okay? Did she hurt you?"

"Not at all. Well, a little bit. But it was well worth it. That was so much fun." I kiss the top of Hannah's head. "Thank you. Next time, I'll tie you up, so you can experience that kind of fun, too."

"No, that's okay. When you asked me where I keep the bungee cords, that's when I suddenly realized I've never once had a bondage fantasy that involved *me* being the one tied up. Every time I've pictured doing that, I'm always the one in control. I can't honestly imagine myself being that vulnerable, not even with someone I trust completely." She brushes her fingertips against my bare chest. "Are you disappointed about that?"

"Of course, not. Like I always say, I only want to do what you're comfortable with. It wouldn't be fun for me, otherwise."

"Tell the truth, though, when you came back into the room with all that stuff in your hands, were you the tiniest bit upset at me for flipping the script on you?"

"*Upset*? Hell no. I was nothing but stoked. Couldn't you tell?"

"Just making sure."

"I've never fantasized about being tied up, to be honest, but I thoroughly enjoyed it."

Hannah cuddles close. "I must admit, I loved the way you shrieked at the hot wax."

I chuckle. "So, you admit Zelda's not the only sadist here? Hannah's got a sadistic streak, too?"

"I guess so. Who knew?"

We both laugh.

I love you.

The words have once again popped into my head. Hannah would say them back to me, if I said them now, I think. I'm ninety-nine percent sure she would, but it's that one percent chance that's keeping my tongue tied.

Hannah kisses my chest. "I'm crazy about you, too," she whispers. "And I adore you, too." She lifts her head and levels me with a dazzling smile. "In fact, I'm falling pretty damned hard for you, Peter Hennessey, if you want to know the truth."

My heart is pounding in my ears. My body vibrating with the urge to say it.

Nope.

I can't do it.

Not yet.

"I'm falling pretty damned hard for you, too, Hannah Milliken." It's a lie, obviously. I'm not falling for Hannah—I've already soundly fallen. In fact, I've crashed through five floors and straight into the basement on my fall. But this phrasing will have to do for now.

Hannah squeezes me and snuggles close again. "I'm going to miss you so much."

"I'm going to miss you, too."

I hold her close, stroking the length of her naked back, until, after a while, her breathing becomes rhythmic and her body relaxed in my arms. "Hannah?" She doesn't reply. "459," I whisper, ever so softly, just in case I'm wrong about her being fast asleep. When she doesn't reply again, I silently mouth the words "I love you." And then, pull my little dominatrix close, shut my eyes, and command myself to join Hannah in blissful sleep for at least a few hours before my early alarm goes off for my flight to Munich.

20

HANNAH

I hug Kat warmly. "I've missed you, girlie pop."

"I've missed you, too," Kat replies with a tight squeeze. "The only good thing about that stupid job was getting to see my Hannah Banana Montana Milliken every day."

We're having lunch at our usual spot for the first time since Kat so spectacularly quit three weeks ago. Now, what used to be an almost daily occurrence for us is a scheduled, special occasion on our busy calendars.

We place our food orders at the counter and head to a corner table.

"How's Colby doing?" I ask as we get settled into our seats. Two weeks ago, Kat's oldest brother, Colby, a Seattle firefighter, had a horrific accident after charging into a burning building to save a baby. From what I understand from both Kat and various news reports, Colby's broken bones and internal injuries were severe enough to land him in the ICU and on a respirator for a full week. In every single media report, they've called Colby a hero, and I couldn't agree more.

"He's doing okay," Kat says with a grimace. "Physically, anyway. Mentally, he's really struggling."

"I can only imagine."

"He's out of the hospital now, thankfully. Staying at my parents' house during his recovery. I've been visiting him every day. That's the upside of being unemployed. I've got plenty of time to drive him to his various appointments—also, to hang out with him and walk his dog. I'm doing everything I can think of to try to cheer him up." Kat thanks me for the flower bouquets I sent, one to Kat and another to her parents' house, and we talk for a bit about the long road ahead for poor Colby.

"The good news," Kat says, "is that the doctors said Colby will fully recover, eventually." She grins. "And lucky for him, he'll get to spend lots of time with his pretty physical therapist along the way." Kat makes an expression I know well—her patented "matchmaker" face. "Something tells me Colby Morgan's got a big, fat crush."

"*Ooh*. Tell me more."

A worker appears with our food and takes the plastic number off our table, and we dig in while Kat tells me what she's observed so far about the palpable attraction between Colby and his physical therapist. Kat and I are both suckers for romance in any form, whether in books, movies, or real life, so of course, we're both enthusiastic participants in the discussion.

When that topic has run its course, I ask about the rest of Kat's big family. It's something I always do, because Kat's stories about her four brothers and parents are always exceedingly entertaining.

"Everyone is doing great," she says, "now that we know our beloved Cheese 'n' Macaroni is on the mend. At first, when we didn't know if he'd survive or not, we were a collective ball of pure agony."

"I can only imagine."

She tells me some of the details of her family's panic and despair in the first days of Colby's horrific accident, and the story brings tears to my eyes.

"But like I said, everyone is doing great now," Kat says. "Oh! Dax and his bandmates just finished making that demo album, and it's freaking fantastic."

I ask her about it for a bit, and then ask, "Do you think Josh might be willing to send it to Reed Rivers?"

Kat winks. "That's already my gameplan, sister. I just have to figure out the right time to ask Josh. He's already done so much for me. I don't want him thinking I'm only with him for all the perks."

"He'd never think that." I understand why Kat is being cautious, though. From a few of our recent text exchanges, I know Kat and Josh had a rough week after karaoke night, due to Josh's failure to mention his imminent move to Seattle. Josh didn't wind up meeting Kat's family the following night, as originally planned, and Kat basically wound up ghosting him for the better part of a week. Luckily, everything seems to be back on track between the pair. In fact, from what Kat's told me, it's now better than ever.

"How are the rest of your brothers?"

"All good." Kat fills me in about her older brother, Ryan, whom the family has nicknamed "Captain" and "Rum Cake." She says Ryan has been working hard as a commercial broker and saving money to open his own bar one day. "The bad news is Ryan's got a crazy girlfriend, apparently," Kat says with a snort. "Olivia. Colby met her before his accident, and he said she's a real humdinger of a bunny boiler."

I laugh. "A bunny boiler?"

Kat says it's a reference to *Fatal Attraction.* "In a fit of jealous rage," Kat explains, "the scorned woman boils her ex-lover's kid's pet bunny in a pot." When I grimace, Kat laughs. "After my brothers saw that movie, they adopted the term for any woman who gives off psycho vibes, basically."

"God, I love your family." It's true. When Kat was my co-worker, I got such regular updates on the Morgan brothers, I felt like I knew each of them personally. In addition to missing Kat terribly these days, I also acutely miss hearing the latest on her family members, too. "How's Peenie Weenie?" I ask, referring to her craziest brother, Keane.

Kat snickers. "Keane the Peen has recently become a stripper—*as his actual job.*"

"*No.*"

"Yep. His stage name is Peen Star."

We both laugh.

"Apparently, he's pretty good at it, based on the money he's been raking in—one dollah bill at a time, of course. In fact, he told Dax, who then told me, he's been making more money as a stripper than he ever did in baseball or bartending."

"No way. That's crazy."

"Who knows, this might be Keane's calling. He's an amazing dancer, a massive flirt, a diehard exhibitionist, and the biggest ham you'll ever meet. If ever there was a man perfectly designed for stripping, it's our family's neon sheep."

"Plus, he's easy on the eyes," I say, "if you don't mind me saying so." I've never met Keane, but from the photos I've seen of him, he's a jaw-droppingly handsome human. Supernaturally gorgeous. But then again, I could say the same thing about all the Morgans.

"Yeah, and he knows it," Kat quips with a roll of her eyes.

"Do your parents know their goofball son has been paying his rent by taking his clothes off?"

"Oh, God, no. Keane swore us all to secrecy. He's positive my mother will clutch her pearls at the news and my father will be 'deeply disappointed' in him." Kat snorts. "But I told him, no, Peenie, Mom will think it's hilarious—or at least, she'll be thrilled you're able to pay your rent without mooching off the parentals anymore. And Dad would need to have actual *expectations* of you in order to be deeply disappointed in you."

"Why is your whole family so freaking mean to poor Keane? Honestly, I find him adorable, at least from afar."

"Oh, he is adorable. Funny and charming and a true original. But he can also be annoying as fuck. When you meet him, you'll understand why our endless razzing of him is well deserved."

"Speaking of meeting your family, are you thinking of bringing Josh to meet your family any time soon, or are you still holding off on that?"

Kat's blue eyes sparkle like sapphires. "As a matter of fact, Josh is coming to my parents' house for dinner *tonight.*"

"Oh my gosh! That's great news!"

"My whole family will be there." Kat leans back and smiles. "So much has happened since we last saw each other at karaoke night, Banana. It's been a whirlwind." She gives me a run-down, including some of the stuff I already knew from texts, and some of which I didn't. She says she froze Josh out for a week after karaoke night, which prompted him to send her endless flowers and beg for forgiveness and ultimately fly Kat down to LA, which is when Kat finally forgave Josh and they agreed to a fresh start and a committed relationship. Also, lucky Kat, she tells me she briefly saw my darling boyfriend during his quick stop in LA after his visit to Fresno. It's something Henn already told me about, of course, but it's fun to hear Kat's version of the visit.

"When is Josh going to move into his new house in Seattle?" I ask.

"He already did—two months earlier than originally planned—because he couldn't wait to live with me." My eyes widen at the implication, but before I'm able to ask the question on the tip of my tongue, Kat squeals and confirms, "I've been living with Josh at his new house!"

I squeal with her. "Congratulations!"

"Thank you. I'm so, so happy." She didn't need to tell me that—it's written all over her face.

"Does this mean you and Josh have now said the magic words to each other?"

Kat's smile becomes even bigger. "We have."

I hoot with glee and ask, "Did you hold out and make Josh say it first?"

Kat flashes me a long side-eye that says, *Girl, duh,* before laughing and saying, "It's always fun to make Joshua chase me—at least, a little bit." She giggles. "What about you and Henny? Have you said it yet?"

I shake my head. "I think we're close, though. I'm betting we'll say it when we see each other in person again."

"When will that be?"

"At Jonas and Sarah's wedding, at the very latest. Henn said he'll fly in for that, no matter what, even if he's not finished with the big job he's been doing on-site in DC by then."

We talk about Jonas and Sarah's upcoming wedding, since Kat's been helping Sarah with the whirlwind planning as her maid of honor. The topic leads to Kat telling me about Jonas' grand proposal in Greece, which she's heard about in detail from Sarah, and when that portion of our conversation ends, we shift to talking about work. Specifically, the gaping hole created by Kat's departure that's yet to be filled.

"I'm sorry I left you there alone," Kat says.

"Girl, I'd quit, too, if I had a million bucks in my bank account and a billionaire boyfriend who wanted me to be able to hang out and play with him all the time." Suddenly, saying that out loud makes me realize something. Kat's not a workaholic type. Never has been. So, now that Josh lives in Seattle, and she's living with him, why on earth would she start her own PR firm, like she talked about doing only three weeks ago? Maybe she'll return to that plan at some point in her life, but why would she do it now, when she's having so much fun with Josh? The man loves to travel, after all. To eat out and attend sporting events and parties all over the world. Clearly, she's going to be insanely busy being Josh's plus-one for all that fun stuff for at least the foreseeable future.

Excitement unexpectedly floods me. If Kat doesn't open her own PR firm, and if Maddy gets into UCLA, it'd be a no-brainer for me to move to LA to be near Henny . . . and I'm suddenly realizing I'm enthralled by the idea. Yes, if Maddy doesn't get into UCLA, then I'd probably lean toward a longer timeline for any eventual move. But either way, if Kat's plans don't include me, that'd surely take me one step closer to eventually living closer to Henn.

"So . . . about Golden Kat PR," Kat says—because, apparently, she's a mind reader. "I'm sorry, Banana, but I've realized I can only handle birthing one baby at a time—per year, anyway. And this year, my one and only baby is going to have to be . . ." A wide grin unfurls across her stunning face. "The accidental Faraday spawn that's growing inside my uterus!"

My mouth hangs open in shock. "You're *pregnant?*"

Kat laughs. "I barfed up a lung when I got home from karaoke and took a pregnancy test . . . and then got the shock of my goddamned life."

I sit in stunned silence for a long moment. If Kat hadn't laughed a moment ago, I'd assume this was very bad news, knowing her. Is she actually *happy* about this unexpected turn of events? Finally, I ask, "How far along are you?"

"Nine weeks or so."

"And . . . you've decided to have it?"

Kat nods, smiling broadly. "I admit I was totally freaked out at first. But I'm actually super excited about it now."

"Well, then, congratulations."

"Thank you."

"You've told Josh?"

"A couple weeks ago. Part of that rough patch I told you about was because Josh reacted like such a shithead to the news. He's never once shied away from his obligations in a financial sense, but he made it clear, at first, he was anything but happy about the news."

"Oh no. That must have been horrible, Kat."

"It was. He was a total dick. Of course, I told him to fuck off. I said, 'I'll happily take your money for our kid, of course, but otherwise, you can fuck right off.'"

"Good for you."

"I told him if he's not all-in with me—and not because of the baby, but because he genuinely wants to be with me—then, fine, I'll move on and find a man who *does* want to be with me. A guy who'll not only fall head over heels in love with me but also with my baby, too."

"Oh, God, I bet Josh shit his pants at that."

"He sure did. But I meant it. I love that stupid man with all my heart, but I'm not going to settle for anyone who doesn't want me. Fuck that. I knew, even if Josh only wanted to be nothing but a wallet to his kid, then my baby would still have me and the two best grandparents ever, plus four amazing uncles who'd spoil him or her rotten. Seven uncles, actually, if you count Zander, Fish, and Colin." She's talking about her brothers' various best friends, all of whom have become honorary brothers to the Morgan family.

"Don't forget the baby will have two aunties, too—Auntie Sarah and Auntie Banana."

"Absolutely! So why would I stoop to trying to force Josh or anyone else to do or feel a fucking thing?"

"I'm so proud of you."

Kat snickers. "It's all a moot point, though. Josh is all-in now. Like, beyond my wildest dreams. I think the thought of another man playing happy family with me and his kid blew the top of his head clean off and cracked his heart wide open." She sighs happily. "He's so cute. He always wants to know, 'How big is the baby *now*?'"

"I never would have believed that possible."

"Me, either. It's a dream come true—one I didn't even dare to dream, if I'm being honest."

"I'm elated for you."

Kat goes on to tell me every juicy detail about Josh's recent transformation from commitment-phobe to excited expectant father and live-in life partner, and I gasp and blurt exclamations throughout her entire story. The whole thing is classic Kat. I swear to God, that woman is a witch. In the end, she *always* winds up getting everything she wants in every situation. And the best part about her magic is that everyone around her thinks it was *their* idea to give her whatever she wants. Truly, she's a genius. Not in a traditional, book-smart sense, perhaps. But when it comes to people—and especially men—Kat Morgan is the wisest of them all.

"I've never been this happy before," Kat gushes. "I'd pinch myself if I wasn't worried it'd somehow make me barf. *Again*." She rolls her eyes.

"You've been sick?"

"*Dude*. I've been barfing morning, noon, and night. I've always been a barfer. As a kid, I couldn't even look at a boat without hurling, and then in college, it wasn't a party till Kat Morgan barfed. My brothers have called me Barf-o-matic my whole life. But still, Holy Exorcist, Batman, this baby has taken my queasy stomach to a whole new level."

"I'm so sorry."

"Thanks. I can only hope I don't barf while Josh is at dinner with my family tonight, or they might figure out something is up with me."

"They don't know you're preggers?"

"Oh, fuck no. And I'm in no rush to tell them. Miscarriage rates are pretty high during the first trimester, so it might not stick, you know? Especially with all the partying I did in Vegas, which is when it happened. Also, Josh doesn't want to tell my family the news until they've had a chance to get to know him first. He said he wants them to like him for him, rather than because he's my baby daddy."

"That makes sense." I bite my lip. "Do you think Josh wants to be more than your baby daddy someday? Have you two broached the topic of marriage?" Without Kat even needing to tell me so, I know marriage with Josh is part of the ultimate dream for her. How could it not be, when Kat's always dreamed of finding her Prince Charming?

I think I see a flicker of a frown on Kat's gorgeous face before she smiles and says, "Marriage isn't in the cards. Josh doesn't believe in it as an institution, and I'm perfectly fine with that. We're deeply committed to each other, and I'm positive Josh will always support his child and me, come what may. He's even having legal papers drawn up to make sure we'll both always be well cared for, if something happens to him. I told him that's great, since I've got zero interest in forcing him to make any promises he's not genuinely thrilled to make."

I return Kat's smile, but my stomach has dropped. Kat's not saying it—maybe not even to herself—but I think she's at least slightly disappointed about this part of her love story.

"That makes perfect sense," I say. "I'm relieved to hear Josh is committed to taking care of you and the baby forever, no matter what."

"He is. He's amazing."

My stomach tightens again. This girl mainlines romance like heroin. Yes, I love romance, too. But whereas I've seen my favorites—*Pride & Prejudice* and *Lala Land*—probably five times each, Kat has seen her favorites—*The Bodyguard, Pretty Woman, Pride & Prejudice*—at least twenty times each. Kat, unlike me, has *always* believed she'll get the same kind of fairytale as her parents one day, and I'm a bit worried she's settling for something less than that, without admitting it to herself.

Obviously, I'd never tell Kat about my hunch. That would be cruel. If I'm right, she'll realize it down the road and do what's necessary for her happiness then.

"Would it be okay for me to tell Henn the baby news?" I ask. "We talk every day."

"Blab away, Banana. Josh is the one who's adamant about keeping things mum until I'm through my first trimester. Honestly, I'm bursting at the seams for the whole world to know."

I laugh. "Something tells me you're going to blab to your family tonight, Kitty Kat."

"Nope. Josh and I have talked about it and decided the timing isn't right yet."

"No offense, honey, but you're not exactly a steel trap under the best of circumstances, so I can't imagine you being able to keep your mouth shut about news this big—especially when you're face to face with your mother."

Kat shakes her head defiantly. "Nope. I made a promise to Josh about tonight and I'm going to keep it, no matter what."

I snort. "Fifty bucks says you won't."

Kat rolls her eyes. "I'm not stupid enough to take that bet. *Puh-lease.*"

We both cackle. God, I love this girl.

The conversation shifts. Kat asks me about Maddy. I tell her she's still waiting on an answer about UCLA. Studying hard at U Dub while working as a wedding videographer on weekends.

"Oh! Did I tell you Maddy's documentary won top honors at a huge film festival the other day?"

"No way! Tell her congrats from me."

"I will. Thankfully, she was able to amend her application to include that new information before the status on her dashboard changed to 'received' yesterday."

"*Yesterday?* Oh my gosh."

"She's praying such a notable award for her film will be the thing to get her in."

"Of course, it will."

"Not necessarily. UCLA is the most-applied-to university in the entire country." I glance at the time on my phone and realize I'm late getting back to my desk. "Son of a beach ball. Rebecca's gonna be on my ass."

"Back to the salt mines you go," Kat says.

We rise and hug. With Kat's permission, I kiss my fingertips and press a gentle kiss onto her flat belly. "Can't wait to meet you, sweetie pie."

"Aw, I love you so much, Auntie Banana."

Outside in the gray Seattle day, we hug again, and I congratulate her again. When Kat says she'll see me at Jonas and Sarah's upcoming wedding, if not before, I reply excitedly, "And you'll see Henny there, too!"

"I can't wait," Kat says. "I'm sorry about Golden Kat PR. I know you were counting on that."

"Kitty, I'm ecstatic for you. All I want is for you to be happy. Don't worry about me. I'll figure something out."

"I know you will."

With a little wave, Kat heads up the street toward her car, while I turn in the other direction to walk the four blocks to my office building. Two steps into my journey, I punch the button to call Henny. The chances are slim I'll reach him at this time of day. Plus, it's a bit silly to call him now, since we'll be talking on FaceTime in mere hours for our nightly call. But I can't wait to at least try to catch Henn to get his reaction to the shocking news of Kat's bun in the oven. In fact, *not* calling Henny right fucking now would take a sort of superhuman strength I simply don't possess.

21

HANNAH

"Hello, beautiful," Henn's sweet voice says when he unexpectedly picks up my call.

"I can't believe I caught you. Do you have a couple minutes to chat?"

"I do. I'm grabbing a quick coffee to give my eyes a chance to uncross. Hang on, baby." Henn speaks to someone on his end of the line, who replies to Henn in a notably congenial tone. "Okay," Henny says. "I'm good to talk now. What's up?"

I snicker. "Have you spoken with Josh recently?"

"No, we've texted here and there with Reed. Why?"

"Josh didn't drop any bombs on you recently?"

"What's going on?"

"Buckle up, babe. I just had lunch with Kat, and she dropped the bomb of the century, which I'm explicitly allowed to pass along to you." I pause for dramatic effect. "Kat's pregnant with Josh's accidental Faraday spawn."

"*What*?"

"That's exactly how she put it. She said she's near the end of her first trimester."

"Holy fucking shit. I'm assuming Josh knows, if she said you could tell me?"

"Kat told him a couple weeks ago. Apparently, he didn't handle it very well. Kat's exact words were that Josh reacted like a total dick."

"Sounds about right. I'm sure he totally freaked out."

"If he didn't want a kid, then I guess he should have wrapped it up tighter, huh? It takes two to tango."

"Indubitably." Henn pauses. "Wow. I'm honestly shocked. Josh has always been insanely careful. In college, he was always paranoid some gold digger would try to trap him with a pregnancy."

My hackles shoot up. "Are you implying Kat might have—"

"No, no, of course not. Just thinking out loud."

"Kat would never do that, Henn."

"Hannah, you have to know I wasn't implying that about Kat. I'm saying Josh is a totally new man with Kat, in so many ways."

My shoulders soften. "I guess so, because Kat said, now that he's gotten used to the shocking news, he's actually excited about the baby."

"Really?"

I tell Henn everything Kat said about Josh's excitement. Also, about the fact that Josh has now declared his love for Kat, explicitly, and also welcomed her to live with him in his new house in Seattle.

Henn whistles at that last revelation. "This is all uncharted territory for Josh. He'd never say 'I love you' or invite Kat to move in with him, solely because of the pregnancy. I hope Kat knows that."

"She does. She gave Josh a get-out-of-jail-free card at first, but he didn't want to use it." I tell the story of Kat telling Josh to fuck off when he acted like a dick at first, and Henn cheers Kat on throughout my story.

"I'll tell you one thing," Henn says. "I pity their poor kid."

"Huh?"

"With Josh and Kat's combined genes, he or she is gonna be butt-ugly."

I burst out laughing. "Yeah, that poor kid's gonna be one tick shy of the Hunchback of Notre Dame."

"It's unavoidable." Henn chuckles. "Hey, is it cool if I call Josh to congratulate him on Kat's Cinnabon in the Oven, or will that get Kat into trouble for being a blabbermouth, as usual?"

"Actually, Kat said, and I quote, 'Go ahead and blab away, Hannah Banana Montana Milliken! I'm bursting at the seams for the whole world to know!'"

Henn lets out a little *tsk.* "Let it never be said our girl doesn't stay true to her brand."

"She's consistent, that's for sure."

"Did Kat say anything about her pregnancy affecting her plan to start her own PR firm?"

"Yeah, she's scrapping the company. For the foreseeable future, anyway, if not forever. Kat said she can only birth one baby per year, and this year it's going to be the accidental Faraday spawn in her belly."

"Are you sad you won't be working with Kat again?"

"Maybe a little. It was a nice fantasy to imagine myself working side by side with her for the rest of my life. But the happiness I feel for Kat far outweighs any selfish sadness I might feel. Plus, the upside is that I'm now one step closer to looking for my dream job, in earnest. Once I know Maddy's whereabouts in the fall, I'll have a better idea of where I should look."

"Cool." Henn pauses. "So, wait, does that mean, if Maddy gets into UCLA, you'll for sure move to LA with her?"

I can practically hear Henn's heartbeat through my phone. "I think it does, yeah. But if she doesn't get in, then I'd be open to moving to LA one day, regardless. Probably in a few years, after Maddy's graduation." I feel myself blushing. "Unless, of course, you're thinking about moving to Seattle. With Josh living here now, maybe you'd love it here."

"Uh, yeah, maybe. I think that's a possibility."

"That's not what you'd prefer to do, though?"

Henn is quiet for a long moment. "I'll do anything to get to live in the same city with you, sooner rather than later. Literally, anything. But, yeah, if I ruled the world, if I had superpowers and could make happen anything I wanted, then you'd move to LA."

"It's awfully hard to beat LA's weather."

"Very true."

"But even if we lived in the same city, would I see you very much, given how much you travel? Plus, wherever I live, I'll have a job, so that will limit our time together, too."

"Babe, first off, your new job, whatever it is, will be remote. You're not gonna take any job unless you've got that option, at least part of the time, okay?"

"Okay."

"Which means whenever I travel, you'll come with me. In fact, when this stint in DC is over, I'm gonna show you the world with all my millions."

My heart skips a beat. *I love you, Henny.* The words are on the tip of my tongue, a breath from breaching my lips. I know if I said them now, Henny would say them back to me, so there's no risk in that sense. But we've made it this far without saying the words for the first time in a phone call. At this point, I feel determined to say "I love you" to Henn for the first time in person, so we can seal our love with a romantic kiss.

"Oh, hang on, babe," Henn says abruptly. To someone on his end of the line, he says, "Americano, with two extra shots." Returning to me, he says, "I'm at the coffee place. What can I get you?" It's been our usual joke these past weeks apart. We say it, or text it, any time either one of us is grabbing coffee.

"A vanilla iced latte with oat milk."

"You've got it." I smile to myself as I await Henn's return to our phone call, and a few seconds later, he says, "So, what else is new, pretty lady?"

"You mean, besides Kat's bombshell baby news? Nothing much, really. Oh! Maddy's UCLA application status changed to 'received' on her dashboard this morning."

"Awesome. My stomach just did a somersault. Was she able to update her application to include—"

"Her big award? Yep! She amended her application two days ago."

"Yeehaw."

"I'm so excited, it might as well be *my* application."

"Mine, too."

"Ever since she told me, I've been crossing my fingers, toes, ankles, eyes, nipples, and fallopian tubes."

Henn laughs. "I'd pay good money to see that. Especially the crossed nipples."

I giggle. "What about you? Any news since we talked last night?"

"Nope. Same ol' same ol'. Except I'm sad to report I'm pretty sure I won't be done here before the wedding. There's still an outside chance, but I think it's a slim one."

"Shoot." I exhale with disappointment. I knew the chances of Henn finishing the project and making it to Seattle long before Jonas and Sarah's wedding were low. But, still, I've been holding out hope he'd come to the wedding and then be able to stay with me for weeks after that. "The good news," I say, trying to keep my voice from reflecting my extreme disappointment, "is that absence makes the heart grow fonder. Just think how much fun we'll have when you're finally free."

"And hopefully, a whole lot richer."

"Nipples crossed. Is it looking like anyone else is poised to swoop in and take the money any time soon?"

"I don't really talk to the other gunslingers all that much, but from what I can surmise, everyone's bees are every bit as fuddled as mine. Who knows, though. They could be keeping their cards close to the vest."

"I don't get why some of you aren't teaming up. Aren't several heads better than one in a situation like this?"

"Yes and no. I think a lot of us have wildly different approaches to the puzzle, so we wouldn't be a good fit. Add to that, some of these people are greedy motherfuckers and they want the pot all to themselves, so I wouldn't be surprised if some of them might try to sabotage someone else, if you let them get too close. That said, I've tried several times to team up with people, but nobody's been interested. So, whatever. I'll figure it out by myself and take the whole prize, if that's how they want to play it." Henn exhales. "To be honest, I'm not sure anyone can solve this fucker, whether it's one brain working alone or fifty brains working together. I can't go into detail, but solving this puzzle is the toughest thing I've ever tried to do. If I don't figure it out by Jonas and Sarah's wedding, I think maybe I'll throw in the towel."

"Oh, honey. Just do your best. That's all you can do. The main thing is you're giving it your all. That way, you won't have regrets later on, no matter what happens."

"That's exactly what's kept me going—telling myself I have to keep going until I've exhausted every fucking idea, even the stupid ones, so I have zero regrets. Plus, I'm pretty incentivized to get the money and buy an amazing house that'll lure you to LA on a bullet train."

"Oh, Henny." My heart squeezes. "You don't need a big, fancy house to tempt me to move to LA. That's not the thing I'm waiting on to figure things out."

"Just saying, it's a good motivator for me when I'm feeling down."

"Have you been able to talk to your therapist while you've been there?"

"No. Maybe I should."

"You can talk over video, right?"

"Yeah. I'll make an appointment. Thanks for the idea."

"And you know I'm always here to talk anytime, too."

"Thanks. I'm doing okay. I'm just really frustrated. Also, lonely and missing you so much I'm in physical pain."

"Oh, sweetie. I miss you, too. So, so much. When I see you in three weeks, I'm going to physically consume you."

Henn laughs. "Sounds like heaven. Are we still FaceTiming tonight, even though we've already talked today? I'd love to see your face before I fall asleep."

"Of course." I smirk. "Actually, if you'd like, I'll let you see a whole lot more than my face tonight. Do you have any interest in giving Face-Time sex a whirl tonight, Peter the Great?"

"Fuck yes! Woohoo!"

"Make sure you've got lube and tissues at the ready," I say. "Because it's gonna be *hawt*."

Henn laughs. "And just like that, I don't think I need that therapy session anymore."

22

HENN

"Hey, gorgeous," I say softly, when Hannah's smiling face appears on my screen. Damn. My heart is already thumping. Anticipation, skating across my skin and sending heat across my cheeks. Ever since Hannah suggested we attempt FaceTime sex during tonight's regular call, I've barely been able to think of anything else. To say I'm excited is an understatement. Even so, I'm consciously trying to keep my face neutral as I greet Hannah, just in case she's changed her mind since this afternoon. The last thing I'd ever want to do is pressure Hannah into doing anything she's not genuinely comfortable with, simply to please me.

"Hey, handsome," Hannah replies with a coy smile. "I could barely concentrate on my work this afternoon after our conversation earlier. Are you still game to get a little frisky with me?"

"Indubitably. You?"

"Indubitably."

A wave of excitement rumbles through me, but I project calm as I say, "Cool."

Hannah's lying in her bed in Seattle, dressed in cute plaid pajamas. I'm lying in my hotel bed in DC, dressed in sweatpants and no shirt. I'm not nearly as predictable as Hannah in terms of my location and clothing during our nightly calls. But still, this isn't an atypical set-up. And yet, tonight, everything about this moment feels extraordinary to me. Unpredictable and exciting, like anything could happen.

"Could you take the lead?" Hannah says shyly.

I'm pretty sure I've told Hannah I've never done this before, either. So, I'm not sure I'm qualified to lead the charge here, any more than she is. But, of course, I try to project nothing but relaxed confidence. "Of course, I'll take the lead," I reply. "As best I can, anyway." When she nods and exhales, I add, "We'll go slow. Speak up, okay? Let me know if you're not feeling something."

"I will. You, too."

"Hard to imagine, but okay." I smile and pause, unsure how we're supposed to get from this stilted awkwardness to mutual masturbation. In person, I'd touch her now. Kiss her. I'd strip off her clothes and caress her bare curves. Devour her breasts and nipples and stroke between her legs while whispering how beautiful she is. How sexy and hot. And *then* I'd forge ahead with third and fourth base. But how the fuck are two FaceTime-sex-newbs supposed to go straight to virtual fourth base without the benefit of touching and kissing? Suddenly, based on the way Hannah is staring at me, I feel like I've been silent for too long. "Sorry," I say on an exhale. "This feels a bit like the blind leading the blind."

Hannah snickers. "Hey, at least, you're a one-eyed man in the Land of the Blind. That makes you far more qualified than me to be our fearless leader."

It takes me a split-second to process her words and understand the joke. Namely, that she's referring to my dick—the one-eyed jack between my legs that's currently opening his singular eye wide and shouting, "Let's get this show on the road, motherfucker!"

I crack up as the meaning of Hannah's joke dawns on me, and she immediately dissolves into laughter along with me—and, quickly, it's clear this is the ice breaker we've both needed. Just this fast, all awkwardness from a moment ago is gone.

"God, you look good," I say. "So fucking hot."

She tugs on her pajamas and winks. "You've got a flannel fetish, do you?"

"No, I've got a Hannah Banana fetish." I sigh from the depths of my soul. "I'd give anything to kiss and touch you right now."

"Me, too. But hang in there. We'll be kissing and touching in three short weeks."

"You think that's short? That sounds like a lifetime to me."

"I'm trying to stay positive, babe. Just think how amazing our reunion is gonna be."

"I can't wait. I'm gonna kiss you like you've never been kissed before."

"Ooh, tell me more." She bites her lip. "In fact, why don't you tell me all the fun things you're going to do to me when we're finally together again."

Well, first off, I'm gonna tell you I love you. That's the thought that immediately pops into my head. But what I say out loud is, "Well, like I said, I'm gonna give you the kiss of your life. And then, I'm gonna rip off your clothes and kiss every damned inch of you."

"I'm gonna kiss every damned inch of you, too." She tilts her head, looking adorably mischievous. "Can I see every inch of you now?"

"You want to see my hunky, hot body, huh?"

"I do."

"Your wish is my command. Hang on." I place my computer on a small entertainment center across from my hotel bed, and when the framing looks right, I grab my phone and find "Birdhouse in Your Soul"— the quirky song I've thought of as our song, ever since our conversation about it in Vegas. As the music begins, I climb onto the mattress and stand facing my opened laptop with my hands on my hips. "Can you see every inch of me?" I call out to Hannah on my laptop screen.

"Yes, although a whole lot of those inches are covered by sweatpants. That's not what I had in mind, sir."

"I was merely confirming we've got the right framing, ma'am. The full Monty is coming." As Hannah hoots her approval, I launch into a gyrating striptease that begins with me playfully pulling on the waistband of my sweatpants and ends with me throwing my boxers onto the floor to reveal my straining hard-on. Through it all, whatever inhibitions I might have started the dance with melt away, thanks to Hannah's enthusiastic hooting, clapping, and cheering.

"You want to see my dick doing its impression of *Cirque Du Soleil*?" I shout to Hannah.

She laughs. "More than I want to breathe."

I begin chaotically jumping up and down on the bed, which causes my hard-on to do all manner of acrobatics, and Hannah guffaws. Am I making a fool of myself? Probably. Should I feel embarrassed she's basically laughing at my dick? Maybe. But I don't care, because there's a method to my madness. A higher purpose to my silliness. Shyness is rooted in a fear of being embarrassed or feeling shame, so I'm hoping by me being willing to thoroughly embarrass myself, I'll put Hannah at ease. Make her realize this is a safe space where we can both let it all hang out. Perhaps there's a smoother, cooler way to get Hannah in the mood to have virtual sex with me, but whatever that is, it's simply not my style.

As the song ends, I stop jumping around and pose in the middle of the bed like a naked superhero, my chest heaving with my exertion, my hands on my hips, and my erection at full mast. "This hard-on's for you, baby! Because I'm imagining putting it inside you!"

Whooping, Hannah barrels toward her computer, her lips puckered, and when she reaches it, she begins furiously kissing what I'm presuming is every inch of my naked body on her screen. To my delight, when she straightens up, she steps back and begins peeling off her pajamas without me even needing to ask—first, her top, and then her bottoms and panties.

"Oh, God, Hannah," I say, my eyes drinking in her naked body. "I've missed seeing you like this. You look so fucking good." I get off the mattress, grab my computer, and bring it back to bed with me. "I can't wait to kiss you. Touch you. Lick you."

Hannah crawls into bed with her computer, the same as me. "If you were here, how would you lick me?"

"I'd start at your mouth. Kiss you passionately. Then kiss your neck. Your gorgeous tits. I'd also lick those beauties and suck your nipples. Maybe even bite 'em."

"Oooh. *Hot.*"

"I'd work my way down, licking and kissing your belly. And by the time I got between your legs, your clit would be throbbing and swollen. You'd be dying for me to lick your bull's-eye, but I wouldn't do it yet. I'd make you wait."

"This is so hot. You wanna touch yourself while you keep telling me?"

My heart rate quickens. "Will you join me?"

Hannah nods. "I've got a vibrator here to help me out, so if you hear a buzzing noise, that's what it is."

Damn. I'd give my right arm to get to watch Hannah using that vibrator on herself, but the framing makes it clear she's planning to use the device off-screen. Oh well. Baby steps. That's what this whole exercise is meant to accomplish, after all. Our first step in what will hopefully become a long journey of exploration for us both.

"Before you get started, can I see the vibrator?" I ask. With a waggle of her eyebrows, Hannah holds it up for me—a pink, rubber dildo that makes me sigh with longing. "What I wouldn't give to be that dildo right now. Can I see it vibrating?"

Hannah turns it on and a soft buzzing noise sounds through my computer speakers. "This is on low," she says. "It'll be at this speed for a while. I always have to start off really slow and get acclimated."

"I'm so fucking turned on."

"Off it goes to the Promised Land to do its job," she says. She pauses. And then, "Oof."

"It's between your legs now?"

"It sure is." She juts her chin at me. "Are you doing your thing off-screen?"

"Oh. No. I was too mesmerized by the sight of your vibrator to think about myself."

Hannah lets out a long, slow exhale and smiles. "Well, get going, babe, or I'm gonna leave you in the dust."

"I'm right behind you." I reach underneath the covers, but before I get going, Hannah surprises me by asking, "Can you widen the frame so I can see?"

"Oh. Yeah. Whatever you want. Hang on." I place the computer at a different angle on the bed, flip the covers down, lie on my side facing the screen, and get to work on myself. "Too much light? Should I throw a shirt over the lamp?"

"No, don't. You look hot." She watches me jerking off for a long moment. "This is really turning me on," she announces. "If I were there with you right now, I'd take that gorgeous cock into my mouth."

My eyebrows ride up. She's a natural! "Oh yeah? Well, if I were there right now, I'd lick and lap at your clit until I had you as wet as a Slip 'n' Slide. And that's when I'd slide my fingers inside you—to your G-spot— and I'd stroke that little spot, over and over again with the tips of my fingers, while my mouth continued licking and lapping at your hard, swollen, throbbing clit. I'd keep going as your pleasure started building and building . . ."

Hannah moans softly, and a second later, the buzzing sound gets louder. The thought that Hannah almost certainly cranked up the speed on her vibe just now sends arousal zinging straight into my dick. I increase the speed of my hand and suddenly decide to switch into present tense. I'm there with her now. *I'm her vibe.*

"Your clit tastes so fucking good," I say, my voice low. "It tastes sweet. Like candy. It's driving me wild to taste you, Hannah. You're turning me on like crazy. I'm drugged by you. Losing my mind."

She moans loudly. "Don't stop."

"Your pleasure is hurtling toward a breaking point, as I lick and stroke you without mercy. I've got you in the palm of my hand. All I have to do is fuck you, and you'll lose your fucking mind."

"Fuck me now," she whispers. "Fuck me hard."

"Okay, I've got your arms above your head and the tip of my cock pressed against your wet opening. As I press my tip inside you, you can feel me breaching you. Do you feel that—the tip of my cock burrowing inside you and stretching you out?"

She gasps. "Yes."

"I'm pushing inside you now. Burrowing inside, all the way in. I'm filling you up. Making you moan."

Hannah groans loudly and the buzzing sound gets even louder. Her face is glowing with perspiration. Her nostrils flaring. "Fuck me hard, Henn. Tell me what you're doing to me as you do it."

"I'm fucking you so hard, your eyes are bugging out. Can you feel the way I'm pounding you? I'm giving you everything I've got, and you're dizzy with pleasure."

Hannah makes a sexy sound. "You feel so good."

"And you feel like heaven on earth. You're a drug to me, Hannah. My addiction. Everything you do, everything you are, every inch of you, it's all perfect. I'm crazy about you. I can't get enough. I . . . I" *No, no, no, Peter. Stop. Not yet. You'll say it to her in person. That's what you've promised yourself.* I inhale a deep breath. "I . . . I . . . I'm coming." I close my eyes as warm liquid spurts out of me and onto my hand, and momentarily lose myself to bliss. As I come, I'm vaguely aware of Hannah making a strangled sound. A moment later, when I open my eyes, the buzzing sound is at a fever pitch and Hannah's face is contorted. Her eyes are closed. Her breathing labored. She whimpers. Shudders. Groans. And finally, quite obviously, has an orgasm that makes my entire body feel electrified at the sight.

"Holy fuck," I murmur as Hannah rides whatever pleasure she's feeling. "Get it, baby."

Finally, Hannah opens her eyes and smiles. The buzzing sound stops. "Mission accomplished," she declares. "You popped my cherry like a boss."

"And you popped mine like a goddess. *Wow, wow, wow.* That was barely tolerable to the extreme."

Hannah laughs. "I wasn't sure if I'd be able to do it, but once we got going, I totally forgot to feel embarrassed and just went with it."

"You were amazing. No, *schmamazing.*"

"So were you. Thank you for taking the lead."

"I'm not sure I did. You seemed pretty damned confident."

"I did?"

"Hell yeah."

Hannah smirks. "You bring out my wild side. Always have. Since night one in Vegas."

"Lucky me. I'm a big fan of your wild side."

She bats her eyelashes. "I can't wait to do this with you in person."

"In three long weeks."

"God, that feels especially long now."

"Doesn't it? Unbearably long."

Hannah bites her lip seductively. "In the meantime, maybe we could do this again."

"Any time. Name it. Count me in."

She giggles. "How about tomorrow night?"

A huge smile unfurls across my face. "*It's a date.*"

23
HANNAH

As I drive slowly along the arrivals area at Sea-Tac, I scan the masses of travelers on the curb for any sign of my boyfriend. Henn offered to grab an Uber to my place, but I wouldn't hear of it. This is going to be a lightning-fast visit to Seattle for Henn—he'll only be here for about twenty-four hours—so I want to be with him every possible second.

There he is.

Emerging from a pair of sliding doors about twenty yards ahead of me with a computer bag in one hand and a garment bag in the other. Squealing with glee, I maneuver my car to the curb and wave my free hand frantically when I've managed to squeeze into a spot. When Henn's searching eyes lock onto mine, a smile as wide as the Grand Canyon spreads across his handsome face.

These past weeks apart, we've talked every day. Grown closer and closer. And I've known for quite some time, through it all, that I'm in love with him. But now that Henn and I are finally in the same place again, breathing the same air, the certainty of my love is bursting out of my skin. In fact, looking at Henn's beaming smile now, as he gallops toward my waiting car, there's zero doubt the little blue birdie that is my soul has found its forever birdhouse. The man bounding to my car is the great love of my life. My soulmate. My heart's forever home. *Indubitably.*

Henn swings open the door and shouts at the top of his lungs, "I love you, Hannah Milliken!"

I laugh. "I love you, too, Peter Hennessey." Oh well. I was planning to say those magic words to Henn back at my apartment. In fact, I've got a little surprise waiting for him there that was meant to be the "big reveal" of my feelings for him. Finally, I thought, I'll be the one to give Henny a grand gesture! But the sweet man's beat me to the punch.

Laughing like a little kid, Henn tumbles into my passenger seat, places his bags in my backseat, grabs my face, and kisses me. *Excitement, love, elation.* That's the nature of the electrifying energy coursing between our swirling tongues. *We're in love, and we've finally said it out loud.* Truly, I can't remember a more romantic, perfect moment in my entire life.

A loud horn sounds behind my car, jolting us from our amazing kiss.

"Take a chill pill, dude," Henn mutters. Laughing, he secures his seatbelt. "Can't he see we're having a once-in-a-lifetime moment here? Jeez."

"Right? How is it not obvious to him we're busy pummeling the shit out of our gobs?"

Henn snort-laughs. "Oh my god. I've missed you so much. I love you so much."

"I love you so much, too."

We lean in to kiss again, but an airport cop appears out of nowhere and halts our forward movement with his frantic, angry waving at me to move along.

"I'm going," I mouth to him, before pulling away from the curb. "So, guess what?" I say excitedly. "Madelyn the Badasselyn is going to UCLA!"

Henn cheers and high-fives me. "I had a premonition that would happen. When did she get the news?"

"This morning. The only not-perfect thing is that she only got in for spring quarter, rather than for fall, which is what she wanted in a perfect world. But of course, the main thing is that she's in."

"Hell yeah. That's all that really matters."

I sigh with deep satisfaction. "I'm so fucking happy for Maddy. UCLA film school has been her dream for so long. She applied as a freshman and didn't get in. And look at her now! Now that she's in, all on her own, I'm so relieved you didn't ask Reed for help. I've been nervous about that decision and worried I'd regret calling you off if she didn't get in—but now that she has, her admission is that much sweeter!"

Henn smiles. "Absolutely. I'm so happy for Maddy."

For the rest of the drive home, we chat enthusiastically. First, about Maddy. And then, about tonight's wedding, with both of us deciding we're going to let loose and maybe even get shitfaced, both in celebration of Maddy's good news and our newfound love.

I ask Henn how he's feeling now about the job in DC, since we generally avoid the topic during our FaceTime chats, and he says he's actually feeling much more confident about the project these days. Confident enough to predict he won't need any more than a week or so to complete the job after returning to DC tomorrow.

"Wow! Sounds like we've got yet another reason to celebrate tonight."

"Not so fast. Let's not jinx it."

We reach my apartment building and, miraculously, find a parking spot right out front.

"It's a sign," I declare. "All good things happen when I find parking out front." As we head to the elevator, I say, "I've got that chicken curry you love in the fridge, if you're hungry. I made a batch last night. Just need to heat it up in the microwave." With so little time before Jonas and Sarah's wedding, Henn and I have already hashed out our itinerary for this afternoon: sex the second we get to my place, if he's not too hungry. Food first, if so. And then, we'll shower and enjoy a pre-game cocktail, and then another one while dressing for the wedding, and then off we'll go to the wedding via Uber, so we can both drink like responsible fishies, all night long.

"I'm not hungry for chicken curry," Henn says with a lascivious waggle of his eyebrows. "And by that, I mean to imply I'm hungry for your pussy."

I giggle. "Oh, thanks for the clarification. I thought you meant you're hungry for a cheeseburger."

As we walk down the hallway, Henn taps out a text to his mom, letting her know he's made it to Seattle safely. We stop in front of my door while he finishes his text exchange, and when I'm sure I have his full attention, I swing open my door with gusto and bellow, "I love you, Peter Hennessey!"

My tiny living room is filled to bursting with helium balloons in red, pink, and white, all of them butting up against my low ceiling and all bearing the phrase "I love you!"

"Oh my god, Hannah. *This is amazing.* I can't believe you did this for me."

"You beat me to the punch at the airport."

"And you beat me to the punch with all this." He slides his hand into his pocket and pulls out a little wrapped box. Gold paper. A perfectly tied, white bow. "Got you a little something."

"Oh, Henny." As Henn puts his bags on a chair, I unwrap the box. When I open the lid, there's a dainty gold-chain necklace inside with gold lettering in its middle, its phrase held in place by the chain on either side of it. The lettering declares "I AM LOVED" with the "O" punctuated at its center by a rather large, sparkling diamond.

"Oh my gosh. I love it." I look up from the necklace, tears springing into my eyes. "It's the best gift I've ever received. Thank you." Henn opens his arms, and I sink into them and against his chest. "I love you, Henny. I truly never thought I'd get to experience this kind of love."

"I love you, too. So, so much."

When we disengage, Henn helps me get the necklace on, and we stand in front of a mirror, looking at it together. I gush about how much I love it, and he looks equal parts enthralled and relieved. Finally, I turn around and slide my arms around his neck and kiss him deeply, until I feel a tell-tale bulge pressing against me from behind his jeans.

"Come on, love," I say. "I'm gonna strip off everything but this neck-lace and fuck the living hell out of you."

———

"I'm gonna come," I choke out. "Oh my god, Henn."

"Not yet, baby."

I've never made love before, in the sense that I've never had sex with a man I actually love. *And it's divine.* Especially when we're surrounded by another batch of "I love you!" balloons scattered across the ceiling of my bedroom. Not to mention, when a gold-and-diamond "YOU ARE LOVED" necklace is clasped to my neck.

As it's turned out, I'm not the one doing the fucking here, despite my sexy little come on earlier. Nope, Henn is definitely fucking me with authority while spooning me from behind and deftly massaging my clit. To top it all off, he keeps whispering sweet nothings into my ear—the best of which is that he loves me. Through it all, a slow and steady pool of molten lava has been gathering force inside me, hurtling toward what's sure to be the most intensely explosive eruption of my life.

I let out a slow, deep moan and tilt my head back for a kiss. As Henn obliges me, he stops massaging my clit in order to pinch my nipples.

"No, don't stop," I murmur. "I'm close."

"That's why I stopped. You're gonna have a *huge* one. The biggest one, ever. This will get you there. Trust me." He pulls out of me and pinches my ass cheek. "Get up. I want you on all fours."

I'm baffled but utterly spellbound by his confidence. I scramble into position, at which point Henn drags me toward the bottom edge of the mattress and roughly spreads my thighs apart. With the tip of his cock pressed against my ass, he says, "Press this vibrator against your clit on low."

I'm surprised he's got the device handy. I didn't see him grab it from my nightstand. But I take it greedily and do as I'm told. It's the same toy I've been using during our regular FaceTime-sex romps, all of which I've thoroughly enjoyed. It didn't occur to me we'd ever have a "threesome" with Henn's stand-in, once we were finally together in person. But now that he's incorporating the toy, I'm all for it.

I turn the vibrator on and get it into position, and Henn runs his palms hungrily over my torso. He licks and bites my neck. Presses his dick between my ass cheeks and tells me I'm the hottest woman alive. That I turn him on like crazy, like nobody ever has. He tells me I'm perfect in every way, which is simply not true, but fun to hear. Soon, I'm spiraling higher and higher, even more so than when he was fucking me from behind a moment ago.

"That's it," Henn says, his voice strained. "You're so fucking hot, baby. Such a good girl." He pauses. "Good girl?"

"*Yes*. Praise me. Good."

Henn shudders behind me. "Such a sexy, smoking-hot good girl."

"Yes! Don't stop. I'm gonna come!"

"Not yet. Not till I tell you. Not till I fuck you."

"Then fuck me, for fuck's sake!"

With a loud groan, Henn flips me over, throws the vibrator onto the mattress and my legs into the air, and plunges himself desperately inside me. He thrusts roughly, like a beast, making my eyelids flutter and zings and zaps of electricity shoot through me. They're warning shots, letting me know the volcano inside me is about to erupt.

"*I love you, Hannah Milliken*," Henn grits out as his body invades mine, again and again. "I love you so fucking much."

"I love you," I manage to choke out.

All of a sudden, I feel a momentary feeling of weightlessness. A tide receding sharply inside me. And then, as my eyes roll back into my head . . . there's nothing but *bliss*. A sensation of electrifying pleasure coursing through me and warping my insides, while rapture zaps every nerve ending. My brain short-circuits with fireworks. I'm Frankenstein's monster and the "on" switch has just been flipped.

I roar as the orgasm throttles me and then gasp for air as it subsides. When the rippling is finally over, I lie motionless on the bed, twitching.

Did I black out for a second there? Because it's now obvious Henn has finished, too, but I don't remember that happening.

"That was barely tolerable," he chokes out through ragged breathing.

"Just barely," I squeak out.

He kisses my forehead, slides off me, and pads into my bathroom, chuckling with delight as he goes. When he returns to the bed, he's not only got a towel in his hand for me but also a huge, satisfied grin on his face. In fact, my handsome dork of a boyfriend is grinning from ear to ear. I flip over and clean myself off while he slides back into bed with me.

"I had no idea sex could be *this* good," he says. "I've heard of supernatural sex before, the kind that makes you see God, but I thought people were exaggerating."

"I always believed them. I just assumed there was something wrong with me for not experiencing it."

"Yeah, I guess I've thought that, too. About myself, I mean. Not about you."

I touch Henn's cheek. "I love you, Henny. I'm so glad you're all mine."

"I am, and I lost the receipt, so no returns-ies." When I giggle, Henn takes my hand and kisses it. Normally, Henn would flex his hand a la Mr. Darcy after doing that. But this time, after taking a long deep breath, he looks up with dark, soulful eyes. There's no joking around to be detected in those eyes. Only an ocean of love and adoration. "Words can be cheap a lot of the time," he whispers. His eyes drift to my necklace. "It can be the same with gifts. If they're not symbols of genuine feelings, then they're empty tokens. Meaningless. Fraudulent, even." He smiles. "I just want you to know, without a doubt, my words and gifts are symbols of the deep love I feel for you. I belong to you, Hannah. And that means I'll always do anything and everything in my power to make all your dreams come true."

24

HANNAH

"**G**o Henny! Go Henny!"

That's what everyone on the dance floor at Jonas and Sarah's raucous wedding reception is shouting while encircling my silly, drunken, dancing fool of an adorable boyfriend. A moment ago, when the live band onstage kicked into high gear, that silly man dropped to the floor like he'd been hit with a stun gun and started performing what appears to be some sort of enthusiastic breakdancing maneuver. In record speed, a chanting crowd formed around Henn, led by Josh and Reed Rivers—which only spurred Henn on even more to turn up the heat on his crazy gyrations.

As everyone chants around me, I scan the faces nearest to me in the circle—Kat, Josh, Jonas, Sarah, and Reed—and their expressions of pure glee are a sight to see. This moment, this night, this life I've found with Henny . . . All of it is better than any dream I could have posted to my board only a few months ago.

As the song comes to an end, Henn bolts up from the floor and takes a dramatic, sweeping bow, at which point everyone in the crowd cheers and applauds him wildly. As the band kicks off a new song, the circle disintegrates. As people begin dancing with partners or in small groups again, Henn takes my hand and twirls me around, his face a portrait of pure joy.

"You were on fire!" I shout above the music.

"Because I'm so happy to be here with my Beautiful Bananaaaa!" he bellows in reply.

When the song ends, I motion toward the bathrooms on the far side of the ballroom, letting Henn know that's where I'm headed. In reply, he motions toward the bar area, letting me know he'll grab us another round while I'm gone.

Off we go in opposite directions.

Outside the bathroom, there's a long line, so I take my place at the back of it. In front of me, there's a gorgeous brunette around my age. She's got long, dark hair, sparkling brown eyes, high cheekbones and full lips, and the most slamming body I've ever seen in real life. If her curves in that clingy dress make *my* eyes pop out of my head, then what kind of reaction does she evoke from heterosexual men?

Is she a supermodel? An actress? One of Sarah's classmates at law school? Is she here as someone's date? If so, whose? Reed was seated at my table for dinner, so I know he's here stag tonight. But he's the only age-appropriate single dude at this wedding with the swagger and power to pull a woman like this. Oh, god. Is she here as the date of Jonas and Josh's uber-wealthy Uncle William? No, no, I think I saw him seated with someone around his age at dinner. Well, shit. I'm dying to know this gorgeous woman's back story.

"Hello," I say brightly to her.

"Hello."

She's giving off a warm and approachable vibe, so I forge ahead.

"Having fun tonight?"

"So much fun. You?"

"I'm having a blast. How do you know Jonas and/or Sarah?"

"I've known Jonas for years. I'm his brother's personal assistant."

"T-Rod!" I blurt excitedly. I'm using the nickname I've heard Josh use several times while telling a story that involves his personal assistant. Holy shit. Whenever Josh has mentioned his assistant, I've always pictured a frumpy, middle-aged woman, not a knockout who could literally walk a Victoria's Secret runway.

"That's me," she says, laughing. She extends her hand. "Theresa Rodriguez."

I shake her hand. "Hannah Milliken. My boyfriend is—"

"Henn."

"Yes!"

"I've heard all about Henn's fabulous girlfriend, Hannah Banana Montana Milliken, from Josh. Apparently, Kat takes full credit for setting you and Henn up."

"As she should. Kat guaranteed we'd be amazing together, and she was right. We went out to dinner with Josh and Kat in Vegas and had crazy sparks from minute one."

Theresa places a palm on her heaving chest, just above her eye-popping breasts. "What a darling meet cute. These days, most people meet online, so they don't get to experience an old-fashioned first date like that."

"Sounds like you're a romantic."

"A diehard one." Theresa sighs as she takes a step forward in the bath-room line. "Well, I used to be, anyway, before finding out my live-in boyfriend of two years was a serial cheater."

"Oh no. I'm sorry that happened to you."

"It's okay. Seeing happy couples like Jonas and Sarah and you and Henn gives me hope true love and romance might actually still be alive and well."

I can't help noticing Theresa didn't mention Josh and Kat as an example of true love. Was that an oversight? Am I reading into that omission? Instantly, my thoughts run wild on me. Has this gorgeous woman had a fling with her handsome, playboy boss at some point . . . and now she's jealous as fuck of Kat?

T-Rod takes another step forward in the bathroom line, so I follow suit.

No, I can't imagine T-Rod has a romantic history with Josh. Kat is no shrinking violet, and she's got a jealous streak a mile wide. Surely, if Kat had smelled even the slightest whiff of romance, or even a simple attrac-tion, between Josh and his longtime assistant, she would have engineered an inglorious and immediate exit for this poor woman. At the very least, Kat would have given me an earful about Josh's gorgeous assistant during our recent lunch. And yet, I've sensed only genuine positivity from Kat whenever T-Rod's name has come up, whether from Josh or Kat herself.

As we take another step forward in the bathroom line, I say, "Did Jonas' speech to Sarah at dinner give your inner romantic a bit of hope?"

"Oh my gosh, yes. That was one of the most romantic things I've ever witnessed in my life."

"Wasn't it? The way Jonas looked at Sarah when he said that thing about their love being the envy of the gods!"

"Gah!" T-Rod sighs deeply. "That's what I want someday—for someone to look at me like *that*."

Henn's face as he gazed at me in front of the fake Eiffel Tower pops into my head. "Henn looks at me like that," I confess with a deep blush. "He's the first guy who's ever done it, and I must admit it feels incredible."

"I can only imagine. Hopefully, you look at Henn like that in return?"

"I sure do. Henn's an incredible person and the best boyfriend, ever. So sweet and funny and loyal."

Theresa nods. "I overheard him joking around with Jonas before the ceremony. Jonas said he was going to name his firstborn after Henn to thank him for finding Sarah for him, and Henn's replies to Jonas were so funny and cute. If you're looking for a diehard romantic, then look no further than Peter Hennessey, right?"

What the fuckity is she talking about? Henn "found" Sarah for Jonas? Huh? What? When was Sarah lost? Whatever Theresa's talking about, her body language makes clear she thinks I already know about it—which means Josh and Kat must also know about it, along with Jonas and Sarah and Henn, or else T-Rod wouldn't say boo about it to me.

I feel sick, all of a sudden. Out of the loop and doubtful of Henn—all the same things I felt on karaoke night when everyone but me knew about the million-dollar finder's fee. Also, worst of all, that everyone at the table was assuming Henn had already told me—his *girlfriend*—all about it.

I force a smile. "Henn is a great friend, and, yes, a diehard romantic, so it wasn't surprising to learn he did whatever he could to help Jonas find love."

"And now look at Jonas and Sarah! Thanks to Henn, they're husband and wife. Talk about a romantic love story."

"I'm so happy for them." *Fucking hell.* I hate pretending I know what we're talking about when I don't, but I'd be mortified to admit Theresa knows more than I do about what my own beloved boyfriend did for Jonas and Sarah. Henn told me he went to Vegas to help Sarah take down her nefarious former employer—but by that time, Sarah was already Jonas' girlfriend, so whatever Henn did to help Jonas find Sarah in the first place, he had to have done it long before Vegas. Color me confused.

A stall opens up and Theresa waltzes into it, leaving me alone with my thoughts. *What the hell did Henn do and when did he do it and why does everyone know about it but me?*

Another stall opens up before Theresa emerges from hers, and I head inside as my head continues teeming with questions.

When I leave the bathroom a few minutes later, Theresa is standing outside the entrance. "The emcee called all the single ladies to the dance floor," she says. "I wasn't sure if you could hear the announcement in there." She's referring to the age-old ritual whereby single women crowd around the bride and elbow each other to catch her bouquet, all in the name of being anointed next in line to get hitched. But since I'm not particularly interested in getting married, not even to Henn, and certainly not any time soon, I reply, "Thank you for looking out for me, but I think I'll sit this one out. My relationship with Henn is still pretty new. You should do it, though, since you're single and looking for love."

"I'm not even dating anyone, though."

"All the more reason to do it, assuming you want to get married one day."

"Oh, I do. I'd love to get married to the love of my life and immediately start having a whole bunch of babies with him." She laughs. "My biological clock is stomping its foot."

I laugh along with her. "You should do it, then. Maybe catching the bouquet will light a fire under the universe's ass to send you the perfect man—someone who looks at you like Jonas looks at Sarah and wants a whole gaggle of babies as soon as possible."

"I suppose it's worth a try," Theresa concedes, as the emcee bellows, "Last call for all the single ladies!" Theresa beckons to me. "Come with me, Hannah. You can cheer me on."

We bound toward the dance floor together, passing Josh and Kat talking to Kat's parents as we go. When I see Kat, I wonder for a split-second if I should make a detour to drag her along with us to the bouquet toss. But quickly, I realize that'd be a cruel thing to do. From everything Kat has told me, she and Josh have now reached a state of joy and peace about their future together, both as a couple and as parents to their growing bun in the oven, including their mutual agreement that their future together won't include marriage. "Josh and I don't need a ceremony or piece of paper to make our love real or complete," Kat told me the other day. "All we need is each other and our private promises, which we've made." It was a lovely speech when Kat made it, and I knew she was trying her damnedest to believe every word of it. But I knew when she said it, she's still dreaming of the fairytale. That was clear to me, even before today's wedding, but that truth hit me even harder during the ceremony earlier, when Kat sobbed her eyes out during Jonas and Sarah's heart-felt exchange of wedding vows.

"Is this everyone?" the emcee booms as Theresa and I arrive at the assembled crowd of tittering single women on the dance floor. As Theresa joins the small group in the middle, I find a nearby spot with the onlookers.

"No, it's not everyone," Sarah says, looking pointedly at me. She beckons to me before looking toward the back of the ballroom where Kat is still talking with Josh and her parents.

I assume Kat's told Sarah everything she's told me about Josh not wanting to get married, but perhaps not. Or maybe Sarah knows Kat is full of shit, the same way I do, and she's thinking this little ritual might help her bestie get what she truly wants. Either way, I think it'd turn out badly for Kat if we drag her out here. And so, I quickly take a step forward onto the dance floor and call out, "I think I'm the last one!"

When Sarah's eyes catch mine, I glance at Kat and then shake my head, and Sarah's face makes clear she instantly gets what I'm trying to say. "Yep, this is everyone," she calls to the emcee. "Let's do this!"

A wedding coordinator whispers something to Sarah and then to the band. There's a drumroll, and Sarah turns her back on the assembled crowd of ladies. The emcee counts down, until right on cue, Sarah heaves her pink bouquet overhead and behind her . . .

Suddenly, I feel like the only single lady out here—a singular single lady. Has everyone else skittered away like cockroaches when the lights come on? It sure feels like it.

I have no choice. I put out my arms to keep the oncoming bouquet from falling onto the floor . . . and *plop.* The blooms fall into my outstretched hands with zero effort asserted by me. For fuck's sake, I didn't even pivot or take a single step! It's as if Sarah aimed this sucker directly at me with sniper-like precision.

When I look up, stunned, with the flowers in my hands, Sarah is jumping up and down and guffawing like crazy. She's laughing so hard, in fact, tears are streaming down her face. I look around, and everyone is having a similar reaction. *This was a set-up?*

"Who's the lucky lady?" the emcee asks.

"Hannah!" Sarah calls out, when it's obvious I'm too shocked to speak.

"Let's hear it for *Hannah*!" the bandleader shouts into her microphone, and everyone on the dance floor cheers. But nobody cheers louder than the bride, who's still laughing herself silly as she crosses the dance floor to hug me.

"Imagine that," Sarah coos. "Looks like you're next, Banana."

"You got me," I say. I'm not upset at Sarah's prank. Only amused. I've certainly never told Sarah about my general lack of enthusiasm about marriage in general, so how could she have known her bouquet would be barking up the wrong tree?

Playing along, I raise the bouquet into the air with a triumphant hoot, and everyone around me claps and cheers. I pose for a smiling shot with Sarah and then hug her again. And when I disengage from Sarah's embrace and turn around to look for Henn, I discover he's directly behind me . . . on bended knee.

"Oh, fuck," I blurt, looking down at him. I love this crazy, silly, sweet man with all my heart. Just this fast, he's become my best friend, in addition to being the best boyfriend a girl could ask for. But I could never say yes to *marrying* him this fast, if at all, especially not when our relationship has been mostly long distance. But do I want to explain all that to Henn *now* in front of all his friends? Hell no.

"Hannah Banana," Henn begins reverently, his dark eyes sparkling up at me. "Please, make me the happiest—"

"*Stop*," I whisper-shout. "Don't, Henny."

"Man in the world and—"

"*Peter, no.* You're drunk. Get up."

Henn abruptly closes his mouth mid-sentence. Blushes. Looks around. And then returns his gaze to mine and forces a smile. "Make me the happiest man in the world and move to LA—now, rather than waiting for Maddy to move in the spring."

I sigh from the depths of my soul. "*Oooh.*" I chuckle out of nervousness. "You got me."

Henn rises and makes a big show of laughing. "I got her," he says to anyone within earshot. "I got her good."

As the crowd dissipates, Henn returns to me. "I really do want you to move to LA now, rather than waiting. That part isn't a prank."

I touch his cheek. "I'm tipsy and you're drunk as shit. Let's talk about this when we're both sober, okay? Also, when we don't have an audience."

"I'm not too drunk to know what I want," Henn says defiantly.

"Honey—"

"No. Hear me out on this. It makes total sense for you to move now, long before spring quarter starts. That way, you can find the perfect place for you and Maddy and make it nice and homey before Maddy's eventual arrival. You said she's anxious about moving to a whole new school and city, right? Well, then, get her home environment all cozy and settled for her, from day one, to alleviate one potential source of stress."

I snort. "Oh, you're good."

Henn doesn't laugh with me. In fact, his face is surprisingly earnest. His dark eyes burning, he ceremoniously takes my hand and places it on his chest. "Do you feel that? That's my heart beating, only for you. It beats differently now that I love you. It beats with a whole new purpose. Hannah, I can't stand the thought of being apart from you a day longer than necessary."

"Oh, honey." My stomach is fluttering with butterflies. "I'll talk to Maddy about the idea tomorrow, and if she seems cool with me moving now—which I'm sure she will because she keeps telling me to stop coddling her—then I'll start looking for a new job in LA next week. Once I've landed a job, then I'll have a better idea of my monthly budget for rent. I can't really put the cart before the horse, you know what I mean?"

A beaming smile unfurls across Henn's handsome face. "You can when Reed is willing to rent you and Maddy one of his best two-bedroom units for the price of a studio!"

"*What?*"

"Have I mentioned Reed owns a luxury apartment building that's only two blocks from UCLA? Well, he does. And when I talked to him over there by the bar a few minutes ago, he said he'd be willing to give you and Maddy a smoking hot deal on rent as a favor to me."

Henn looks so excited about his revelation, I feel bad reacting with anything but enthusiasm and gratitude. But I can't let Reed do this for me. It's way too much for me to accept from him. "Honey, I can't let Reed do that. He'd probably be losing thousands on that unit every month."

"Pfft. Reed doesn't care," Henn insists. "He owns the apartment building, free and clear. No partners. No loans. That means he can do whatever he wants. If it makes you feel better, he frequently puts up his new bands and artists in that very building, free of charge, in between tours or when they're recording an album."

"Reed only does that because his artists eventually make him money."

"He said he genuinely wants to rent the apartment to you and Maddy. He said he *insists.*"

My heart is beating wildly. I must admit, the thought that Maddy and I could live in such a stellar location—and for so little—is an awfully tempting proposition. "I'm not saying yes, okay, but if I did, how long do you think Reed would let us live there at a discounted rate? Do you think two years would be too long?"

"Nope. Reed said you and Maddy could live there as long as you want. The only glitch is that the two-bedroom he has in mind for you won't be available for about six weeks."

"That'd be great timing, actually. It'd give me enough time to find a job in LA before moving."

"Reed also said he knows several people at movie studios. He said he'll make some calls and find out if anyone is hiring PR people."

"He did not say that!"

"He did."

I palm my forehead. "He truly wouldn't mind doing such big favors for me?"

"They're not big to him. But even if they were, I've done some big favors for Reed over the years, so he's happy to return them. That's how our friendship works. We're always doing stuff for each other."

I feel on the cusp of hyperventilating with excitement. "Would it be okay for me to thank Reed for his generosity—and also confirm he truly doesn't mind?"

"Come on." Henn takes my hand and leads me toward Reed, who's chatting in a far corner with none other than T-Rod.

When we get a few feet away from the pair, there's an intensity in Reed's body language that stops me short. I yank on Henn's hand to stop his progress and shout above the music, "Maybe we shouldn't interrupt Reed now. He looks like he's hitting on Theresa—*hard*!"

Henn laughs. "What else is new? He hits on T-Rod every time he sees her. She never takes the bait, though."

"She's newly single," I shout back over the music. "Maybe she'll be interested this time."

"Yeah, Reed already knows she's single. Trust me, he keeps tabs on her."

Well, that answers the question I had earlier about Josh and his long-time personal assistant possibly being more than friends. I don't know Josh all that well, but I've heard enough about the longtime, brotherly bond between Henn, Josh, and Reed to know Reed would *never* hit on a woman Josh had been romantically involved with. The realization is a relief to me, frankly, given my allegiance to Kat. I'd hate for her to be walking into any kind of messy situation that might cause her insecurity or jealousy in her relationship with Josh—or maybe even heartbreak—down the line.

"Come on, Hannah," Henn insists. "Reed's just flirting, as usual. I promise he won't mind us interrupting."

I hesitate for several reasons. For one thing, I don't care what Henn says, Reed is clearly doing more than flirting with Theresa. He's trying to charm that clingy dress right off her smoking hot body, and I certainly don't want to be the one to interrupt his flow. Also, Henn is drunk as fuck right now, so I don't trust his judgment completely.

"Let's give them a minute," I say, still pulling on Henn's hand.

We continue watching the pair, and as we do, I remember that surprising thing T-Rod told me before the bouquet toss—specifically, that

Henn found Sarah for Jonas. Frankly, before I chat with Reed about an apartment and job in LA, shouldn't I pull Henn aside and ask him to explain all that to me? Not only T-Rod's comment itself, but more importantly, why, once again, I'm feeling like everyone knows more about my boyfriend than I do.

"Hannah!" T-Rod says. Her gaze has found me. "Congrats on catching the bouquet! Were you shocked?"

Well, that's that. There's no choice but to go over there now.

As Henn and I approach, I reply, "I think Sarah had an agenda."

"I think you're right." Theresa motions to Reed. "Do you know Reed?"

"Yes, we met earlier. Actually, I came over here specifically to thank you, Reed. And to make sure you're genuinely okay helping me out so much." To my relief, Reed knows exactly what I'm talking about, which means Henn didn't flat-out lie to me about Reed's offers in order to lure me to LA. Indeed, Reed graciously confirms he's happy to help, not only regarding the apartment but with my job search, too.

"It's settled then!" Henn declares triumphantly, pumping a fist toward the ceiling. "Hannah Banana is movin' to LA!"

I laugh. "Not so fast, Henny. I haven't made a firm decision yet. I still want to speak to my sister about the idea."

Henn is far too drunk and happy to listen to reason. He's so happy, in fact, when the band starts playing a new song, he grabs my hand jubilantly and pulls me toward the dance floor, scooping up shots off a roaming server's tray for both of us along the way. When we arrive at our destination, he twirls me around and sings along to the song at top volume, making it abundantly clear he's celebrating what he believes is my impending move to LA.

25
HANNAH

"My goodness, someone's inebriated," I murmur as I steer Henn toward the front door of my apartment. I'm drunk, too. But Santa Maria! Henn brought new meaning to the phrase "he really tied one on" at the wedding tonight. Clearly, he needed to let off some steam from the high-stress environment and long hours of his mysterious job in DC—the one he's sadly flying back to continue in mere hours. I discern the shape of my keys at the bottom of my purse and murmur, "Found 'em."

After unlocking my front door, I lead my lilting boyfriend inside, and we laughingly kick our way through the morass of fallen "I love you!" balloons on my living room floor, their helium magic long gone by now.

"We're in a giant snow globe!" Henn booms, as he gleefully kicks another balloon.

I'm not surprised he's such a happy drunk. In my experience, alcohol is like truth serum—it only brings to the surface whatever lies beneath. I barely remember living with my father, since my parents divorced when I was seven, but I distinctly remember him becoming a total prick whenever he drank. Angus was like that, too, although I thankfully didn't know him long enough to witness the phenomenon more than once. How lovely to find out the only thing buried deep inside Peter Hennessey is even more sweetness and silliness.

Although . . .

T-Rod's comment about Henn finding Sarah for Jonas suddenly pops into my buzzed brain, along with that same icky feeling I had on karaoke night. I meant to ask Henn about the subject earlier tonight, but I forgot about it when we started throwing back another round of shots.

"Should I make us a snack?" Henn says, veering toward the kitchen.

"No, love, we're going to bed. That's where drunk people who have to leave for the airport at noon should go."

"I'm not drunk," Henn insists, but he lets me guide him toward the bedroom. "I'm *purr*-fectly buzzed. Like a tipsy cat with a buzzing bee in his bonnet." He winks. "You're the only bee in my bonnet, Hannah Banana."

I believe he's referencing a lyric from "Birdhouse in Your Soul"—the song Henn and I discussed during one of our earliest dates. But even if he's not thinking consciously of that particular song, it's still an adorable thing for him to say to me.

"You're the only bee in my bonnet, too," I reply. "Now, come on, sweetie. This way."

"This is why Hannah Banana Montana Milliken is my Bert and I'm her Ernie. Because she looks out for me."

"Yes, she does." I guide him to my bed and onto his back. "I'm Hannah, by the way. There's no need to talk about me in third person."

He looks around, thoroughly confused. "Where's Josh? Is he still here?"

"He was never here."

"Yes, he was."

"No. He helped you into the Uber and that was that. I've been the only one with you, ever since."

"That's a false statement, sir. You're forgetting about Earl."

I chuckle. "You mean our Uber driver?"

"Yes, Earl. A very nice bloke, was he."

For some reason, Henn's using a British accent again. The same way he did during the Uber ride. "Yes, he was. But Earl wasn't British."

Henn scoffs. "Then why did he talk to me in a British accent the entire ride home?"

"That was you, love. *You* talked in a British accent. The whole damned ride."

Henn snorts. "Why'd I do that, if Earl wasn't British?"

"God only knows. So, listen, honey. I have a question for you. When I was taking to T-Rod tonight—"

"I have question for you, too, Banana. Do you know how to say your name in Spanish?" He grins proudly. "It's *Plátano*. That means banana, according to Sarah. She also joked, since you're a *female* banana, I should call you *Plátana*. Isn't that cute? By the way, did you know Reed told me *not* to propose to Hannah Banana la *Plátana* Milliken tonight? Yup. Man, I should have listened to him, huh?"

My eyebrows are jutting up against my hairline by now. "So . . . when you kneeled down after I caught the—"

"Yep. That was the plan. But when Hannah looked like she wanted to barf, I quickly decided to pivot." He grins. "*Pivot!*" As I well know, it's a reference to one of our favorite episodes of *Friends*—the one where Ross, Rachel, and Chandler try to maneuver a big couch through a tight stairwell. Henn and I have watched the episode together and laughed through the whole thing. But right now, I don't have time for any kind of detour. Even a pleasant one. On the contrary, while the tequila-infused truth serum in Henn's veins is still working its magic, I need to lure Henn into spilling every detail about his aborted proposal tonight.

"Back to what you said before," I coax. "Tell me more, honey."

Henn adopts a British accent again. "Compared to a Qwerty keyboard, a Dvork keyboard enables the typist to type twenty times faster." Jesus Christ. It's the same thing he did during our Uber ride, when he regaled the driver and me with non-stop computer-related trivia.

"No, no, tell me more about your plan to propose to Hannah tonight. Tell me everything about *that*."

"Oh, *that*. Why are you talking about yourself in third person?" Another snort. "Well, first off, plan is too strong a word. It was more of a spur-of-the-moment *idea*. A notion, you might say, that popped into my bean when the lady with the microphone called all the single ladies to the dance floor. I told Jonas and Reed, 'If Sarah can somehow get her bouquet into Hannah's hands, then I'll do it. If not, then it's not meant to be, and I'll wait for fate to take the wheel another time."

My heart is thundering. "And then what happened?"

Henn shrugs. "Jonas ran off to talk to Sarah, who I think asked T-Rod to get you because you were in the bathroom, and Reed stayed behind to try to talk me out of it." He scoffs. "I wish I'd listened."

I touch his face. "You didn't do anything wrong, honey. It was a swoony, sweet, adorable gesture. The thing is I'm not entirely convinced marriage is the right thing for me with anyone. It has nothing to do with you, personally."

Henn looks shellshocked. "You never want to get married?"

"I wouldn't say never. I'm not *against* marriage. I think marriage is a lovely, romantic ideal." I pause, remembering myself saying yes to Angus during the darkest period of my life. Talk about a sign I needed to get my ass back into therapy. I exhale and say, "Practically speaking, though, I think a person can get all the upsides of marriage with a life partner without risking a messy divorce later on if things don't work out. Divorce rates are high, you know? And breakups are hard enough without involving lawyers and legal paperwork."

"But the risk of it getting messy later on is the whole point. Don't you see? Both people are saying, 'I believe we'll defy the odds, baby! I'm in it to win it with you, no matter how hard it might get—no matter the risks or the odds!'"

Henn looks like I've punched him in the face, so I snuggle close to him on the bed and hug him. "Thank you for being ready to say all those things to me." I run my hand through his wavy hair. "I can promise you this: if I ever do decide to get married, it'll be to you and nobody else."

I thought my pronouncement would thrill Henn, but he looks only confused. "What about the photo, though?" he asks. "I thought it meant you're dreaming of a husband and a baby."

I furrow my brow. "What photo?"

"On your dream board."

My lips part in surprise. I have no recollection of showing Henn my dream board, but I guess I must have. Was I drunk, so I forgot the next day? Or is it that I'm too drunk now to remember?

"The photo on my dream board means I want to find my life partner," I say. "My soulmate. And, yes, I'd love to have a baby with him, too." I stroke Henn's hair again. "I'm just not positive I need marriage as part of that dream."

Henn takes my hand and kisses it. "Because of your parents' divorce?"

"Maybe. Probably."

"Any other reason, you think?"

Oh, I dunno. Maybe that I said yes to marrying a fucking scammer, and now I'm deathly afraid my picker is wildly defective? "Nothing specific that I can think of, no. Like I said, never say never. I'm just not willing to jump into a legally binding forever too quickly. What's the rush?"

Henn processes that. "Fair enough."

"I'm glad you understand. So, about T-Rod."

"Remember when we saw Reed talking to her? It turns out, he was asking her out."

I gasp. "On a date? What'd she say?"

"She said, 'Thanks, but I'm not dating right now because I'm nursing a broken heart.'" Henn snickers. "I don't think anyone's ever turned Reed down before. I think he's now—how shall I put this?—even more *intrigued.*" He chuckles. "Oh, and did I tell you Reed told me not to propose tonight?"

"You mentioned that. What, specifically, did Reed say about that?"

"He goes, 'It's way too soon, Peter!' And I was like, 'But she might say yes!' And he goes, 'And what if she does? Do you really want your future wife to get engaged to you for the one and only time without a fucking ring on her finger? Think, Peter, think!'"

"Well, he had a valid point there," I mumble under my breath.

"Reed always calls me Peter when he thinks I'm a dumbfuck."

"You're not a dumbfuck." I stroke his hair again. "You're a sweet, kind, romantic man who's had a lot to drink."

"Nah, I'm a dumbfuck. I should have listened to Reed, instead of Jonas. I thought because Jonas had just gotten married to his dream girl *he*'d be the expert in the situation. I mean, for fuck's sake, Reed's never even been in love. Plus, he's said a million times he'll never get married, the same as Josh." Henn chuckles. "Although in Josh's case, I guess he was just waiting for the right woman, without realizing it. Never say never, right?"

I gasp. "Josh wants to marry Kat?"

"Oops."

I sit up and stare down at Henn's wide eyes. "Tell me everything right fucking now."

Henn grins. "You're pretty."

"Tell me about Josh wanting to propose to Kat."

He sighs. "Kat's mom told me that's what he wants to do. Apparently, she gets loose lips when she's drunk, same as me. *Ha.*" He puts his hand to the side of his mouth and whispers, "Josh's plan to propose to Kat is a big secret. I promised Kat's mom I wouldn't tell anyone, so don't tell Kat or anyone else what I told you."

"I won't say a word. Did Kat's mom say *when* Josh will pop the question to Kat?"

"He doesn't know yet. He asked for Kat's parents' blessing tonight. I think that's as far as he's gotten in his planning."

"Oh my god. Kat's going to be so happy."

"You can't tell her."

"I know. I won't."

"I'm not even gonna tell Josh I know. If he follows through with it, then I'll act totally surprised. Like *this.*" Henn opens his mouth and widens his eyes, apparently demonstrating his "shocked" face.

"*If* Josh follows through with it?"

Henn shrugs. "Maybe Josh was drunk when he asked the Morgans for their blessing. Maybe tomorrow he'll wake up and freak out and change his mind."

I narrow my eyes into laser beams. "I swear to God, if Josh Faraday changes his mind about marrying the only female member of the Morgan Mafia *after* impregnating her, and *after* asking her parents for their blessing, then he'd better flee the country, because Kat's brothers won't simply let that shit go."

Henn snort-laughs. "The Morgan Mafia?"

"That's what Kat and her brothers call themselves. For all that family's razzing and teasing, they've got each other's backs like you wouldn't believe."

"That's the kind of family I want to have with you, Banana." He chuckles. "We could be The Hennessey Hoodlums."

My heart skips a beat. "That's sounds lovely. Like a beautiful dream. But let's not get ahead of ourselves and forget to build a healthy, strong relationship in the present, okay?"

"Speaking of which, have you thought any more about taking Reed up on that two-bedroom?"

I bite back a smile. I texted Maddy earlier tonight and she lost her ever-loving mind about Reed's offer. First off, because she loves me and adores Henn and knows I'll be happiest living in the same city with him. But also because my sister's genuinely ecstatic about Reed's offer for herself, too. What student transfer wouldn't want to live two blocks from her new campus in a luxury two-bedroom apartment with her big sister at a steeply discounted rate?

"Yes, I've heard from Maddy, and the move is a go, just as soon as the apartment is available and I've landed a job—"

"Woohoo!"

"*Assuming* Reed doesn't change his mind about giving me an apartment for such a cheap price."

"Reed won't change his mind. He's been wanting to do a big favor for me for a very long time."

The comment reminds me of something I wondered earlier tonight but forgot to ask about when our partying kicked into high gear. "Why, exactly, does Reed want to do a big favor for you? What kinds of favors have you done for him in the past?"

Henn pauses. "Oh. Uh. Just some computer stuff. Setting up his record label's system and such. When Reed was first launching his new company, he didn't have two dimes to rub together that he wasn't pouring into his first and only band, so I did a bunch of stuff for him for free."

I stare at Henn for a long moment, trying to read his facial expression. It's hard to do when he's drunk. He looks kind of loopy. Even so, I can't help feeling like he's holding something back. Consciously not saying something. "That was generous of you."

"That's what friends do. They do favors for each other. Which is why you shouldn't feel bad about Reed helping you out, as a favor to me."

"Speaking of favors for friends, T-Rod told me tonight you did one for Jonas. Specifically, you 'found' Sarah for him. What does that mean?"

Henn twists his mouth. "Sorry, that's not really my secret to tell."

"It's not a secret if T-Rod knows about it."

"But I didn't tell T-Rod. Josh must have told her."

"That only proves my point even more. If Josh, T-Rod, Jonas, and Sarah know about this thing you did, then how is it too big a secret to tell me?"

Henn presses his lips together but says nothing.

"This feels like karaoke night all over again, Henn. Like I'm the last person to know something about you, and yet everyone assumes you've already told me. I understand you not telling me about work-related stuff. But something like this, a favor you did for a friend of ours, and everyone in our friend group already knows about it, I can't help feeling like you don't consider me as close a confidante as the others. And that's a truly horrible feeling." A surge of unexpected emotion rises inside me. "You wanted to propose to me tonight, but you're not willing to tell me something everyone already thinks I know."

Henn sits up and looks down at me on the bed, his face awash with concern. "You're my confidante, Hannah. I just now blabbed to you about what Mrs. Morgan told me in confidence, didn't I, even though I promised her I wouldn't tell anyone?"

I sniffle. "Yes, and that made me feel really close to you. Like you trust me. Like I'm special. That's my whole point."

Henn sighs. "I get it. I'm sorry. I think maybe the difference is that the thing with Jonas happened before I'd even met you, and Mrs. Morgan blabbed to me tonight. Do you see what I mean? So, yeah, it popped into my head to tell you what Mrs. Morgan said, whereas telling you about something that happened before we ever met never even crossed my mind."

Angus's face pops into my head and I quickly shove him away. "That makes sense," I concede. "I guess the thing that hurts my feelings the most is when it feels like everyone else in our friend group knows something and assumes I already know it, too. That's happening in present day for me, even if the thing they know about happened before we met."

"Okay, that's fair. I guess if T-Rod knows about this, then it's only fair you should, too."

"It's not about fairness. It's about intimacy. I don't like feeling like you're keeping me in the dark about stuff and then I have to pretend we're closer than we are to save face."

"We are close, love. I love you with all my heart and soul. You don't believe that?"

"I do. And I love you, too. But I think we've both got a ways to go to build full trust. The kind where you know you can say anything, no matter what, without holding back."

Well, that arrow hit the bull's-eye. It's written all over Henn's face. With a sigh, he lies back down. This time, on his side. With a sigh, I assume the same position, so we're now lying nose to nose on the moonlit bed.

"Okay, here's the story," he whispers. "This is highly confidential. For your ears only."

My skin electrifies. "I'll never tell a soul."

Henn proceeds to tell me the story, which in summary is that, when Jonas signed up for a high-end dating service, he unexpectedly received an anonymous email from someone at the service in response to his detailed application. Henn doesn't know what the anonymous email said, exactly, but whatever it was, Jonas was hooked like a fish on a line when he read it. Henn says, "Somehow, Jonas was positive it was written by a woman— a smart, sexy, sassy one."

"Enter Sarah."

"Yep. Josh called me and told me his brother was obsessed with finding the sender of an anonymous email. And, of course, I'll always do anything for Josh. First off, I traced the sender's IP address, and found out it was linked to the University of Washington's system. Which meant the sender was a student or employee there. Based on some verbiage in the email, Jonas deduced the sender was probably a law student, and he also figured out the sender's first name was Sarah. So, bada-bing-bada-boom, I did a little internet research, and next thing you know, I'd tracked down a law student at U Dub named Sarah Cruz."

I clutch my heart, swooning. "And now, thanks to you, Sarah Cruz is Sarah Faraday!"

"Well, I only led the horse to water," Henn says. "Once she got there, Jonas had to convince her to drink."

I laugh with glee. "Oh, Henny. That's such a romantic story. Thank you for telling me." I lean in to kiss him, but Henn pulls back. I crinkle my brow. "What?"

"I feel like I should tell you something else. The whole truth about the favor I did for Reed. Now that I've told you what I did for Jonas, I should tell you that story, too." Henn swallows hard. "This most definitely isn't my secret to tell, so you can't tell anyone, ever."

"I won't."

"Not even if we break up and you hate my guts."

"I could never hate you, Henn. And I promise, no matter what, I'll never tell."

Henn props his cheek on his palm and smiles. "Reed didn't ask me to do this favor. Didn't even know I did it, until much later. But I knew he'd put everything on the line for his first band. I knew it was make or break for him. Do or die. If his first band's debut single flamed out and sank like a stone, Reed would lose everything, and I couldn't let that happen. So, I gamed some algorithms during release week on the song, made sure the music video racked up huge views during its first twenty-four hours." He snickers. "Radio stations took notice of this new band's debut music video racking up millions of views in lightning speed, so they started playing the song, which then meant listeners were downloading and streaming it in droves, which sent the song to the top of the charts that week, which then launched the band—and Reed's label—into the stratosphere." He snickers. "And the rest is history."

I gasp. "You're talking about Red Card Riot?" They're one of the hottest bands in the world these days, and I think they were River Records' first band.

"Bingo," Henn says. "To be clear, the whole idea wouldn't have worked if the song hadn't been fire. All I did was give it a big push out of the gate. But my push wouldn't have led to anything, if the song didn't have legs to take it from there."

"'Shaynee'?" By now, the whole world knows that's the massively popular song that introduced the band to the world.

"That's the one."

"What do you mean you gamed some algorithms?"

Henn says a bunch of stuff I don't understand. In a nutshell, I think he's telling me he somehow infiltrated YouTube's backend and made the system tabulate views that didn't actually occur.

"You're saying you *hacked* YouTube?" I ask, feeling utterly astonished.

"I am."

I stare at him with my mouth hanging open. I'm shocked, but perhaps I shouldn't be. After my first dinner with Henn, I googled "cybersecurity" and found out experts in Henn's field keep the bad guys out of online spaces by staying one step ahead of them. In other words, cybersecurity experts know how to *protect* online systems because they can predict how the bad guys will try to hack them. Is it really a surprise that Henn would occasionally veer off-course from his day job to perform an illicit hack to help his best friend in a do-or-die situation? That's what Henn did for Sarah in Vegas, too, although Henn did characterize that job as a "one-off." But maybe he wasn't being literal about that. Perhaps, Henn meant he does stuff like that only very rarely—when he believes wholeheartedly in the cause, and he's doing it as a favor for a very close friend. Frankly, if that's the case, it's something I could easily get behind.

I close my hanging mouth. "That's amazing, Henn. You're an incredible friend."

Henn looks nervous. "You're not freaked out about what I did?"

I shake my head. "You gave a harmless push to a song for one day, in order to help your best friend launch his record label and the band he'd gambled everything on." I flash him side-eye. "It was harmless, right? You didn't hurt anyone?"

"Not a soul. What I did was technically illegal, though. Online trespassing. I went somewhere I didn't have authority to go."

"Did you steal data or money?"

"Of course, not. I'd never do that. I was in and out and nobody was ever the wiser, to this day."

"And you've never done another favor like that for Reed? You haven't commandeered the entire music industry since then, have you?"

"Pfft. Absolutely not. If Reed wanted to hire me to game the system for him, I'd say no. But see, Reed would never ask me to do that. He's actually really pissed at me for helping him out that one time without his consent. He's grateful, too. But mostly pissed."

"Not so pissed that he won't help your girlfriend get an apartment and a job in LA."

"He'd do that, regardless. But, yeah, he feels indebted to me. He shouldn't. I'm sure 'Shaynee' would have been a huge hit, regardless."

"Maybe not. I guess he'll never know."

"Hence, the reason he's pissed at me. Understandably. I sometimes think I know best, and then, it turns out I'm actually an idiot. A well-meaning one, though."

I touch his cheek. "I think maybe we've discovered your imperfection."

"Does it scare you away?"

"Not even a little bit."

Henn sighs with relief. "That's great news." He closes his eyes and murmurs, "God, I have to pee."

"What?"

His eyes are still closed.

"You have to pee? Henny." I nudge his shoulder, and he opens his eyes. "You have to pee?"

"So much."

"Well, come on." I pull him up by his two lead arms and guide him into my bathroom and straight to the toilet. When I've got him positioned, he does nothing, so I unzip his pants, hand him his flaccid dick, and point to the spot where he should aim. He wobbles slightly in place for a moment, before sighing deeply and peeing for approximately ten years, like Tom Hanks in *A League of Their Own.*

"Wow," I murmur. "That's got to be a world record."

When Henn's bladder is finally empty, I help him out of his clothes and take off mine, and then guide him into the shower with me. After rinsing the night's sweat, grime, and spilled drinks off both of us, I dry us off and lead him, naked, back to my bed, where I tuck him in next to me under the covers.

"Wait!" Henn shouts, abruptly sitting up. "I rented a Sybian for you tonight as a surprise. No pressure, of course, but if you're down, then we have to go to the place to pick it up before closing time!"

I pull him back down. "It's way past closing time, love. Plus, we're way too drunk. Thank you for the thought, but it's not gonna happen tonight."

"If it were here now, would you try riding it?"

"Probably. Actually, yes. I'm pretty damned sure I would."

"Gah! I'll change my flight and stay another night!"

"No, no. I'd never forgive myself if one of the other programmers swooped in and got the reward while you were here, watching me ride a Sybian. Now, close your eyes and let's get some sleep before we head to the airport. I'll ride a Sybian to celebrate when you finally finish this job."

"No pressure."

"I know. I want to do it. But not tonight."

Henn waggles his eyebrows. "You know what we *could* do tonight? We could decide to sleep when we're dead and use the rest of our time together to pretend *I'm* a Sybian."

I pull a face. "Are you even capable of that, with all the booze in your system?" I reach under the covers and touch his penis, fully expecting it to be flaccid, but to my surprise, it's rock hard. "Oh. *Hello*."

"Let me be your Sybian, cowgirl."

"Yeehaw." With that, I slide on top of him, straddle his hips, and then lean down and kiss him passionately. As we kiss, he strokes me, until soon, I'm aroused and wet and ready for action. With a wicked smile, I slide myself down onto his shaft, prompting Henn to start making a weird buzzing noise.

"What the fuck are you doing?" I ask, laughing.

"I'm your Sybian. They're pretty noisy, from what I've seen in videos."

"You're such a dork."

"It takes one to know one."

"Yes, it does."

"I love you, Hannah," he whispers, all traces of playfulness gone from his tone.

"I love you, too." I lean down and kiss him again, and we begin to move together. As we make love, Henn showers me with compliments. He tells me I'm beautiful. Gorgeous. Sexy. Hot. Smart. Funny. Perfect. And right before I climax, he says something I would have thought would freak me out, but surprisingly, only turns me on: "And one day, my pretty Plátana, I'm gonna make you my wife."

26

HENN

*F*uck my life.

I'm no longer losing hope that I'll be able to solve the Rubik's cube that is this godawful, endless project. I'm now officially hopeless. Done. Fried. Exhausted beyond anything I've experienced before. I'm a human bag of smashed assholes.

I thought I'd be the genius to figure this shit out, after a whole lot of smart hackers before me couldn't do it. But it turns out I'd vastly overestimated my talents. I'm a mere mortal, as it turns out, and a deluded one, at that. I'm not Superman, after all. I'm Don Fucking Quixote trying to conquer a windmill.

At present, I'm shuffling my sorry ass down the hallway of my budget hotel in DC—the place I've called home for what feels like half my fucking life—after a particularly long and brutal day of trying to crack an uncrackable code. It's now clear all my hard work, all the time away from Hannah and the life we could be building together, has been for naught. Pointless. Futile. The worst mistake of my life.

I was so sure my Big Idea would do the trick today—that, finally, after weeks of methodical coding and tinkering—that fucking encryption would finally become my bitch. And yet, when the time came today, the big payoff I was expecting didn't happen. Which means I'm now officially stumped because that was my last idea. All that's left inside my brain now is useless mush, along with a whole lot of frustration and regret.

My head hung low, I reach the door of my hotel room and drag myself inside the drab room. After putting down my keycard and jacket with a heavy sigh, I text Hannah to see if she's still up and available for our nightly FaceTime call. We normally talk much earlier in the evening than this, so I'm not surprised when she doesn't reply to my text. She's probably already fast asleep. *Shit.* I wish I'd had my phone with me in that small work room, so I could have at least texted her a simple "Goodnight. I love you" a couple hours ago. But, unfortunately, I totally lost track of time when I thought I was on a major roll.

I head into the bathroom and take a hot shower, letting my thoughts wander as I stand under the streaming water. If I hadn't left for this stupid gig, but had instead stayed in Seattle with Hannah until Jonas and Sarah's wedding, would Hannah have looked terrified or elated when I kneeled before her that night? Would I be engaged today to the love of my life, if it weren't for this stupid boondoggle of a fucking job? I guess I'll never know.

I thought coming here to chase the money would be well worth it. I thought I'd use the reward money to buy a kickass dream house in LA, one that Hannah wouldn't be able to resist moving into with me. And now, all I've got to show for my lengthy time away is homesickness, lovesickness, and a deep-seated fear that my absence at the very beginning of my budding relationship with Hannah has inflicted irreversible damage onto it. Have I snuffed out our once-in-a-lifetime spark by being gone and inattentive for too long at a critical juncture? Hannah's given me nothing but support during all of this, but there's only so much intimacy a couple can feel over nightly FaceTime calls.

I get out of the shower and check my phone. Still no reply from Hannah. Which means, yeah, she's almost certainly fast asleep.

I get into a pair of pajama pants and flop into an armchair with a beer, my laptop, and a couple of phones. As I throw back the beer, I scroll through the messages and job requests I've missed throughout the day, but nothing appeals to me enough to reply. That is, until I come across a missive received through my dummy website—Your Nerd for Hire. A chain of department stores wants to hire me for a cybersecurity gig.

Apparently, they got hacked earlier this year and had all their data stolen —a logistical and PR nightmare—so now they want to make sure their new system is as unhackable as it can possibly be. They write, "We hired the best cyber-security team money can buy to create our new system. And now, we'd like to hire you for a full week, during which you'll attempt to hack our new system through any possible means."

Ha. This is a gig I would have been thrilled to take right out of college. For quite some time now, though, a gig like this has been far beneath me. At least, that's what I would have thought before today's embarrassing failure. Frankly, the way I'm feeling right now, this kind of thing might be all I'm good for—trying to hack a department store's new system. In fact, it's the perfect gig to find out if I'm as mediocre a hacker as I now think I am. Hell, I'll be quitting this project in DC tomorrow, anyway. Why not take this gig to distract me when I'm back in Seattle and hanging out in Hannah's apartment while she's at work?

I write back and tell the client I'll do the gig with one caveat: I'll only do it on a contingency-fee basis. If I can breach their system within one workday, then they'll agree to pay me a lump sum equal to whatever they've paid their supposedly "expert" cybersecurity team. But if I can't breach their system in one day, then I promise I'll keep working on it for free until I'm successful or, in the alternative, willing to certify the system as unhackable.

After pressing send on my reply, I finish my beer and then click into my file on Hannah's sweetheart swindler, Greg Smith aka Angus Well-born. I haven't had much time over the past several weeks to even think about the guy, let alone try to hunt him down. But now that I'm going to quit this project tomorrow, I might as well poke around and see if I can make some headway. There's got to be some recent instances, somewhere, of the dude using his real name. Like, maybe his mother has used it on some paperwork that's been filed in the public record? Or maybe someone has sued him for something? Demon Spawn gave up looking for him a while ago, so I guess that's where I'll jump into the hunt—by looking through every instance of "Greg Smith" in the public record, and then cross-checking the birthdate to see if it's the right one.

As I'm scrolling through a large batch of Greg Smiths in King County, my phone buzzes with an incoming text from Josh.

Josh: Yo, Peter. Do you have a couple minutes to chat with our Ocean's Eleven crew + Kat's brother, Ryan, tonight? Ryan could use some Henny magic along the lines of what you did for Jonas, all in the name of potential true love. No worries if you're too busy. I know you're swamped these days.

Me: You know I'm a sucker for true love. I'm in the middle of something, but I can talk in about 30 min.

Josh: I'll call you then. Thanks, brother.

Me: BTW, I'll for sure make it to the C&C party now. Put me down as a yes.

Josh: Awesome! What about the gig in DC?

Me: It's over. I'm leaving tomorrow.

Josh: Congrats!

I stare at the word on my screen, feeling sick to my stomach. What I wouldn't give to deserve Josh's congratulations right now. I've never quit a gig in my life, due to abject failure. It's a horrible feeling.

Me: Thanks. Talk to you in 30.

Sighing deeply, I return to my laptop and resume scrolling through endless entries about "Greg Smith." And with perfect timing, just as I've fruitlessly reached the last entry of the batch, my phone rings with an incoming call from Jonas. It's not a surprise, really. Josh mentioned he's with the whole crew.

"Hey, Jonas."

"Hey, Henn. I'm at Josh's house with Sarah and Kat's brother, Ryan. Kat felt sick and Josh went to comfort her in their bedroom."

"Aw, poor Kitty Kat. I thought her morning sickness had faded a bit."

"If so, it's not completely gone. She looked downright green when she bolted out of here. Hey, can I put you on speaker phone?"

"Of course."

The next thing I know, I'm greeted by Sarah, and then introduced to Kat's brother, Ryan Morgan. We talk about Kat's pregnancy sickness for a bit, at which point Ryan says his sister has always been a barfer. "One of her many nicknames is Barf-o-Matic," he says, making everyone on the call, including me, laugh.

I tell Jonas and Sarah how much fun Hannah and I had at their amazing wedding last month, since this is the first time I'm speaking to them since that night, and they both go on and on about how much fun they had. At my urging, they tell me about their honeymoon, which Josh and Kat joined for a short time before splitting off on their own trip to Argentina. And, finally, it's time to get down to the actual reason for their call.

Sarah takes the lead in explaining Ryan's situation, which, in a nutshell, is that Ryan met a scorching-hot brunette at a bar in Seattle tonight—a flight attendant named Samantha who blew Ryan away in every conceivable way.

"We both made it clear we were feeling a major connection," Ryan says. "I know it sounds crazy, but it felt like a once-in-a-lifetime kind of thing." He sighs deeply. "Unfortunately, before Samantha and I had exchanged numbers or even last names, my crazy ex blasted into the bar and made a huge scene, and Samantha understandably bolted like Cinderella at midnight. After quickly dealing with my ex, I ran outside to find Samantha, but she was gone."

"Did she leave a glass slipper that we might be able use to track her down?" I ask.

"That's exactly why we're calling," Sarah chimes in. "To see if we can construct some kind of glass slipper you might be able to use."

"I'm willing to try."

"Whatever you can do would be greatly appreciated," Jonas says. "Ryan reminds me of myself after receiving Sarah's first email."

"You mean he's totally and completely obsessed?"

Jonas laughs. "Exactly."

Ryan says, "I know there's no guarantee Samantha's supposed to be the great love of my life. *But what if she is?* I've never felt chemistry like that before. Not even close. If I never see her again and never find out what could have happened, I'll always wonder what if."

"I'm sold," I say. "Tell me everything you know about this woman, no matter how seemingly trivial or inconsequential."

"You should probably take notes," Sarah pipes in to say. "We've been brainstorming for the past half hour, so we've compiled a list for you."

"True to form," I say, chuckling. It's very on-brand for Sarah Cruz to approach the situation in this manner. The woman is a thorough researcher, a brilliant analyst, and an all-around smart cookie. I open a tab on my screen for note taking. "Okay, hit me."

Sarah says, "Samantha is a twenty-seven-year-old Argentinian-American. Brunette with brown eyes. A Virgo."

"Oh, good. Virgo helps narrow down her birth date."

Sarah says, "Samantha speaks English and Spanish. Works as a flight attendant for Delta Airlines, based out of LA."

"Was she in Seattle for work or pleasure?"

"For work," Sarah says. "She was in uniform at the bar. She said she flew in from LA today."

"All good info. Do we know if Samantha flew from LA to Seattle on her regular route?"

Sarah says something to someone on her end of the call. And then, "We don't know."

Ryan chimes in with, "Samantha and I didn't talk about work all that much. But I think her still being in uniform suggests she came straight from her flight to the bar, so she must have landed not too long before she got there."

"Good thinking. That'll help me narrow down which flight she was on, if need be. Around what time did she get to the bar?"

"Around eight-thirty," Ryan supplies.

"Got it. What else?"

There's some chatter on their end of the line, followed by Sarah saying, "That's it, unless you've got questions."

"No, I think I've got what I need. Great work, guys. No promises, but I'm guessing if I take a gander at Delta's employee files for a bilingual, Virgo flight attendant named Samantha who flew from LA to Seattle this afternoon, I'll be able to find her pretty easily."

"Holy shit," Ryan says. "Thank you. Wow." There's no mistaking his excitement.

"No promises, though. I don't know what kind of search functionality I'll find in the database. We're positive she said she works for Delta, right? It'd suck if I'm looking around in the wrong database."

"She didn't actually say it, but only because we didn't talk about work, like I said. But she had little triangles on her scarf, and when Sarah and I looked online, the logo definitely belonged to Delta."

Delta. My eyes saucer as a lightning bolt hits my brain. *How did I not think of this before?*

"Of course, I insist on paying you for your time," Ryan says.

Delta. If I attack each layer of encryption by looking at their data transmissions in the form of *differences* between sequential data, rather than complete files . . . Oh my fuck. This could work.

"Uh, no need," I stammer. "Kat's family to me, which means you are, too."

Ryan pushes back, and I quickly shut him down. But I can barely register our conversation because my brain is whirring and clacking. Could this be the elusive idea to finally crack the code that's been stumping me, plaguing me, *torturing* me for weeks?

"I've got to run," I blurt, cutting Ryan off mid-sentence. "Ryan, will you be at Climb & Conquer's grand opening party next week?"

"I will."

"Me, too. I'll try to have the info for you by then." This new idea is a Hail Mary, but whether it works or not, I'll surely make it to Jonas and Josh's big party. Hopefully, with victory and two million bucks in my pocket, rather than a humiliating goose egg.

Ryan is thanking me profusely, but I'm already tuned out. *Delta.* Holy fucking hell. Please, let this be the answer I've been waiting for.

I say goodbye to everyone and hang up, and then run around like a chicken with my head cut off. I throw on clothes, grab my phone, keycard, and jacket, and sprint out the door at top speed. There are always security personnel at the facility, day and night. I won't be the first hacker to head down there late at night after inspiration has struck, but hopefully, at least for this project, I'll be the last.

———

It's late morning as I stand outside the facility with tears of joy and relief in my eyes. I'm so hungry and dehydrated, I feel like I'm about to fall over. So sleep-deprived, I can't see straight. But there's no way I'm going to wait till I get back to my hotel room to place a call to Hannah. Seattle is three hours behind DC, so Hannah's probably getting ready for work right now. *Please, please, pick up, Hannah.*

Thankfully, she does. After only two rings.

"Hi, honey. Sorry I was already asleep when you texted last night."

I'm shaking. On the cusp of bursting into tears. "I did it," I whisper-shout, wiping my eyes.

"What?" she says. "I couldn't hear you, honey."

I take a deep breath and find my voice. "I did it. That thing I came to DC to do? I did it, baby. Just now."

"Oh my god. Congratulations! I knew you could do it!"

"We're set for life now, baby. I did it all by myself, which means the full reward is mine."

"Oh my god!"

"Go into work today and quit. You hear me, baby? I want you to quit that soul-sucking job and clear your calendar for this entire week, because I'm coming straight to you."

Hannah gasps. "Do you want me to meet you in LA?"

"No. We've got that grand opening party for Josh and Jonas in a week, remember? I'll fly to Seattle on the first flight I can get, and from the second I land till we go to that party, I'm gonna be stuck to you like lovesick glue."

27
HANNAH

"What do you want to do next?" Henn asks.

We're sitting at a corner table in a small Mexican restaurant. Henn has just finished paying the check. Since he arrived in Seattle four days ago, we've spent every moment together, exactly as planned, and it's been divine. Perfect. Fabulous. Every bit as magical as our first week together, months ago. Even more so, because we're even more comfortable with each other now than we were back then. Plus, it's been a blast to celebrate Henn's whopping payday that landed in his account this morning.

I'm not surprised Henn is asking me what we should do next. Henn is pretty easy going, and I love playing cruise director, especially in my hometown. So, I often take the lead in terms of our activities, unless Henn says he's got a surprise for me or something specific he wants to do.

"I'm uncharacteristically devoid of ideas," I admit. "I'm down to do anything you're in the mood to do. Anything at all."

One side of Henn's mouth tilts up. "*Anything*?"

"I mean, within reason. If you're itching to push me off a cliff, or into a pit of vipers, then I'd like to amend my answer."

Henn leans forward, his smirk morphing into a full-blown smile.

"What if the thing I'm itching to do is heading back to your place and watching you ride a Sybian?"

Well, well, well. I suppose I should have expected him to ask about that at some point, given our prior conversations on the topic, but I honestly forgot such a machine even existed.

Henn looks like he's trying very hard not to look too excited. But there's no need. I'm pretty damned excited, too. I ask, "Do you know where we can get one?"

"I've already got one rented, as a matter of fact. I made the arrangements this morning while you were in the shower as a surprise." Henn bites his lower lip. "No pressure, of course. I figured if the timing felt right tonight, and if the idea sounded like fun to you, then we'd go pick it up together. If not, that's fine by me."

I can feel physical heat creeping across my cheeks and neck. I know I'm the one who first brought up the topic of the infamous orgasm machine. But saying I'm curious about a kinky machine and actually committing to riding one like a cowgirl—in front of another person, no less—are two different things. The former is an offhanded remark. The latter requires a level of sexual confidence I'm not certain I possess. On the other hand, I've been extremely curious about the thing since Kat mentioned it to me in Vegas, once I googled the hell out of it that very night in our hotel room.

"Let's do it," I say on an exhale. Why not? I'm sincerely excited to try to ride the thing, if I can muster the courage to board it in front of Henn. But even more than that, I can't imagine a better way to celebrate Henn's amazing accomplishment than by fulfilling a kinky fantasy for him. Yes, I'm the one who brought this idea up, months ago, but it doesn't take a genius to see he's going to enjoy this every bit as much as I am, if not more.

I get the feeling Henn wants to fist-pump the air in response to my affirmative reply. But, instead, he swallows hard, rises from his chair, and calmly extends his hand to me. "Come with me, pretty lady. Your chariot awaits."

When we enter my bedroom, Henn puts the box we picked up at a sex-toy shop onto my bed. At my request, the guy at the store explained their meticulous process for sanitizing the machine between rentals, including showing me the process in the back of the store. I had to admit, it was a damned good process. Foolproof, really. Especially because all parts designed to touch a woman's body are removable and forged from rubber that's easily cleaned. In the end, I had to admit renting the machine was a thoroughly acceptable option from a practical standpoint—that the cleanliness of the machine didn't present a hurdle whatsoever.

The hurdle that remains, however, is my nerves. The fact that I feel anxious about surrendering complete control over myself. As much as I want to lean into my sexuality and ditch some of my inhibitions, I can't help feeling self-conscious and shy about engaging in mutual masturbation of this magnitude. That's what this experience would ultimately be, wouldn't it, since what else would Henn do but touch himself while I'm riding a machine designed to pull full-bodied orgasms out of me?

It was one thing to mutually masturbate and dirty talk via FaceTime while Henn was in DC. Somehow, the screen and miles between us gave me a kind of false confidence I'm not feeling now. For those shenanigans, I was able to employ my simple, trusty vibrator—a device that's familiar to me and under my complete control. Plus, I controlled the framing of the live stream Henn was viewing, so if I wasn't comfortable with him seeing something, he didn't see it. But with this device—and in person, no less— it feels like I'll be jumping from the Little Leagues to the World Series in one fell swoop.

"Ready for the unboxing?" Henn asks with a waggle of his eyebrows. When I nod, he reaches into the box and pulls out the machine—a black, half-domed box that's about a foot-and-a-half long and a foot wide with a saddle on top. There's a place to attach a dildo and a rubber pad that vibrates against a woman's clitoris when turned on. Henn reaches in and pulls out a small control box and power cord and places them next to the machine.

"Wow," I whisper. I've already seen all of this online and at the sex-toy shop. But seeing them laid out, all nice and pretty, in my bedroom and realizing the time has come for me to actually ride this thing is making me blush like a vine-ripened tomato. The good news? It's also sending excitement across my skin and straight into my clit.

"The guy said to lay out towels, remember?" Henn says. "So, should we . . .?"

"Yes. Absolutely. Better safe than sorry." I've never squirted before, but the guy at the sex shop warned women sometimes do it for the first time when riding this machine.

As Henn scurries excitedly into my bathroom to collect the towels, I shift my weight nervously and wring my hands. Why am I so damned nervous about this? Henn is the best, most patient lover imaginable. And I can't deny the arousal zinging between my legs. So, what's my hang up?

When Henn returns, he gleefully lays out towels onto my bed and places the machine on top of them. He plugs in the power cord, lays the control panel next to the box, and pulls out a bag from the box. "Pick your prick, cowgirl." He's holding up a hygienically sealed bag of rubber dicks. They're of varying sizes and colors, but all have been crafted realistically with veiny shafts and mushroom tips.

As I take the bag from Henn, I can't help chuckling. "The struggle is real," I say, surveying my options. "How am I supposed to pick but one prick?"

"You're not limited to one for the duration," Henn says. "We've got this thing for three days, baby. All you have to do is pick the lucky prick that gets to kick off our fun. The lucky kick-off prick."

I twist my lips. "Aha. Winner, winner, pricky dinner." I pull out a dildo that looks a lot like Henn's—Caucasian-colored, circumcised, and average in terms of length and girth. The only thing noticeably unlike Henn's dick is how unnaturally straight it is. Henn's penis isn't bent, but this thing is stick-straight in a way human penises can't replicate. Other than that, however, this fake dick will serve as a nice stand-in for my boyfriend's real one.

"You don't want to try something totally different than your usual fare?" Henn asks. "This is meant to be fantasy fulfillment, and you've got my dick in real life, any time you please." He takes the bag of dicks from me. "What about this purple one? That looks fun. Or maybe pick one that's way bigger and thicker than mine?"

"No, this bad boy is perfect as a starter kit. If I get really comfortable with your stunt double, then maybe we can experiment with something like ol' Nessie here after that." I point to a massive dildo that rivals the ratios of the Loch Ness monster, and Henn chuckles.

Henn puts the bag onto the bed and embraces me. "We don't have to do this, you know. You said this is a fantasy of yours, so I thought it'd be a fun surprise for you. I'm not hell-bent on it, though. Don't feel like you have to do it for me."

"I don't. I genuinely want to do it. But that doesn't mean I'm not also nervous about it."

"Fair enough."

I smirk. "And by the way, let's not pretend this isn't a huge fantasy for you, too, even more than it is for me. That much has become abundantly clear, sir."

Henn snickers. "Guilty as charged."

"Guilty in the first degree."

"So guilty, I'm probably on death row."

"Oh, for sure. You're a dead man walking."

We both laugh.

"Seriously, though," Henn says, "no matter how excited I am, it won't be fun for me if you're only doing it for me. I don't want to force you."

"You're not. I want to do this, as long as we take it slow. This is way outside my comfort zone."

"Slow-going it shall be, my pretty *Plátana*. If you want to stop at any time, say so and I'll press the instant kill button."

"*You're* going to be working the control box?"

Henn looks surprised. "Well . . . yeah. That's kind of the whole point. That's not okay with you?"

I take a deep breath. The look on Henn's face makes it clear he's *dying* to control my pleasure, and not merely observe it. "No, yeah, that's fine. Unless it turns out it's not. At which point, I'll tell you so."

"Deal." For a moment, he looks like the adult version of a kid on Christmas. But, quickly, he clears his throat and assumes a more neutral facial expression. "Okay if I set it up?" When I nod, he gets to work, anticipation wafting off him like a physical thing. He attaches my chosen dildo and slathers it in lube. He tells me to straddle the box, still in my clothes, so he can adjust the height on the vibrating pad that's going to press against my clit. He slathers that sucker in lube, too, and, last but not least, reminds me to pee before we get started, like the guy at the sex-toy shop instructed.

When I return from the bathroom, the only thing left for me to do is take off my clothes and board the thing. But I'm frozen in place. With a smile, Henn pulls me to him in the middle of the room and kisses me deeply. After a moment, his mouth travels to my cheeks. And then my neck. When he returns to kissing my mouth, he slowly begins removing my clothes. And by the time the last article of my clothing hits the floor, I'm aroused and wet as can be, despite my nerves. Henn reaches between my legs and strokes me to full arousal, making my knees buckle. Finally, I stroke the bulge behind his pants and whisper, "Get naked with me."

Without hesitation, Henn peels off his clothes. When we're both naked, he climbs onto the bed and picks up the control box, while I straddle the machine and place the tip of the dildo at my entrance.

"Don't start anything moving until I say," I whisper.

"You're in charge," he replies, his voice as strained as his hard penis.

I close my eyes and take the tip of the dildo inside me, and when I open my eyes and behold Henn's excited face, it's all I need to take in the rest. This adorable, generous man has showered me with gifts and grand gestures for months. It's his turn to be on the receiving end of an amazing gift now.

I settle into the saddle with the dildo inside me and my clit pressed firmly against the rubber pad. From what I understand, the dildo inside me will swipe methodically at my G-spot, as slowly or quickly as desired, while the pad vibrates, ever-so slightly or as powerfully as a small jet engine. My choice. According to the internet and also that guy at the sex shop, the combination of the two kinds of stimulation, once set to whatever velocity works best for me, will create a sweet spot of pleasure that will supposedly pull multiple, intense orgasms out of me, one after another in a cascading domino effect, until I literally can't take it any longer. Apparently, not all women can achieve the desired domino effect, despite their best efforts, but even if that's not achievable, I'll surely nonetheless experience an orgasm unlike anything I've felt before.

"Okay, turn on the vibrating pad," I whisper. "Lowest setting."

Henn turns a dial, and a low vibration awakens my clit.

"*Whoa.*" Reflexively, I back off the rubber pad. But after taking a deep breath, resume my position and settle into it. "Oh, that feels good. A little more."

Henn nudges the dial.

"More."

"Look at you go. Already a pro."

"Wow. That's nice. This will probably get me there, all on its own."

"Yeah, but that's not the goal. The whole point is to get you to experience a full-body orgasm. For that, we need the dildo to do its part, too, at the same time."

I take a couple deep breaths. "Okay, then, let's . . ." Before I can get the end of my sentence out, a small orgasm unexpectedly ripples through me, making me moan. "Oh my god. I just came," I announce.

"Holy shit." Henn's hard cock visibly twitches. With a shuddering exhale, he crawls to me, control box in hand, and kisses me deeply, and I return his kiss with fiery passion. Certainly, in the long history of Sybian riders, what just happened to me was the equivalent of me making it down the bunny slope at an Olympic downhill event. But still, it broke the seal for me, so to speak, enough to realize I can do this. I can have an orgasm in front of Henn, live and in person, with the lights on and my body fully bared and the framing not controlled. Yeah, I can definitely do this and thoroughly enjoy it, too.

"Yeehaw," I whisper into Henn's lips. "Let's keep going. Turn it back on. Keep the vibrator at the same level and turn on the dildo to low."

"You've got it, cowgirl." Henn settles back next to the machine and turns a dial, and everything I've asked for becomes a reality. Over and over again, the dildo swipes at a pinpoint location inside me while the vibrating pad continues its delicious, lowkey work on my clit.

"Oh, jeez," I say, as pressure quickly begins building inside my lower abdomen. "This is wild. Oh, shit. The pressure inside me is getting intense."

"Try not to lean forward," Henn remarks, his dark eyes burning. There's pre-cum beaded on the tip of his dick now, I can't help noticing. Clearly, he's already thoroughly turned on. "Don't try to relieve the pressure," he says. "Push through it, if you can. That's the advice in chat rooms."

Chat rooms? Oh, Henny.

I follow his instructions and suddenly feel my insides warp like nothing I've felt before. It's like two elevator doors are trying to slam shut, but something is making them glitch.

"Something's happening to me," I report. "Something's gaining momentum inside me. Something big. Oh my god. This feels . . . crazy."

"Crazy good?"

"Not sure yet. Oh, wow. Yes. I think so."

Henn crawls to me and swirls his tongue against my hard nipple as I continue riding, making me moan from the depths of my core. At my reaction, he nibbles on my nipple, this time making me groan so loudly, he echoes my groans in reply.

"More," I choke out.

"On which?"

"Both. Everything. *More*."

Henn touches the control box, and the force of vibration on the rubber pad and speed of the dildo swirling inside me increase. Almost instantly, a strangled sound lurches out of me. My skin erupts with goosebumps. Sweat forms on my brow. Pressure shifts inside my ear canals, like I've suddenly reached a different altitude.

"What's happening to me?" I grit out. "I think a tsunami is coming." As I say the words, the walls of my vagina contract so sharply, the sensation takes my breath away. To my surprise, however, the contraction doesn't release. On the contrary, my walls keep tightening. Coiling. Clenching with force. "Oh, fuckity," I say. "It's too intense. I don't know if I can do it."

"Do you need to stop?"

"No. I'm just . . . Oh my god. Something's . . . happening." I close my eyes, and the next thing I know. I feel Henn's breathing against my ear.

He whispers, "Close your eyes and imagine that dildo is me and you're fucking me hard. Move your hips like the goddess you are and imagine I'm underneath you, going batshit crazy at how sexy you are."

I move my body and imagine what he's suggested, while Henn licks and nips at my nipples—and through it all, that vibration and swiping inside me continue ravaging me.

"Fuck me hard," Henn whispers. "You're Zelda, fucking me to get confidential information out of me. You're Zelda, not Hannah. Come on, Zelda. Fuck the living hell out of me."

He's a genius. The minute I imagine myself as my *femme fatale* alter ego, something shifts inside me. Confidence surges. All of a sudden, my core begins clenching even more fiercely, coiling tighter and tighter. I'm on the brink of a tsunami crashing down on me. On the very cusp.

"More dildo," I command.

My eyes are closed, so I can't see Henn move the dial, but I can certainly tell he's complied when the swiping inside me increases in speed and my entire body jolts deliciously in response.

With my eyes still shut, I move my hips forward and back with increased fervor. I'm Zelda, fucking classified information out of James Bond beneath me. I'm in charge. A femme fatale. I've got goosebumps. My heart is thundering in my ears. Sweat is trickling down my back.

Henn's hands and mouth are all over me. When his mouth isn't directly on me, he's whispering about how hot I am. That he can't get enough of me.

A bizarre numbing sensation overtakes my feet. My hands. My cheeks. My toes curl.

A growl lurches out of me.

"I think I'm gonna . . ." I can't complete my sentence—thankfully, since I was about to say "throw up"—because, suddenly, the most intense orgasm of my life is shattering every inch of me. Every nerve ending. The pleasure is so intense, in fact, I feel like I'm being electrocuted by it.

As my body quakes with a full-bodied seizure, I tumble off the machine and onto the mattress and writhe as waves of pleasure twist and throttle my deepest core muscles. We don't need the towels Henn carefully laid out because nothing is shooting out of my cooch, as far as I can tell. But, still, it's the most intense orgasm of my life.

When I turn my head to look at Henn, his eyes are on fire. His hand, furiously working his straining shaft. "Holy shit," he murmurs. "That was incredible."

I take a deep breath, shuddering with aftershocks. "I think once is enough for me tonight. It's too intense for me to do it again."

"Let me be your Sybian now." To my surprise, he motions to his chin, rather than to his straining cock. "Come on, love. Ride my face. *Please.*"

He's invited me to try this particular sex act several times. Each time, I've deflected by turning the tables and taking him into my mouth. I've never sat on anyone's face before, out of self-consciousness. What if I were to bear down too hard on his face and smother him? What if I'm heavier in that position than he'd anticipated, and the whole experience winds up being a huge turn-off for him and an embarrassment for me? That's my usual thought process in moments like these, even with Henn. But not this time. Now that I've ridden an orgasm machine for Henn so successfully, I'm feeling adventurous. Wild. Invincible.

Breathing hard, I crawl to him on the bed, straddle his face, and grab my headboard. "Slap my ass hard if you can't breathe," I call down to him.

"What if I slap your ass because I'm in heaven?"

"We need a signal," I insist. "I don't want to find out later I fucked my dead boyfriend's face for a full ten minutes before realizing it."

Henn chuckles. "If I happen to die, it'll be because I've died and gone to heaven."

"We need a signal, Henn. Hurry up, or I'm going to lose my nerve."

"Okay, if I'm dying, I'll poke your ribs. Otherwise, if I slap, grab, pinch or otherwise assault your ass, keep going and never stop."

"Deal." I take a deep breath and lower myself onto Henn's face, at which point he gets to work on me enthusiastically—with so much energy, in fact, I'm quickly screaming his name and moaning as my body warps and twists against his mouth. This orgasm isn't quite as physically intense as the one I just experienced on the Sybian, but it feels even hotter to me than that one. It's a thrill to know I'm face-fucking the man I love for the first time after riding a kinky orgasm machine in front of him. Who am I right now? Talk about a sign Peter Hennessey makes me feel safer and freer to explore my sexuality than ever before. The man truly is Peter the Great.

As I come down from my orgasm, I flop onto the bed on my back, moaning and writhing. Henn grabs my hands and raises them above my head, and the next thing I know, he's thrusting inside me, pounding me. Railing me like never before. I dig my nails into his back as he thrusts, entranced by the movements of his body in mine. The lack of inhibition I feel in this moment.

When he comes, it's with such force, I can actually feel his dick rippling inside me and his heart pounding behind his sternum. He kisses me deeply, and the next thing I know, he's pulled out and his fingers are now inside me, swiping at the same spot the Sybian stimulated earlier. Swipe, swipe, swipe, Henn's fingers go. And a moment later, a blast of white light bursts behind my eyelids, momentarily blinding me the same way coming indoors from a sunny day does.

When the pleasure subsides, my body goes slack. I feel boneless. Like a jellyfish. I've never had four orgasms in one sexual encounter before. Not even two, before Henn.

"My gob is beyond pummeled," I whisper.

"It's beaten to a bloody pulp?"

"It's been horrifically, brutally murdered."

Henn laughs. "Mine, too." He scoops my sweaty, wet noodle of a body into his arms and kisses my mouth passionately. And then my cheeks, neck, temples and hair. "I'm so fucking in love with you, Hannah Milliken," he gasps out. "You're better than any fantasy. You're perfect in every way. Incredible. Supernatural. The sexiest woman alive. Thank you, thank you, *thank you*."

28

HENN

"And that's why Climb & Conquer is all about reaching higher than you ever thought you could reach, literally and metaphorically," Jonas says into his microphone. "It's about becoming better than you ever thought you could be."

The large, packed crowd, including Hannah and me, erupts into enthusiastic applause. We're at the grand opening celebration for Climb & Conquer—the national chain of rock-climbing gyms the Faraday brothers are launching today with much fanfare in Seattle.

For today's festivities, the Faraday brothers—or whatever party planner they hired for today's event—has done a spectacular job. There's a live band on a raised stage with a dance floor immediately below it. Also, various tented booths along the walls of the large gym that include food vendors, craft beer, and a face painter for the kiddos. There's also a booth with a banner inviting people to "Join the C&C Team!" with staffers standing at the ready to answer questions and accept applications. And, last but not least, given what we're all here to celebrate, there's indoor rock climbing, too. No shortage of towering rock walls of varying skill levels for people to climb, all of them manned with smiling personnel in bright blue C&C-branded T-shirts.

When Hannah and I arrived at this party a few minutes ago, Josh and

Jonas were already onstage in front of an idle band, trading the microphone for their welcoming remarks. And so, Hannah and I quickly wormed our way toward the front of the packed crowd to a spot where our friends onstage would be able to see us and know we'd made it to their big day. It's where we're still standing now.

"As part of our genuine commitment to extraordinary aspiration," Jonas continues from the stage, "Climb & Conquer has identified certain designated charities we'll be supporting with a portion of our proceeds."

As Jonas lists the charities, I zone out. Let my eyes wander. I notice Sarah and Kat standing to the side of the stage, smiling at their men—and when I notice Kat's baby bump, I can't help smiling from ear to ear. Kat didn't have any noticeable bump the last time I saw her at Jonas and Sarah's wedding—but it's unmistakable now.

I nudge Hannah's arm and whisper, "Kat's showing."

Hannah nods. "I saw. She looks like when actresses wear a fake baby bump on TV."

"Jennifer Aniston on *Friends*."

She giggles. "That's exactly who I was thinking of."

I return my attention to the stage, where Jonas is still talking about the mission of Climb & Conquer, but a moment later, my gaze drifts again. This time, to Josh's smiling face as he listens intently to his brother. Damn, I'm proud of Josh today. It took balls to ditch the empire his father left for his two sons to start something totally new from scratch. Something the Faraday brothers could build together, with passion, from the ground up. It just goes to show, it's never too late to follow your dreams. You simply have to figure out what they are and go for it.

I look at Hannah next to me and the sight of her quickens my heart rate. Getting to love Hannah, to build a life with her, that's *my* dream. That truth has never been clearer to me.

Onstage, Jonas says something that draws my gaze back to him: "Simply figure out what your passion is and resolve to make excellence your habit."

As the crowd erupts in applause, I look around the massive, sparkling gym and notice Kat's parents in the crowd. They're standing with two muscular guys who look like slightly different, but equally handsome, combinations of Mr. and Mrs. Morgan. One of the dudes is on crutches, so

I'm guessing he's Kat's oldest brother, Colby—a firefighter who suffered a horrible accident several months ago. Is the other guy—the one with tattoo sleeves on his arms—the Morgan brother who asked for my help in finding Samantha the Flight Attendant? If that guy is, indeed, Ryan Morgan aka Captain, then he's not going to like what I have to tell him.

I nudge Hannah. "Babe, are those two guys with Kat's parents Colby and Ryan?"

Hannah looks to where I'm indicating and confirms their identities.

Onstage, Jonas says, "And so, without further ado, let's let the band play while you guys climb and conquer our rock walls and have a great time."

As everyone claps and cheers, Josh grabs the microphone from his brother and shouts, "Thanks for coming, everyone. Happy Birthday, Climb & Conquer!" He cues the band behind him which then launches into the classic party song, "Shout," causing a flurry of whooping partygoers to storm the dance floor and begin throwing their hands into the air.

"Should we go over there and congratulate Josh and Jonas now?" Hannah asks. But she's no sooner said the words than the Faraday brothers begin posing for photos on the side of the stage, while Sarah and Kat look on with pride. "Nah, let's go later," Hannah says, answering her own question. "It looks like it's going to be a minute before they're free to chat. Should we grab some food and beer while we wait?"

"Lead on, pretty lady."

A few minutes later, we're standing to the side of a large rock wall, drinking and eating and people-watching. "Oh, look. Kat and Sarah are heading to the dance floor," Hannah says excitedly. "Let's go dance with them!" I glance across the expansive, crowded space and discover Jonas giving an interview with a TV reporter near the stage, while Josh's personal assistant, T-Rod, looks on.

"I think I'd rather say hi to Josh first. But go ahead."

Hannah's now bopping in place to the beat of the live music, raring to go. But she says, "Are you sure?"

"Absolutely. Put on your dancing shoes while I find Josh. I'll join you later."

Hannah squeals happily. "Okay. See you later!" And off she goes. I'm not surprised. Hannah not only loves to dance, she hasn't seen Kat or

Sarah since the wedding, and I know she's been bursting at the seams to catch up with them.

As Hannah gallops away, I scan the crowded space, looking for Josh. Where is he? He's nowhere near the spot where Jonas is talking to that TV reporter. After a moment, Josh suddenly emerges from the crowd, heading straight for me. *Uh oh.* He looks stressed. Is that because of today's event or something else? When I wave at him and begin walking toward him, Josh motions for me to meet him behind a nearby rock wall.

When I get to Josh's chosen destination, he hugs me and pats my back in greeting. "Hey, man," he says. "Thanks for coming today. You didn't have to do that."

"I wouldn't have missed it. Plus, it gave me an excuse to come see Hannah."

"So, hey, man," Josh says. "Do you think you could do me a favor? I need to find someone. Could you get me dialed in?"

Well, that settles it. He's definitely stressed. It's not like Josh to jump straight to asking me for a favor. Not that I mind. I'd give the man the shirt off my back, no questions asked, and no niceties required. "Sure," I say without hesitation. "Who is it this time, boss?"

Josh tells me the name of the guy and everything he knows about him —his full name, the college he attended with approximate dates, the fact that his father is a senator and his mother some sort of philanthropist—and I tell him it shouldn't be hard for me to find the guy with all that info to work with.

"Thanks, man. As soon as possible, please."

"Yeah, I figured. When have you ever asked me to find someone 'whenever it's convenient for you, Henn'?"

Josh chuckles. "Sorry."

"No worries. Whatever you need. Always."

Josh takes a deep breath. Runs his hand through his hair. "So, what's been shaking with you? Work good?"

I can't imagine Josh genuinely wants to hear about my work. Clearly, something big is on his mind, and my Spidey senses tell me his anxiety has nothing to do with this grand opening party, which is plainly going fantastically well. But, hey, he asked, so I answer. I tell him I just wrapped up a job with the feds in DC, and also tell him the funny story of the work

I did for that department store chain. "They truly believed they were impervious to hacking," I say with a chuckle. "They'd supposedly hired the best cyber-security team money could buy to protect their data, but I dug around and broke 'em wide open in less than a day."

Josh laughs. "I'm not surprised. And how's everything else? Things with Hannah good?"

"Better than good. *Awesome*. She's moving to LA next month."

"Really? Wow. That's fantastic."

"Yeah, the long-distance thing is killing us, man. And since Kat's decided to put her PR company on the back burner for a while to become a mommy, Hannah's decided to look for a PR job in the entertainment industry."

"Awesome. Hey, you should ask Reed if he knows someone who might be able to help her with her job search. Reed knows everyone."

"Yeah, I already talked to him. He's on it. So, how are things with Kat? Have you two been nesting, getting ready for baby?" Josh hasn't said a word to me about his plans to propose to Kat, and I'm hoping his silence on the topic doesn't mean he's changed his mind. I know my best friend better than he knows himself sometimes, and I truly think he'd be far happier in life married to Kat and being part of her big, boisterous family than he's even capable of imagining. In fact, if I could hand-pick a family for Josh to join, it'd be the Morgans.

As if reading my mind, Josh glances furtively at Kat across the crowded gym where she's dancing with gusto with Sarah and Hannah. A wide smile unfurls across his face before he returns his attention to me. "I'm going to ask Kat to marry me," he whispers. He touches his pocket and smiles. "Got the ring right here."

That's got to be the source of the stress I've been detecting from Josh. If I had an engagement ring in my pocket for Hannah, I'd be bursting out of my skin. "No shit?" I say, feigning surprise. I give Josh a warm hug. "That's awesome. When are you gonna do it?"

"As soon as you get me that info."

"Aaaah. *Interesting*. What does one thing have to do with the other?"

Josh briefly explains how the information gathering/hacking project he's asked me to do will play into his proposal, and I can't help hooting with laughter.

"Very cool," I say. "Okay. I'll put a rush on it, boss."

"Thanks."

I shake my head. "Wow. I never thought I'd see the day Josh 'YOLO' Faraday would get married and settle down."

Josh shrugs. "I never thought I'd see the day, either. And now, it's all I want." He exhales. "Let's just hope Kat says yes."

I smirk. Not too long ago, Josh gave me some supremely bad advice about bagging babes in Vegas, and I can't resist throwing that shit back into his face now. "Bah," I deadpan. "Just dick it up and she won't be able to resist you."

Josh rolls his eyes. "Yeah, well, I've recently learned the whole dick-it-up-strategy might not be *quite* as effective as I originally thought." He steals another look at Kat on the dance floor, where she's gleefully throwing her baby bump around and singing along with the band. "At least, not with Madame Terrorist."

"I'm really happy for you, Josh," I say, patting his shoulder. "You've definitely come a long way from the dude who got YOLO inked onto his ass-cheek, thanks to losing a bet about a quote from *Happy Gilmore*."

Josh cracks up. "God, I hope so. Hey, what was that quote we were arguing about, by the way? I can never remember what it was."

We launch into conversation about that movie, and which scene inspired the ass tattoo Josh got while wasted, until, finally, Josh remarks that he'd better get back to his adoring public.

After we've said our goodbyes, I leave our hiding spot to look for Ryan Morgan . . . and what do you know, only a few seconds into my search, I see Kat heading straight toward me with her brother, Ryan, in tow.

———

Well, that sucked donkey balls. I'm walking out of a private office in the back of the gym with Ryan Morgan after breaking the news that I couldn't find his flight attendant in Delta's database, despite my best efforts. I assured him I'll keep trying until I find her—that my plan is to hack every airline that had flights from LA to Seattle on the day in question. But, unfortunately, that's going to take some time.

Kat stayed behind in the office when Ryan and I departed. Apparently, Josh is going to meet her in there any minute now for a private celebration. So, it's just Ryan and me heading down the short corridor leading back into the party now.

"Are you sure I can't pay you for your time?" Ryan asks. "This is going to be so much more work than you initially envisioned."

"Bah. Like I said, your money's no good to me."

Ryan thanks me again, the same way he did a few minutes ago in the office, and says he's going to look for his brother, Colby. I point in another direction and explain I'm going to look for my girlfriend, who's probably on the dance floor as we speak. And off we go in opposite directions.

Holy shit.

I stop short after turning a corner. No way. It can't be. And yet, I truly think it is. I've stared at this man's face in photos so many times, I know his features as well as my own.

It's Greg Smith aka Angus Wellborn aka The Asshole. *He's here.*

I've been searching high and low for this fucker for quite some time now. And suddenly, here he is, mere feet away, standing in line for the expert rock wall. And the best part? The gift from Steve Jobs? *He's wearing wireless earbuds.* Which means hacking him via Bluetooth will be like taking candy from a baby.

As my heart rate skyrockets, I look around for Hannah, praying she's nowhere nearby, and thankfully, she's nowhere to be found. Is it pure coincidence this fucker is here today, or did he somehow know Hannah would be here and came to stalk or harass her? To my knowledge, she didn't post on social media about her plans for today. And I swept her devices the day after I landed in Seattle, as always, to make sure she hadn't been hacked or otherwise compromised by this fucker or anyone else—and she was clean.

I take a deep breath. *Calm down, Peter.* Seattle is a huge city, filled with millions of people, and this asshole's got a history of living here. Plus, this is a well-publicized party that's probably right up his alley, given that he fancies himself a fitness enthusiast. Indeed, all logical signs point to this being nothing but a coincidence. Either way, though, I definitely need to take care of business, *pronto*, and then quickly get Hannah the fuck out of here before she runs into him or vice versa.

I amble toward the guy casually, while nonchalantly swiping into my phone. Quickly, I pull up a Bluetooth scanner that's loaded onto my phone for opportunities exactly like this one, and then stop about three feet behind my target.

"You like working here?" he asks a pretty staffer in a bright blue "C&C" T-shirt.

"So far, so good," she says. "We've only had training for the past month, but our bosses are super cool, and the entire staff already feels like one big family."

"Awesome," the fucker says. "I just applied. Hopefully, I'll be joining the family soon."

"Oh my gosh, good luck!" the staffer says.

"I've been a personal trainer for years, but recently become obsessed with climbing."

"It's addicting, isn't it?"

The Asshole nods. "This would be my dream job."

"What's your name? I'll put in a good word for you."

"Thanks so much. Sean Goodman."

"I'm Lena," she replies. "And you're up, Sean." She motions to the towering wall. "Show me what you've got."

As "Sean" gets strapped into a harness, my scanner locks in. Fuck. It's connected me to three nearby phones, all of them with Bluetooth currently activated, and none of them bearing an identifier that would definitively tell me which one to choose. I swiftly breach all three devices, figuring I'll sift through my options later and figure out which is his, and then quickly shove my phone into my pocket.

Boom. I got you, motherfucker.

As much as I'd love to stand here and glory in my victory, there's no time for that. I need to find Hannah and get her the fuck out of here.

I head toward the dance floor and, luckily, find Hannah whooping it up with Sarah. Unless my girlfriend is giving an Oscar-worthy performance, she hasn't seen The Asshole yet, thank God, and I'm determined to keep it that way.

When I reach Hannah on the dance floor, I tap her shoulder, lean in to be heard above the live music, and tell her I need to leave immediately. "Explosive diarrhea," I say. "I just came from the bathroom. I'm a ticking time bomb."

"Oh no. You poor thing. I was wondering where you disappeared off to. Do we have time to say goodbye to—"

"No, no time. I might blow again any minute."

"Oh dear. I'll tell Sarah to say our goodbyes to everyone." She taps Sarah on the shoulder and says something into her ear that makes Sarah grimace and then blow me a kiss. I hold my stomach and make a "yeesh" face, and Sarah gestures as if to say, "Go, go, gooo!" before blowing me another kiss.

As Hannah and I head toward the nearest exit, I tap out a text to Josh, telling him to scrap any application he receives from "Sean Goodman" and to put him on their never-hire list. For good measure, I forward a snapshot of the guy, too. "I'll explain later," I write.

We've made it. We're outside in the chilly air, heading straight for Hannah's car.

"Hang in there, sweetie," Hannah says, patting my arm. "If you need to stop on the way to my place, let me know."

"I think I'll make it there. Sorry to make us leave."

"Don't apologize. I'm sorry you're not feeling well. After dropping you off at my place, I'll go back out and get you some supplies—Imodium and Saltines and Gatorade and all that stuff."

Perfect. When Hannah goes out, I'll go *in.* To Greg Smith's phone, that is. And then into his laptop and all other devices, which will surely be connected to his phone in some way.

"Thanks so much," I say. "You're the best."

"Would you prefer chicken noodle or Won Ton soup?"

I'm pretty sure the Chinese place is farther away than wherever Hannah might go to get chicken noodle, so that's what I request. The more time I can get to secure the bastard's devices while she's out, the better.

Aw, fuck.

I just realized my choice of cover story will probably preclude me from having sex with Hannah tonight. Well, that's a damned shame. Oh well. It'll be worth it, if I can finally infiltrate The Asshole and set myself up to exact appropriate revenge on him for the way he treated Hannah—and God knows how many others. In fact, I'd trade one sexless night to make sure I'll be able to avenge my beloved Hannah every fucking time.

29
HENN

"I shouldn't be gone more than two or three hours," Hannah says. "I'm itching to get back home to start packing." She's heading out with her sister to run some errands, while I stay here in her apartment to help Josh with his proposal to Kat. Josh asked me not to jinx his big moment by telling anyone about it in real-time, not even Hannah, so I told her I'm staying behind to do some "time-sensitive online research" for Josh today.

After counting off the errands she'll be running with Maddy this afternoon, Hannah asks, "Do you think you'll be finished with Josh's thing in time to have dinner with me around six?"

I glance at the time on my phone. Based on when Josh and Kat boarded that private jet, I should be hearing from Josh any minute now, and I can't imagine the project will last all that long, once we get started. "Yeah, that should work."

"Awesome," Hannah says cheerfully. "Say hi to Josh for me."

"Will do. Say hi to Maddy for me."

"You'll see her later. She's coming back here to help me start packing."

Hannah kisses my cheek, grabs her purse, and heads out, at which point I return to my laptop to make sure Josh's target and the target's wife are both still at their expected locations.

Since landing in Seattle almost two weeks ago, I haven't felt much like working. Now that Hannah is unemployed, and I'm a multimillionaire who doesn't actually *need* to work, I've been spending all my time hanging out with my girlfriend lately. In fact, the only times I've pulled out my computers since landing in Seattle, besides that one time I quickly hacked Greg Smith after the Climb & Conquer party, was to work on this job for Josh. But even then, I only worked on it when Hannah wasn't around, like when she went to get her hair done or to her book club one night. I haven't even felt the urge to poke around Greg Smith's devices all that much yet.

That last thing is probably for the best, actually. Whenever I do start poking around Greg Smith's devices in earnest and figuring out the degree of punishment to fairly inflict upon him, I think it'd be best for that *not* to happen in too close a proximity to the Climb & Conquer event. The chances are slim to none he'll figure out he's been hacked. But on the off chance he realizes it, I wouldn't want him remembering that nerdy dude who stood a little too close as he got harnessed up to climb the expert rock wall at the party.

Josh: Plane landing in five. You still there?

Me: Not going anywhere. You feeling good, brother?

Josh: I'm FANTASTIC. Kat has no idea what's coming. She thinks today has been a consolation prize to make up for the fact that I'll never, ever propose to her. LOL.

Me: Genius.

I check the location of Josh's target and the target's wife, yet again, making sure both are where we want them to be, and then send Josh a text letting him know all systems are still go.

Mom: Checking in. How are you?

Jesus Christ. I love this woman so much, but she's got the worst fucking timing.

Me: I'm in the middle of something important and time sensitive, Mom. I'll call you later.

Mom: In the time it took you to send that text, you could have filled me in on the status with Hannah. Is everything still going wonderfully with her, I hope?

Fuck my life. I wouldn't normally have told my mother about my relationship with Hannah until we were living together and the revelation was unavoidable, precisely because I don't like having to answer questions like this. But I couldn't help myself during one particularly lonely night in DC. I was missing Hannah so much that night, I'd decided to get shitfaced on whiskey from the minibar. And then, as often happens when I drink excessively, I got the "dial-ies," as I call them, followed by an acute case of word vomit. When Hannah didn't answer my call, I drunkenly called my mother and babbled to her all about the amazing girlfriend I couldn't wait to see again.

Me: Yes, everything is going great. I'm still in Seattle with her. We're getting ready for her move to LA.

Mom: HANNAH IS MOVING TO LA? Fabulous news! To live with you?

Me: No, not yet. Gotta go.

Mom: Are you two driving or flying from Seattle to LA?

Me: We're driving her car while a moving company takes all her furniture and boxes. Gotta go, Mom. I'll call you later.

Mom: You're going to have to make at least a couple overnight stops during the drive. One of them should be in Fresno.

Shit. As a matter of fact, Fresno is perfectly situated for the last overnight stop of our trip.

Me: Maybe. No promises. I'll talk to Hannah and let you know. Gotta go. Bye.

Mom replies, but I ignore her message this time, when I get one from Josh.

Josh: Leaving airport now. Kat is already fast asleep. Plan A or B, brother?

Me: Plan A. The target is at his house and wifey is still at the hairdresser. No Plan B required.

> Josh: Well, how considerate of him to be home in time for my visit.

Seeing as how Kat is fast asleep, I ask if we can talk. I want to go over some of the details about what's to come, and a voice conversation would be easier for that. Plus, I'd love to hear Josh's voice when I tell him the brilliant thing I did to make sure our porn-addicted target has remained at his house after arriving home from his golf game.

> Josh: Calling now.

My phone rings, and I connect the call. "Yo."

Josh replies in a soft tone, obviously taking care not to awaken his future fiancée sleeping next to him in the car. "Nice of the bastard to be sitting at home, waiting for me."

"He's always home at this time of day after a round of golf at the country club," I explain. "But just to make double-damn sure he was gonna be there for you today, he *might* have received a VIP-invitation to a live chat with his favorite porn star. *Wink.*"

Josh chuckles. "Fucking genius."

"So I've been told. How close are you?"

"We're in the limo now," he says softly. "I'd say we're about fifteen minutes out."

"Cool." I glance at my laptop, which is now showing me the target's various devices in split-screen. "The dude's not going anywhere. He's watching a gangbang-*bukkake*-porno on his iPad while simultaneously live-chatting with a porn star on his laptop."

"He's *double-fisting* porn?" Josh whispers.

"I think he *might* have an addiction."

"Ya think?"

"So, hey, I went through the dude's computer like you asked me to. You were right—he's totally cheating on his wife. Like, compulsively."

"Yeah, I figured. A leopard doesn't change his spots."

"The guy's a scumbag," I say. "I literally *hate* him."

"Welcome to the club."

"I went through his wife's phone and laptop just to get the lay of the land and she's a total sweetheart—a genuinely good person. Clearly, she's got no idea who she's married to."

"Not surprised at all."

"So, are you gonna rat him out?"

"I wish I could so badly," Josh says on an exhale. "But, no, I wasn't planning to, for the sake of the wife."

I exhale the same way Josh did a moment ago. I get Josh's thinking on this, logically. It's not our place to enlighten this woman about her shitbag of a husband. But it's awfully hard for me to stand by and do nothing when I know for a fact an innocent woman is unknowingly married to a serial cheater. On the other hand, however, I was floored five years ago by the reaction of my pregnant childhood friend, Josie, when she found out about *her* serial cheater of a husband. Not only did she *not* leave him after finding out about his many infidelities from an "anonymous woman" he'd supposedly cheated with—cough, cough, aka *me*—but she also chewed out said anonymous woman for "butting her nose in where it didn't belong out of pure jealousy" and for supposedly "maliciously photoshopping" the genuine screen shots that unequivocally proved her husband's escapades.

"Yeah, I guess that's the right call," I say to Josh. "It's not really our place to ruin her life. But it kills me. They're trying to have a baby—doing hard-core fertility treatments. I hope one way or another she finds out she's married to a cheating scumbag before she gets pregnant with the guy's kid."

I can't help thinking my childhood friend's reaction to the truth about her cheating husband might have been different if she hadn't already had kids with the guy. If so, isn't it my duty to save this poor woman from locking herself into a co-parenting relationship *forever* with this fuckstick? If she were drowning in a swimming pool, I'd jump in to save her without a thought. Isn't this basically the same thing?

"So you think we should rat him out, after all?" Josh asks. He's always been able to read me like a book.

I pause, considering the totality of the situation for a moment. "No," I finally concede. "It's really not our place, man. That's not the mission."

"Damn. I would have loved to decimate that cocksucker in every conceivable way."

"Oh, well. I guess even a guy as awesome as you can't have everything, Josh."

"Actually, I'm beginning to think he can."

My heart rate quickens. "Wait. So you *do* wanna tell the wife about his extracurricular activities?" I was secretly hoping he'd say that.

"No, sorry. I wasn't referring to ratting him out. Kat's asleep on me. I was looking at her face when I said that."

I chuckle. Who the hell is this head-over-heels romantic and what has he done with my commitment-phobic, emotionally stunted, eternal bachelor of a best friend? "Oh, well, I can see why you'd say that, then."

"Kat's totally drooling right now," Josh whispers, but his tone is as if Kat is gracefully doing pirouettes across a white-sand beach at sunset.

I snicker. "Yeah, but I bet it's really *pretty* drool."

"Actually, it is." Josh chuckles. "But, anyway, okay, yeah, I agree. We don't tell the wife she's married to the world's biggest scumbag."

"Not today, anyway. I might not be able to control myself tomorrow. I make no promises."

"Hey, you gotta follow your conscience, dude. I trust you. But just not today."

It's the right call. If I revealed this guy's douchebaggery to his wife today, he'd wrongly conclude it was Josh who'd hastened his undoing, which could risk the guy coming after Josh to retaliate. And that's not something I'd ever want to set in motion. If there's one thing I've learned over my years of fucking over douchebags through anonymous hacking, it's that you've got to do it in a way where they can't put two and two together and track down their tormentor. Yeah, the smart thing would be to fuck this guy over in a couple months or so, and in a way that'll make his wife—and therefore the target—think she'd stumbled across evidence of the target's misdeeds, organically, through sheer coincidence. I smile wickedly at the thought, my heart already skipping a beat about all the fun I'm going to have when the timing is right.

Josh asks, "So can we somehow make sure the wife's not there when Kat and I arrive?"

I look at the box on my screen that's displaying the wife's current location and inform Josh she's still at a high-end hair salon. "Don't women's hair appointments at hoity-toity salons take at least an hour or so?" I ask. "Her appointment's at one of those really fancy places where they give you cucumber water and wash your hair, so she should be gone a while."

Josh laughs. "*That's* your definition of a fancy salon? They give you water and a shampoo?"

"Hey, I go to Supercuts, man. What do I know?"

"You *do*?" His tone is dripping with sarcasm. With a laugh, Josh adds, "I totally couldn't tell that from looking at you, Henn."

I laugh with him. Josh can be an entitled prick at times, simply because he doesn't know any better, thanks to his upbringing. And yet, he's *my* entitled prick. The coolest, most fiercely loyal entitled prick of a best friend anyone could ever ask for. "So, here's the sitch, man," I say, ignoring Josh's mockery about my lowbrow grooming habits. "When you get there, the name Frank Farmer is on the approved visitors' list at the guard station. Just text me when you're there and I'll go in and freeze the bastard's hard drive."

"Will do. We're almost there. Sit tight and wait for my signal, okay?"

"Yup. No worries. I'll just be sitting here, watching him watch porn. Don't you worry about a thing except bagging that babe."

"I'll do my mighty best."

"Is that a note of *anxiety* I detect in your voice, boss?"

"Yeah, this is life or death, man. I don't wanna fuck it up."

Another smile unfurls across my face. During our first year of college, Josh let down his guard and told me about his acute anxiety regarding his brother, Jonas, who, at the time, was struggling with severe mental health issues following several traumas. But since then, Josh has rarely admitted to feeling anxious or vulnerable about a damned thing. He's certainly never displayed anything but suave confidence when it comes to women.

"Aw, come on, you can't fail," I say. But because I can't resist the chance to tease him once again about the moronic advice he gave me in Las Vegas, I add, "Just dick it up and the babe will be eating out the palm of your hand."

"Gee, thanks for the tip."

I snicker. "No prob."

"I'll text you when we're there."

"Roger."

I'm expecting Josh to reply with "rabbit," since anyone who's hung out with Kat Morgan for any length of time acquires the silly habit. In fact, Kat once told me in Vegas that replying "rabbit" in response to "roger" is "sacred Morgan law." When Josh doesn't say it, however, and I call out his name, I realize he's already ended the call.

"Okay, then," I murmur, leaning back into Hannah's couch. For several minutes, I watch the target's porn as he watches it on his end, until, finally, I get a text from Josh that informs me they've arrived at the guy's house and that I should do the thing we discussed earlier in precisely three minutes.

I text Josh to let him know I'm on it, and three minutes later, do the thing. For a while, I stare at my screen and wait for word from Josh. And when I finally hear from him, Josh says the target just went back inside his house and is now looking at his computer.

> Josh: He was threatening to call the police. Send him a message loud and clear, would you? Make sure he knows he's at my fucking mercy.

> Me: Gotcha, boss. When he comes back out, the tiger will be nothing more than a pussy cat. I promise.

There's a noise at the door, the jangling of keys, and two seconds later, Hannah and Maddy burst into Hannah's apartment, both of them carrying flattened cardboard boxes.

"Hello there, handsome chap!" Hannah chirps happily.

"Hi, Henny!" Maddy says.

When the ladies come over to greet me, I hug them and quickly return to my screen so as not to leave Josh hanging. I think my work here is done, but Josh's actual proposal should be coming any minute now, and I don't want to miss his text saying as much.

Hannah says, "There are more boxes in my car, Henny. Would you mind bringing them up for me?"

"Sure thing, just as soon as I'm finished here. I should be done any minute now."

"Do you want a glass of wine? We're going to have some."

"No, I'm good. Thanks."

Hannah heads to the kitchen with Maddy, and the pair sets about pouring themselves wine. As the sisters chat and bustle around the kitchen, it occurs to me this is probably one of those instances when I should tell Hannah about what I'm up to. It's not a normal thing for me to reveal my hacking activities to anyone who isn't directly involved in hiring me, but I've promised Hannah the awkwardness and hurt she felt on karaoke night would be a one-off, and I'm nothing if not a man of my word.

Surely, at some point soon, Josh will regale his new fiancée with the story of how he pulled off today's complicated marriage proposal, including the part where he epically humiliated Kat's cheating ex with a little help from me. And once that happens, Kat will almost certainly talk about what happened with or in front of Hannah. And when that happens, Kat will assume Hannah's already been fully briefed on the topic by me, her beloved boyfriend. And it'll be karaoke night, all over again. Only worse. Because this time, unlike then, Hannah's already made it clear it hurts her feelings when our friend group knows something I've done, and I haven't told her about it myself.

I briefly consider waiting to tell Hannah what I've done until after Maddy leaves, but quickly decide I don't have the luxury of that kind of time. Plus, Maddy is family to me by now, and there's no doubt I can trust her with this particular information. "Hey, Banana," I call toward the kitchen. "Come over here, babe. You're gonna want to see this. Josh is proposing to Kat, as we speak."

"*What?*" Hannah shrieks. She races to the couch, practically spilling the red wine in her goblet as she runs. With a bloom in her cheeks, she plops down onto the couch next to me, peeks over my shoulder at my screen, and peppers me with questions about what she's seeing.

As Maddy makes her way to an armchair, I say, "Josh asked me not to say anything until he was sure everything was going off without a hitch, but now that it is, I think I'm in the clear to spill the beans." After making sure both women understand the confidential nature of what they're seeing on my screen, I tell them both the whole story.

"Josh is such a baller to propose to Kat like this!" Hannah gushes when I finish my explanation. "She's going to *love* it!"

Suddenly, my phone pings with a text from Josh.

> Josh: I bagged the babe. She said YES. Fuck yeah! Exit The Asshole's system now.

After Hannah and I whoop loudly and fist-bump each other, I reply to Josh, congratulating him and letting him know I'll leave the target's system without a trace. True to my word, that's what I do . . . except that I can't resist leaving an encrypted back door in place, in case my future self decides to lead his clueless wife to the truth one day. Plus, if the bastard is stupid enough to try to fuck with Josh in retaliation for the humiliation he suffered on his doorstep today, then I'll use this back door to remind him I've got his balls in the palm of my hand.

As I'm still constructing my back door, Hannah says, "I wonder how long it'll take Kat to let us know she's engaged? Five minutes? Ten? What's the over-under?" But she's no sooner said the words than a text from Kat lands in our group chat with Kat, Josh, Jonas, and Sarah.

> Kat: JOSH ASKED ME TO MARRY HIM AND I SAID HELL YES! WAHOOOO!!!!! I'M GOING TO BE MRS. FARADAY, BITCHES!!!!!

I breathe a sigh of relief from the depths of my toes. Phee-to-the-fucking-yoo I told Hannah about my part in Josh's proposal *before* Kat's text landed on Hannah's phone. Otherwise, Hannah would have received this text and instantly realized Kat's with Josh, getting engaged, at the exact time I'm sitting on her couch doing "online research" for Josh. Jesus. In that scenario, I'd have been well and truly fucked.

Before anyone in the group has replied to Kat's exuberant text, we get a photo of the happy couple, huddled up and smiling in the back of a limo. In the shot, Kat's holding up her hand to show off a gigantic rock on her third finger, with both faces exuding pure joy.

"Holy fuckburgers!" Hannah blurts. "Look at that rock!"

"Oooh, lemme see," Maddy says. She takes Hannah's phone, and immediately gasps. "That's not a *rock*. That's a mother-trucking beach ball."

Both women crack up, and then return to the happy business of gushing over the photo, the ring, the joy on Josh's and Kat's faces. As they chatter away, a surprising emotion grips me. *Extreme embarrassment.* Now that I'm seeing Hannah's reaction to Kat's good news, I can't believe I was ever stupid enough to even *think* of proposing to Hannah, spur-of-the-moment at Jonas and Sarah's wedding. Drunk or not, no matter how much I'd been missing Hannah, no matter how much I couldn't bear the fact that I had to immediately hop a flight back to DC, I should have known better than to kneel before her on a fucking whim without a ring. Reed was exactly right. Whenever the time comes, and it will, Hannah deserves a well-planned, thoughtful proposal with a fat diamond ring—a proposal that's every bit as perfect for Hannah as the one Josh pulled off for Kat today.

I know Hannah said she's not positive she believes in marriage. But even drunk, I knew she was reacting to the trauma of her parents' messy divorce. Probably, the trauma of that scammer taking advantage of her, too. Even drunk, I knew that photo on Hannah's dream board was a depiction of our future selves, married with a baby—and witnessing Hannah's gushing reaction to Josh and Kat's engagement only solidifies that belief, all the more.

Kat's all-caps text is met with a flurry of congratulatory replies and gifs in our group chat, until, after a while, Josh and Kat sign off to celebrate privately. With an audible sigh, Hannah puts down her phone and smiles. "Just goes to show, you can never say never. I'm sure Josh thought he'd never get married, and yet here he is."

I smile. "There's no doubt in my mind, if Josh hadn't met Kat, he never would have gotten married to anyone. I'm convinced she's literally the only person in the world who could have changed his mind about marriage."

Hannah clutches her heart. "How romantic."

"I love that so much," Maddy says softly.

Aw. Am I imagining sadness in Maddy's tone? Is sweet little Maddy Milliken thinking about her deceased boyfriend, Justin, and wondering if he was her only shot at the fairytale? God, I hope not. She's only twenty-two, and a total cutie. Surely, there's someone out there who'll pull her out of her shyness the same way Justin apparently did.

"Oh, the boxes in your car," I say, rising from the couch. "Where are your keys, babe?"

"On the kitchen counter. I'll come with you. There's a lot."

As I grab the keys, Maddy says she'll stay behind to start constructing the boxes the girls brought up earlier, and a moment later, Hannah and I are striding down the hallway toward the elevator. As we walk, Hannah suddenly grabs my arm, stopping my motion, and then wordlessly takes my face in her palms, and kisses me passionately.

"What was that for?" I sputter. "Not that I'm complaining."

Hannah's blue eyes are blazing. "That was to thank you for helping your best friend make *my* best friend's dream come true." Her smile widens. "And even more so, for trusting me enough to tell me all about it."

30

HENN

I lay down my cards with a yawn. "Bedtime for Henny. Today was a long day of driving."

Hannah and I are staying with my mom in Fresno on the last night of our leisurely, four-day drive from Seattle to LA. Tomorrow, after we've finally made it to Hannah's new apartment, we'll meet the moving truck and begin the exciting, probably exhausting, process of moving my girlfriend into her new digs in my city. *Hallelujah.*

I'm expecting Mom and Hannah to yawn and rise from the card table, too, but to my surprise, Mom looks at Hannah, bright-eyed and bushy-tailed, and says, "Are you too tired to play one more game with me?" *Well, I'll be damned.* Mom's never been much of a night owl. And that's been especially true since Dad died.

"I'd love to, Mrs. Hennessey," Hannah replies.

"Wonderful! And call me Carol."

Hannah beams a glorious smile at my mother from behind her thick glasses. "I'd love to, Carol."

I open my mouth, intending to say, "Well, I suppose I could be convinced to stick around for one more game, too." But Mom beats me to the punch.

"Goodnight, honey," she says to me. To Hannah, she says, "You know what we should play? *Backgammon*."

Whoa. Mom and Dad used to play backgammon every night before bedtime. They'd pop some popcorn, pour a glass of wine or whiskey, and sit down at this very table to play and laugh and tease each other relentlessly. Despite my best efforts, I haven't been able to coax Mom into playing her favorite game since Dad's passing. And now, after only a half-day spent with Hannah, she's inviting her to play the sacred game with her?

"Is it hard to learn?" Hannah asks.

"My darling, it's easy peasy lemon squeezy. You'll pick it up in no time."

Hannah shoots me a snarky look that says, "Yes, I noticed she said *lemon* instead of *pumpkin*," and I chuckle in response. Since that first night in Vegas, we've playfully argued about that phrase several times, with both of us being willing to die on our respective hills.

"Well, off to bed I go," I say. "Kick some ass, Banana. Mom always wallops me in backgammon."

"Oh, before you go, Peter," Mom says. "Would you be a doll and make us a big bowl of popcorn?"

My breathing halts. Backgammon *and* popcorn? I never would have believed it. I swallow hard and try to sound casual. "Sure thing. Butter and salt?"

"Yep, the usual. If that's okay with you?"

"It's perfect," Hannah confirms.

"Would you like refills on wine?"

After both women say they'd love it, I grab their empty glasses and head to the adjacent kitchen, while Mom scurries excitedly from the card table to a nearby cabinet where she keeps the backgammon set.

"I've always wanted to learn how to play backgammon," Hannah says behind me.

"I used to play it all the time with my husband, David," Mom says, as I'm crossing the threshold into the kitchen. But rather than enter the heart of the room, I stand at the wall, hidden and eavesdropping, as Mom continues talking. "David and I always loved teasing and taunting each other while playing," she says. "But all in good fun. Let me know if I get too mean, and I promise I'll stop."

Hannah giggles. "Don't tamp down your trash-talking on my account, Carol. My sister and I do the same thing while playing any game. Fair warning, I can give as good as I get."

"Oh, good," Mom says. "Light-hearted teasing makes any game so much more fun, doesn't it? As long as nobody gets *too* mean."

"Agreed. A little light ribbing is the goal. Nobody should be running out of the room bawling over a game of cards or backgammon."

Both women laugh together, causing tears to prick my eyes. I can't believe how light-hearted and happy Mom seems around Hannah. She's like her old self. My heart squeezing, I set the wine glasses on the island and grab the popcorn popper from a cupboard. But when I hear another burst of laughter from the other room, I suddenly feel too overcome by emotion to carry on with my task. Breathing hard, I lean over the kitchen counter and try to pull myself together. The last thing I want to do is walk into that room with tears streaming down my face. Not when Mom's sounding so carefree and happy.

I rub my eyes and glance around the kitchen at the various ghosts of my dad. The one at the kitchen table. Another at the coffee maker. One standing on this very spot, making popcorn. And after a bit, I feel in control of my emotions and able to get back to work.

"Any questions?" Mom is saying to Hannah when I walk into the room bearing popcorn and wine. "Ooooh, that looks delicious. Thank you."

"Can I do anything else for you, ladies?"

"Not for me," Hannah says. And when Mom says the same, I wish them a good night, warn them both to play nice and not get into fisticuffs, and shuffle toward the hallway leading to the bedrooms.

"Oh, wow, that was impressive!" Mom says behind me.

"I can do it from clear across the room," Hannah replies. "It's my superpower."

"Well, this I've got to see!"

I'm assuming Hannah has tossed a popped kernel up and into her mouth—a parlor trick she deftly performs whenever we watch a movie with popcorn. But the excitement in Mom's voice makes me want to see

Mom's reaction to the feat. When I turn around in the entryway to the hall-way, Hannah is getting into position across the room from Mom.

"Your toss doesn't have to be perfect," Hannah says, "but it can't be awful, either. If it's really low or super far away from my head, I won't be able to get there in time."

"I'll do my best," Mom says, grabbing a fistful of popcorn.

"That's all anyone can do, Momma Carol," Hannah says.

Mom vibrates happily at Hannah's endearment and then takes a deep breath like she's poised to throw out the first pitch at the World Series. Finally, after a slow and steady exhale, Mom lobs a popped kernel into the air—and nowhere near my adorable, bespectacled girlfriend's face. Hannah gamely lurches toward the kernel, trying to snag it with her gaping mouth, but it's futile. Superman couldn't have caught that sorry-ass toss.

"I'm so sorry!" Mom says.

"No worries. Try, try again!" Hannah replies.

Another toss. Same result. Rinse and repeat. Until finally, Mom's toss is only sort of terrible, and Hannah deftly scoops up the kernel with her mouth.

"Amazing!" Mom shouts gleefully. And that's it. The ladies are off to the popcorn-catching races in earnest now. In fact, Mom can't get enough. For the next several minutes, I watch from the entryway on the far side of the room, undetected, as Mom tosses kernel after kernel at Hannah, who leaps, zigs, zags, and dives to retrieve anything even remotely near her head. Finally, in a shocking twist I didn't see coming, Hannah coaxes Mom to give it a whirl, despite Mom's protestations that she'd be horrible at it.

"The fun is in the trying," Hannah assures Mom. "Not the actual succeeding."

"Oh, I love that," Mom says. "I should cross-stitch that onto a pillow."

Away they go. For the next few minutes, Hannah throws popcorn kernels at Mom, who misses every single one. And yet, both women guffaw throughout the entire exercise, proving correct Hannah's cross-stitch-worthy comment.

After a while, Hannah moves ridiculously close to Mom and aims a kernel at her gaping mouth with the precision of a sniper, and Mom miraculously catches it, at which point, the women whoop and cheer and hug and then breathlessly tumble into their chairs at the card table.

As the ladies roll to see who'll go first in their backgammon game, I slip into the hallway and head to the guest bedroom, feeling a bit choked up. In the shower, however, I'm able to pull myself together.

Dressed in pajamas, I slide into bed with a laptop, figuring I'll look at some long-ignored Bluebird stuff. With all the fun I've been having with Hannah lately, not to mention all the packing and preparing for her move —and now, this fun road trip—I've barely worked lately, other than doing an incognito favor for Kat's younger brother, Keane, at the request of Josh and Ryan Morgan a few days ago.

I look at the time. With Hannah occupied for at least the next half-hour, maybe even more, now would be a good time to finally poke around the devices of one Greg Smith aka Angus Wellborn aka Sean Goodman. Out of an abundance of caution, I didn't dive in right after the Climb & Conquer party, but instead performed the hack, gathered some basic data to ensure future access if he upgraded devices or whatever, and left it at that. Now that a month has passed, however, I think it's safe to go back in and take a long look around.

There's a laptop and iPad connected to the guy's phone. *Click. Click.* I've now got access to everything. I scroll through his emails and texts and quickly surmise he's been doing what he did to Hannah to countless others. The dude is the second coming of the Tinder Swindler. The good news, of course, is that he's firmly moved on from Hannah. In fact, based on the sheer volume of his atrocities, I think it's fifty-fifty he wouldn't have even recognized Hannah as one of his past victims if he'd seen her at the Climb & Conquer party. Not that I ever would have taken that chance, since Hannah surely would have recognized him and possibly had a massive panic attack.

I poke around some more and determine the target is a personal trainer who works at various big-box gyms under various names. Looks like he's usually the dude assigned to welcome new members, at which point he tries to convince them to buy a package of one-on-one training sessions. When he's successful at that task, some new clients—married women, dudes, law enforcement officers—get nothing but the services they've signed up for. But some of them—young, single women—wind up falling in love and getting scammed. As a side hustle, he also steals credit card numbers from the gym's membership database.

Moving on.

Wow. Greg Smith loves him some conspiracy theories. In fact, he can't get enough of them. He also spends a shit-ton of time playing Call of Duty and watching any video with a "sensitive content" warning. If someone is dying or getting the shit kicked out of them in a video, this idiot wants to see it.

Porn.

Greg Smith is addicted to it. Especially stuff that's degrading toward women, if not downright violent. Does he have some kind of rape-fantasy fetish? If so, has he acted it out or kept it in check? Practically every time I've been hired to prove the accusations made by an alleged victim of sexual abuse, the alleged rapist and/or pedophile—the guy who's typically been screaming his denials at the top of his lungs and is often a pillar of his community—almost always fucks himself by keeping some kind of trophy of his sins. Sometimes, it's photos or videos of himself in the act. Other times, it's of one of his victims in a prone state. At times, it's random child pornography. One way or another, though, they almost always tell on themselves. Has Greg Smith told on himself, too? I look and look, but nope. That kind of thing isn't here. Well, that's a relief.

I notice a phone number Greg's been texting photos and reminders to in a way that suggests it's a second number owned by him, but I can't get into that second phone from here because it's not connected to these other devices. Is it a burner phone? If so, why does he keep it separate? I send the number a phishing text—a link to a cheap penile enlargement pill—and then create a new document entitled "To Do List: Greg Smith."

One, I'll create a host of fake female accounts on Facebook and use them to post Greg's photo in groups dedicated to warning women about scammers, liars, and cheaters. I'll plan to post in ten groups per day, until I run out of them or lose interest. I suppose I could hire Demon Spawn to do some posting for me every day, if I get too bored. Yeah, that's a good idea.

Two, I'll send Greg's photo and evidence of his credit card theft to every major big-box gym in the United States. Hopefully, some of them will contact law enforcement to report him. If they do, it's unlikely anyone will follow up, unfortunately. Romance scammers and identity thieves at

Greg Smith's level don't usually attract a whole lot of robust investigation from frontline resources. But even if law enforcement doesn't wind up giving a shit, I don't want this guy getting hired as a personal trainer at any of the biggest places, ever again. After I've contacted the biggest national gyms, I'll move on to medium- and small-sized gyms, assuming I'm still interested in the project. Or perhaps I'll add that task to Demon Spawn's To Do List, if it comes to that.

Three, I'll slowly mess with Greg's finances. Create a drip-drip-drip of banking errors and miscalculations that will make him feel like there's a hole in his bucket. Sadly, all he'll need to do is open a new account under yet another fake name to elude me for a little while. But I'll find him again, if I feel like it. And when he gets all new devices, I'll hunt him down and hack him again. Next time, even more easily, now that I've got his data.

Four, I'll continue my Used Car Crusade, which Demon Spawn has been diligently implementing for months now, and which I'm more than happy to continue funding, on the off chance my dastardly plan is actually having its intended effect. The chances are low, I know, but it's so fun imagining everything working as planned, I can't resist keeping it going.

Five, I'll send the asshole a phishing link to that burner phone every day of my life, until he ditches it or clicks on my link, all in the name of assuring myself I've turned over every stone. I doubt that phone would reveal any information beyond what I've discovered here, but since I'm a thorough guy, I don't mind persisting on this front.

And that's it. My entire To Do List for Greg Smith, with all tasks intended to administer death by a thousand papercuts over the coming months, until I feel like he's been adequately punished and/or I lose interest.

As I'm typing the last item of my To Do List, the door of the guest bedroom opens, and Hannah appears.

"Hey," I say, abruptly shutting my laptop. "How was backgammon?"

"So fun." After carefully placing her thick glasses and phone onto the nightstand, she crawls on top of the bedspread and snuggles up to me. "Your mom is so funny. You've got her sense of humor."

"In other words, she's a total weirdo?"

"A darling one." She boops my nose. "Just like you."

I laugh. "I wish you could have met my dad. I'm the perfect combination of both of them. He would have loved you so much."

She strokes my arm. "I feel like I met your dad tonight. As we played backgammon, your mom told me all about him. Man, did she love her David."

"And her David loved her. He had the biggest heart." A lump forms in my throat, preventing further speech, so I simply bring Hannah's hand to my cheek and close my eyes. Bringing Hannah here has felt so right. I feel closer to her now than ever.

"Is it hard coming here and seeing all the places he used to be?" she whispers.

"Yeah, but it's awesome, too." I tell her about how Mom and Dad used to eat popcorn and play backgammon every night before bed, and she instantly understands the poignancy of Mom asking her to perform the ritual tonight. In fact, Hannah is so moved, she tears up.

"I feel so honored," she whispers. "I had no idea it was such a big deal."

"My mom already adores you."

"I adore her. How could I not? There's so much of you in her. Or I guess, the other way around." She leans in to kiss me, and soon, we're making out—and then making love, quietly, with both of us giggling every time one of us makes a sound that could conceivably travel to my mother's bedroom across the hall.

When we're done, and Hannah's lying naked in my arms, a palpable serenity washes over me. A sense of peace and rightness. I've known since day one Hannah was meant for me. But seeing her with my mom and getting to witness how seamlessly she fits into my family has taken my certainty to a whole new level. She's The One. Indubitably. The only question now is how long this eager beaver will be able to wait to tell her so on bended knee.

31
HANNAH

"Babe, you were Buffy and that interviewer a vampire," Henn says. It's his way of pumping me up about the job interview I had today with the PR department of a major movie studio. For the past twenty minutes or so, while baking cookies in my new kitchen in LA, I've been telling Henn every detail I can remember about the interview, while Henn offers non-stop words of encouragement.

"The job is as good as yours," Henn declares after I've wrapped up both my storytelling and the task of putting mounds of cookie dough onto cookie sheets.

"If I get the job, I don't know how I'll ever thank Reed for getting me the interview."

"Not to diminish Reed's act of kindness," Henn says, "I don't think it took a whole lot of time or effort on his part. All he had to do was text Isabel and ask her to call the head of the PR department at the studio. I bet Isabel was thrilled to do a favor for Reed. She probably thought it would help her accomplish her dream of making Reed finally fall madly in love with her." From what Henn's told me, Reed's been dating the up-and-coming actress, Isabel Randolph, off and on for several years now, and it's become painfully obvious to everyone but Isabel she's far more invested in the situationship than Reed.

"Even so," I say, "I feel like I should do something nice to thank Reed for helping me so much. This apartment is incredible and even getting to interview for my dream job was a dream come true."

"Babe, you've already thanked him enough, both in person and on Instagram."

I turn on the oven light and peek at the rising cookies in the oven. "Does Reed like chocolate chip cookies? I could make him—"

"Sweetheart, no. Have you seen the man? He'd never risk softening his abs of steel for the fleeting pleasure of a cookie in his mouth. Truly, you've thanked him enough." Henn leaves his bar stool to pull me into his arms and give me a little peck. "If it makes you feel any better, I'll eat the crap outta those cookies."

"Thank you. It does."

Henn kisses my cheek. "Do you want me to hang some more stuff on the walls? I'm feeling kinda handy." He grabs my ass. "Oh, wait. That would be *handsy.*" When I laugh, he squeezes my ass again. "I can't get enough."

"Too late. You already offered and I'm dying to hang those prints from the flea market." I pinch his ass. "But I'll definitely take a rain check on you're handsiness, sir." I put my hands on my hips and look around. "Where did I leave the hammer and nails yesterday, that's the question?"

We search the spacious apartment and finally find the items on a shelf in the hall closet of all places. At my urging, we head to my bedroom next, where I've decided said prints shall go. Where, exactly? I have no idea. For several minutes, Henn asks me which one goes where, and I make him move the frames up and down and over, repeatedly, trying to make my decision. Before I've decided, however, Henn's phone rings—and when he looks at the screen, he says, "Sorry. I should take this." He puts down the framed print in his hands and presses his phone to his ear. "Why, hello there, Captain Morgan. How's it going, sir?"

"Bahwoo?" I say softly, imitating Scooby Doo being offered a Scooby Snack. "Captain Morgan" is the nickname of Kat's tattooed brother, Ryan. So, that's my silly way of saying, basically, "When did Henn meet Ryan?"

Henn chuckles at my goofy reaction—by this time, he understands all my Scooby-Doo-inspired shorthand. Smiling at me, he says to Ryan, "Well, let's just say if I were a superhero in a comic strip, my name would be 'Captain I'm-So-Fucking-Awesome!'" Henn winks at me, confirming *I'm* the source of his awesomeness. The phone still pressed against his ear, Henn takes a seat on the edge of my bed, so I sit next to him. Henn says, "So, I take it you're calling because you're losing your fucking mind about Samantha?"

I pull another Scooby Doo face, this one conveying my confusion about Samantha. *Who's that?*

After pausing to let Ryan talk, Henn says, "Well, first off, you sound like the Energizer Bunny on crack right now. And second off—wait, you're not on crack, are you?" Henn pauses to listen and chuckle. "Oh, good choice. Love that guy. And, second off, when I met you at the Climb & Conquer party, you looked like a man on the verge of a nervous break-down back then, so I can only imagine how perilously close to the edge of the cliff of insanity you're teetering a full four weeks later."

Well, that answers question number one: how Henn met Ryan. It happened at the Climb & Conquer party. Was I on the dance floor when that happened? Probably. I bet Kat made the introduction when I was dancing with Sarah. For a long time, Kat was nowhere to be found.

"Holy shit," Henn says, responding to whatever Ryan has said on his end of the call. "It's been *six* weeks since the party? Wow, time flies."

The timer on my phone goes off, telling me it's time to pull my cookies out of the oven. With a little squeeze of Henn's thigh, I pop up and head into the kitchen where I don oven mitts and pull the sheet pans out, muttering happily to myself about how perfectly the cookies have turned out.

After a few minutes, Henn walks into the adjacent living room and sits on the couch, his phone still pressed against his ear. "Plus, besides all that," Henn says, "Hannah finally moved to LA, so I've been having fun with her. Fun fact: when your amazing girlfriend finally lives in the same city with you, working twenty hours a day doesn't seem nearly as exciting as it used to." He pauses again. "Yeah, thanks, but your happiness for me isn't keeping you from going batshit crazy, is it? You're completely obsessed, aren't you?" Henn pauses. "Yeah, that's what all madmen call it."

I begin transferring my freshly baked cookies to a wire rack for cooling. But midway through my task, my phone pings with an incoming text from Kat, asking for my advice on some jerseys she's planning to give to all guests at her destination wedding in Hawaii next month. Kat says each guest's jersey will be emblazoned with a cute nickname across the back, and she's wondering if she should use "Henn" or something else for Henn's jersey.

Kat: Henn is technically his nickname. But since literally everyone calls him that, it feels more like his actual name. Should I come up with something silly and cute for him?

Me: What about Henny or Peter the Great?

Kat: I like Peter the Great!

Me: Actually, wait. On second thought, don't use that. I only call him that in sexual situations.

Kat: Bwahahaa!! You think that will deter me? Honey, it only seals the deal.

Me: If you use that, he'll know I told you and he'll feel embarrassed to wear it all week in front of everyone.

Kat: Embarrassed to be called great in bed? Pfft.

Me: Henny is shy about stuff like that.

Kat: Okay, fine. I'll use Henny, but only because you're my favorite bridesmaid.

Me: Gasp! What would Sarah say?

Kat: Loophole! She's my matron of honor.

Me: Haha. Clever girl.

I ask Kat how the rest of the wedding planning is going, and Kat calls me, rather than texting the whole thing.

"It's going as easy as pie," Kat says, "thanks to T-Rod being such a fucking superstar." Josh's trusty, longtime personal assistant has taken the laboring oar on the couple's whirlwind wedding planning, including commanding a literal army of wedding planners to bring Josh and Kat's vision to life in record speed. From what Kat's told me, the happy couple quickly settled on hosting a weeklong destination wedding in Maui, with everything for everyone paid for by Josh. But since they also decided to get hitched *before* the arrival of their baby girl, and also with enough time to get back home and nest for a bit before they become parents, that only gave poor T-Rod and her wedding army a two-month window after the proposal to throw the whole thing together.

Kat tells me about some of the exciting activities they've already nailed down for guests to enjoy throughout the exciting week: a helicopter tour of the island, snorkeling, a luau. "And on the second night," Kat says, "right after the luau, Dax's band is going to give everyone a private concert in the dance club at the resort."

"*Everyone?*" I say with notable snark. "Or, mostly, a certain owner of a certain record label?" Apparently, Dax's band's demo ultimately made its way into Reed's hands, thanks to Josh. But as much as Reed loved what he heard, he said he wanted to watch a live performance by 22 Goats before making a decision on signing them. Last I heard from Kat, Reed's been traveling a ton since he first heard the demo and still hasn't gotten around to visiting Seattle.

"You know me so well," Kat says with a snicker. "I figured, hey, if Reed hasn't had time to make it to a 22 Goats show, then I'll bring a 22 Goats show to him."

"Clever girl."

"Oh! I forgot to tell you my wedding dress came in. I'm going to a fitting with my mom and Sarah later today."

"How exciting. I wish so badly I could be there with all of you." These past two weeks in LA have been wonderful. But not living in the same city as Kat anymore has been the only downside. Well, that and being away from Maddy. But when it comes to my sister, I know she'll be moving here soon, so the pain of missing her isn't nearly as acute.

"I wish you could be here, too," Kat says. "Did your bridesmaid dress come in yet?"

"Yep. I've got my fitting in less than an hour, as a matter of fact."

"Oh, good. Sarah and my mom are both getting fittings today, too."

"If we trade photos of everyone, it'll feel like we're all together."

"I'll set up a group chat."

"Perfect. Give your momma and Sarah big hugs for me. I miss them."

"I will. Love you, girlie."

"Love you, too."

After we say our goodbyes, I finish transferring my cookies onto a rack, and when I'm done, I amble into the living room and take a seat next to Henn on the couch, where he's *still* conversing with his new best friend, Ryan Morgan.

Henn says, "Yeah, it looks like it's going to be an amazing week. But that's Josh Faraday for you—he doesn't do parties half-assed." Aw. How cute that my boyfriend's been talking to the bride's brother about the wedding, while I've been talking to the bride about the same topic in the next room.

Henn pauses briefly. And then, "Hey, Ryan? Sorry to cut you off, but didn't you say you left some poor woman with perfect breasts sitting at a table when you called me?"

I make my patented Scooby Doo face again. *Excuse me?* How'd they go from talking about a romantic wedding to Ryan leaving a woman with perfect breasts sitting at a table? I've got whiplash, dudes.

Henn chuckles, but I'm not sure if he's laughing at my expression or something Ryan has said. "Any time, Captain Ahab," Henn says. "Oh, and dude? Let the poor girl down easy. I don't think you realize just how studly you are. You're kind of the shit, man, hate to break it to you. Try to be kind about letting her down."

I smirk. No lie detected there. I've never seen a more traditionally handsome, charming, charismatic man than Ryan "Captain" Morgan. On top of all that, Kat's told me he's been doing quite well for himself as a commercial broker lately, so I'm sure Ryan's got his pick of "perfect breasted" women wherever he may roam.

After ending the call, Henn plops his phone onto my coffee table and grins at me. "That was Kat's brother, Ryan."

"I figured that out. I didn't realize you'd met him at the Climb & Conquer party."

"Yeah, in person, but I'd spoken to him on the phone before that. Jonas had told Ryan about how I'd found Sarah for him, and Ryan was hoping I might do the same for him in relation to a flight attendant he'd met in a bar. They didn't exchange last names or numbers, apparently, but Ryan couldn't get her off his mind."

I snort. "Well, it's no wonder, considering her perfect breasts."

Henn chuckles. "No, the woman with perfect breasts is Ryan's dinner date tonight. I can neither confirm nor deny the perfection of the flight attendant's breasts."

"So, you found the flight attendant for Ryan, and he realized she wasn't everything he'd hoped, and now he's dating a woman with perfect breasts?"

"No, I haven't been able to find the flight attendant for him yet, unfortunately. The woman with perfect breasts came up because Ryan said he's on his first date since meeting the flight attendant almost two months ago, and it's made him realize he doesn't want anyone else but her."

"I'm tempted to say that's adorable and swoony, but I'm going to withhold that comment until I find out how, exactly, perfect breasts came up in that context."

"Ryan said, 'I'm sitting in a restaurant across from a woman with perfect breasts and all I can think about is wanting to see Samantha again.' He sounded pretty tortured."

"Not so tortured he didn't notice his date's perfect breasts."

Henn laughs. "Touché."

"Still, that's a pretty romantic story."

"I think so, too. That's why I told Ryan I'll keep looking for the flight attendant. One way or another, I'll find her."

"Aw, you're such a sweetheart."

"What can I say? I'm a sucker for true love."

I crawl onto Henn's lap and straddle him on the couch. "Add that to the list of things I love about you. Damn, this list is becoming unwieldy. Thoroughly unmanageable." I lean down and kiss him—and predictably, our kiss quickly becomes heated. Which, in turn, leads to full-scale making out. Before our passion leads to actual sex, however, I remember the fitting for my bridesmaid dress. When I look at the time, I've got to go.

"My apologies to your boner," I say. "I have to go to a fitting now."

Henn leans his head back and sighs. "Fitting?"

"For my bridesmaid dress. Remember?"

"Oh yeah. Can I come? Is it bad luck for me to see you in the dress before the big day?"

"I think that only applies to the bride and groom. We're not main characters in this wedding movie, babe. We're not even co-stars."

"We're lowly extras?"

"No, I'd say we're humorous sidekicks."

"I can live with that."

"Me, too."

Henn bites his lip. "Can you imagine yourself as the main character in a wedding movie at some point?"

I bite back a smile. For a while now, I've been able to imagine myself marrying Henn one day, perhaps because finally living in the same city with him has given me some much-needed confirmation that we're as compatible as we seemed when our relationship was long-distance. Also, Kat's excitement about her upcoming wedding has been infectious. Without meaning to do it, I keep finding myself comparing Josh and Kat's choices and selections to ones I'd make when it's *my* turn to get married to Henn.

"I can imagine it pretty clearly, as a matter of fact," I answer coyly.

Henn's eyebrows shoot up. "When you imagine it, is it my face on the groom's body or a question mark?"

I take his hand. "Of course, it's your face. I can't imagine marrying anyone else."

Henn is lit up with excitement. "Okay, baby. When we get back from Josh and Kat's wedding, how about we start seriously looking for a house for me to buy. Whatever I get, I want you to love it as much as I do, so you'll want to move into it with me, eventually."

"I'd love to go house-hunting with you. But, Henny, I'm probably not going to move in with you for at least a year."

"I know. But even after Maddy moves down, you'll sleep at my place a couple times a week, right, and I'll continue sleeping here regularly, too?"

"Of course." I look down at the time. "Shit. I really have to go. I noticed a little Sushi place down the street when I was there last time. If you come with me, we could eat there after my fitting."

"Cool. But only if you promise something." Henn winks. "That we're gonna feast till our stomachs' delight."

32

HANNAH

Am I sleeping?

Is this a beautiful, Hawaiian dream?

Nope. It's real life, bitches! Courtesy of our generous hosts, the soon-to-be Mr. and Mrs. Faraday.

It's the first full day of Josh and Kat's weeklong wedding extravaganza in Maui, and it's already the best vacation of my life. This morning, Josh and Kat and all two hundred of their wedding guests were bussed to the top of a dormant volcano called Haleakala, where we were treated to a sunrise guided bicycle tour down to the bottom. When we returned to the resort, the whole group descended upon the resort's massive swimming pool area for lunch, cocktails, and a bit of relaxation before tonight's festivities. While some went to the main pool, Henn and I headed to the lazy river to float around in innertubes, cocktails in hand, with a group that included Kat, Josh, Reed, Jonas, Sarah, and a few of Josh's and Kat's respective college friends. And that's where we've been ever since. In a few hours, it'll be time to head to the suite to get ready for tonight's luau and subsequent concert by 22 Goats—the rock band fronted by Kat's little brother, Dax, and his two best friends, Colin and Fish. But for now, we're soaking in the Hawaiian sun and enjoying our cocktails and everyone's company.

"Bathroom break!" Sarah calls out next to me from her inner tube. I open my eyes and discern she's talking to her husband, Jonas. Not to me. But her comment makes me realize my bladder is full.

"Wait for me, Sarah! I'll come with you." I try to extricate myself gracefully from my innertube, but wind up inelegantly capsizing. When I come back up, Sarah is cracking up.

"The *Colombiana* judge gives you a ten out of ten," she quips when I reach her on the steps of the lazy river.

"It takes a lifetime of training to be able to do that," I retort.

Laughing together, we head to a nearby restroom and then to a bar by the main pool for another fruity drink, which is when we notice Josh's personal assistant, Theresa Rodriguez—T-Rod—sunbathing alone on a lounge chair.

"Hey, Tessa," Sarah says as we approach her. Sarah gestures to two loungers next to T-Rod's. "Are these open?" T-Rod says they are, and we make ourselves comfortable. Sarah says, "We were taking a bathroom break from floating around the lazy river and saw you lying here all alone."

"Oh, I'm just hanging out, watching the dolphin show." Theresa motions to the large swimming pool in front of us, where all four of Kat's hunky brothers, plus their good friend, Zander, a muscular Black man with an infectious smile, are presently splashing around with a cute little girl. We watch the group for a moment and laugh when their game becomes clear: the little girl is a dolphin trainer and the Morgan brothers, plus Zander, are her pod of eager—and hot as fuck—dolphins performing tricks at her adorable command.

"Who's the little girl?" Sarah asks.

"Coco," Theresa says. "One of the Morgan cousins just married her dad."

"Aw," I say. "Those boys are so sweet to make Coco feel so included."

"The Morgan boys are all really sweet like that," Sarah says, and Theresa nods her agreement.

"Their momma must have taught them well," I say. I'm thinking about Henn's sweet mother, Carol, and how well she's taught her son to be kind and gentle and thoughtful. Surely, if Henn had a cute little step-cousin-in-law who'd recently joined his family, he'd treat her with the same kindness these Morgans are showing Coco.

For several minutes, the three of us watch the dolphin show, commenting and laughing about this or that "trick," as well as Coco's infectious squeak of a voice. But when godlike Ryan Morgan places Coco on the ledge of the pool and coaxes her to jump into his opened, muscular, tattooed arms, we all simultaneously stop talking and gasp at the swoony sight.

"Oh my God, that was hot," I blurt. "Muscles and tattoos and pierced nipples and a leaping, laughing little girl? Jesus God, I suddenly want to grab Henn and drag him to our room."

Sarah snickers. "I used to have the biggest crush on Ryan."

I flash Sarah a Scooby Doo "Bah-w*oo*?" face, and she chuckles and shrugs. "Ryan's gorgeous."

No lie detected there. I return my gaze to the pool, where the hunky Morgan brothers are now throwing their tiny dolphin trainer to and fro like a beach ball, and ask, "How the heck did you pick just *one* Morgan brother to have a crush on? They're all freaks of nature, just like Kat. Freaks, freaks, freaks. It's not fair how much hotness is contained within one family. I feel like I'm watching that volleyball scene from *Top Gun,* only *way* better." After the other two women agree with my assessment, I ask Sarah, "Does Ryan know about your old crush on him?"

"Hellz no," Sarah replies. "I never said a word. I did tell Kat about it at the time and asked her to find out if maybe he was interested in taking me out, but she refused."

"Why?" I ask, astonished. It's not the reaction I'd expect from Kat, considering how much she loves both Sarah and matchmaking.

Sarah rolls her eyes. "Kat said Ryan would break my heart and then it would be weird at birthday parties and stuff." She explains in further detail, concluding with, "Imagine how weird it'd be now if we *had* gone out."

"Plus, think about the butterfly effect," I reply. "What if dating Ryan back then would have somehow kept you from meeting Jonas when you did."

"I shudder to think about it," Sarah says. "Nowadays, Ryan feels like a brother to me—the same as Josh or Henn. He's objectively gorgeous, of course—I mean, just look at him—but the minute I met Jonas, I instantly knew the difference between having a crush on a guy, even a massive one, and meeting the true love of my life. Once you've finally experienced true love, there's just no comparison."

At Sarah's words, my heart floods with love for Henn—with certainty that he's the love of my life. My soulmate. In fact, I'm suddenly realizing I'm ready for Henn to ask me to marry him when we get home. We wouldn't have to have a whirlwind engagement like Jonas and Sarah and Kat and Josh did, and we don't need to live together to be engaged. So, why wait?

It's a surprise to be feeling this way, but there's no denying it. Is my biological clock suddenly going off because of the giggling cutie pie playing dolphin in the swimming pool? Have I had too many mai tais today? Has this week's dreamlike wedding extravaganza inspired me? Whatever has brought me to this point, I'm positive it's real and what I genuinely want. I want to be engaged to Henn when we get home and then ultimately to have the kind of happy marriage Jonas and Sarah do. The kind Josh and Kat will undoubtedly have, as well.

I smile at Sarah. "You and Jonas are so amazing. Hashtag-relationship-goals."

"You and Henny, too," she replies. "I predict you'll be following in Jonas' and my footsteps before long."

Am I that transparent? "Oh, for sure," I say, and as the words leave my lips, I'm certain I mean them.

"Really?" Sarah says, sitting upright in her lounge chair. "Have you two talked about marriage?"

I feel myself blush. "Yeah, right after I caught the bouquet at your wedding, Henny and I talked about it. And a couple times after that, too. We're definitely going to get married. The only question is when." I explain that my sister is coming to UCLA in the spring and I'm going to live with her for at least a while. Also, that Henn has decided to start looking for a house in LA when we get back and has invited me to move into it with him, whenever I'm ready.

"Well, whenever you guys decide to get engaged," Sarah says, "maybe Tessa would be willing to share some of her amazing spreadsheets with you. Before helping Josh and Kat with their wedding, she helped Jonas and me find some vendors quickly, too." She smiles at Theresa lying next to her. "Tessa is such a superstar."

We both look at Theresa, but she's clearly distracted by the Morgan brothers' shenanigans in the pool.

"Hey, T-Rod," I say, prompting her to look at me and blink rapidly. "I keep noticing Kat and Sarah and Mrs. Morgan calling you Tessa. And yet it seems like Josh and Henn and all those guys keep calling you Theresa. Do you have a preference?"

"Tessa, honestly," she says. "That's what my friends and family have always called me."

"Okay, then. Tessa it is." I'm hoping she understands the subtext of my comment. Namely, that I consider her a friend. I don't know Theresa—er, *Tessa*—all that well, but she was incredibly friendly with me at Jonas and Sarah's wedding, and I've only heard good things about her from Kat. I think it might prove difficult for Tessa to fully relax this week, given that she's a guest of her longtime boss and probably used to scurrying off to deliver on Josh's every instruction, so I want to make it abundantly clear she's more than welcome to join our friend group as a full-fledged member.

In response to my comment, Tessa smiles gratefully at me, which makes me think she's understood my intended meaning and is grateful for it.

A squeal of happiness pulls our attention. It's Coco in the pool. She's sitting atop Ryan Morgan's broad shoulders while battling Keane and Zander in a splashing, chaotic game of chicken.

"Oh my God," I say. "My left ovary exploded when the Morgan brothers played dolphin—and now my right ovary's gone, too."

"He's so freaking hot," Tessa whispers.

"Yep," Sarah agrees.

"A man who loves kids," I murmur. "Gets me every time."

With a high-pitched growl, Coco pushes on Keane's chest with all her little might, and the totem pole that is Keane and Zander topples backward dramatically into the pool. As Keane and Zander punch the surface of the water like sore losers, Ryan guides a giggling Coco to standing atop his broad shoulders like a cheerleader, his strong hands gripping her calves.

Once he's got Coco safely situated, Ryan takes his tiny teammate on a victory lap around the shallow end of the pool.

When Ryan and Coco's victory tour makes its way to our side of the massive pool, Tessa, Sarah, and I applaud and cheer effusively.

"Hey, ladies," a male voice says.

I look to my right and discover the source of the voice. It's Reed Rivers. He's standing before us, shirtless and in swim trunks. *Good lord.* At this rate, Henn is going to get a workout this afternoon.

Reed pulls up a chair and sits down, his dark gaze noticeably raking over the length of Tessa's bikini-clad body before landing on me. He flashes me a polite smile—one that bears no resemblance to the wolf-like smolder he just flashed Tessa—and asks me how I'm liking my new apartment in LA.

"Oh, I love it," I say. "Thank you so much for the amazing deal you're giving me on the place. I can't thank you enough, Reed."

Reed replies to me the way he always does—by politely insisting it was nothing and I've already thanked him enough. "Congratulations on the new job," he says. "When do you start?"

"A couple weeks after we get back from Maui. It's yet another reason I'm indebted to you. Thank you for passing along my résumé. It's my dream job."

Reed mumbles something, but he's obviously distracted by the sight of Tessa in her black string-bikini. I can't say I blame him. She's distracting to me, and I've never known myself to be sexually attracted to women before. But who wouldn't want to tap that? Theresa Rodriguez is a supernatural, sensuous, head-turner.

When Reed's gaze remains on T-Rod, I smirk at Sarah and tilt my head toward the lazy river. Obviously, Reed didn't come over here to chat with me about my new apartment and dream job. He's got something else on his mind.

"And what about you, T-Rod?" Reed asks. "Are you having fun so far?"

"Oh, yes. I'm having a blast. I thought it'd be hard for me to relax and be a guest this week, but as it turns out, it's shockingly easy." She holds up her drink by way of explanation and Reed chuckles.

Reed leans back in his chair, giving the three of us women a delightful view of his tanned, tattooed torso. "So, hey, T-Rod, I wanted to chat with you about the logistics for my surprise gift at the reception."

"Oh, yeah, I got your text. Having that musician play shouldn't be a problem. I've already got a crew coming for tonight's concert, so I'll ask them—" She abruptly stops talking when Josh and Kat, along with a small group that includes Henn, approach. Clearly, Tessa doesn't want the bride and groom to overhear any details about Reed's surprise wedding gift, and since I have no desire to be a cockblocker to Reed Rivers a second longer, I jump up, poised to blurt that Sarah and I will distract the oncoming group and lead them away.

Sarah beats me to the punch, though. "I'll drag them to that bar over there," Sarah says, leaping up. "Come on, Hannah Banana—help me lure them away."

Oh, thank God. I salute Reed and wink at Tessa, before following Sarah toward the oncoming group. When Sarah reaches Kat and Josh, I can't hear what she says to them, but whatever it is, it works. Suddenly, the entire group, other than Henn who's stopped to wait for me, is now following Sarah.

"Hey, Peter the Great," I say, taking his hand. He pivots like he's going to follow the crowd, but I pull on his hand. "Nope. We're not going that way."

"We're not?"

"I mean, we can, if you'd prefer to have a drink with our friends, rather than having some hot vacation sex in our bungalow."

Henn doesn't hesitate. "I think I'll take door number two, please."

33

HENN

It's Day Four of Josh and Kat's weeklong wedding extravaganza, and I'm having the time of my life. How could I not, when I'm in paradise with Hannah and my best friends and every meal, cocktail, and entertainment has been arranged and paid for?

Already this week, we've enjoyed a jaw-dropping array of activities: a sunrise bike ride down a volcano, snorkeling, a helicopter tour of the island, a luau, karaoke, horseback-riding, kayaking, ATV-ing, relaxation by the pool and in the resort's lazy river. We also watched a private concert in the resort's club by Dax's band, 22 Goats, that was so fucking awesome, Reed immediately signed them to his label. Verbally, anyway. Legal paperwork to come, apparently. And we've still got three days left! Plus, Hannah and I are going to Kuai for five days after this. Talk about a dream vacation. I don't think I've ever felt so relaxed and happy as an individual or as a couple. Hannah and I have been glued at the hip this whole week and loving every minute.

Today was the first time Hannah and I have spent any substantial time apart, actually, because Hannah had a spa day with the bride and a gaggle of bridesmaids. As Hannah did her thing today, I went parasailing over the ocean with a group that included Josh, Jonas, a couple fraternity brothers, and the two oldest Morgan brothers—Ryan and Colby.

I picked parasailing for today's activity, instead of jet skiing with Reed and a group that included the boys from 22 Goats, because I knew Hannah wants to go jet skiing with me in Kuai. It turned out to be a good choice. My group had so much fun together, in fact, a sub-group of us—Josh, Jonas, Ryan, Colby, and me—headed to a bar at the resort afterward to throw back some pre-dinner drinks. That's what we're still doing now, a full hour later.

Currently, we're talking about sex. Not specifically in terms of sex we've personally enjoyed. That'd be an awkward topic in this group, given that Josh's sex partner these days is Colby and Ryan's little sister. No, we've been talking about the fact that our generation seems obsessed with unlocking the mysteries of the female orgasm in a way our forefathers didn't appear to be. We've all agreed that shift probably has a lot to do with the internet—the sheer volume of information out there now. We've also agreed it's a frustrating thing that so much of the information out there is faulty, unreliable, or dead-ass wrong.

"I sometimes think Colby and I should do the world a favor and make an instructional video about this technique we came up with," Ryan says. "Once we perfected it, we told the younger guys about it, and it worked like a charm for them, too. We've all gotten it so dialed in at this point, we call it The Sure Thing."

Colby chuckles. "As Keane likes to say, it makes women have honey bunches of O's."

Everyone chuckles.

"I'd definitely watch a video about that," I say. "And I'm sure I'm not alone. I bet it'd go viral."

Colby scoffs. "Speaking for myself, I've got no desire to become the viral face of The Sure Thing. The guys at the firehouse would razz me about it till the end of time. No thanks."

"I've got no desire to be The Sure Thing Guy, either" Ryan says. "I want to become a respected business mogul like Josh and Jonas here, not a fucking internet sex guru."

"You know who'd make a perfect internet sex guru?" Josh says. "*Keane*. With that face of his and the crazy way he talks, he'd be a natural."

Colby says, "Actually, it'd make perfect sense for a male stripper called Peen Star to talk about sex online."

"Some of those YouTubers make bank," I chime in. "Like, millions per year." I don't know Keane. I haven't even chatted with the dude one-on-one this week. But Kat told me her younger brother turned to stripping after an elbow injury dashed his baseball dreams, and I'm rooting for him from afar to find his groove again.

Ryan chuckles and addresses his older brother. "Bee, you're high if you think Keane has the attention span to run a fucking YouTube channel. That kid can barely remember to check his texts on a daily basis. Oh, and by the way, Keane's stripper name isn't Peen Star anymore. He recently changed it to Ball Peen Hammer for some reason."

I flash Ryan a secret smile. The man's a true gent. When Ryan and Josh called me recently and asked me to help extract Keane from a "stripper predicament," we all agreed the situation was on a strict need-to-know basis, especially regarding my identity as the hacker who'd stepped in to help. Apparently, Ryan is so damned trustworthy, he didn't even tell Colby about the situation, since I know for a fact Ryan knows precisely why Keane changed his stripper name.

What happened is this: one of Keane's clients—a much older woman who'd hired Keane to dance and strip at a small, private party—thereafter decided she basically owned the kid. According to Ryan, Keane had been perfectly willing to let said older woman treat him like a sex slave for one crazy night of weird, kinky fun. Why not? Keane's a horny, single, twenty-three-year-old, and life is short. But see, for Keane, it was a one-time lark. A curiosity, never to be repeated. Not so much for the older woman. Apparently, she had so much fun that night, she decided she wanted it to become a regular thing, at her pleasure and on command. When Keane refused, she went ballistic. Threatened to ruin his life and fledgling stripper career with false accusations of inappropriate behavior and coercion.

Lucky for Keane, an anonymous hacker friend of Josh's—cough, cough, *me*—swooped in and saved Keane's stupid, horny ass by easily infiltrating the woman's devices, getting some nasty dirt on her, and making it clear she had no choice but to leave the kid alone or else. And that was that. Just like that, Keane got a clean slate and fresh start. He smartly changed his stripper name, switched to a more reputable booking agent, and vowed he'd never do anything to get himself into a similar jam again. At least, that's what Ryan told me on the boat today when we were awaiting our turn to parasail.

A cocktail waitress appears with another round of drinks, and we all thank her and dive in.

"So, what exactly is The Sure Thing?" Jonas asks. "A fingering technique, or . . .?"

"Yeah, though it starts with oral and ends with penetration," Ryan says. As we all hang on his every word, Ryan describes the technique in astounding detail, which, in essence, hinges on finding and manipulating a woman's "A-spot"—a spot that's apparently deep inside a woman and in a different place than her G-spot—to the point where she ultimately experiences a cascading domino effect of full-bodied orgasms that leave her "speaking in tongues" and quite possibly "bursting into tears of sheer ecstasy." In other words, these Morgan boys have apparently figured out how to give a woman the same orgasmic experience as a fucking Sybian, without the need for a power cord or dildo. Hot damn.

"Jesus Christ," Jonas murmurs, taking the words right out of my mouth.

"If you do it right, she'll have at least three orgasms in a row, each one more intense than the last," Ryan says. "And then, when you finally go in with penetration, she'll come again while you're inside her, and you'll both basically pass out."

We all stare at each other, momentarily rendered speechless.

Jonas breaks the silence. "Is it really a sure thing? It works *literally* every time?"

"Once you get it going, yeah," Ryan replies. "To be fair, it can take a little trial and error to figure it out at first, especially with a new partner. But once you get it going, yeah, it's a sure thing. To be clear, it's not the kind of thing you'd want to do every time you have sex with someone. Leave it for now and again, special occasions, because it's pretty exhausting for both people. Plus, you don't want to turn it into the usual, or it might lose its effectiveness."

"Interesting," Jonas says. "How many orgasms in a row is your record?"

"Eight," Ryan says, and the whole table collectively gasps.

"Five for me," Colby says. "But even that was plenty wild."

Jonas and I ask a bunch of questions, which Ryan answers with an occasional assist from Colby. Ryan concludes with, "The point isn't *quantity* of orgasms, even though she's definitely gonna have a bunch. It's *quality*. The point is giving her the most intense O's of her life. Do that, and she'll become addicted to you in a way she's never been with anyone else."

"Sign me up," Jonas says, chuckling.

"Me, too," I say. "Holy fuck."

It's suddenly obvious our normally gregarious Joshua hasn't said a word in a very long time, but instead has been sitting in uncharacteristic, awkward silence, sipping his drink this whole time. Obviously, Josh is in the unenviable position of listening to Ryan's amazing spiel . . . while thinking about using the technique on Ryan's little sister.

Jonas nudges his brother's shoulder. "Having fun, Joshua?"

"So much fun."

As we all crack up, my phone buzzes with an incoming text from Hannah.

> Hannah: I'm back in the bungalow. Wanna come here for a pre-dinner cocktail?

> Me: I'm having cocktails with a fun group. Wrangle Kat and Sarah and join us. We're in the bar by the main pool.

> Hannah: Sweetie, I've been drinking rum punch all afternoon while listening to Kat's crazy stories about her sexual escapades with Josh. "Come have a cocktail" was code for "come put your cock inside me."

> Me: Coming now.

As I look up from my phone, I try my best to look normal. Unhurried and nonchalant and not like a dude who's growing a boner underneath the table. "I think I'm gonna head to my room for a bit," I say. "Hannah's back from the spa and wants to chill with me before dinner."

Everyone at the table chuckles and/or snickers. Apparently, despite my best efforts, my excitement is written all over my face.

As I rise from the table with my hands clasped in front of me to hide my growing hard-on, Josh raises his glass to me. "Godspeed, Henny. Hopefully, The Sure Thing will live up to its name for you."

34
HENN

When I try to enter our bungalow with two rum punches, the front door cracks only a few inches, thanks to the security bar being latched on the inside.

"Room service!" I call out playfully through the crack. "I've got a cocktail and a cock for you, ma'am!"

The door abruptly slams shut. There's the sound of the security bar being unlatched. And then, Hannah is standing before me in the doorway in a slinky, red sundress I've never seen before—one that features a low neckline that wildly accentuates her gorgeous cleavage and spaghetti straps that show off her sun-kissed shoulders to maximum effect.

"Wow," I murmur. Hannah has looked incredibly sensuous and sexy to me this entire week, but thanks to whatever she did at the spa this afternoon and the way that dress clings to her, she's looking even sexier than usual.

"Mr. Bond," Hannah says in a clipped German accent. "I should have known you'd follow me to Maui, given the sensitive information I've recently acquired."

A wide smile spreads across my face. I'm not sure what's prompted her to reprise her role as Zelda the Foreign Operative, but obviously, I'm thrilled to play along. "Hello, Zelda," I say, adopting my best James-

Bondian accent. "It took me a while to track you down. You're quite the world traveler. But I've heard tell of the information you're harboring, and I knew it was my duty to extract it from you, at all costs."

Hannah giggles and widens the door. "Come in. May zhe best spy win."

Inside the room, I offer her one of the rum punches, and we clink and guzzle half our beverages before placing our cups down and falling into a giddy embrace.

"That dress is fire," I murmur, falling completely out of character. "Wow, Hannah."

"I saw it in the window at the gift shop and couldn't resist. You don't think my boobs look too front-and-center in it?"

"There's no such thing as *too* front-and-center. They look like the stars of the show, as they deserve to be."

When she leans in and kisses me again, I reach behind her and unzip the dress, causing its front to fall forward and off. I slide her shoulder straps down, and, suddenly, I'm staring at two mouthwatering headlights accentuated by the new tan lines Hannah has acquired over the past few days of fun in the sun. I pull on the dress, sending it crumpling onto the floor, and then dive head-first into Hannah's cleavage.

As I devour her, Hannah runs her hands through my hair. "I want you to tie me up," she purrs. "Tease and torture me into telling you all my biggest secrets."

I look up, shocked. The last time we role-played, Hannah balked at being tied up because, she said, she's not willing to surrender complete control of her body. So, what's changed?

Hannah smiles wickedly. "A few of Kat's wild stories inspired me to want to expand my horizons a bit." She touches my cheek. "I trust you, Henny. I know I'm in the best possible hands. I'm ready to experience complete surrender."

I don't know what I did in a past life to deserve a gift this epic—and mere minutes after Ryan Morgan gave me detailed instructions for giving Hannah "honey bunches of O's" with my fingers, culminating in experiencing her all-body orgasm while burrowed inside her. But, hey, whatever it was, I'm deeply grateful to my past incarnation. I take a deep breath. "I'm always game to do anything you want. I love you so much."

"I love you, too." Her eyebrow quirks up. "Back in character, okay?"

I nod and assume my stupid accent. "Mark my words, Zelda, by the time I'm finished with you, I'm going to know *all* your secrets."

"Ha! Impossible. But give it zhe best attempt."

I finish undressing her and then guide her onto the bed. "Wait here," I command, before striding around our hotel suite in search of something to tie her with, as well as proper implements of torture. We didn't pack any sex toys or bindings for our trip to paradise, but it doesn't take me long to gather substitutes.

I use belts to bind Hannah's wrists to the headboard and two of her long sundresses for her ankles, and then pull off my clothes and stand before her, my cock hard and my chest heaving. During Ryan's explanation about The Sure Thing, he emphasized the importance of anticipation. Taking one's time. Keeping her guessing. Also, using lots of dirty-talk and compliments. So, I follow his every instruction to a tee.

"You look fucking incredible," I say, ditching my fake accent.

"So do you," she whispers.

I'm not a perfect specimen, like the dudes I had drinks with earlier. I often joke I've got "heating pad abs," instead of "six-pack" ones. But the look in Hannah's eyes makes me feel like I'm a golden god in her eyes— like she's as genuinely turned-on by the sight of me as I am by the sight of her.

I grab an ice cube from one of the rum punches and run it across her belly and inner thighs, before licking up the trail of liquid it leaves behind. From there, I kiss and lick the sensitive flesh between her legs, taking great care to avoid her actual bull's-eye for now.

When Hannah begins writhing and pulling against her straps with increasing enthusiasm, I decide she's ready for some direct stimulation. I flicker my tongue against her hard, swollen tip, teasing her, and she moans far more loudly than I would have expected. Wow.

I lean in and blow on her clit before licking her in earnest, and as she moans and purrs, I slide my fingers inside her and massage her G-spot. Holy shit, in no time at all, Hannah's innermost muscles begin rippling against my fingers. It's not the spot Ryan described, but it's only round one, and I'm pretty sure I'm doing this right. So far, so good.

I crawl up to Hannah's face and whisper, "Your secrets will be mine,

Zelda," before kissing her passionately. As we kiss, I caress her breasts. Stroke her hip bone. And then brush my fingers gently against her slit, up and down. I begin a steady stream of dirty talk, as instructed. I tell her she's delicious. Looks hot. That she turns me on and drives me crazy and I can't get enough. And when she's gyrating and writhing against her bindings and purring in near-desperate anticipation, I take a deep breath and decide it's time to go for it. I'm not positive I can find Hannah's A-spot on my first try or stroke it exactly the way Ryan described to maximum effect, but I'm sure as hell going to try my best.

While whispering a steady stream of compliments into Hannah's ear, I slide my fingers inside her, and to my surprise, quickly find the seam Ryan described. It's at the farthest reaches inside her, and thanks to her extreme arousal, it's swollen and wet as hell. I move my fingers the way Ryan described, over and over again, stroking the supposedly magical spot without mercy or variation as I await clear signs from Hannah's body that she's teetering on the bitter edge, like Ryan described.

Suddenly, I'll be damned, a sharp tightness seizes around my hand— and then a violent internal shudder that suggests Hannah's deepest core muscles are on the cusp of contracting and then releasing in explosive fashion. As my fingers move inside Hannah, they're beginning to make a sort of sloshing sound, thanks to her insane level of arousal. This is unreal. I feel high.

Despite my skyrocketing excitement, I manage to stay the course and follow instructions. I whisper to Hannah that I've never been this turned on before, which is true. I tell her she's so fucking delicious, I almost lose it every time I eat her out. Also, true. And after a few more minutes of steady, concerted manipulation of that same spot, Hannah arches her back, keens like a wild animal, and comes with a loud roar. I've only heard her roar like that once before—when she rode a Sybian for me months ago. But, wow, I must admit it's way hotter, and far more gratifying, to hear that reaction as a result of something *I* did to her with zero assistance from a machine with a fake dick and a power cord.

When Hannah comes down from her pleasure, she begs me to fuck her. Ryan said that often happens. He said most guys mess up at this point because they're too turned on to resist giving their woman exactly what she's begging for. "Tell her no and stay the course, and you'll both be handsomely rewarded later on," Ryan said.

"Not yet," I force myself to say, even though my body is on fire, and I want nothing more than to plunge myself inside Hannah now. My breathing ragged, I crawl between her legs and lick her, making her moan and pull against her bindings. When she seems like she's on the right path again, I commence The Sure Thing again, from the very beginning. And once again, exactly like Ryan said, Hannah has another orgasm. This one, far quicker than the last one. It's also more forceful than the last, apparently, based on the way Hannah's now babbling incoherently and whimpering.

Again, Hannah begs me to fuck her. This time, desperately. But somehow, I find the willpower to stay the course and go through the steps again. And when Hannah comes the next time, she bursts into tears of pure ecstasy. *Well, I'll be damned.*

Practically panting with arousal, I release Hannah's bindings, place a pillow underneath her lower back, and sink myself deep inside her. As my body invades hers, Hannah growls and squeezes my ass, while I grunt and groan and begin fucking her more aggressively than I've ever done before. Oh my god, I'm fucking Hannah with everything I've got, and she's receiving me the same way—moving her pelvis to maximize my movements. Gripping my ass like a lifeline. We're in a frenzy of heat, both of us hurtling together toward white-hot bliss.

I press my lips to Hannah's ear and whisper that she's all mine. Every inch of her. That I'm taking what I want from her, because she belongs to me. It's not stuff I'd typically say. I'm far more inclined to tell her I'm all hers, that she can have all of me. But in the midst of our role-play, these sentiments feel like the thing to say. Or maybe I'm discovering a new side of myself, the same way Hannah says she does with me.

"Oh, God," Hannah blurts, and a second later, powerful waves of pleasure begin clenching my cock, catapulting me into the most intense release of my life. It feels so fucking good, I think I'm in serious danger of losing consciousness.

I collapse on top of Hannah, breathing hard, and she exhales loudly underneath me like she just crossed the finish line of a full-length marathon.

"How the fuck did you do that to me?" she says. "Oh my God, Henn."

"The name is Bond. James Bond." I roll off her onto my back and try to catch my breath. "That's the torture technique they taught us at . . . British Spy School. What's that called?"

"M16."

"That's right. That's what they taught us at M16 for fucking state secrets out of sexy foreign operatives."

Hannah snuggles up to me and slides her thigh across my pelvis. "Well, the technique is wildly effective. I suddenly feel powerless to keep my biggest secret from lurching out of me."

Hannah didn't use her silly accent when saying that, so I don't use mine in reply. "Do tell."

Hannah runs her fingertip across my bare chest. "I'm ready to get engaged to you, when we get back to LA. Honestly, I'm excited to take that next step with you."

My heart is exploding in my chest. This is the best thing she could have said to me. Also, a total surprise. I don't know what I thought she was going to say, but it certainly wasn't that.

"I'm thrilled to hear it," I say. "Are you sure?"

She smiles and nods. "I wouldn't want a quickie wedding. I'd want to be engaged for a while, since I've promised to live with Maddy for the foreseeable future."

"Fine by me."

"But I'm not scared of marriage anymore, Henn. I'm not even neutral about it. I'm excited to get engaged when we get back to LA, and then marry you one fine day." She lifts her head. "Is that what you want, too?"

"You know it is."

"Just checking." She smirks. "To be clear, I'm not hereby proposing to you. I'm asking you to propose to me, if that's what you'd like to do."

I laugh. "Thanks for the clarification, but I figured that out. If what you're really saying is you'd prefer for me to do it right—with a ring and all the bells and whistles—then don't worry, that's exactly what you'll get."

Hannah squeals. "Really?"

"Yep. And then, I'll be perfectly happy being engaged for a while. No rush."

She kisses my cheek. "Thank you! This way, I can get settled in my new job and have fun living with Maddy for however long, and *then* we'll start thinking about planning a wedding and moving in together."

"Awesome. When we get back, I'll start looking for a house in earnest, like we talked about. Something you'll love as much as I do. And you'll have a standing invitation to move in with me, whenever you want."

"But first, you're going to propose to me."

"Right. I got that part."

"Thank you."

I laugh. "No, thank *you.*"

Hannah beams a breathtaking smile at me. "My life feels like a dream." She runs her fingertip across my lip. "I love you so much. Thank you for always being so understanding, Henny."

"Who the bollocks is *Henny*? I'm Bond. James Bond. And like I warned you, Zelda, you never stood a chance."

35

HENN

"How many cards, Zander?" Josh asks, chewing on the end of his cigar. Besides Josh and the Morgan's honorary brother, Zander, our group for poker tonight is comprised of Jonas, Reed, Ryan, a couple fraternity brothers, and me. We're playing poker in Josh's bungalow on the night before his big wedding day as a spontaneous bachelor party of sorts. It's hard to say this is *the* bachelor party, however, since the whole week in Maui has been one long, amazing party.

"Three," Zander replies, tossing his cast-offs toward Josh, our current dealer.

"How are you feeling on your last night as a free man, Josh?" Jonas asks.

Electricity shoots through me. Now that Hannah's told me she's ready to get engaged, any mention of marriage—which happens a lot during a destination wedding—hits me like a thunderbolt. I can't wait to get home and start planning my proposal in earnest. Should I do it at The Griffith Observatory, where they filmed *Lala Land*?

"I'm feeling like a kid on Christmas Eve," Josh replies to his brother. "Oh, hey, by the way, Kat doesn't want me to see her on our wedding day till she walks down the aisle in her dress, so can she sleep with Sarah tonight and you sleep here?"

"Yeah, Sarah already told me," Jonas says. "It's fine. I mean, not sleeping with my wife tonight is a huge sacrifice, but I'll consider it one of my wedding gifts to you."

Josh scoffs. "It's your wedding gift to Kat and Kat alone. I don't want these stupid sleeping arrangements any more than you do."

Jonas chuckles. "Happy wife, happy life. It's the key to the kingdom."

Wife.

There it is again. That same thunderbolt of excitement and anticipation.

"Yo, Henn, it's your bet," Reed says, yanking me from my thoughts.

I look down at my cards for the first time. "Yeah, yeah, I know—I'm thinking." Damn. My cards suck. "Why'd you have to deal me such shitty cards, Joshua? I'm out, thanks to your piss-poor card dealing."

Reed shoves a stack of chips into the pot with a gleeful smile. "Looks like Mr. Faraday dealt me all your good cards, Henny-Baby."

"Bah, you're bluffing," Josh says. "I can read you like a book, Rivers —and it's clear to me you've got nuttin'." Josh shoves a bunch of chips into the kitty to match Reed's. "You might have a Midas touch when it comes to selling music to the masses, but you're about to become my little bitch when it comes to cards."

"I guess we'll find out soon enough who's the little bitch, won't we?" Reed quips.

My mind races back to the Faraday brothers' exchange a moment ago —the one about sleeping arrangements for tonight—and I'm reminded of something Hannah told me: she'll be spending all day tomorrow dressing and primping with Kat, Kat's mom, and the other bridesmaids before the wedding at sunset. When Hannah told me that, I figured I'd go snorkeling or kayaking with Reed and whoever, since getting ready for me will take all of twenty minutes. But suddenly, I'm realizing tomorrow would be the perfect opportunity for me to buy a ring for Hannah and pull together a proposal for tomorrow night. There are lots of stars in the sky here in Maui on a clear night, and we've already re-enacted *Lala Land* in Seattle. So, why not seize the opportunity to give Hannah a romantic proposal under the stars on a tropical beach?

"No need to thank me," Reed says when I tune back into the table's conversation. He's speaking to Ryan Morgan across the table. Reed adds, "I didn't do it as a favor. I did it because I like making truckloads of money off of great music and your brother checks off all the boxes." Ryan must have thanked Reed for signing his brother's band while my mind was wandering.

Ryan says, "Well, regardless, I still feel the need to express my personal gratitude to you. I would have hated to be stuck on an island for a week with Dax if you'd turned him down."

Their conversation continues for a bit, with Reed eventually divulging T-Rod unexpectedly played an instrumental role in convincing him to sign 22 Goats. Reed explains, "She was pretty passionate about the topic, that's for sure. And she was right, actually. I must say, the girl's got good instincts."

I'd normally find this topic of interest, I think. *But not right now.* Not when I'm practically bursting into flames of excitement about possibly proposing to Hannah tomorrow night. I wouldn't steal Josh and Kat's thunder, of course. I'd do it once the reception was in full swing, long after the ceremony. I'm positive Josh would be thrilled with the idea, but what about Kat? So far, she seems like the chillest bride, ever. Jonas and Sarah were certainly on board for me to propose at *their* wedding reception, so I'd think it's likely Josh and Kat would feel the same way.

Reed laughs sharply, distracting me from my racing thoughts. He says to Josh, "Why you always gotta be such a hard ass about your precious little assistant, Faraday? You're assuming I'd be a total dick to her. Maybe I wouldn't be. Maybe T-Rod would be the girl who finally slays my demons, once and for all. Maybe she'd *save* me, man."

I can't resist pushing back on that line of bullshit. "Not bloody likely," I quip, and everyone at the table laughs. I add, looking at Reed, "That's not a knock on T-Rod's demon-slaying capabilities, by the way, but a commentary on the virility of your particular strain of demon."

Reed scoffs. "Bah. I'm a total softie, deep down." He winks at me and then slides a stack of poker chips into the pot. "Raise you a hundred."

"You're not a softie, bro," Josh retorts. "A great guy? Yes. The best friend, ever? For sure. But a softie? Hell no. Your bet, Zander."

Poor Zander looks stressed. Clearly, the bets in this poker game are getting way too rich for his blood. At the opening cocktail party that kicked off this week, someone mentioned Zander being a personal trainer —and not a celebrity one in LA or whatever. Nope, he's just an ordinary guy who shares an apartment in Seattle with his lifelong best friend, a male stripper who makes his rent one crinkled dollar at a time. It stands to reason, then, that card players like Josh and Reed aren't anywhere close to Zander's usual poker crowd.

"I'll spot you whatever you need to stay in, Z," Ryan says.

"Thanks, Captain. Much obliged."

"No, no, Captain," Josh says, still chewing on his cigar. "Zander's bets are on me tonight."

"No, I got him," Ryan insists. "He's my brother."

Josh waves Ryan off again. "Then he's mine, too. Keep your money, Ry. I've got him. I've had some massive poker losses to Reed over the years that I want to vicariously avenge." Josh slides a mammoth stack of chips over to Zander. "Get him, Z. Make him cry."

"Jesus, I'm getting it from all sides," Reed mumbles, but his tone is playful.

Zander thanks Josh profusely and immediately shoves all his newly acquired chips into the pot to match and then raise Reed's bet.

"I like your style, Z," Reed says. "But, seriously, Faraday, why are you always so damned protective of T-Rod? She's a big girl. Let her make her own decisions. If I take a shot and it doesn't work out, I promise I won't leave her any worse for wear. In fact, even if her heart gets smashed into a thousand pieces, I promise she'll nonetheless thank me for the ride."

For the first time during this playful banter, Josh looks genuinely irritated with Reed, though he manages to keep his tone relaxed and playful. "I'm not gonna risk anyone taking a shot with her and smashing her heart, motherfucker. She's like a sister. Plus, on a selfish note, it's in my personal interest to keep that woman from getting her heart broken. Last time she did, it took months for her to fully bounce back, and I happen to like T-Rod running my world at full capacity."

Jonas pipes in with his two cents about T-Rod's ever-expanding skill set, as well as his opinion that Josh hasn't been maximizing it lately. And again, I tune out.

Okay, here's my plan. I'll propose to Hannah tomorrow night, *assuming* Josh and Kat are both totally cool with the idea *and* I can get a ring in time. With the wedding at sunset and Hannah primping all day with the ladies, I should have plenty of time in the morning to get my ass to a jewelry store in Kahului or wherever before I have to be anywhere for photos. I'm sure a big diamond ring will be ridiculously expensive in a tourist trap like this, but so what? My priority isn't getting a good deal on Hannah's ring; it's having something jaw-dropping to slide onto her finger tomorrow night, so I don't have to go to bed one more night than necessary without getting to call Hannah Milliken my fiancée.

I tune back into the conversation at the table, just in time to hear Josh saying to his brother, "I'll give it some serious thought, I promise. Thanks for putting a bug in my ear."

Jonas smiles. "Hey, you've got the charm and I've got the brains, remember? I wouldn't wanna fall down on my job."

Josh turns his attention to Reed, upon whom he bestows an exaggerated, mock-glare. "And in the meantime," he says, "keep your paws off her, you fucking menace."

Reed rolls his eyes. "Fine. But only because it's you."

Smirking, Josh looks down at his hand. "From here on out, nobody goes near Theresa Rodriguez unless they're planning to make her happy for the rest of her fucking life, and that's final. Got it?"

There it is again. That same thunderbolt as before. Hot damn, I can't wait to get down on my knee tomorrow night and ask Hannah for the honor of trying to make her happy for the rest of her life.

"Okay, what you got, Rivers?" Josh asks. "Time for the rubber to finally hit the road, fucker."

Reed snickers and lays down his cards. "Three aces, son. Read 'em and weep."

Josh lays down his cards with a laugh. "I've got a pair of fours. I was totally bluffing."

Everyone laughs along with him.

"What you got, Zander?" Josh asks. "Please tell me it's something that's gonna beat this fucker and make him cry."

Zander lays down his cards with a flourish while flashing a huge smile that shows off his straight, white teeth. "Full house, gentlemen. Read 'em and weep."

Everyone at the table cheers and hurls taunts at Reed as our unlikely victor, Zander, rakes in his mountain of chips. And just like that, our poker night comes to an end. The party over, guys start rising from the table, murmuring about our big day tomorrow. Jonas says he's going to say goodnight to Sarah and grab an overnight bag before returning to bunk with Josh tonight, and Ryan and Zander and the others say goodnight and head out. Suddenly, it's only Josh, Reed, and me remaining in Josh's bungalow. *The Three Musketeers.*

"Hey, Joshua," I say. "Would you make me a martini?" Josh was a bartender in college, and he still loves playing bartender to this day.

"Coming right up." I follow him to a bar in the corner, while Reed checks his phone at the table.

As Josh begins making my cocktail, I take a deep breath and ask, "What would you think about me proposing to Hannah tomorrow night during the reception? Would that be okay with you?"

Josh looks up, his face aglow. "That'd be fucking awesome."

"Are you sure?"

"I'd be thrilled."

"I think we should confirm Kat's equally cool with the idea. She might have a different take."

"Kat might have a different take about what?" Reed asks. He leans his forearms on the bar. "Make me one of those, too, bartender."

"You got it. Henny asked if I'd be cool with him proposing to Hannah tomorrow night during the reception."

Reed flashes me a snarky look. "Please, tell me you've got a ring this time."

"No, but I will. I'm gonna run out and get one tomorrow morning— assuming Kat says she's on board."

Josh rolls his eyes. "Kat will consider it her personal triumph if you propose at our wedding. Do you know how many times I've had to listen to that woman saying she's a gifted matchmaker? And yet, as far as I know, you and Hannah are her only success story."

"Could you text Kat now about it, just to be sure? I'm feeling antsy."

Josh pulls out his phone and taps on it. And mere seconds later, he shows me the string of gifs Kat's already sent in reply: various people jumping for joy and popping champagne bottles. Josh deadpans, "It would appear my lovely fiancée is mildly in favor of you proposing to Hannah tomorrow night at our wedding reception." As he's putting down his phone on the bar, it pings, and when he looks at the screen, he says, "Kat says she'll throw her bridal bouquet to Hannah and tell everyone else not to catch it. She says you should propose to Hannah right after that."

I frown. "I already did that at Jonas and Sarah's wedding and had to pivot in abject humiliation at the last minute. If I did that again, would it come off like a cute call-back, only with completion this time, or like I'm a loser who's only capable of pulling off one proposal idea?"

"What the fuck are you talking about?" Josh asks, which makes me remember he and Kat weren't anywhere nearby when I drunkenly kneeled before Hannah at his brother's wedding. Quickly, I explain everything to Josh, with Reed piping in to tell his version of events here and there. And when Reed and I are done telling our tale, Josh says he thinks Kat's idea is still a good one.

Josh reasons, "Who better to catch Kat's bouquet, than the woman who's about to get engaged a minute later? That's the only person who'd make any sense."

I consider the situation and finally say, "Okay, tell Kat all systems go on the bouquet toss. But I won't propose to Hannah in front of everyone on the dance floor this time. After she catches the bouquet, I'll take her outside onto the beach, straight to a telescope I'll have arranged in advance, and I'll do it there."

"Why do you need a telescope?" Reed asks, so I explain the gift I've been wanting to give Hannah since our first week together.

"I'm texting T-Rod now," Josh says, tapping on his phone. "Asking her to get a telescope set up for you."

"Thanks so much. Tell T-Rod thanks from me."

"Doing it now."

Reed asks, "Do you want some company when you shop for the ring tomorrow morning, Henny?"

"Absolutely. Thanks."

Josh smirks at Reed. "What do you know about engagement rings?"

"Not a fucking thing, thank God," Reed replies with a wicked grin. "But I bet I'm still better at choosing one than Henn."

"Indubitably," I say. "You're hired."

Josh slides two martinis across the bar and picks one up for himself. "Cheers, fellas. Sounds like tomorrow is going to be a fucking awesome day for more reasons than one."

36
HENN

"Hey, Uncle William, will you tie Henn's bowtie?" Josh asks. "I'd do it, but I'm so nervous my fingers won't function."

Uncle William laughs. "Sure thing. Come here, Peter."

"If this bowtie were a motherboard," I say, "I swear it'd be my bitch."

"It's hard to tie a bowtie," Uncle William assures me. "Much harder than it looks."

I smirk at Reed, who was making fun of my incompetence earlier. "See, Reed? It's not me that's the problem—it's the bowtie."

Reed laughs. "Keep telling yourself that, man."

"All the chairs are filled," Jonas murmurs. He's peeking out a crack in the bungalow door toward the beach. "Everyone looks really excited."

"Gah. Don't tell me that," Josh says. "I'm nervous enough already."

You want to talk about a guy being nervous? That's what I'm thinking as I touch the ring box in my pocket for the twentieth time. But, obviously, I know better than to say it out loud. This is Josh's big day, not mine. At least, until after that bouquet toss later tonight. Right now, Josh's nerves are the only ones that matter.

"What do you have to be nervous about, Faraday?" Reed says. "You're marrying the greatest girl, ever."

"Which is exactly why I'm nervous. I don't wanna fuck this up for her."

Exactly, I think, running my fingers across the square-shaped bulge in my pocket again. I'm not worried Hannah will reject me tonight, since, thankfully, she's explicitly told me she'll say yes. No, the source of my nerves is wanting the proposal to be everything Hannah wants it to be, especially after the debacle at Jonas and Sarah's wedding.

"Hey, Jonas," Josh calls to his brother at the door. "Were you nervous right before you went out to marry Sarah?"

Jonas shuts the door. "Oh, yeah, I was shitting." He strides toward the group, twirling the wedding band on his finger as he walks. "I wasn't nervous about getting married—I was just freaking out I was gonna fuck up my vows."

"*Exactly,*" Josh says. "What if I spontaneously start spewing gibberish up there? Or pass out? Or worst-case scenario, what if I spontaneously shart in front of everyone?"

Everyone bursts out laughing, except for Uncle William who looks deeply confused.

"What's *sharting?*" he asks, his brow furrowed.

I put my hand on the old man's shoulder. "It's when you think you're gonna fart, but you unexpectedly shit instead."

Uncle William cracks up and shakes his head. "*Joshua.*"

"Well, let's look at this logically," Reed says. "When was the last time you sharted?"

"Hmm," Josh says. "Maybe when I was ten?"

"Okay, then, realistically, the odds are extremely low it will happen within the next thirty minutes for the first time in twenty years."

"God willing," Josh murmurs.

"Unless, of course, it's been so long, you're now statistically *overdue,*" I chime in to say, as Uncle William continues working his magic on my bowtie.

"Not helpful, Henn," Josh says. "In what universe would you ever think that's a helpful thing to say?"

I laugh. "Sorry."

Jonas puts his hand on his brother's arm. "You've got this. If *I* can say my vows without sharting, then you most certainly can."

"All done," Uncle William says, patting me on my shoulder. He turns me around to face the groom, like I'm Josh's little puppet boy. "Acceptable, Joshua?"

"Suave perfection," Josh confirms. "You're Cary-Grant-meets-Steve-Jobs, Henn."

"Oooh, thank you."

Reed sidles up to Josh with a bottle of Patron. "A little something to calm the jitters?"

"Just a little sip," Josh says, accepting the bottle. "Any more than that and I might spontaneously shart from being too relaxed."

We all gather around and take turns swigging the pricey tequila.

"Pretty good," Uncle William says after taking a sip. "But at the reception, we're all drinking my Scotch."

Conversation turns to the fancy Scotch the old man has brought to share—apparently, the bottles are rare and highly valuable—until the wedding planner pokes her head into the bungalow and tells us it's almost time to take our positions on the beach. "We have to time this with the sunset," she reminds us, "so you've got to be in position in five."

When she leaves, Josh turns to the group. "Ready, men?"

Everyone says yes, we're ready and raring to go, at which point we pass around the bottle of Patron once more.

"Hey, bro," Josh says to Jonas. "You got a Plato quote for me to think about when I'm up there, just in case I suddenly feel like I'm gonna spontaneously shart?"

Jonas taps his steel chin and thinks for a half-second before replying, "Courage is knowing what *not* to fear. And the one thing *never* to fear is spontaneous sharting."

Everyone bursts out laughing.

"Thank you," Josh says. "You're a beast of a best man, Jonas Faraday." He takes a deep breath. "Now let's get out there and get me a smokin' hot wife."

Absolutely, brother, I think. *And me, a smokin' hot fiancée.*

37
HANNAH

As the band cranks onstage, I throw my arms up and my head back and shake my booty with gusto—all while singing along at top volume with my best friends. I'm dancing in a group with the usual suspects and having the time of my life. Dinner is long over. All toasts and speeches given. Dancing kicked off maybe an hour ago and promises to continue for hours to come.

When the song ends, I signal to Henn that I'm going to the bathroom, and when I emerge from that task and see Henn and all of our friends still going strong on the dance floor, I decide to get in line at the bar behind two of Kat's brothers—Colby, the firefighter, and, Dax, the future rockstar.

As I come to a stop behind the pair, I wonder if I should say hello, since we've crossed paths in large groups several times this week but haven't conversed directly. Should I congratulate Dax on his band getting signed to River Records? Should I tell Colby I saw news reports about his heroism earlier this year, and I'm relieved to see him recovering so well from his injuries?

Nah. I can't hear what the brothers are saying in front of me, due to the loud music, but I can plainly see they're engaged in animated conversation. I can't imagine they'd appreciate being interrupted, only to make awkward small talk with a well-meaning stranger.

I swipe into my photos, figuring I'll use this time to send Maddy a few images and videos from today's festivities. As I do, the band's loud, upbeat song ends and a slower one ensues, and suddenly, I can make out Dax's voice in front of me.

"Oh, I'm sure she loved it," Dax says. "You not only told her you're in love with her, but you *showed* her how much by not being able to hold it in, no matter how hard you tried."

Colby says something I can't discern, so I lean in a bit closer while still looking down at my phone, just in time to catch Colby saying ". . . swear this week away from Lydia and the kids has driven me batshit. That's the only explanation for my uncharacteristic lack of restraint during that phone call."

Dax chuckles. "If you're batshit, then what does that make Ryan—a psychopath? Only a psychopath would say yes to letting some friend of Josh's hack into no less than *nine* airlines to find a woman he'd only met *once* in a bar."

My eyes widen. *Excuse me?*

"Ryan told you about that?" Colby asks.

"No, The Blabbermouth did."

"Of course, she did."

Dax says, "Hey, do you know if the hacker who helped Ryan is the same one who helped Keane out of his stripper jam last month?"

Say what now?

Colby says, "Keane got himself into a stripper jam? Jesus Christ. Tell me everything."

"Oh, shit," Dax says. "Kat told me not to tell anyone about that."

"Well, it's too late now," Colby says. "Tell me *everything* or I'll beat it out of you."

Fuck. They've got their drinks now and they're walking away. Fuckity! I want to hear the whole story.

"What can I get you?" the bartender asks with a smile.

Crap. It's too late now. The Morgan boys are long gone, and there's no way for me to race over to them to eavesdrop without giving myself away.

"Um, two mai tais, please." That's the drink Henn and I have been throwing back all night, so I placed the order without thinking. But when I get the drinks handed to me, I realize I'm not ready to head back to the dance floor with them yet—not after what I just overheard.

I put the drinks down on a table and stand motionless, my head spinning. *Henn hacked nine airlines to help Ryan find that flight attendant?* During the opening night cocktail party here in Maui, Henn said something to our entire friend group about Ryan emailing him earlier that day with additional information to help Henn's "search." But even then, Henn once again made it sound like he only did some internet research for Ryan. Some clever sleuthing. Not a full-scale hacking operation of nine freaking airlines. Does everyone in our friend group except for me know about that jaw-dropping detail?

Also, what kind of hack did Henn perform for Keane? Henn hasn't said a word about that to me, whatever it was. Not a single word. Does everyone but me know about that one, too?

T-Rod.

She can be my bell-weather! If she already knows about both those things, then I'll know for a fact I'm not crazy to think Henn should have told me about them, too. If T-Rod knows, then it would be bullshit if Henn tries to defend himself with his usual line: "It's not my secret to tell."

My heart is racing. I need to know if this is karaoke night, all over again, and I need to know it right fucking now.

Determination hardening in my veins, I scan the crowded reception, looking for T-Rod. But I don't see her anywhere. Come to think of it, I haven't seen her for a while, maybe since the dancing kicked off. Did she go to her room to pass out after two months of hard work in planning this whirlwind week? Yeah, I bet she did. Shoot.

I glance toward the dance floor where Henn is currently dancing like a maniac with Josh, Kat, and Reed. There's really no point in me asking Kat about this, since she's probably the one who requested Josh ask Henn to help her brothers in the first place. Yeah, Kat is too close to the situation to be of any use to me in this instance.

But what about Sarah? T-Rod's far more tangential to our friend group than Sarah, so T-Rod knowing this stuff would have been more telling than Sarah knowing it. But still, Sarah's not married to Henn's best friend since college. Also, Colby and Keane aren't Sarah's brothers, like they are for Kat, so I definitely think Sarah is the next best litmus test after T-Rod.

I scan the tent and spot Sarah sitting at a table with Jonas and Jonas's uncle. I peek at the dance floor to make sure Henn is still whooping it up over there. When he is, off I go toward Sarah's table.

When I reach my destination, I make polite small talk with everyone briefly, before calmly asking Sarah if she's got a minute to chat with me in private. When she says yes, we head into a corner to talk.

"Is everything okay?" Sarah asks.

"It's fine. I'm being sneaky, honestly. Trying to get some information about my brilliant but humble boyfriend. Henn would rather die than brag or boast about himself, but there's something I'm wondering about." As Sarah sighs with relief, I say, "I know Henn sometimes does favors for really good friends. Or, in this case, for the *brother* of a really good friend—"

"Oh, you're curious to know the details of the favor Henn did for Jonas?"

I press my lips together. That's not what I was going to ask Sarah about, but now that she's mentioned it, I'm realizing it'd be worth my while to hear the "Henn found Sarah for Jonas" story from *Sarah's* perspective. If Henn told me a sanitized version of the favor he did for Ryan, then it stands to reason he also told me a sanitized version of the one he did for Jonas.

"You read my mind," I say with a smile. "Henn made it sound like what he did for Jonas was no big deal, but I suspect he's being humble and there's more to the story than he's telling me."

Sarah snorts. "That's so Henny. Trust me, what he did was a very big deal. Don't let him tell you otherwise. Also, I call bullshit. Henn knows it was amazing, or else he wouldn't have joked that he'd prefer we name our first-born Hennessey rather than Peter." She laughs. "Did he tell you he said that?"

I laugh along with her, even though my stomach is tightening. "No, he didn't. He never toots his own horn. Ever. All he said was that he found you for Jonas after you'd sent Jonas an anonymous email."

Sarah glances at the dance floor. "Yeah, that's it in a nutshell. Apparently, Jonas went into full-on obsession mode, so Josh called Henn and asked him to find the sender of the email." At my urging, Sarah elaborates a bit, and to my relief, what she says tracks everything Henn's already told me . . . That is, until Sarah gets to the part of her story where she says, "So, that's when Henn went in and grabbed the law school's student roster and got the contact info of anyone named Sarah and passed it along to Jonas. And the rest is history."

Went in.

It's that phrase that's sticking with me. Does that mean Henn *hacked* into the University of Washington to get that student roster for Jonas? I think that's what Sarah is saying.

I clear my throat. "So, uh, when Henn hacked into the University's system to get that student roster . . ." I pause, figuring Sarah will correct my assumption if I'm wrong. When she doesn't, I finish my sentence with, "Do you know if it was hard for him to do?"

"I can't imagine there's any hack that's all that difficult for Henn to pull off," Sarah replies without missing a beat. "The man is a fucking genius."

"That he is."

Holy crap. When Henn told me the story of how he'd found Sarah for Jonas, how did I not realize then that Henn had hacked the University of fucking Washington to do it? The same way he hacked into nine motherfucking airlines to find a flight attendant for Ryan. And performed some hack that helped Keane out of a "stripper jam." The same way Henn hacked Sarah's former employer to bring them down. And how he hacked YouTube to give a boost to the first music video ever released by River Records. Oh! And Henn hacked that ex-boyfriend of Kat's to help Josh with his unconventional marriage proposal, too. The list goes on and on.

In a flash, all the dots that have been separately floating around in my head converge and connect. *Henn is a hacker.* A full-time one. A professional one. All this time, I've thought my boyfriend is a cybersecurity specialist who occasionally dabbles in hacking to perform a harmless favor for a good friend for a good cause. In the name of true love, for instance. But suddenly, the evidence of Henn's hacking activities all around me is making me realize . . . *Henn doesn't dabble. Henn is a professional hacker for a fucking living.* He doesn't do it occasionally, here and there, but as his fucking day job. Why else would all these people constantly approach him for favors of this nature? I don't know much about hacking, but I know enough to realize a hacking hobbyist wouldn't be able to pull off hacking *nine* freaking airlines. Isn't that a huge job to pull off?

How did I not realize all this before now? Am I epically stupid, or has Henn been carefully choosing his words whenever he tells me stuff, specifically to keep the full truth from dawning on me? I'm one thousand percent positive Henn told me he's in cybersecurity and has never once corrected that statement. I'm also positive he's never once said the words "I'm a hacker" to me. *Holy shit.*

"So, is that everything you were wondering about?" Sarah asks, her eyebrows raised.

Oh. Clearly, I've been in my own little world for a bit too long. "Oh. Yes, it is. Thank you." At this point, it doesn't matter if Sarah knows what Henn did for Ryan or Keane or anyone else. Based on what Sarah has told me about Henn's favor for Jonas, it's now clear Henn has lied to me. Or at least, he's been less than truthful. *And I need him to explain why.*

Sarah says, "I'm so glad you asked me about this. You of all people should know how brilliant, generous, and romantic your boyfriend really is. I don't think there's anything Henn wouldn't do to help someone he loves, especially when there's the possibility of true love at the finish line."

"That's true. That's Henn. He'd do anything to help someone he cares about."

"Or, as was the case with Jonas, the *sibling* of someone he cares about," Sarah adds.

"Absolutely." As the word leaves my lips, a horrifying realization crashes into me. *Maddy.* Her recent admission into UCLA. *No, no, no.* Henn wouldn't have. He couldn't have. *And yet, I'm almost positive he did.*

No. My heart doesn't want to believe it, even as my gut screams at me that Henn did, in fact, go behind my back and do the exact thing I'd asked him *not* to do. Henn hacked a major university in Washington to help his best friend's brother find true love, after all, so what would stop him from hacking into a major university in California to help his girlfriend's sister make her dreams come true? I'd made it clear Maddy getting into UCLA would make my own move to LA a no-brainer, didn't I? So, Henn had every incentive to help Maddy in order to help himself. *Motherfucker.*

I thank Sarah for the chat and mumble something about needing to find Henn. Obviously, I'll hear him out. Try not to jump to conclusions. I could be wrong. But what are the odds of that, when it seems like every time I turn around, there's another hack performed by my boyfriend that our friend group knows about, which Henn hasn't bothered to tell me about himself? Why is he so secretive with me? Is it because he knows if he tells me one thing, that'll be the thread that unravels the UCLA sweater?

"Ladies and gentlemen," the emcee onstage says into a microphone. "Can we get all the single ladies to the dance floor? It's time for the bouquet toss!"

I look toward the dance floor and discover Kat beckoning enthusiastically to me, with Henn standing next to her, his face awash in excited anticipation. *Fuck.* They've arranged for me to catch the fucking bouquet again, haven't they? The same way they did at Jonas and Sarah's wedding.

Panic floods me. I can't do this right now. I have way too many questions for Henn. Too many doubts about him and his basic honesty. His character. Do I even know the man I've fallen head over heels in love with?

When the emcee repeats his refrain, Kat beckons to me again, so I shake my head at her, letting her know I'm not coming. From Kat, my gaze shifts to Henn, who's saying something to Josh. *Fuck.* I can't walk over there like nothing is wrong. In fact, I can't stay here another minute, or I'm going to make a scene. Biting back tears, I turn on my heel, hike up my long bridesmaid dress so I don't trip over its hem, and sprint out the nearest exit.

38

HENN

Where the heck is Hannah going . . . and now of all times? She can't leave. She's got to come over here and catch the bouquet, so I can lead her outside and show her our cuddling stars, and then get down on my knee and give her the ring that's been burning a hole in my pocket all day and ask her to become my fiancée.

"Hannah!" I shout. But it's too noisy in the crowded reception tent and Hannah's too far away to hear me above the happy chaos. Does Hannah need to grab something from our room, and she's cluelessly chosen this most inopportune time to do it?

I take off running at top speed toward the exit where Hannah disappeared, and when I get outside into the balmy Hawaiian night, it's just in time to see Hannah turning a corner and disappearing again. Is she feeling sick? Did she get her period unexpectedly, and now she's sprinting to change into some clean panties in our bungalow? That last idea seems legit. Honestly, I can't fathom any other reason Hannah would take off so suddenly, right after the announcement of the bouquet toss, without saying a word to me.

"Hannah!" I yell. I pick up my pace and round the corner and yell her name again. And this time, thank God, she stops and turns around about thirty yards away from me on a hibiscus-lined path.

"Are you okay?" I walk toward her, my heart stampeding. As I get closer, tears on her cheeks glint in the moonlight. "Oh my god. What happened?" When I reach her, I open my arms, figuring whatever's happened, she could probably use a hug. But to my surprise, she doesn't fall into my arms. In fact, she takes a full step backward.

I drop my arms, as my stomach comes alive with knives and knots.

"I have a question," she says coolly. "And I want you to answer with complete honesty."

Uh oh. "I'll certainly try."

"See, that's not a normal response, Henn. Most people would simply say okay."

My stomach feels like it's physically somersaulting. She knows full well there are things I can't talk about. But I don't think it would help my cause to remind her about that now. I ask, "What's the question?"

Hannah shifts her weight and crosses her arms over her chest. "Did you hack into UCLA and do something that made the admissions office think Maddy had been admitted?"

Oooooooh, shit. I stare at Hannah, my lips pressed together, weighing my options. The ground suddenly feels like it's shifting beneath my dress shoes. How the fuck did Hannah even think to ask me that question? And why now, of all times, mere seconds before I was going to pull her outside and make her my fiancée?

In the face of my silence, Hannah clenches her jaw. "It's a simple yes or no question."

Welp.

Here we go.

I guess I've always known, deep down, this day would come. I just thought I'd be the one controlling its timing. I thought I'd be able to sit Hannah down one day, when I felt good and ready, and tell her all my secrets. All the things I do and why. And she'd hug me and thank me for my honesty. And off we'd go into the sunset together without missing a beat. But it's now abundantly clear I've waited too long and missed my chance to lead the charge.

"It's actually a yes *and* no question," I say. "Yes, I hacked into UCLA. No, I didn't do anything on Maddy's behalf once I got there. Once I pulled up the admissions data, she'd already gotten in on her own." Hannah looks deeply skeptical, so I add, "I swear to Steve Jobs, I didn't do anything to get her in." At any other time, that bit about Steve Jobs would amuse Hannah. Make her smile, at least, if not chuckle. *But not this time.* Which means this moment—this conversation—is probably about a whole lot more than my hack into UCLA. It's the conversation I've been dreading. The one I'm now realizing, indubitably, *I* should have been the one to instigate. "I swear she got in on her own," I sputter. "I swear on my mother. On my father, too."

"How do you expect me to believe a word you say?" Hannah says. "You knew how I felt. I told you, explicitly, I didn't want you to do anything. But you did it, anyway. Because no matter what, you wanted me to move to LA."

"I know it looks bad for me, but if I'd changed her status from rejected to admitted, do you think I'd have admitted her for spring quarter? Hell no! I would have given her exactly what she wanted: admittance for the fall. Nobody wants spring quarter. That sucks ass. It's a consolation prize."

Hannah folds her arms over her chest. "Unless putting Maddy in for spring decreased the chances of someone noticing the nefarious thing you'd done."

Damn. That's an impressive leap of logic, even if it's not true. In fact, I had that very thought when I sat in front of my screen, struggling mightily with my thumping desire to switch Maddy from spring to fall admittance. In the end, I decided not to touch it, for a variety of reasons, including the one Hannah's just identified.

"I feel like I should get some credit for resisting temptation," I say, feeling a bit like I'm playing violin on a sinking ship. "I wanted to switch her to fall, so fucking badly, to guarantee I'd have my beloved girlfriend in LA with me. But I restrained myself, out of respect for your wishes."

"If you respected my wishes so damned much, why'd you hack into UCLA in the first place?"

"I was simply poking around, out of curiosity. I do that kind of thing all the time. I hack systems, just to see if I can. If I were a rock climber, then I'd climb every steep rock formation I came upon. It's the same sort of impulse."

She's not buying it. "What would you have done if you you'd gone in there and found out Maddy had been rejected?"

"Luckily, we don't need to wonder about that, because she got in on her own."

"So you say."

"I swear she did, Hannah."

"Let's say I believe you. There's still no point in going in at all, if you weren't fully prepared to get her in through any means necessary. That's the part I can't wrap my head around, Henn—the fact that you'll say one thing to my face and then do the opposite behind my back."

"But I didn't."

"You were *prepared* to do it, if necessary, though. And that's the issue. It's a matter of trust and integrity. I would have sworn on my life you'd never bald face lie to me about anything. Yes, you're tight-lipped and mysterious about your work. But I never thought for a minute you'd flat-out lie to me about something important like this. It's making me question everything."

I'm floored. Panicked. Freaking out. "It doesn't have to be that big a deal. It's like, imagine there's a Christmas present you've *really* wanted all year long, and then you see a wrapped box under the tree in the exact shape of that thing. Add to this scenario the fact that you know, for sure, you can take a peek without anyone finding out. Ever. Well, you'd take that peek, wouldn't you, and you wouldn't consider yourself a bad person or lacking integrity for doing it, right?"

Hannah levels me with tear-filled blue eyes. "I'm not going to argue silly hypotheticals with you, when the reality is you lied to me to get something you wanted. It's that simple."

"In my defense, you never told me *specifically* not to hack UCLA to get Maddy admitted—which, I repeat, I didn't wind up doing. You only told me not to ask Reed to—"

"Are you fucking kidding me?" she bellows, going from zero to sixty in a heartbeat. "Please, tell me you're not serious right now."

My heart is lodged in my throat. I don't think Hannah has ever screamed at me before. It's jarring. "I was joking." I attempt a smile. "Unless, of course, my logic is persuasive to you?"

"There's nothing funny about this. What if UCLA figured out you'd broken into their system?" She's shouting again, which prompts me to look around nervously. She adds, "You could have gotten Maddy's offer rescinded, Henn!"

"Not a chance in hell. And, please, lower your voice."

"You could have ruined my sister's life."

"Absolutely impossible. The odds of me getting found out on a simple hack like that are the same as the world's best downhill skier having a catastrophic, career-ending injury on a bunny slope."

"And why would that be? Because you're a professional hacker?"

"Correct. I'm one of the world's best."

"Well, gosh, that's news to me, since you've only ever told me you're in *cybersecurity*."

"That's what I said in the beginning, yes, because that's what I always say, and I've never once told the truth to anyone I've dated before. But you know full well I've slowly let you in on a whole lot more than that. Really early on, I told you about what I did for Sarah in Vegas. You knew back then I'd hacked into a global crime syndicate and stolen all their money and data and turned it over to the feds. You knew that, Hannah."

"Yes, I knew you'd performed *one* specific hack. But not because you're a *hacker*."

I pull a face of confusion. "I don't understand the distinction."

"You told me it was a one-off, remember? And that you're in cybersecurity. I thought in Vegas you did a one-time hacking-type thing as a favor to a good friend for a good cause."

I furrow my brow. "I never said the Vegas thing was a one-off. It was the first time I'd worked with the feds, but the work itself was right up my alley."

Hannah looks deeply confused. "When we went outside the karaoke bar, you literally promised me it was a one-off."

"Oooh. I meant it was a one-off that everyone except you would know about something I'd done."

"Well, if that was your promise, then you've broken it, repeatedly, as I've learned tonight. Apparently, you're perfectly comfortable with everyone but me knowing about all your various hacking activities, but when it comes to me, you actively hold back details and tell me a litany of half-truths. The only question is: *Why? Why* do you actively keep things from me, Henn? Is it because you're scared if I knew the truth, I'd leave you?"

"Back up. What did you learn tonight? What are we talking about here?"

"You told me you went looking for Ryan's flight attendant, but you didn't bother to mention you hacked into *nine* fucking airlines to do that. Or that you performed some kind of hack to help Keane out of a stripper jam. You told me you found Sarah for Jonas, but you made it sound like internet research. You certainly didn't mention you'd hacked into U Dub to find her. Could it be you didn't want me knowing about your hack of U Dub because you didn't want me connecting the dots from that particular university to another one, hmm?"

"I didn't get Maddy in."

"So you say."

I wipe my sweaty palm against the front of my pants, and it brushes against the ring box in my pocket. "Can we go to the room to finish this conversation? I'll tell you whatever you want to know about all that stuff, but I don't want to do it out here."

Hannah wordlessly turns on her heel and tramps down the pathway toward our bungalow, so I follow her in thick silence. I can't believe the night I *thought* was going to be the best of my life could turn out to be the worst.

When we reach our room, I open the door for Hannah, and she marches swiftly inside.

Quickly, I decide the best defense is a good offense. "Maybe I should have been more forthcoming with actual words," I say, before Hannah says whatever is on the tip of her tongue, "but I certainly showed you who I am. I let you sit right next to me while hacking that dude for Josh's proposal, didn't I? I thought you understood."

"I thought you were a cybersecurity guy doing a *favor* for a friend. I didn't realize that's what you *do*. What about Your Nerd for Hire? Your website lists cybersecurity and IT services."

I shrug. "It's a dummy website at this point. I mean, it functions—I get inquiries off it sometimes—but I mostly ignore them."

"Why have you never told me that?"

"If it makes you feel any better, even my own mother thinks I'm in cybersecurity."

Rage contorts Hannah's features. "You're not fucking your mother, Henn."

In any other situation, that would have been the perfect set-up for a dark, twisted, horribly inappropriate joke. Something like, "At least, not since I met you!" But now isn't the time for jokes. "I should have sat you down and told you what I do," I concede. "I was actually going to do that soon, when the timing felt right. But since I've never told a girlfriend about this stuff, I guess I didn't have a good feel for when that should be. I knew I had to do it before we got married, but how soon before that wasn't clear to me."

Hannah sighs and plops on the couch. "Just tell me what you do for a living, for fuck's sake. Tell me who you are."

I sit next to her. "I'm a hacker for hire. I get hired to hack bad people who deserve to be taken down. I go in, get information that proves their malfeasance, and leave without a trace. I have to be very careful and secretive because, if any of my targets were to find out who I am or what I do, they could come after me or someone I love in retaliation." I give her a rundown of the sorts of douchebags I regularly take down. Human traffickers, rapists, pedophiles. Cheating husbands who've hidden assets. "When I turn over the information to my clients, I get paid a bounty," I explain. "It's an honest living. I could steal money, but I don't. I like earning my money legitimately." I try to take her hand, but she pulls away. "Please, Hannah, the main thing is that none of this stuff changes who I am or how I feel about you. And it certainly doesn't change how perfect we are for each other. How compatible. We're Bert and Ernie—Denver and Stockholm—whether I'm Denver on the side or Denver for a living."

Hannah's blue eyes light up. A lightbulb has plainly gone off in her head. "Oh my fucking god. You've hacked *me*, haven't you?"

Oh, fuck.

"That's why we've always been so freakishly compatible! Because you went in, without a trace, and gathered whatever intel was necessary to make yourself a cheat-sheet on Hannah Milliken!"

Oh, fuck, fuck, fuck. For a half-second there, when I was talking about all the good stuff I do to make the world a better place, I thought I saw forgiveness brewing in Hannah's deep, blue eyes. But just this fast, I know this confession is going to decimate any chance I might have had of being forgiven tonight . . . or maybe ever.

"Have you hacked me or not?" she demands.

"Yes, I've hacked you," I admit, my heart thundering. "Only once, though. And what I found only confirmed—"

Hannah lurches to standing, looking heartbroken. "No wonder you knew 'Birdhouse in Your Soul.' Nobody ever knows that song."

I stand. "I knew the song through my dad, exactly like I told you. Hannah, I hadn't even hacked you yet when we had that conversation. I hacked you the next day. And when I did, I quickly discovered hacking you was a pointless exercise because everything I saw only confirmed we're totally compatible and perfect for each other in every way."

She scowls: "I never showed you my dream board, did I?"

"No. But that's a perfect example of what I'm saying. When I saw it, I was like, damn, this girl wants exactly what I want. She's perfect for me."

Hannah's nostrils flare. "That whole dinner in Vegas, I kept thinking, 'Where did this perfect man who loves the hand-flex in *Pride & Prejudice* come from? And now I know—"

"No. I genuinely love *Pride & Prejudice* and the hand-flex. Please, Hannah. Don't spiral out of control and assume everything I've ever said or done—"

She screams, "I'm not the one who's out of control, Henn. It's you! You thought you could hack me into falling in love with you. You thought you could control my emotions by gathering data on me."

"No. Not at all. Well, yes, a tiny bit. At first. But it immediately became clear—"

"That whole first dinner, it felt like you had the Hannah Milliken Spark Notes or something. And you did!"

Panic is spiraling inside me. Why isn't she listening to me? Why is she jumping to worst-case scenario? "I hadn't even hacked you at that point. I did it the next day. Do you remember getting an email from your favorite makeup line—fill out a short marketing survey and get a bunch of free stuff? That was me! And you got the email the day *after* our first dinner together." The thought occurs, "And by the way, all that stuff I sent you for filling out the survey? It wasn't cheap!" But thankfully, I know better than to say it out loud.

"But Kat got that offer, too," Hannah says, looking perplexed.

"Yeah, I figured if you weren't naïve enough to click my link, then Kat would be, and then I'd be able to get to you through her."

"So, now you're calling me *naïve*?"

"In terms of phishing, yes. If Kat clicked the link, then I knew I could get into your devices through hers, thanks to the remote server you both used to log into work."

Hannah looks like she feels physically ill. *Violated.* "Have you been keeping tabs on my devices every fucking day? Do you eavesdrop on my conversations and texts and—"

"No, no. Never. Like I said, I only peeked at your stuff once and never again. I swear on my mother and father that's the truth. But even then, I didn't look at anything confidential, like your finances or medical info. I didn't even look at any of your texts or emails." An idea hits me like a thunderbolt. "You once told me you googled me. Well, what I did is the hacker equivalent of that. But like I said, everything I saw only made me realize I shouldn't have bothered because we were so compatible. Did I get some good ideas for gifts and dates I could plan? Yes. I admit that. But that's it. Beyond that, everything that's ever happened between us has been real and organic."

Hannah flops into an armchair. "Tell me every gift or date you've planned that derived from something you learned about me through hacking me. Don't leave a goddamned thing out."

This is a nightmare. I take a deep, long breath and puff out my cheeks on my exhale while plopping myself down onto the couch. I gather my thoughts, briefly, and then proceed to tell Hannah everything I've ever done, big or small, that had anything to do with something I learned through hacking her. It's not a whole lot, really. The flowers. The tickets to the comedy show. Our late-night, private visits to the video arcade and planetarium. Also, I admit I saw a couple necklaces she'd purchased that made me think to buy her one as a gift one day.

The only thing I don't mention is that motherfucker, Greg Smith. Hannah still hasn't told me about him, and there's no way in hell, when I'm fighting for my life here, I'd ever admit I've known about that motherfucker since basically day one of our relationship. If I tell her that, and that I perused her draft protective order, then I'm sure she'd ask if I've hacked him, and then I'd also have to admit I've been gleefully administering vengeance upon him in a slow drip for the past two months. No fucking way.

When I'm done talking, Hannah silently stares at me for a long moment, apparently trying to figure out how she feels about all of it. About *me*. What does she believe? And what she can forgive? Finally, without saying a word, Hannah puts her face in her hands and bursts into tears.

"Aw, baby." I get up and touch her hair. "I'm exactly who you think I am. This doesn't change anything. I love you so fucking much."

"I don't know what to believe," she says between sniffles. "There's so much about you I don't know." She shakes her head. "I can't believe you got down on your knee at Jonas and Sarah's wedding with the intention of proposing marriage to me before you'd even bothered to tell me that you're not, in fact, in cybersecurity."

Bile rises into my throat. "Yeah, that was a mistake. I realize that now. I'm sorry."

"What were you doing in DC all those weeks? Was it something horrific and horrible that would make me want to break up with you? Is that the real reason you won't tell me anything about that?"

Oh, Jesus. She's lost all faith in me, obviously, and in anything I've ever told her.

"No, it was something good and noble. It's the thing I'm most proud of that I've ever done, as a matter of fact, and I'm dying to tell you and everyone I love about it. But I can't."

Hannah wipes her eyes. "That's the thing that hurts the most. I feel like I'm not even the bull's-eye in the circle of everyone you love. I feel like you tell Josh and Reed way more than you tell me. And yet, I'm supposedly the one you want to marry."

I'm speechless. How did this situation spiral out of control like this? I never saw it coming.

"I need time to think about all this," Hannah says. "Will you please sleep in Reed's room tonight? I want to be alone." She wipes her eyes again. "Also, I'm going to Seattle tomorrow. I need to see my therapist in person. I want to cry on my sister's shoulder, too."

I can't believe my ears. "What about our trip to Kauai?" Since Hannah's new job doesn't start till next Monday, we've planned to island-hop to Kauai tomorrow for a luxurious five-day trip, just the two of us. While buying Hannah's ring this morning, I excitedly told Reed those five days in paradise with Hannah were going to be our "engagement-moon"— a perfect way to celebrate Hannah saying yes. I was a fool.

"I want to go home," Hannah says, her lower lip trembling. "I need time."

I can barely choke out my next words. "How much time? Do you mean you're moving back to Seattle? Is this it for us?"

Hannah swallows hard. "I'm not prepared to answer those questions right now. All I know is I need to cry on the shoulder of someone I trust completely. And since tonight is Kat's wedding night, I need to go home to do that."

My heart throbs painfully, as the full impact of Hannah's words stab me there. I'm not her shoulder to cry on, because *I'm* the one who hurt her. It's a crazy thought, when I'd do anything to protect her from pain.

"Could you please go to Reed's or wherever now?" she says softly. "I need to be alone to cry."

Fuck. I want to stay and try to convince her to forgive me. I want to beg and plead, to open my laptop and prove I never peeked at her devices before that first dinner in Vegas and never again after that first time. I want to remind her about her new job starting a week from Monday—to force her to admit she'll be coming back to LA after only a brief visit to Seattle.

But the pained, crumpled, exhausted look on Hannah's face makes me press my lips firmly together, rise, and start gathering stuff for my sad little slumber party at Reed's bungalow tonight.

Before I've finished packing, Hannah heads silently into the bathroom and closes the door. When she's gone, I stand frozen, staring at the closed door with my duffel bag in hand. Once I leave this room and tell Reed what's happened, this nightmare will become real. And I don't want that to happen. No, I want Hannah to burst out of that bathroom, slide her arms around me, and tell me all is forgiven. That she loves me, no matter what.

The shower turns on behind the closed door. A moment later, I hear muffled crying mingling with the sounds of the water—and I know it's time for me to leave. Hannah won't be coming out to forgive me tonight. Nope. She's inside that bathroom feeling heartbroken and betrayed because of what I did. What I didn't say. The trust I didn't have in her. That's really what this all boils down to, isn't it? I didn't trust Hannah enough to reveal my whole self to her. *And she knows it.*

―――――

"What happened?" Reed asks, approaching me at his bungalow's doorstep. He looks like a father who's finally located his missing toddler at the mall. He came here in response to my cryptic text from a moment ago. And by the looks of him, he rushed to get here.

Without saying a word, I gesture for Reed to open his bungalow door. If I speak, I'll cry. And I don't want to do that out here.

Inside the bungalow, I plop down my duffel bag, flop onto the couch, and empty my pockets onto the coffee table. First, the piece of paper I so excitedly printed off earlier this afternoon in the hotel's business center, and second, the ring box containing the sparkler Reed and I picked out for Hannah this morning. "I fucked things up with Hannah," I murmur. "She's flying to Seattle tomorrow morning."

"What the fuck?" Reed sits next to me and grabs the folded paper from the coffee table. "What the fuck?" he repeats after reading it, this time indignantly. "Hannah turned you down after seeing this and the ring? What's her problem? What more could she possibly want?"

"She didn't turn me down. I never even got the chance to ask her." I ramble the whole story, and to my surprise, when I finish talking, Reed looks deeply relieved. "If all you did wrong is you hacked her to try to impress her and didn't tell her the full truth about a few things she doesn't need to know about, anyway, then big fucking deal. That's a Tuesday for me, man."

Even in my misery, I can't help but chuckle. "Those aren't small things for normal people, Reed. I know you don't know this, but honesty is the bedrock of a healthy relationship. If there's no honesty, then there's no trust. And if there's no trust—"

"Spare me the therapy-speak," he says. "You were honest *enough.*

There's no rule that says you have to tell your romantic partner every-fucking-thing you ever think, feel, or do. That's a myth. You're a hacker, so, obviously, you're gonna hack her. You wouldn't ask a bird not to fly, would you? Well."

I'm not surprised by Reed's take on the situation. He's never valued honesty in his romantic entanglements. On the contrary, they're all messy and complicated and toxic as fuck. Funnily enough, I'm constantly the one encouraging Reed to let down his guard and give honesty a try. And yet, at the end of the day, it turns out I'm more like him than I ever thought possible. These past months with Hannah, I've been meting out bits and pieces of the truth-elephant—a leg here, an ear or trunk or tail there—without ever revealing the whole animal to her. Why'd I do that?

Because you were scared. Because you didn't want to risk losing Hannah if she found out the full truth too quickly, before deep trust had been established.

At the end of the day, I wasn't protecting *Hannah* by keeping certain details to myself, like I told myself. *I was protecting myself.*

Reed pats the side of my leg. "Give her time and space and she'll forgive you in a week." He holds up the paper—the one I've been dying to show Hannah for months now, ever since the magical night at the planetarium in Seattle. "God can be a cruel motherfucker at times," Reed says. "But even a cruel God wouldn't be so cruel as to create the male and female versions of the exact same dork, if he didn't want them to hook up and make a dork-baby to continue the species."

"This is your way of *comforting* me?"

Reed laughs. "Chin up, Peter. She'll forgive you, eventually. Sooner rather than later. I'm sure of it. And as we both know, I'm never wrong about anything."

39

HENN

Five days later

I stare at Hannah's diamond engagement ring—the one I didn't get to give her in Maui when all hell broke loose. And when I'm done torturing myself like that, I move on to torturing myself by staring at my phone again and willing Hannah to reply to my many texts, voicemails, and flower deliveries.

"Stop pining over her and watch the game," Reed barks. "It's getting good. We're closing the gap."

We're sitting on his couch, facing his TV. I've been staying at Reed's new, hilltop mansion since we left Maui together five days ago, and he's clearly grown sick of my misery and despair.

I've got earbuds in again. Today's song playing on repeat is "Birdhouse in Your Soul." Yesterday, I had Milli Vanilli's whole album on repeat. The day before that, the soundtrack to *Lala Land*. I figured listening to music that reminds me of Hannah would take the edge off my torture. But when it only turned up the dial on it, I kept at it because that's what I deserve. To be tortured. In fact, I've decided to keep torturing myself like this until Hannah forgives me.

I thought I'd hear from her after sending that salmon dinner for three to her mom's place last night. Before that, I was sure she'd respond to the balloon bouquet and box of cupcakes. Or any of the flowers. But nope. So far, I've received no response from Hannah, other than *one* text five days ago that told me she'd landed safely in Seattle and would be staying at her mom's place. "I'd appreciate you giving me space to sort out my feelings and thoughts," she wrote. And I wrote back, "I'll respect your wishes, but please know I love you and I'll do whatever it takes to earn your trust again." Little did I know then the space I was promising to give her would extend for five days with no relief in sight.

I've now realized I stupidly thought I could control everything in my real life as expertly as I control everything in my virtual life. That's where I went wrong. And that's what I'm dying to tell Hannah.

As the birdhouse song reaches its conclusion again, I check my screen, in case I've missed a call or text from Hannah. Still, nothing.

"Maybe she's not staying with her mom, after all, so she hasn't gotten any of my deliveries," I say. "She wouldn't be staying with Maddy at the dorms, I don't think. But maybe she went to a hotel."

"Well, that's easy enough to figure out," Reed says, much to my surprise. I wasn't really talking to him, even though he's sitting next to me on his couch. I was basically thinking out loud.

"Huh?"

Reed motions to my phone. "Hack her and check her location."

I roll my eyes. "I can't do that."

"Sure, you can. That'd be like falling off a log for you."

"Yes, I *can* in terms of ability. But I *shouldn't* in terms of ethics. At some point, I'm going to need to look Hannah in the eyes and promise I only did it once and will never do it again. And I can't very well do that if I went in and hacked her again *after* she freaked out about it in the first place."

Reed shrugs, conveying he's wholly unimpressed with my logic. "If I wanted a woman and hacking her would get me that woman, then I'd do it. It's not that deep. If I could make my dick a foot longer, I'd do that, too."

I laugh, despite my intense pain.

Amalia, Reed's beloved housekeeper, appears at the end of his couch and asks if we'd like some chicken tortilla soup she's made in the kitchen.

"You know my answer to that," Reed says. He looks at me. "It's my favorite thing she makes."

"Which is why I made it," Amalia says. She winks at Reed and then looks at me, her dark eyes pleading with me to finally come eat something.

"No, thank you. Maybe later."

"He'll have a big bowl," Reed says. "But no need to bring it here. We'll come to the kitchen and get it ourselves."

As Amalia heads off, Reed rises from the couch. "Come on, brother. You have to eat something."

"I can't. I feel sick."

"The minute you smell this soup, you'll be ravenous."

With a loud exhale, I rise from the couch, but as I do, a phone call rings in my earbuds. "It's Hannah! Oh my fuck!" Without waiting for Reed's reply, I sprint toward a pair of French doors leading to Reed's sprawling backyard and press the button to connect the call as I go. "Hi, Hannah!" I blurt excitedly. I wanted to sound like a normal, sane human who isn't presently having a cardiac event, but I'm sure I didn't succeed.

"Hi, Henn," Hannah replies softly.

I come to a stop on Reed's patio, practically panting with excitement. Reed is in the midst of constructing an entertainer's paradise out here, so there are construction workers galore around me in every direction. But they're not close enough to overhear me, and I doubt they'd care if they could. I want to dive right into asking if Hannah's gotten my gifts. Heard and read my pleas for mercy and forgiveness. But instead, I ask simply, "How are you?"

"Exhausted. Sad. Confused. You?"

"Depressed. Remorseful. So fucking sorry." I press my lips together and command myself to leave it at that. But I can't. Against my will, a torrent of words suddenly spews out of me, concluding with, "I'll do anything to earn back your trust again. Whatever I need to do to convince you I'm worthy of a second chance, I'll do it. And I'll never let you down again. I promise."

Hannah pauses for an eternal moment. "I called to thank you for all the flowers and treats and food and stuff. The salmon dinner for my mom, Maddy, and me was particularly thoughtful. We loved the cupcakes, too. Thank you for everything. And for all the notes. And flowers and balloons. And voicemails. Thank you for everything."

I take a deep, shuddering breath. "Did you all feast till your stomach's delight on the salmon last night?" That's what I put in the note that came with the salmon meal. I was hoping the verbiage would make Hannah remember our amazing first meal together in Seattle, the one that confirmed our magical night in Vegas wasn't a fluke.

"Honestly, I could barely eat a bite, as great as the food was. I'm feeling really depressed, to be honest."

"I haven't been able to eat, either. I'm staying with Reed, and he and his housekeeper, Amalia, are practically threatening to force-feed me at this point."

To my surprise, Hannah chuckles. "*Reed Rivers* is taking care of you in your time of need?"

I laugh with her. "He's actually much sweeter underneath it all than you'd ever guess."

"I'm relieved to hear you're not alone in your apartment, if you're feeling depressed."

"Reed insisted I come stay with him. To put it mildly, I wasn't in good shape when I landed on his doorstep in Maui."

"That was a rough night for both of us."

"When it comes to me, any and all rough nights are well deserved. I'm so sorry."

"I know you are. You've definitely made that clear. I must say, you've been groveling immaculately."

"I've meant every word."

She's silent.

"You don't believe me?"

She pauses. "No, I do."

I wait, but that's all she's going to say about that, apparently. "Have you seen your therapist yet?"

"No. She was out of town, so the first appointment I could get is tomorrow morning. She's really insightful and helpful. I'm sure I'll leave the appointment with full clarity. Or at least, a whole new level of clarity I don't currently possess."

"Can we make a date to talk after your appointment tomorrow? How about I fly to Seattle right now, so I can pick you up from—"

"No, no, don't come here. And yes, we can make a date to talk. I think that's a great idea. I'm tempted to talk to you about everything now, but I really think it makes more sense to wait until tomorrow."

"What time's your appointment?"

"Ten."

"Thirty minutes?"

"An hour."

"Okay, I'll be waiting by the phone from eleven on tomorrow."

"I might need to grab a quick sandwich right afterwards. Sometimes, I get really hungry after therapy."

"The same thing happens to me. It's like all the emotions that have been twisting my stomach into knots have been released, and suddenly I'm starving."

"Exactly. I promise I'll call you after the appointment, but it might not be at eleven on the dot."

"No worries. Take your time. As long as I know you'll be calling me to talk things through at some point tomorrow, I'm all good."

"Thank you. You're so sweet. Well, I'd better go. I've been using my mom's car while I'm in Seattle, and I need to run some errands now to be able to pick her up from work on time."

"Okay. Tell your mom I said hi. Unless she hates me now."

"Henn, nobody hates you. Least of all me. The issue isn't whether I've stopped loving you. I haven't. I still love you with all my heart. The issue is whether I can *trust* you. It's whether I love the real you or that dude from 'You.'"

I roll my eyes. "He's a mediocre hacker at best. Also, he's a psychopath, while I'm merely a sociopath."

She laughs. "Didn't mean to offend."

"Well, you did."

"I'll call you tomorrow." Her tone has become surprisingly flirtatious. "Bye for now, Peter."

"Bye for now, Banana."

She still loves me. That's what she said. And I could *feel* that it's true. In fact, based on her tone at the end there, I think Hannah's already decided she's going to forgive me, and seeing her therapist tomorrow is a mere formality. As a matter of fact, now that I've heard her voice, I'm not even worried about her therapy appointment tomorrow. If her therapist is anything like mine, all she's going to do is coax Hannah's truth out of her —get Hannah to admit out loud what she already knows she wants in her heart. *And what Hannah wants in her heart is me. Hallelujah.*

When the line goes dead, I shove my phone into my pocket and whoop with glee. I feel alive again—the most alive I've felt in five fucking days. She loves me! As long as we've got that, then we can fix the rest. I know we can.

With a happy sigh, I head back inside Reed's house. But only two steps into his living room, I get a notification that stops me dead in my tracks.

Greg Smith.

He finally clicked one of my phishing links.

Holy shit.

I've been trying to get into that fucker's burner phone for two months now. And now, out of nowhere, he's clicked a link and given me access.

"What'd Hannah say?" Reed says, approaching me.

I tell him the gist of my conversation with Hannah. And then, since I'm losing my mind about what just happened with Greg Smith, I tell Reed all about him, too, including everything I've been doing to torture the guy for the past two months. "You want to watch me hack into his burner phone?" I ask.

Reed looks equal parts relieved that I'm feeling so much better and amused by what I've told him about my campaign of terror. "Of course, I want to watch you hack him," Reed says. "Fuck the soup. I love watching a genius at work in any context. Even better, if he's a *vengeful* genius."

————

I sit on the edge of the bed that's been mine these past five days at Reed's house and open my laptop while Reed sits next to me and peeks over my shoulder.

"Okay, I'm in," I report. "Easy peasy."

"And?" Reed asks.

"Gimme a second." I click around for a while. "Looks like he uses this phone to hire sex workers. Lots of 'em. Huh. That's interesting, considering how many women he's scamming at any given time. You'd think he'd be too exhausted from being a fake boyfriend to hire a sex worker."

"Maybe it's a relief for him to have sex with women he doesn't need to pretend to like."

"Good point. I bet that's exactly right."

I click around for a bit more. But that's it. He uses this phone exclusively to contact sex workers, and nothing else.

"Well, damn," I say. "After all that phishing, and all that anticipation, this phone turns out to be a big, fat nothing-burger."

"What'd you expect to find?" Reed says.

"I don't know. I thought maybe there'd be something here I could decimate him with. But nobody in law enforcement is gonna give two shits about any of this."

"So, what are you gonna do?"

"Nothing. I mean, I'll keep doing all the stuff I told you about. The cars. The postings. Making sure he can't get hired and can't get a date. I'll keep fucking around with his finances, too. But there's nothing here I can throw into the mix."

Reed shrugs. "Oh, well. Sounds like there's still plenty of fun stuff you can do to him, until you lose interest." He grips my shoulder. "Come on, Peter. Let's get some soup into you."

———

"Okay, I'll be there," Reed says on his phone call. We're at his kitchen table, our soup bowls almost empty. A moment ago, he got a call he's been waiting for all morning, and now, suddenly, he's got that tell-tale look in his dark eyes—the look that says, "I'm about to make a shit-ton of money, baby." Still on his phone call, Reed says, "Text me the name of that club. I'll be there in time to come backstage before their show starts. Yep. See you then. Thanks." He hangs up and smiles at me. "Go pack your pathetic little duffel bag, Pietro. You're coming to Chicago with me to sign my next band tonight. *Fugitive Summer*. Remember that name, 'cause they're gonna be huge. They've got a lead singer named Savage who's like manna from heaven."

"I can't go. Hannah could change her mind about waiting to talk to me tomorrow and call me tonight instead, while we're still in the air. I don't want to miss her call."

Reed pulls a face of pure disdain. Being lovesick isn't something he has any personal experience with, and, clearly, he's reached his limit with me after watching me succumb to the condition for the past five days. "We're flying private," he says, "which means you can talk on the phone all you want. We'll also have fantastic Wi-Fi, too, if you're wondering."

"I'm tempted, but it makes no sense for me to come, since I might need to hop a flight to Seattle tomorrow."

"It's futile to resist me," he says. "Under any scenario, it makes more logical sense for you to come to Chicago with me now, rather than staying here in LA to sulk and listen to that fucking song on repeat."

"How do you figure? The flight from LA to Seattle is shorter than the flight from Chicago to Seattle."

"Let's say Hannah calls you tomorrow from Seattle and all is forgiven, and she wants to kiss and make up. Well, in that case I'll send my plane to pick her up and bring her to Chicago and you two will get to enjoy a romantic getaway in the Windy City. My treat. On the other hand, if she calls and you need to fly to Seattle on a moment's notice, then you'll actually get there faster from Chicago than from LA, despite the longer flying time, because you'll be taking my private jet instead of a commercial flight. Plus, you'll have a whole lot more fun for the next twenty-four hours if you come with me now, and that's not nothing, considering the sorry shape you're in."

"Okay, you've convinced me. I suppose I could buy another used car for Greg Smith in Chicago while I'm there."

"Atta boy. Come on. We need to pack our bags and go ASAP to make it to the show on time." As we head out of his kitchen together, Reed asks, "Does Hannah know about all those used cars you've been buying for that scammer guy?"

"No. She has no idea I even know the scammer exists."

"She's never told you about him?"

"No."

As we walk through Reed's expansive living room, I can tell he's holding something back. Not saying something that's on the tip of his tongue. "What?"

Reed shrugs. "You don't think that's a bit hypocritical of her?"

"How so?"

"Hannah's upset you've kept some details about your life to yourself, and yet this whole time she's never told you about her asshole ex."

"He's not her ex. He's a scammer, Reed. A sweetheart swindler. Hannah was his victim. I'm sure she's embarrassed and humiliated about what happened, not that she should be." He doesn't look convinced, so I add, "I purposefully kept Hannah in the dark about some things because I was scared the truth would scare her off, and she's kept a humiliating trauma to herself. They're not the same. Add to that, I didn't only keep some things from her, I've also actively done some pretty shitty things, like hacking her and hacking UCLA after she expressly told me not to help her sister."

Reed's obviously not buying it. "Meh. Every shitty thing you did only proves how much you care about her. Women complain all the time that men don't care enough. They only do the bare minimum. And then—"

"Yeah, women who date *you* complain about that stuff. And rightly so."

He laughs. "The point is you did everything within your extensive superpowers to impress, help, woo, and protect that woman, and you're supposed to *apologize* for it? Well, I say fuck that. She should be thanking you for caring so damned much, and also apologizing for not telling you about the scammer. If Hannah wants total honesty from you, then she should be willing to give as good as she gets."

"Wow. It's a good thing we're not a couple because it'd be scary as fuck being in a relationship with you. You'd have me turned upside down and back again, convinced *I'm* the one who's fucked up all the time."

"It's a talent, what can I say?" We stop at the bottom of the grand stair-case. It's a fork in the road, since Reed has to go upstairs to his bedroom to pack for Chicago, while I need to go to the end of a first-floor hallway to my guest room. "Look, I like Hannah," Reed says. "She's a sweetheart who's perfect for you. All I'm saying is, whenever you talk to her again, keep in mind there's only so much groveling and apologizing you should be doing here. She's not picture-perfect here, either."

"Okay, thank you for that amazing insight and pep talk. I'll keep it in mind. But please, let that be the last relationship advice you ever give me, because you're truly the last person I'd ever want to emulate in a romantic relationship. No offense."

"None taken. I wouldn't want to be you, either. If a woman didn't want me anymore, then that would be it. There'd be no groveling or begging to get her back. I'd move the fuck on."

Now, it's my turn to roll my eyes. "That's because you have abandonment issues, Reed. You flee when things get rough to avoid the other person fleeing first. Also, you've never even fallen in love, so you have no idea what you'd do in my shoes."

Reed doesn't look offended by my comment. In fact, he looks unfazed. With an audible shrug, he looks down at his watch. "Okay, meet me back here in five. We've got to move fast."

"Roger." As Reed silently ascends the staircase, I call up to him. "*Rabbit*. That's what you're supposed to say in reply whenever someone says roger. According to Kat, anyway."

Reed doesn't stop moving. "You're annoying the fuck out of me, Peter," he throws over his shoulder. "How 'bout that for a reply?" And he's gone. He's rounded a corner at the top of the stairs.

"That works, too," I murmur, before heading into the hallway toward my guest room. "Jeez, Mr. Rivers. Tell me how you really feel."

40

HANNAH

"Henn knew about all kinds of stuff nobody I've ever dated has known about," I say to my therapist, Bettina. "The birdhouse song. The hand-flex from *Pride & Prejudice*. And on and on."

My therapist hands me a tissue. "He definitely seems particularly well-suited to you."

"It's more like he was made for me. And that's what makes this so much harder, because I know for a fact I'll never meet anyone like him again."

"Do you think maybe you're getting ahead of yourself here? Leaping to catastrophic outcomes, when there might be a few stopping points along the way?"

"Do you think that's what I'm doing?"

"I do."

"I'm just confused. I thought he was The One. My Mr. Darcy. The birdhouse for my soul's little blue birdie nightlight." I lean back in my comfy armchair. I've already cried all the tears, and now I'm just exhausted. I've been babbling everything going on with Henn for the past thirty minutes, sometimes with coded language, so as not to reveal too much about Henn's online activities, and there's nothing left to say. At this point, I need input. Advice. Help sorting out all these big feelings.

Bettina offers me another tissue and I use it to blow my nose like it's a clown horn. "I have a question," she says. "Are you now in *doubt* about Henn being the birdhouse for your soul's little blue birdie nightlight, or are you now *certain* he's not?"

"Oh, no, I'm not certain he's not. In fact, I still mostly believe he is. I'm confused, though. In need of clarity. I can't imagine anyone better for me. Henn isn't one in a million—he's one in a quadrillion. But I'm not sure if I can trust him after everything that's happened. And if I can't, then there's no point in continuing the relationship."

"Are you *certain* you can't trust him again, or are you *worried* you can't?"

I think about that. "I'm not certain of anything. I think I'm mostly worried it'd be stupid or naive to trust him again, and I don't want to make the same mistakes I've made in the past."

"What mistakes would that be?"

"You know, like with my father. When he told my sister and me lie after lie through the years, I always believed him or gave him another chance, until I *finally* realized in college my life, my self-confidence, my mental health—they were all better without him."

Bettina nods sympathetically. My fraught relationship with my father is what brought me onto her couch in the first place, long before Maddy's accident brought me back again.

"Is there anything else in your past you're worried you'd be repeating with Henn, if you were to choose to trust him again?"

"I can choose to do that?"

She smiles. "Yes. But more on that later. What other mistakes are you scared about repeating?"

"Well, Angus. Not that I think Henn is anything like him. In fact, Henn is the polar opposite of Angus in every way."

"Okay, then it doesn't sound like you're worried you're being gullible with Henn, the way you were with Angus."

"Correct."

"You said you're almost positive Henn was telling the truth about seeing that stuff on your phone only *after* your first date. So, it sounds like you feel violated that he looked through your phone, understandably, rather than actually disbelieving you two are genuinely compatible."

I pause. "Yes, I think that's true."

"In that case, do you think that's a boundary you could set with Henn in the future—that he'd never look at your phone again without your permission? And if so, do you believe he'd respect that boundary?"

"Yes, he's already said, repeatedly, he'll never do it again, and I believe him. But let's not forget he also asked a friend to help my sister get into UCLA, even though I asked him not to do that." Obviously, I couldn't tell Bettina that Henn hacked into UCLA, any more than I could tell her he'd hacked me to see my phone, but I think my substitute stories work just as well for my purposes.

Bettina nods. "He's made mistakes, for sure. The question is—and correct me if I'm wrong—are those mistakes the death knell of the relationship, or a launching pad for discussion and boundary-setting going forward?"

My heart is racing. I think Bettina thinks my relationship with Henn is salvageable, despite the shit he pulled! What a relief.

When I say nothing, Bettina asks, "In other words, do you think it's within Henn's character to learn from his mistakes and respect your stated boundaries? If you were to tell him, 'Hey, you did X thing and that's a dealbreaker for me,' do you think, going forward, he'd respect that?"

The answer is suddenly obvious to me. Crystal clear, in fact. "Yes. Henn said he'll do anything for a second chance. He's even offered to go to couple's therapy with me, if that's what I want to do."

Bettina smiles. "Do you *want* to give Henn a second chance, Hannah?"

My chin trembles. Shoot. I thought I was done with tears, but they're suddenly springing into my eyes. "So much, it hurts. I miss him so, so much. *I love him.*" That's it. My tears are flowing again.

Bettina hands me the whole tissue box this time. "Then give yourself permission to use this as a teaching moment and give the man a second chance."

I wipe my eyes. "You don't think it'd be stupid and naïve for me to do that? I can be really naïve, Bettina. I know that about myself."

"I think you'd be following your heart. And I think he's shown remorse and a willingness to change and learn. Nobody's perfect. Not Henn. And not you." She looks at me pointedly. "On that note, there are probably some things you haven't gotten perfectly right, either. Things you maybe haven't gotten around to telling Henn yet that maybe you should have by now?"

My stomach twists. "Uh. Yeah. That's probably a true statement."

"*Probably?*" She suppresses a smirk. "How much have you told Henn about your relationship with your father?"

I shift in my seat. "I've told him a few things. But I haven't talked his ear off about it or anything."

"Why not?"

"It just never comes up."

This time, Bettina tilts her head and flashes me one of her patented looks—the one that says, "You're full of shit."

Now, I'm literally squirming in my seat. "It's not something I like talking about, that's all. The fact that my father would rather gamble at a casino than pick me up for my tenth birthday, like he promised, makes me feel like there's something wrong with me to this day. It's embarrassing."

"You did nothing wrong."

"I know that, intellectually. But I'm just saying that hurt doesn't go away, and I don't like going into detail on things that make me sad."

"Interesting," Bettina says. She leans back. "How much have you told Henn about Angus?"

"*Angus?*" My stomach tightens. "Why would I tell Henn about that?" When Bettina doesn't answer, I add, "Okay, in my defense, the only people I've ever told about him are you and my friend, Kat. I haven't even told my sister."

"You haven't told Maddy *anything* about all that?"

I shake my head. "The whole thing happened when she was rehabbing from her car accident."

"And what's the reason you haven't told Henn about it?"

I think about it for only half a second before the answer pops into my head, clear as a bell. "Because I'm embarrassed."

"Could it be you don't want Henn to think less of you for falling for Angus' manipulations?"

I exhale. "Correct. I don't want Henn to think I'm a gullible idiot who was so desperate for love and male validation, I fell for a romance scammer. Who does that?"

"A lot of people do. More than you'd ever believe." Bettina pauses. "I think the real question here is why both you and Henn haven't told each other everything. Sounds to me like you've both been holding back. Playing it safe. Putting your best foot forward. But isn't it way past the time in your relationship when you two should be doing that?"

I nod. "That's an excellent point."

"Do you think maybe Henn was scared to show you everything because he sensed *you* weren't showing *him* everything? And by that I mean the imperfect parts of yourself—the darkest, most vulnerable parts, the most traumatized parts—and, yes, the most embarrassed and humiliated parts, too?"

Motherfucking hell. I hate it when I come in here and sit in this chair, expecting to be told I'm totally right and everyone else is totally wrong, only to find out I've played a big part in my own problems.

Bettina smiles at whatever she's seeing on my face. And then, "Have you and Henn ever had a fight before the one in Maui?"

"No. This was our first."

"Have you two ever had so much as a quarrel before this?"

I stop to think. "No, nothing comes to mind."

"A disagreement—even about something minor or petty?"

"Well, I did tell him one night after karaoke that something he did hurt my feelings. But he immediately threw himself on his sword and promised never to do it again." I roll my eyes. "So much for that."

"Anything else?"

I search my memories. "Henn doesn't love *Lala Land* like I do. He says he *liked* it but wouldn't put it on his top ten list and also doesn't feel the urge to see it again. Of course, I told him he's a *monster.*"

Bettina's visibly unimpressed. "Anything else?"

I purse my lips. "He doesn't like Nutella. Also, monstrous. I found that out when he rented out my favorite crepes place and hired the owner to give us a private crepe-making lesson."

"How thoughtful."

"Yes, it was. Although, to be clear, I think he knew I'd like that surprise, based on what he saw on my phone."

"Which you believe he'll never do again, if you make it clear that's a dealbreaker."

"Correct."

"Is there something bigger than food and movie preferences you've disagreed on?"

I think carefully, but all that comes to mind is karaoke night. And that's it. Other than what happened that night, all I can think about is how compatible Henn and I are on important stuff. How affable and flexible Henn always is on small stuff. He has opinions, of course, but there's no hill Henn's been willing to die on that I'm not already firmly standing on beside him. Is *that* what I'm worried about—that all those hills we've been firmly standing on together have been a lie this whole time? No. My heart knows for certain that's not the case—that, in fact, Henn is exactly the man he's shown himself to be all this time. *My perfect match.* As a matter of fact, now that I've been able to talk this through, my heart knows Henn couldn't possibly have tricked me *this* well, based solely on what-ever he saw on my phone in the beginning. To the extent he's been guilty of putting his best foot forward a little too much, then I'm guilty of it, too.

"You know what?" I say, straightening up in my seat. "I have full clar-ity. I love Henn and I want to be with him."

Bettina smiles. "I think that's a great outcome for you, although I strongly suggest you work consciously on letting down your guard. Showing Henn your flaws and imperfections and making him feel safe enough to do the same."

"Thank you. I'll do that."

A gentle buzzer on Bettina's phone goes off, signaling the end of our session.

"We can keep going, if you need to," she says, picking up her phone. "I don't have anyone else until eleven-thirty."

"Nope, I'm good." I rise from my armchair. "Thank you so much. I'm excited to call him and tell him I love him and I'm sorry for not being more open and forthcoming with him in the past."

"Wonderful. I can't wait to hear how it goes. If you need help with any of those conversations, take him up on his offer to do couple's therapy."

"I will. Thank you." I give her a hug. "You're the best, Bettina. Thank you for squeezing me in."

"Any time."

As I leave Bettina's office and enter the parking garage, I feel like I'm floating on air. Like the weight of the world has been lifted off my shoulders. I grab my phone, eager to call Henn, but there's no signal in the parking garage, so I shove it back into my pocket. I'll call him from the car, the minute I've exited the structure, and tell him I'm coming home—to LA—tomorrow. I'll tell him when I get there, he should plan to come to my apartment and hunker down for a sleepover, during which we're going to have a long, much-needed talk. Not only about the stuff he's never told me, but about the stuff I've never told *him*. I'll tell him I'm ready to give all of myself to him, no holding back.

Smiling from ear to ear, I pull out my key fob and unlock my mother's car as I approach. But as I reach out to open the driver's side door, someone grabs me roughly from behind. I open my mouth to scream, but something is smashed against my mouth and nose. A cloth. It smells weird. Toxic. *What is that?*

For a split-second, I struggle against the strong arms holding me. I try to scream and kick. But it's useless. My limbs are heavy. My vision is blurring. A weird sweetness has entered my mouth, making me want to gag. Suddenly, my legs give way beneath me . . . and that's the last thing I'm aware of before my vision turns to black.

41

HENN

"It's four o'clock, Seattle time," I announce. "Hannah's been out of her therapy session for five hours."

Reed calmly cuts the stupidly expensive steak on his gilded plate. "Apparently, she doesn't wish to speak to you yet."

I lean back in my chair, too anxious to eat another bite. "I could have sworn she was ready to forgive and forget yesterday when we talked. Did her therapist talk her out of forgiving me today?"

I'm sitting at a table in a Chicago steak house with Reed, feeling deeply hungover and anxious as fuck. In about an hour, we're supposed to board Reed's private jet to fly to New York next, because Reed wants to say a quick hello to his mother and then hit some big, industry-related party, which he's planning to drag me to as his plus-one. We've both agreed, however, if I hear from Hannah before then and she says something, anything, that gives me hope, he'll fly to New York on a commercial flight—*gasp*—and give me his plane to hightail it to Seattle. When I made that deal with Reed hours ago, I thought for sure he'd be flying to New York on his own. But as the minutes continue ticking by without a peep from Hannah, I'm beginning to think the Big Apple is in my imminent future, along with a whole lot of heartbreak.

"Did Hannah promise to call you at a specific time?" Reed asks, cutting another sliver of steak.

"No." I peek at my phone again. Still nothing. "She said her appointment was at ten and would take an hour and she'd call me at some point after that. She did mention possibly grabbing lunch before calling me, but how long could that possibly take?" I run my hand through my hair. Would Hannah feel wooed or smothered if I showed up uninvited in Seattle and threw myself at her feet? I'm sleep-deprived, adrenaline-fueled, hungover, and verging on panic—not a great combination for optimal decision-making—but my gut tells me Hannah would feel wooed. "I should go to Seattle, whether I hear from her or not."

Reed calmly cuts another piece of his food. "Don't chase her, Peter. You've already groveled enough."

"Says the man who can't hold down a healthy, committed relationship to save his life."

"By *choice*. If I wanted a committed relationship, then I'd have one. But I don't." He calmly stabs a bite of veggies with his fork.

"Well, I do." I pick up my phone. "I'm gonna check flights."

"Have you considered the possibility that Hannah might not have called you yet because she's currently sitting on a flight to LA as a surprise?"

My heart stops. That's definitely something Hannah would do! And it would absolutely explain her uncharacteristic radio silence. "You're a genius, Reed Rivers."

"So I've been told many times."

I palm my forehead. "Except that you're a fucking idiot. Why'd you make me come to Chicago, when Hannah could very well be landing in LA this very minute?"

Before Reed has replied, his phone rings, and he picks up. "Hey, O. What's up?"

"O" is Owen, Reed's trusty assistant. As Reed launches into his phone call, I check my phone to make sure I haven't missed a call or text from Hannah. When it's clear I haven't, I post about Greg Smith in a few new Facebook groups, just to pass the time. Contact a few more gyms. Check in with Demon Spawn to see if he's planning to purchase another used car in the near future, and if so, where. You know, the same sorts of things I've been doing for a few months now. When I grow bored of my Greg-Smith-related shenanigans, I give in to temptation and glance at my texts again, but there's still nothing from Hannah. Fuck it. I'll send her one.

> Me: I hope therapy went well. Please call me as soon as you can to let me know you're okay.

"Can I get you gentlemen anything else?" our pretty waitress asks.

I look up and open my mouth, but Reed beats me to it.

"Just the check," he says, though he's still on his call.

"Let me get this one," I say.

"Don't be an asshole," Reed says, before returning to his call.

I stare at my phone, willing Hannah to answer my text. When she doesn't, I can't resist calling her. Unfortunately, though, my call goes straight to voicemail.

"Hey, Hannah, it's me. I'm wondering how therapy went. Call me right away, please. I'm worried about you. I love you."

Reed ends his call and scowls at me. "You called her? Come on, man."

"I think her phone is turned off." I grimace as my stomach twists with knots.

"She'd have to turn it off if she's on a flight," Reed says.

"True." I shift in my chair. I must admit it's possible Hannah went straight from therapy to the airport, but my gut tells me she wouldn't do that without calling me first.

"Is it possible to hack a phone when it's been turned off?" Reed asks. "If so, hack her and check her location, and all your questions will be answered, my friend."

I roll my eyes. "Yes, it'd be *possible* for me to turn on her phone remotely to hack her, since I've already got access," I say. "But if I pull that shit, then I won't be able to look her in the eyes and say, 'I only hacked you that one time, once in the beginning, and I swear that will be the one and only time.'"

Reed shrugs. "Or you could *not* look her in the eyes when you tell her that."

"Jesus Christ. Are you a psychopath?"

Reed laughs. "I look at Violet's location all the time without telling her. And I know for a fact Josh and Kat set it up so they can see each other's locations anytime they want."

"You pay your sister's phone bill. She's on your plan. That's not the same thing as hacking my girlfriend. And Josh and Kat gave each other *consensual* access to their locations. That's not the same thing as me remotely turning Hannah's phone on and accessing that information without her permission. Do you truly not understand that?"

"Of course, I do. All I'm saying is it'd be a minor infraction to avoid the major bummer of you flying to Seattle to surprise Hannah, if it turns out she's sitting on a flight to LA to surprise you."

I process his logic. Weigh the pros and cons and ethics of the situation. And finally say, "There's actually a normal, mortal way to gather the same information that won't breach Hannah's trust and privacy." I hold up my phone and smile. "I'll call Hannah's sister. Hannah would never fly to LA without telling her she left Seattle. In fact, if Hannah is on a flight right now, then Maddy probably took her to the airport." I snicker. "And lucky for me, Maddy's a terrible liar."

The waitress appears again, this time with our check, and Reed interacts with her. While he's handling the bill, I place the call to Maddy.

"Hello, Henn."

"Hi, Maddy. Have you heard from Hannah recently?"

"I was just about to call you to ask the same question. She hasn't answered my texts all afternoon and my call went straight to voicemail."

My heart slams into my toes. "Same here." Every nerve ending in my body spasms with acute worry. "Do you think maybe she caught a flight to LA on a whim?"

"She'd never do that without telling me. Plus, she's got my mom's car today and promised to pick her up from work at six. We're doing pizza and a movie at my mom's place tonight."

"She had a therapy session at ten and promised to call me after that. But it's been crickets."

Maddy pauses. "Maybe she went to see a movie after therapy? She does that sometimes, if the session was brutal."

I feel two diametrically opposed emotions at once: relief that Maddy's offering an explanation that would mean Hannah is safe and sound, but also panic that Hannah's therapy session, which was all about me and what I did, might have been brutal for her.

"That would explain our calls going straight to voicemail," Maddy adds. "If Hannah's in a movie, she would have turned off her phone."

"Yeah, that makes sense. I was thinking maybe she went on a little tour of Henn and Hannah's Seattle after her appointment. Like, maybe she decided to visit all the places she and I went during our first week together and remember The Happier Times. But a movie actually makes a whole lot more sense than that."

"A little tour like that would make sense, too. That'd be a very main-character-having-deep-and-nostalgic-thoughts kind of thing for her to do. She loves that kind of thing."

We both chuckle. "Yeah," I say, "if there's one thing Hannah Banana loves, it's being the main character in her movie."

"Yes, she does."

I exhale a long breath of relief. "So, I take it you haven't received a distress signal from her, right? You've checked to make sure of that?" Months ago, during dinner with the three Milliken women, our foursome got to talking about our mutual obsession with all things true crime. That conversation led to one about how terrifying it is that monsters walk among us, undetected. Which then led to me helping all three women load a clever, one-touch distress signal onto their phones—an app that looks like a calculator on its face, but when opened, sends an instant text message to the people selected, as well as a pinpoint location and instructions to send help. In this case, Hannah's distress-signal text would go to the other two women and me.

"Nope. I haven't gotten a thing," Maddy confirms, and I exhale with relief again. In theory, I would have received the same distress signal as Maddy, if Hannah had sent one. But not if Hannah had taken me off the recipient list because she's pissed at me.

"Whenever Hannah calls or texts you," I say, "will you do me a favor and tell her to please contact me, if only to tell me she's okay? We were supposed to talk today, so I'm hoping she'll want to talk to me beyond confirming she's safe. But if not, she needs to give me at least that."

"Of course. But I bet she's planning to call you after picking up my mom from work, at the latest. Hannah would never leave you hanging overnight."

"I wouldn't think so."

When I hang up with Maddy, Reed has already paid the waitress and is staring at me with raised eyebrows. "So, what's your destination, brother?" he asks. "LA, Seattle, or New York?"

"Seattle. Hannah will be at her mother's place tonight. I'm gonna skip the phone call and talk to her in person. Don't worry, I'll grab a commercial flight."

Reed shakes his head. "No, I'll take you in my plane. I've got some stuff I can do in Seattle."

"Thanks, but that's not necessary. I'm sure there are plenty of—"

"No, you need to get there as soon as possible, and I really do have stuff to do there. Owen said all the signed paperwork came in from 22 Goats, so I should probably take them out to celebrate and talk next steps. I want to bounce some music video ideas off them. Plus, I want to move them into one of my apartment buildings in LA while they're writing and recording their debut album, and it'd be more productive to have those conversations in person."

I shrug. "Okay, if it's genuinely not a problem for you to fly me there, then I'll take you up on the ride."

"Not a problem at all. Happy to help." Reed stands, and when I don't immediately follow suit because I'm checking my phone for a text from Hannah, he snaps his fingers impatiently at me. "Come on, Peter. I'm happy to help but not to *wait*."

"Sorry."

42

HANNAH

O*uch.*

My brain is on fire.

When I open my groggy eyes, I'm bound to a chair by my chest and legs. I try to scream but something affixed to my mouth muffles the sound. Is that duct tape on my lips? I think there's a gag in my mouth, too. I try to touch whatever is keeping my lips firmly shut, but my arms are tied behind my back at my wrists. There's only one person in the world I'd let tie me up. But not like this. *Have I been abducted*?

No.

It can't be.

I must have fallen asleep while listening to a true crime podcast.

Wake up, Hannah.

I blink several times, but my bindings are still there. My shabby surroundings the same. I'm in a dilapidated barn or large shed. There's a card table on the far side of the space with an opened metal folding chair next to it. The chair is slightly askew, like someone slid it back when getting up and didn't push it back in.

Someone.

My abductor.

Due to my bindings, I can't turn to look behind me to see if my captor is back there, so I hold my ragged breath and listen carefully for any sounds. But there's nothing but silence and the faint sounds of twittering birds and wind outside. Either my abductor left me here for who knows how long and for God knows what purpose, *or* he's standing right behind me at this very moment, silently savoring my panic and confusion and fear.

Have I been raped?

I close my eyes and zero in on the sensations between my legs, but nothing feels out of the ordinary or painful, other than my bladder feeling uncomfortably full. Although, I suppose, that's not a guarantee I'm untouched. Tears well in my eyes at the thought of what might have happened to me while my body was prone and unconscious.

The air passing in and out of my nostrils is loud and erratic. My heart is beating so hard, it's surely going to create hairline fractures in my sternum. Is my abductor going to rape and murder me and then harvest my organs? Or will he rape me and sell me into sex slavery?

Calm down, Hannah. Figure out how to escape.

My phone.

Where is it?

Henn loaded that distress signal onto it that looks like a calculator! My heart sinks. Clearly, that's not going to help me. Even if my phone is miraculously still on me, I wouldn't be able to press any buttons on it with my hands tied behind my back.

Fuck.

I'm going to die today.

No, you're not. Look around. Figure out your escape.

There's a small window in a far corner that's been hastily covered by a thin red handkerchief and some duct tape. One side of the fabric is fluttering slightly, suggesting the window is opened. Or maybe there's no glass in the opening at all? Either way, the quality of light behind the fluttering red swatch of fabric tells me it's still daylight outside, although there's no way of knowing if it's still the same day as when I was taken or if night has come and gone who-knows-how-many times. Is that weak light a sign that it's dawn or dusk? I guess I'll find out soon enough, when the light brightens or turns to black.

My eyes drift to the small card table. There's a small, flat-ish object on it that I can't make out from here. Also, an opened laptop, a large, plastic bottle of water, and a small black duffel bag on the floor next to the chair.

Fuck.

I'm going to die today.

My favorite true crime podcaster always warns, "Don't let your abductor take you to a secondary location, or else your odds of survival plummet." And yet, here I am, bound and gagged in a secondary location. Fuck.

All of a sudden, a loud thwapping noise behind me splits the silence, making me jolt and shriek behind my gag. Heavy footsteps draw closer behind me, sending shivers of terror across my skin.

"You're awake," a deep male voice says behind me. "For a minute there, I thought maybe I overdid the chloroform and turned you into a vegetable forever." The footsteps stop. My captor is standing above me. *It's Angus.* Or Greg Smith. Whatever the hell this man's name is. Holy fuck, I feel like I'm seeing a ghost. Why? And why *now*? I would have bet he'd forgotten all about me by now. In fact, with all his presumed victims, I would have bet anything he wouldn't even recognize me if he passed me on the street. And yet, two years later, after zero contact, he's kidnapped me out of nowhere? Has he been stalking me this entire time?

Standing before me now, Angus looks nothing like the charming, handsome, smooth operator from two years ago—the personal trainer who so deftly wielded his traditional good looks and perfect physique to maximum advantage. No, the present iteration of this man looks manic, unkempt, unhinged, and wild-eyed. Plus, he's even more muscular than when I knew him, which only makes him seem even more menacing to me.

Angus bends down until his nose practically touches mine. "Are you in the mood to die today, Hannah? Because today will be your last, if you don't help me get every fucking thing I want."

Warmth spreads between my legs and across the denim on my inner thighs. The scent of urine fills the air and mingles with the scent of Angus' sweat.

Angus looks down at the pee spreading between my thighs and chuckles. "Glad to see you're taking this so seriously."

I nod, letting him know I'm taking this as seriously as a human being can take anything.

"I've figured everything out," Angus says. "There's no point in denying anything. Do you understand me?"

I nod again, even though, obviously, I don't know what he could possibly be talking about.

Satisfied with my compliance, Angus marches across the small space to the card table. He digs around in the duffel bag on the floor and pulls out a black knit something. A cap? He then picks up the unidentified object off the table. Oh, God. *It's a knife.* A big, scary, serrated one that could end my life in point-two seconds flat, if Angus were to drag its blade across my neck with any kind of force. If I hadn't already pissed myself, I'd surely be doing it now.

Angus grabs the metal chair with his free hand and strides toward me. As he approaches, I notice a phone peeking out of his pocket. Unless he's got his own phone with the same hot pink case as mine, then that's my phone. *Hallelujah!* Surely, it's been sending pings to nearby cell towers this whole time, which means the police can use my phone to triangulate my location. That's what happens in so many of my true crime podcasts.

Although . . . come to think of it, the police would only be triangulating my location if my family has reported me missing by now. What time is it? Has the time come for me to pick up my mother at work?

Aw, fuck. As Angus comes to a stop in front of me, I can plainly see my phone screen in his pocket is pure black, which means the device is turned off, or, worse, its battery dead. Fuckity. Thanks to my true crime obsession, I know phones have to be turned on to be trackable. So much for the police triangulating my location.

"Eyes here, bitch," Angus barks, as he places the chair immediately across from me.

I jerk my gaze from the blackened screen in Angus' pocket to his angry eyes as he takes a seat before me. He lays his two objects—a black, knit cap and that scary knife—onto his lap and says, "I'm going to talk now, and you're going to listen carefully. And when I'm done talking, you're going to realize you've only got one option, if you want to see another day. You're going to call your rich boyfriend on FaceTime, so I can see his face and make sure you're not trying to pull a fast one, and you're going to convince that motherfucker to a) stop fucking with me, and b) pay me five million bucks in exchange for your life."

My thoughts come fast and furious, as my breathing becomes shallow. Angus knows about Henn? *How?* My Instagram is set to private. But regardless, I don't post about Henn or tag him in photos because Henn abhors social media and doesn't have any accounts. Also, why does Angus think Henn can afford to pay five million bucks to save my life? Yes, Henn has done well for himself lately, but he doesn't have that kind of money. Although I suppose Henn could hack a bank to get the money or perhaps ask Josh or Reed to give it to him. Yeah, the more I think about it, I guess Henn could get his hands on that kind of ransom. *But how does Angus know that?*

Wait.

Angus wants Henn to stop "fucking with" him. So, that means Henn not only knows about Angus, but he's also hacked Angus and has been doing something to inflict pain upon him. Oh, God. *The draft protective order!* It's still on my laptop. Henn must have seen it when he hacked me. Goddammit! Bettina had me feeling guilty for never telling Henn anything about Angus, but Henn has known about him from the earliest days of our relationship and never once asked me about him. Motherfucker! Has Henn been screwing with Angus for months and months as some sort of revenge plot for what Henn read about in that draft protective order? And is that what set Angus off and motivated him to hunt me down and drag me here? Ha! I guess Henn isn't quite as talented a hacker as he thinks, if someone as stupid as Angus figured him out.

"Listen up!" Angus booms, so I return my darting eyes to his angry face and nod effusively. "*Listen to me,*" Angus says, a bit more calmly. And when I nod again, he settles back into his chair and begins his tale. "At first, I thought it was an honest mistake—a glitch—when all those impound notices started coming to my mom's place for cars registered in my name. So many fucking cars. I thought there had to be another Greg Smith who hadn't paid a bunch of parking tickets and impound fees. But then, two notices turned into twenty. Then fifty. Then a hundred. Collections agencies started hounding my mother. And then, bounty hunters showed up with warrants for my fucking arrest."

What the fuck? Henn hacked into the Department of Motor Vehicles to make it look like a hundred different impounded cars were registered to Greg Smith? I'd actually think the strategy kind of brilliant, if it hadn't landed me here. But wouldn't someone at the Department have noticed a massive hack like that?

Angus leaps up and shouts, "I can't even visit my own mother, or else someone's gonna arrest me for not paying impound fees on a hundred-fifty cars that aren't even mine! And I can't use my real name anymore, either. Not even for stuff relating to my mother, or twenty different bounty hunters are gonna find me and drag me to jail."

I wince as his hot breath and spittle hit my face. The black knit something and knife both fell to the floor when Angus leaped up, and looking at them now, I can tell the black thing is a knit mask—the kind skiers wear in blizzards and bank robbers wear in movies.

Shit. I think that ski mask is a bad omen for me. Surely, it means Angus is planning to obscure his identity from Henn when we call him on FaceTime later, which therefore means he can't let me go at the end of all this, even if he gets the money he wants. How could he let me go, when I've seen his face and could identify him to police? I'm sure Angus decided it was worth it to show me his face, even though it means he now has to commit murder, simply because his ego demands I know it was *him* who so cleverly bested Henn.

"I told you to listen to me!" Angus bellows, and it's only then that I realize my mind has been wandering while he's been speaking. I return my eyes to his, but it's not soon enough. All of a sudden, I feel the shocking sting of a fist punching the side of my face.

I scream behind my gag. I've never been hit before, and the experience isn't one I'd recommend. Zero stars. Even in my terror, however, my true-crime-obsessed brain is gathering information. Namely, if Angus feels this comfortable screaming at top volume, then we must be in the middle of nowhere, since this structure doesn't look soundproofed in the least.

With a deep exhale, Angus retakes his seat across from me and resumes his rambling monologue. "And then, I didn't get an interview at Climb & Conquer, even though that chick said she'd put in a good word for me. I couldn't understand it. I've gotten every job at every gym I've ever applied to. Every fucking one. And I couldn't even get an interview at that one, even though I climbed the expert wall at the party like it was nothing? It made no sense."

My head is spinning. *Angus attended the Climb & Conquer party*? How? Why? Is that proof he's been stalking me all this time, or was it pure coincidence that he was there, and I never saw him? Did Angus see me and that's why I'm sitting here now, bound to a chair?

Wait.

Henn and his explosive diarrhea.

Mother trucker!

Henn must have seen Angus at the party and told me that gross excuse to get me out of there on a bullet train. I'd find it funny that Henn fell on his sword like that to keep me from bumping into Angus, if I weren't sitting here now. Except, of course, for the part where Henn only knew about Angus in the first place because he'd secretly hacked me the day after meeting me . . . and then embarked on some kind of vengeance crusade on my behalf that somehow led Angus straight to me. *Son of a beach ball.*

Angus runs his hand through his hair. "I couldn't figure out why I didn't get an interview, and why nobody was answering my emails, so I went to Climb & Conquer's Instagram to message them there. And who did I see in the background on one of their shots from the party? *You.* Cuddled up with the hot blonde girlfriend of one of the brothers. It took me a minute to even remember your name, but when I did, I sent a request from a fake profile, and that's when I went through your Instagram and saw you cuddled up at the other Faraday brother's wedding with your rich boyfriend. I couldn't believe my eyes. Not only did Hannah-What's-Her-Name go to a billionaire's wedding, but she was there with *that* guy?" He shakes his head in disbelief. "I did a little research and found out you'd worked with blondie, which meant blondie must have set you up with her boyfriend's rich best friend. Well, that explained it. Obviously, I knew you had to be nothing but a fuck buddy to him because why would someone like *him* want someone like *you* as an actual girlfriend? But, anyway, I made a mental note to keep tabs on your relationship with him, just in case I could somehow benefit from your access to him in the future."

I'm baffled. Angus thinks Henn is out of my league, based on looks alone? It's the least of my problems at the moment, but I'm offended.

Henn is adorable and gorgeous to me, and his smile lights up every room, but it's his personality that makes him a perfect ten. He's certainly not out of my league in terms of looks, sir.

"And then, weird shit started happening," Angus continues. "I couldn't get a job at any of my usual gyms. My photos were being posted everywhere with warnings about me. My bank accounts were glitching. Freezing me out. It was small stuff at first, but it never let up. I'm thinking, 'Am I under attack or having a string of bad luck?'" His dark eyes narrow. "And that's when I went back to your Instagram and saw what finally helped me figure the whole thing out." He gets up from his chair and begins pacing the small space. "There was a selfie of you in your new apartment in LA. And what did you say in the caption? You thanked your rich boyfriend for his generosity."

Well, he's got that wrong. I thanked *Reed* in that caption, not Henn.

"And then, there was another selfie—this one bragging about landing your dream job. And who'd you thank in the caption *again*? Your rich boyfriend, again. And then, to cap it all off, there you were with him at blondie's wedding in Maui to his best friend. How sweet for you both. Double dates for life, huh?"

If my jaw weren't firmly taped in place, it'd clank into my lap. *Angus thinks Reed is my rich boyfriend.*

Angus says, "I did some research on your rich boyfriend and Reddit is full of stories about him being a vindictive prick. Did you know he dropped a band from his label simply because their lead singer fucked his ex? Nice boyfriend you've got there, Hannah. You can really pick 'em, eh?" He chortles. "So, that's when I finally figured everything out: Hannah-What's-Her-Name cried to her rich, vindictive boyfriend about me, so he hired a hacker to fuck with me. God, I'm good."

I can't believe it. This unhinged lunatic reached the correct conclusion through totally incorrect reasoning. It's just my luck. Fucking hell.

Angus rambles for a while about how brilliant he is for figuring me out. And then, about what he wants me to say to my rich boyfriend when we call him, shortly, on FaceTime. In conclusion, Angus says, "When you call him, you're going to convince him there's no point in denying what he's done because I'm smarter than him and his fucking hacker and I've figured it all out. You got that?"

I nod.

"You'll tell him to pay up, if he ever wants to see you alive again."

I nod again, even though my brain has now shifted into rapid-fire problem-solving mode. What's my survival strategy here? If Angus frees my hand and gives me my phone to make the FaceTime call to Reed, then I'll somehow get to that distress signal button. That's a no-brainer. But I think the chances are low he'll free my hand. More likely, he'll keep me tied up and use my contacts to call Reed on my phone. If he does that, that'd be a good thing for me, in theory, since my newly turned-on phone will start pinging nearby cell towers. In reality, however, that phone call to Reed will probably get me killed before anyone can find me.

First off, Reed probably won't even pick up my call, since it'd show up to him as an unknown caller. Yes, *I* saved *Reed's* number when Kat included him in a group chat once. But I can't fathom why *Reed* would have saved *my* number. How many times will Angus let Reed fail to pick up his "girlfriend's" call before Angus realizes Reed isn't, in fact, my rich boyfriend, and won't, in fact, pay to keep me alive? But even if Reed does miraculously answer my call, I'll be dead, regardless, because Reed's natural, immediate reaction to the crazy shit Angus has instructed me to say will quickly make Angus realize Reed isn't, in fact, my rich boyfriend. Shit. There's no way in hell I'm getting out of this mess alive, is there?

Oh, yes, you are. Calm down and think, Hannah. Think!

Angus stops pacing, pulls out a small phone from his other pocket—one that's not mine—and resumes his seat across from me again. "I hope for your sake you know Reed's number by heart," he says. "Because we can't turn on your phone to get the number." He rolls his eyes. "I fucked up in the parking garage and forgot facial recognition doesn't work on closed eyes. So, I couldn't get Reed's number off your phone back there. And then, I realized after we got here, if I turn on your phone now, someone could use the signal to find you."

Fuck, fuck, fuck. Now what?

"I'm going to take the tape off your mouth now," Angus says slowly, like he's talking to a skittish kitten in a tree. "*Don't scream.* No one but me will hear you, if you do. But I don't want to hear it. If you scream, I'll punch you even harder than last time. Understand?"

I nod and he removes the tape.

"I don't know Reed's latest number by heart," I blurt. "He changes his number every month for security reasons. But I do know his assistant's number, so I can call him and—"

"You're not calling anyone but Reed on FaceTime."

"If Reed is going to pay you five million bucks for my life, then he's going to need his assistant to help him get those funds in order. Even rich people don't have five million bucks in cash sitting around. They have to move things around. Sell stocks and stuff. I guarantee Reed will need to tell his assistant what's going on to get you that money because his assistant is his right hand in everything he does. Well, since that's the case, then what's the harm in me calling his assistant first on FaceTime and calmly asking for Reed's number? He knows I always forget to save my boyfriend's latest number. It happens every month. He won't think anything of it."

Angus looks like he's actually considering saying yes to this change of plans. At the very least, he's not presently punching me in the face, so I forge ahead. "I promise I'll get you the money and get Reed to call off the hacker, too, if only you'll let me call Reed's assistant first. What could go wrong? You'll be there when I talk to him, watching to make sure I'm not saying something I shouldn't. I know if I mess up you'll kill me, so I won't mess up."

Angus's nostrils flare. "I don't want you telling the assistant what's going on. You'll play it off like it's any other day. Be cheerful. Ask for the number. Hang up."

"Absolutely."

"What's his name?

"Owen Boucher." Thank God, I happen to know that, thanks to over-hearing part of Reed's phone call in Maui and then looking the guy up on the River Records website for kicks.

Angus strides over to his laptop on the card table and clacks away. Presumably, he's googling Owen's name. Hopefully, he's finding Owen on the River Records website, because, as I recall, the smiling photo of him there looks vaguely like Henn. Close enough, anyway, that Angus won't notice the switch-a-roo, especially since FaceTime doesn't provide the clearest view of a person. Regardless, what choice do I have than to give this idea a try? This is literally the only thing I can think to do to try to save my life.

Still bent over his computer, Angus says, "Is Owen's number the one listed on the River Records website?"

"No. That's the number that goes to the receptionist. Reed always talks to Owen on an unlisted number. That's the one I've memorized because Reed told me not to save it into my phone because it's a direct line for Reed's use only."

Angus straightens up and heads toward me again. As he moves, I realize my phone screen sticking out of his pocket is no longer black—it's illuminated. *My phone has been turned on*! Holy fuck! Is that Henn? Has Henn realized I'm missing and he's checking my location? If so, Henn has finished his work by the time Angus is sitting across from me again. In fact, my phone is back to black by the time Angus is leaning back in his chair. Oh, shit. Did I imagine my phone being turned on? Was that a hallucination brought on by wishful thinking?

"You'll play it off casually with Owen," Angus instructs. "Nothing out of the ordinary. Everything's great. You simply forgot to save Reed's latest number, as usual, and need the new one."

"Got it."

"If the assistant doesn't immediately give you Reed's number, or if I get a vibe you're giving him a coded message, or if you scream for him to call the police, I'll slit your throat from ear to ear while he's watching. Understand?"

Tears threaten, but I swallow them down. "Yes. Owen might not answer a call from an unknown number, though. If he doesn't pick up, maybe you could text him first to let him know—"

"I'm not stupid. I've rigged my phone to spoof your number, so it'll look like you're the one calling. Now, what's the assistant's number?"

43
HENN

"Why did Hannah go all the way out there?" I ask, staring at my laptop screen.

We're on Reed's private jet. He's sitting across the aisle from me, looking at his own laptop. "You broke down and hacked her?"

"I'm far more worried about her safety at this point than I am about her being pissed at me for checking her location." I turn my laptop screen toward him. "Look. She's in the middle of nowhere."

"Does she know anyone who lives out there?"

"Not that I know of." I turn my laptop around and quickly power Hannah's phone off again. Hopefully, she didn't notice my snooping. If she did, I can only hope and pray she understands why I did it and forgives me. "Shit. I thought knowing her location would calm my nerves, but it's only freaking me out, even more."

My phone rings with an incoming FaceTime call from Hannah. *Oh, thank God, she's safe.* Granted, based on timing, Hannah's almost certainly calling to chew me out for hacking her phone again, but I'll take that bullet every time in a situation like this to confirm she's okay. Even though Reed is sitting across from me on the plane, he won't hear the ass-chewing I'm about to get, since I'm wearing my earbuds. And so, I connect the call from where I'm sitting.

"Hannah." I force myself to press my lips together and wait for her to speak. My instinct is to ramble a long string of apologies and explanations, but there's an outside chance the timing of her call is coincidental, so why throw myself underneath a bus if it's not absolutely necessary?

Hold up. Hannah's appearance is deeply concerning. She looks ragged. And she's got what looks like a welt on the side of her face. Is her cheek slightly swollen? And what's that redness around her mouth? It looks like she's recently ripped a Band-Aid off from that spot. Suddenly, all the explanations and apologies rattling around inside my head vanish, replaced by nothing but acute worry and anxiety. My heart pounding, I blurt, "What happened to your cheek?"

Hannah's eyes flicker to a spot beyond the phone. And that's when I realize the angle-and-distance ratio of the camera to Hannah's face is off. Too far away. Hannah's not holding the phone. *Someone else is doing it.*

"Hey, Owen," Hannah says with a tight smile.

Owen?

"I'm so dumb," she says with a roll of her eyes. "I bonked my cheek on my car door like a dunce. But that's not why I missed my lunch with Reed today. What happened is . . ."

I yank out my earbuds, letting the rest of Hannah's sentence fill the space between Reed and me, while frantically gesturing out of frame for Reed to listen. In my periphery, Reed looks up from his laptop as Hannah continues speaking.

She says, ". . . I ran into an old friend after my therapy appointment and then totally lost track of time when we got to talking. Is my darling boyfriend, Reed, furious with me for being such a flake and forgetting to call him sooner?"

My brain is rapidly processing every batshit crazy thing Hannah's said and combining it with her batshit crazy location and that concerning welt on her face. The redness on her chin and around her mouth. "Uh, yeah, Reed was pretty furious at first," I say. "But after a while, when you hadn't called or texted in hours, his anger turned to worry, so I'm sure he'll forgive you out of sheer relief that you're okay."

Hannah's eyes flicker to that same target beyond the phone again, so I quickly glance at my best friend across the aisle. Reed's dark eyes are transfixed on mine. He's on high alert. Breathing hard, the same as me.

Clearly, something horrific is going down with Hannah. My worst nightmare. And Reed knows it as well as I do.

"I'll call Reed to explain everything now," Hannah says. "That is, if you'd be so kind as to give me his latest number. I'm sure it won't surprise you to learn I've once again forgotten to save Reed's latest monthly number in my phone." She forces a chuckle. "I promise to save it next month when he changes it again and never bother you again."

I chuckle with her. "We both know you won't save it. But don't worry, you're never a bother. I've got to earn the big bucks Reed pays me somehow. But, hey, if you want to talk to your boyfriend, there's no need to hang up and call his phone. He's sitting right here. We just now boarded his jet for Chicago. We're checking out a possible new band tomorrow night."

Intense relief floods Hannah's face. "Oh, how fun. I wish I could be there with you both." She glances at that same target beyond her phone again and nods subtly. "Um, yeah, that sounds good. Put Reed on, Owen. Thanks so much."

"You bet. Bye now. I'm so glad you're okay."

"Thanks. I'm fine. Just forgetful and easily distractible."

I move across the aisle toward Reed, prompting him to slide one seat over. Quickly, I take the newly vacated seat and hand Reed my phone.

"Hey, baby," Reed says. "Why the fuck didn't you make our lunch and why the fuck didn't you call me before now?"

"Sweetheart, is Owen still there? I need to talk to you alone."

Reed looks to his left, even though I'm sitting to his right. "Hey, O. Can you give me a sec? Thanks." He waits a beat. "Okay, we're alone. This better be good, Hannah."

"What I'm about to tell you is going to piss you off, but you have to promise you won't contact law enforcement. My life depends on you following that instruction."

"What happened to your face?" Reed asks.

"I've been abducted, and my captor wants money in exchange for my life. You'll need to do everything he says to a T. My life depends on it."

Jesus Fucking Christ. *Greg Smith.* Who else could it be? But why? How? And why the fuck does he think *Reed* is Hannah's boyfriend?

Hannah is now giving Reed a bizarre, disjointed speech that basically boils down to this: her captor wants Reed to pay five million bucks in Bitcoin of all things in exchange for her release.

While Hannah talks, I open my computer and punch through a virtual back door I left ajar on the fucker's laptop. He wiped his entire system clean recently, and probably congratulated himself on kicking his pesky hacker out by doing so. But of course, he didn't do any such thing. I'm impossible to shake, once I've got you, especially when my target is a high priority one like this fucker.

Once inside Greg Smith's laptop, I quickly check the device's pinpoint location and surmise it's in the same place as Hannah's phone. In theory, he could have spoofed his location, but that's extremely unlikely, considering both devices line up and he almost certainly thinks he's shaken me. To be sure, however, I try to check the phone he had with him at the Climb & Conquer party, but its battery is dead or dismantled. He must have ditched that phone and got himself a new one when he realized he'd been hacked. Okay, what about that burner phone? I click into that one, and, yep, it's still live. And not only that, its location is the same as Hannah's phone and Greg's laptop. *Bingo.*

On his FaceTime call with Hannah, Reed says, "Okay, put the fucker on now. I want to talk to him, man to man."

His face covered by a black ski mask, Greg Smith appears. "Hey there, Reed," he says. "It turns out I'm a whole lot smarter than you and your hacker gave me credit for, huh?"

"Let's skip the part where you taunt me and cut straight to you convincing me you'll actually return Hannah to me, safe and sound, if I send you the money. I swear to God, if you touch a hair on her head—"

"If you're not convinced, then don't pay me and see what happens," Greg barks. "I normally like keeping my boxes separate, but I swear to God, I won't hesitate to slit this bitch's throat if you don't follow my instructions."

"I'll pay it," Reed says. "But only if I'm sure, when I press submit on the transfer, Hannah's alive and in perfect health. I'll need to see Hannah on FaceTime as I'm pressing the button."

"I can do that," Greg replies.

"It'll take me a day to pull that much cash together," Reed says. "Give me until—"

"Nope. Payment by midnight West Coast time, or she's dead."

I motion to Reed to keep him talking, so he asks a question about logistics. As Greg babbles his answer, I race toward the back of the plane with my laptop. I can't believe I led this maniac straight to Hannah. True, it seems he got to her by connecting dots I can't even fathom right now. But the fact remains, I'm the careless idiot who set the wheels in motion for this catastrofuck to happen. And now, God help me, I'm going to do whatever it takes to get Hannah back, alive and well.

Once I'm situated at the back of the plane, I pull out my back-up phone and shoot my main FBI contact a message. Lucky for me, she's second in command of the whole operation—the Deputy Director with direct access to the Director himself—which means she's a damned good person to have on speed dial at a time like this.

> Me: This is Peter Hennessey. I've got a life-or-death emergency requiring your immediate, urgent assistance. Please drop whatever you're doing and call me at this number.

It's a ballsy thing to tell someone that high up at the FBI to drop what they're doing and call you back. But I don't give a fuck. I saved the country from total catastrophe on her watch, and she's already told me she owes me one. So, this is how she can repay me.

While awaiting her reply, I click into Google Earth and check out 3-D imagery of Hannah's location. Looks like a rundown barn or large shed in a rural area that's about two hours outside of Seattle. *Hang in there, baby. Help is on the way.*

My phone rings after a minute or two, though it feels a whole lot longer.

"Deputy Director Leach?"

"Identify yourself."

"Bluebird. Peter Hennessey." I spit out the code I used to punch in to access the system in DC.

"What's going on, Peter?"

I tell her everything as succinctly as I can, concluding with, "I'm begging you to please call in whatever favors you can with local law enforcement in Washington state and get them to—"

"Kidnapping is a federal crime," Deputy Director Leach replies calmly. "Squarely within our jurisdiction and expertise. No local law enforcement needed."

Relief floods me. "Oh, thank God."

"Tell me everything you know."

I babble every detail, big and small, and she tells me to send her everything I've got, including Hannah's location, whatever data I've collected on Greg Smith, and links to get into his devices.

"I'm on it. I've sent you the pinpoint location already. The rest will take a few minutes."

"Perfect. I'm sending the location to the head of the Seattle office with instructions to call me right away for instructions. He'll assemble a team in lightning speed, and we'll be off to the races. Keep this line free, in case we need to talk to you again."

"Yes, ma'am. Standing by."

"Is Reed still talking to him?"

I rise up in my seat enough to peek toward the front of the plane. "Yes."

"Good. Can you patch me into the cell Reed is using?"

"Yes."

"Do that and send me a number where we can text Reed while he's talking. We'll give him real-time instructions on what to say."

"Working on that now."

"Perfect. Okay, my guy in Seattle is calling me on another line. I'll be in touch."

When the line goes dead, I race to the front of the plane and sit next to Reed, safely out of frame from his call with Greg. Quickly, I send a text to Reed's own phone that's sitting in his lap, telling him to keep an eye out for incoming instructions from the FBI. I gesture to Reed to pick up the phone in his lap, which he does, and after slyly stealing a peek at his screen as Greg continues rambling, Reed flashes me a covert thumbs-up.

That mission accomplished, I get to work on my laptop. First things first, I patch the FBI into Reed's on-going FaceTime call on my phone, as promised. Once that's done, I start pulling together information about Greg Smith to send to Deputy Director Leach.

"I'm done talking about this," Greg suddenly barks, cutting Reed off mid-sentence. "The price is five mill in Bitcoin, transferred to me by midnight, or she's dead. If I don't hear from you in time, I'll kill her. That's not a bluff, Reed. Trust me on that. In fact, it's taking all my self-restraint not to kill her now, just to teach you a lesson for fucking with me."

"Don't do that," Reed says—and it's the first time he's let a bit of panic seep into his tone. "Think about what you'll be able to do with five million bucks in the bank. Where you'll be able to go. Take it from me, being rich makes you feel like a god. You can do whatever the fuck you want."

"I already do."

"Well, then, you'll be able to do it in grand style."

I hold my breath as the black-ski-mask-covered figure on the screen fidgets, and then exhale deeply and says, "You've got till midnight. Don't fuck around or you'll find out I'm not bluffing."

The call ends abruptly.

"Fucking hell," Reed murmurs, letting out a long exhale.

Before I've pulled myself together enough to reply, the phone in Reed's lap buzzes with an incoming call.

"This is Reed," he says. "Yes, Peter is here, too. Hang on."

Reed pushes a button, and Deputy Director Leach's voice comes through on speaker phone.

"You did great, Reed," she says. "You kept him talking long enough for us to confirm his location is the same one Peter sent to us. The Seattle team is leaving now, partially by helicopter and partially by car."

"Don't let him hear the helicopter," I call out. "He said he'd kill Hannah if we contact law enforcement."

"The pilot will touch down at a safe distance. We've got this, Peter. This is something we train to do. Reed, an agent will contact you shortly on this line to talk about the game plan for later—for when you call him to say the transfer is ready. It was great thinking to demand to see Hannah's face while pressing submit. It's also a good thing you said you need time to liquidate some things. That will buy us some time to get into position."

"Should I transfer the five mill he wants into Bitcoin?" Reed asks.

"Do you have that kind of cash available?"

"I've got that much and more, sitting in an account."

"Or I could spoof the transfer," I pipe in to say. "I've still got access to his laptop, remember? I can make it look like he's receiving the money, when he's not. He won't know the difference."

"Let's not fuck with that, just in case," Reed says. "Even if I have to make the transfer for real, I'll get my money back at some point, won't I?"

"I'd say the chances are ninety-nine percent," Deputy Director Leach says.

"Then let's do it for real," Reed says. He looks at me. "Nothing's infallible, Henny. This situation proves it. Let's not take any chances."

Tears spring into my eyes. "Thank you." I can barely get the words out over the lump in my throat.

Reed asks a few questions about the tone he should strike during his next call, and while he and the Deputy Director talk, I slump in my seat, put my face in my hands, and try not to fall completely apart.

"Yep, sounds good," Reed says. "We'll wait to hear from you. Thanks." When he ends the call, I've still got my head in my hands. Reed says, "She's gonna be okay, Henny." When I don't look up or respond, he touches my arm and says, "Peter, listen to me. They know what they're doing. She's gonna be okay."

"How could I have been so stupid and arrogant?" I choke out from behind my hands. "So *careless* with the one person who matters most to me in this world?"

"You weren't careless. He's a nut job. A conspiracy theorist. This is a case of a broken clock being right twice a day." When I don't reply, Reed adds, "Nobody—not even a genius like you—could have foreseen he'd connect all those weird dots."

"I should have foreseen that as a possibility. I should have factored that into my calculations."

"Henny, no. He's a whack job who connected dots that weren't even connectable."

I lift my head and wipe my wet cheeks. "What if he kills her before they get there? Or they get there, and he kills her because we called law enforcement?"

"They're experts at this kind of thing. Let's choose to trust them."

"Experts aren't infallible. I'm an expert hacker and look how badly I fucked this up." A sob lurches out of me. "If anything happens to Hannah, I won't survive it. If he kills her, I won't deserve to live another day."

"*Don't talk like that,*" Reed says sharply.

His voice is so commanding, I'm instantly rendered breathless. What was I thinking, saying something like that to Reed, when I know full well his father killed himself? "I'm sorry," I murmur. "I just need her to be safe."

"I know." He grips my arm. "And she will be."

I lean my forehead against Reed's broad shoulder and crumple into him. As I cry quietly, my friend pats my shoulder and tries his best to comfort me. Reed gets a bad rap for being cold and calculating in his business dealings. Also, cranky and rude in his personal life. But this right here is the friend I've known and loved since college—the brother who'd give me the shirt off his back—or, in this case, five million bucks from his bank account—without a second thought.

After a while, I pull myself together. Sit up. Wipe my eyes. "Breakdown over. My FBI contact asked for everything I have on Greg Smith. I should triple-check I've sent her everything."

"Hey, when this is all over and Hannah's back safe and sound," Reed says, "can we keep my name out of it? The last thing I want is for word of my involvement to leak to the press and for some nut job to get the bright idea I'll pay five million bucks as ransom for Violet, too." He's referring to his half-sister who's ten years his junior—a talented fashion designer who's in art college on the East Coast. Frankly, I don't think it's crazy for Reed to think news of him paying five million bucks in exchange for his best friend's girlfriend might inspire a copycat kidnapping involving his sister.

"I won't say a word about your involvement to anyone," I assure him. "And when we get Hannah back, I'll ask her to stay mum about it, too." I exhale. It felt good to say *when,* rather than *if.*

"We can tell Josh and Kat the full story when they get back from their honeymoon, obviously," Reed says. "But nobody else, okay? Let's make sure the FBI knows my concerns, too."

I nod and look at the time. "I should call Hannah's sister and tell her what's going on. I don't want Hannah's mom freaking out and calling the police when Hannah doesn't show up to pick her up from work."

"While you're doing that, I'll tell Owen to book a block of rooms in the closest hotel to the FBI building in Seattle. We might need a command center."

"Good thinking."

"I'll also tell Owen to send a car to bring Hannah's sister and mother to the hotel. I'm sure they'll be too distraught to drive after talking to you."

"Thanks. I'll send you their contact info." Reed hands me my phone— the one Hannah called me on that he's been holding ever since—and I share the pertinent info with him. That settled, I take a deep, long, steadying breath and place the dreaded call to Maddy.

44
HANNAH

The sun has set now, based on the dusky quality of the light behind the red handkerchief taped to the window. There's a hanging bulb in the center of the space, which I'm hoping Angus will turn on soon. If he makes me sit here in the dark, on top of everything else, I might lose it.

At the moment, Angus is sitting at the card table. He's been over there, engrossed in something on his laptop, since the call with Reed ended however long ago. The fact that he's been ignoring me is great by me. Fantastic. *Except* for the fact that I'm now so thirsty, I'm worried I'm going to pass out or die from dehydration. I've almost called out to Angus at his computer a couple times to ask for a sip from that water bottle on the table. But both times, I've decided I'd rather pass out or die a slow death than draw his attention back to me and risk him slashing my neck with that knife for the fun of it. I heard what he said to Reed earlier—that he's itching to kill me, simply to teach Reed a lesson for "fucking with him"— and the thing is, when he said it, I believed him.

All of a sudden, Angus jerks his head up from his laptop, making me jolt beneath my bindings. With a furrowed brow, he grabs the knife off the table and slowly creeps to the handkerchief-covered window, where he pushes the edge of fabric aside, just enough to surreptitiously peek out. He visibly holds his breath for a long moment as he scans whatever is out there. Until, finally, he returns to the table, puts down the knife, and resumes his engrossing work.

My heart is thrashing. Is someone out there in the darkness—but well hidden—or is Angus simply hearing things because he's a paranoid lunatic?

A notification goes off, and Angus grabs his phone off the table.

"Your boyfriend's got my money ready for transfer," he announces with a snicker. "Let's show him you're still alive and well."

I nod and say nothing. Angus never reapplied the duct tape to my mouth after our phone call with Henn and Reed, but I'm too terrified of him at this point to say a single unnecessary word.

Angus puts on his black ski mask, grabs his laptop and the knife, and strides with purpose toward me. When he reaches me, he carefully places the opened laptop on my lap, its screen facing me and displaying some sort of banking site, and then he bounds behind me and leans down like he's posing with me for a happy selfie. "When I call Reed," he says, "you're gonna say, 'I'm fine. Send him the money now or else he'll kill me.' Understand?"

"Yes."

"If you say or do anything other than that, your boyfriend will get a front-row seat to me slitting your throat. No warnings. No hesitations. No do-overs. I'll slice your head clean-off. Got it?"

I'm trembling. "Yes."

He reaches down and presses a couple buttons on his computer's keyboard, and Reed's scowling face appears in split-screen with the banking site.

"Are you okay?" Reed asks.

"Yes," I confirm. "Send the money now, or he says he'll kill me without a warning."

To emphasize the point, Angus presses the knife into my throat with force, causing my flesh to sting at the point of impact and a loud whimper to lurch from my throat. Angus barks out, "Send it now or she's dead!"

"Wait, don't hurt her! I'm sending it now! Hang on."

"She's dead in three . . . two—"

A loud popping noise rings out, like a firecracker, only louder. At what seems like the same time, Angus suddenly keels over before finishing his countdown. As his large frame clatters to the floor, simultaneous crashing noises—one emanating from the far window and another from behind me —fill the space and bounce off the walls. Was that a gunshot? Sheer terror compels me to throw my weight to one side to avoid more gunfire, if that's indeed what that popping noise was, and my chair crashes onto its side with me still bound to it.

As I hit the ground, there's no mistaking the sounds of multiple sets of energetic footsteps. Shouting voices. A male voice yells, "FBI! Hands where we can see them!"

They couldn't possibly be talking to me, right, since my hands are still bound behind me? Just in case, I yell, "My hands are tied up!"

Another male voice yells, "Got him right between the eyes. Instant karma. No pulse."

More footsteps abound. More yelling. From Angus' laptop on the floor, Henn's voice shouts my name frantically, so I scream over the din, "I'm okay, Henny! I'm not hit!"

"Oh, thank God." He's sobbing. "I love you so much."

"I love you, Henny! Come to Seattle! I need you."

"I'm already on my way, baby. I'll be there soon. I love you so much."

"She'll call you back," a male voice says. And that's it. Henn's voice is gone, without either of us being able to say goodbye or I love you one more time.

I feel hands gripping me. My body being tilted upright in the chair. I look down and discover Angus lying motionless on the floor. His ski mask is off—it's been cast off on the floor near him. His eyes are wide open, and a puddle of dark, maroon blood is gushing from a nasty-looking hole in his forehead. Like the voice said, the hole is right between his wide-open eyes. Damn. I'm no medical examiner, but even I can tell that's a dead man. He's dead as a door nail. Holy shit.

Someone kneels before me. "Let's get you free, huh? Look here, Hannah. Don't look at that."

I wrench my shocked gaze away from the empty eyes on the floor. The oozing blood and brain matter. "Thank you," I choke out, blinking back tears. "Can I have some water, please?"

"You can have anything you want."

"I want my boyfriend, Peter Hennessey. And my mom and sister, too. *Please*." It's the last thing I say before bursting into loud, uncontrollable sobs.

45

HENN

I look up from my phone. "Hannah's taking a bathroom break from giving her statement. She says she's almost done."

I'm sitting with Reed in the back of a car. We're being driven from the airport to the FBI office in downtown Seattle, where I'll finally see my Hannah. From the scene of the crime, Hannah was whisked by helicopter to a downtown hospital, where she was given IV fluids and food and examined from head to toe. Thankfully, it was all good news. Physically, anyway. The rape kit turned up no evidence of sexual assault, and she suffered no broken bones, either on her face where the bastard punched her, or on her arm from when she fell onto her side while strapped to a chair. In a matter of weeks, all Hannah's physical injuries will all be completely gone and forgotten. The real question is how long it will take Hannah's mental injuries to follow suit, if ever.

Hannah will most likely grapple with PTSD for some period of time, but she told me via text she's already planning treatment for that. However long it takes, whatever she needs, I'll be right by her side. Supporting her. Loving her. Giving her a shoulder to cry on and an ear to fill. Assuming she wants me there. My greatest fear is that I'll finally get to see Hannah, and she'll have decided she doesn't want anything to do with me, since I'm the one who summoned this shit storm in the first place.

"Are you going to catch some heat for the hacking you did to Greg Smith?" Reed asks in a whisper. We've been keeping our voices low during this car ride, so our driver won't overhear us. He's a special agent, and therefore presumably in the know about the details of our involvement here, but better safe than sorry.

I shake my head. "My FBI bestie said she's designated me as a confidential informant."

"She can do that?"

I nod. "She recently took a big chance hiring me for a really high-level project, and she doesn't want it getting out the guy she placed that much trust in for a job that big is a loose cannon who'd recklessly hack a romance scammer for sport, simply to avenge his girlfriend."

"Sounds like your FBI bestie is a good friend to have."

It's an understatement. After my first call with her today, Deputy Director Leach immediately hopped a flight from DC to Seattle, and she's been deftly overseeing the investigation ever since. Under her capable leadership, her team on the ground quickly obtained a search warrant for a small dwelling near the barn where Greg Smith held Hannah, and what they gathered there has been a "treasure trove" of evidence, I'm told. My FBI connection couldn't give me any details over the phone, but she uncharacteristically said she was "eager" to update me in person.

Reed asks, "So, if you didn't hack Greggy-poo, according to the official version of events, then what motivated him to kidnap Hannah?"

That's an easy one, since I've already discussed it with Deputy Director Leach. I reply, "Greggy-poo saw Hannah at the Climb & Conquer party by chance, and after covertly observing her gallivanting with her billionaire best friends, he started stalking her online afterwards, out of curiosity and envy. When he saw she was living the kind of life he wanted for himself, he became increasingly full of rage toward her, so he hatched his plan."

"Sounds plausible enough," Reed says. "More plausible than the truth, actually. The guy was definitely full of rage."

"Yes, he was. May he rot in hell."

Our car pulls into a parking garage attached to the FBI building, and I nearly leap out before it's come to a full stop. Reed and I are bustled out of the car and brought through a back entrance. As we're striding with our escorts down a long hallway under fluorescent lights, my phone pings with a text from Hannah.

"Hannah's finished giving her statement," I report excitedly. "Perfect timing."

We're led into an elevator. As we ascend, nobody speaks. Anticipation in the small space is thick. Anxiety, too. At least, on my part. In fact, it's skating across my skin and churning my stomach. What if Hannah's been processing everything that's happened since our brief conversation after her rescue, and she's now decided she wants nothing to do with me? Amid the chaos right after the raid, Hannah yelled the four most beautiful words in the English language—"I love you, Henny!"—but what if she's changed her mind about that, now that she's had some time to reflect on my culpability?

When we exit the elevator, we're led down another hallway to a closed door. The agent opens it for us, and there she is. *Hannah Banana Montana la Plátana Milliken.* The great love of my life. Wrapped in a blanket, looking pale and small and disheveled—like a little sea otter that's been through a storm.

"*Hannah.*" I rush to her, completely forgetting the plan I'd formulated in the car to let her dictate the terms of our reunion. To my relief, Hannah springs up and hurls herself into my waiting arms. As I wrap her up, she breaks down in sobs, so I hold her close and kiss her hair and whisper that I love her. That I'm sorry. That everything is going to be okay.

After a while, we disengage from our embrace and discover we're now alone in the small room with the door closed. Apparently, everyone here earlier decided to give us some privacy.

We sit down on a couch and talk furiously for several minutes. I apologize again and again, and Hannah says this wasn't my fault, that Greg Smith made ridiculous leaps of logic that nobody could have foreseen.

"I should have told you I knew about him," I insist. "I shouldn't have held that information back from you."

"Well, that's true. But I should have told you about him at some point, too. Frankly, we've both been holding back. We have to commit to not doing that going forward. We need to trust each other with everything from now on."

"I promise."

"So do I."

"Are you willing to be my girlfriend again, if I make that promise and keep it forever?" As I ask the question, my heart is stampeding in my chest.

"I'm not only willing," Hannah says, touching my cheek. "That's all I want, Henny. I only want to be with you. It's you or nobody for me. You're my person—the birdhouse for the little blue birdie that is my soul. I love you more than words could ever say."

Tears have filled my eyes. I can barely speak. Somehow, I manage to say, "I love you. You're my soul's birdhouse, too."

We hug again, until we're interrupted by a knock at the door. After we've told our unknown guest to enter, my badass FBI bestie, Deputy Director Leach, appears in the doorframe.

"Sorry to break this up," she says. "But I've got some news to share— something I'm certain you're both going to want to hear."

———

My mouth is hanging open. I look at Hannah, and she's equally flabbergasted. The Deputy Director has just dropped a bombshell on us. Namely, that it's now clear, based on evidence collected today—specifically, horrific photos and videos stored by Greg Smith on several different hard drives—that Hannah's kidnapper was far more than a run-of-the-mill romance scammer and identity thief. Yes, those were his main hustles. His day job, so to speak. But by night, he was a hunter. His prey? Sex workers. At least seven of them, the FBI believes, across three states—Washington, Texas, and California. Probably more.

According to Deputy Director Leach, a sample of Greg Smith's DNA was immediately extracted from his dead body today and run through the national DNA database—CODIS. Lo and behold, they got a hit. A perfect match to unknown DNA taken off the recently recovered body of a sex worker who'd gone missing outside of Dallas this past year, only about fifteen minutes from where Greg Smith's mother lives. A perusal of Greg's burner phone revealed that number was the last to call the victim before she went missing. Presumably, she agreed to a meet-up with the person who'd called from that previously unidentified number and then was never seen or heard from again.

There were no other matches to Greg's DNA in CODIS today, but the Deputy Director's team knew there were quite a few other unsolved cases of missing sex workers with strikingly similar facts to the case in Texas. With no bodies recovered in those cases, there was no possibility of matching DNA in those cases to Greg's. And so, they instead checked to see if the last incoming calls to any of those victims' phones matched that same burner phone recovered today. *Jackpot.* They hit pay-dirt in a whopping *six* of those cases.

My FBI bestie says to Hannah and me, "Since Greg was the last person to contact all six of those missing women, the same way he was for the victim in Texas, we feel confident we've found our killer in those cases, too."

"Jesus," I whisper.

Hannah says, "Do you think he targeted sex workers because he thought nobody would miss them or look for them too hard? That's what I heard on a podcast once."

Deputy Director Leach nods. "Very likely. Remember when he was talking to Reed and he said, 'I usually like keeping my boxes separate, but I'll kill her if necessary'? We're confident he was referring to the fact that he normally prefers killing sex workers—women he thinks nobody will look for."

I look into Hannah's wide eyes and squeeze her hand. I'm feeling sick to my stomach as I process the full magnitude of the danger she was in today.

Hannah says to the Deputy Director, "I thought his comment about boxes was weird at the time. But then again, he'd said a whole lot of weird and incoherent things, so I didn't focus too much on that particular one."

"When our team heard that," Deputy Director Leach says, "we were pretty certain what kind of monster we were dealing with. I'm betting in the coming days we'll find out he was involved in even more sex crimes. His type of offender usually starts with rape before escalating to murder. Perhaps he raped some women who didn't feel comfortable coming forward at the time but who might be willing to do so once they find out he's no longer a threat."

I run my palm down my face and exhale loudly. "I can't believe it was me who unleashed a monster like that onto Hannah."

"How could you know?" Hannah says. "And don't forget you're also the one who heroically saved me from that monster."

"I'm not a hero. You can't call an arsonist a hero, just because he eventually put out his own fire."

"Love, no," Hannah says. Now it's her turn to grab *my* hand and squeeze. "You need to forgive yourself, honey. Yes, I endured one terrifying day and a couple physical wounds that will heal in a matter of weeks. But I got off easy, compared to all those poor women he killed. If me going through one horrible, scary day means a monster is now off the streets forever, and future women are safe from him, then it was well worth it." Hannah squeezes my hand again. "Henny, you saved who-knows how many lives today, in addition to mine. You're a hero. And so is Reed. *Indubitably.*"

I lose the battle with my emotions, and Hannah hugs me close and whispers all manner of beautiful sentiments into my ear. Words of love and forgiveness. Gratitude for how quickly I realized she was in peril. She says she's excited about our future together—the new chapter we'll be embarking on together in LA.

"I'm gonna buy an amazing house for us," I whisper through sniffles, pressing my forehead into the dark hair covering her neck. "It'll be your dream house. I promise I won't pressure you to move in until you're ready. Enjoy living with your sister for however long. But whenever you're ready, you'll have a standing invitation to move in and make it your own."

"That sounds incredible. Whenever the timing feels right, I promise I'll do exactly that."

Deputy Director Leach clears her throat. "Sorry to interrupt. I should get Peter's statement now, so you two can get out of here and reunite Hannah with her family again. I'm told they've been energetically asking to see her again for some time now." Thankfully, Hannah's mom and sister were able to meet her at the hospital when she arrived earlier, so they've already had their tearful reunion. But I'm sure that wasn't nearly enough time for the three Milliken women to talk and hug.

"Reed smartly thought to put your mom and sister up in a hotel down the street," I say. "We've got a room there, too, so you can hang out with them as long as you want tonight and tomorrow."

"Thank you so much."

"Thank Reed. He arranged everything."

"Is he still here? I'll thank him now."

"He left a while ago," the Deputy Director supplies. She looks at me. "He said he'd text you his goodbyes."

I look down at my phone and sure enough, there's a lovely text from Reed saying all manner of kind things, including that he'll be in Seattle for a few days if Hannah and I need anything at all.

I read Hannah the text and then address my FBI bestie. "Did Reed talk to you about his name not being mentioned in connection with all this?"

"He did. It's taken care of."

"Thank you." I take a deep breath and slap my thighs with my palms. "Okay, let's do this. What do you need to know from me that you don't already?"

"Your statement won't be contained in the general file, since you're a confidential informant. But I just need to memorialize what happened today, in your own words." The Deputy Director asks me a question to get us started, and I answer it fully and succinctly. Rinse and repeat. About fifteen minutes into our conversation, Hannah's head lolls forward, and it's clear she's fast asleep. Gently, I pull her into me, against my chest, and cuddle her sleeping frame throughout the remainder of my interview.

"Anything else you want to add?" the Deputy Director asks me.

"Nope."

"Okay, then, I've got everything I need." She motions to Hannah. "Get that girl to her family and to bed."

I gently awaken Hannah, and we say our goodbyes and thanks.

Hannah asks, "Will something bad happen to Henny for all the hacking stuff he did to Greg Smith?"

The Deputy Director smirks. "No. I've handled it." She looks at me sternly. "But this is a one-off, Peter. I won't be able to protect you, if you do something like this again."

"I won't. I promise."

She winks. "Actually, if I'm totally honest with you, the job you did for us in DC probably earned you enough credits to mess up another three or four times." She leans forward and narrows her eyes. "But let's not test that theory, okay?"

I chuckle. "From this day forward, you won't even know Peter Hennessey exists."

"Well, let's hope that's not true, since I'm sure we'll be calling you again with another job. But until then, keep your nose clean, please. For God's sake, no more missions of personal vengeance." After I've reassured her, she walks us to the door and hands us off to the special agent standing there. With a pat to my shoulder, she says, "Take good care of this brave woman. She's going to need lots of rest and TLC." To Hannah, she says, "I know today was terrifying, but you did an amazing job of keeping yourself alive. We were all thoroughly impressed with your quick thinking and grace under pressure."

"Thank you," Hannah says, tears pricking her eyes.

The Deputy Director smiles. "Among all the swirling emotions you're probably feeling, Hannah, I hope one of them is pride in how brilliantly you handled yourself today."

46

HANNAH

"I've never been so exhausted in my life," I murmur to Henn as we traipse down the short distance from my mom and sister's hotel room to ours.

"We'll get you into bed, and you can sleep as long as your body needs."

"You'll stay with me?"

Henn squeezes my hand. "I'll never leave your side again, if you don't want me to."

I smile. "Well, that won't be necessary. But I appreciate the sentiment."

I've showered by now. All physical traces of today's trauma, other than my bruises, have been washed down the drain. I'm wearing comfy pajamas and slippers Maddy brought for me, and my hand is firmly joined with Henn's, the same way it's been since we were reunited at the FBI building. Well, other than during my shower and when I wolfed down a meal from room service.

To my surprise, I'm doing amazingly well emotionally. Spending three relaxed hours with my family—Mom, Maddy, and Henn—did wonders for my soul. So did that cheeseburger, fries, and chocolate shake with extra whipped cream. I'm sure I'll have some nightmares and other after-effects to overcome in the coming weeks and months, but I'm determined to address that sort of thing in therapy. As it stands now, however, I'm feeling confident I'll wake up tomorrow after a good night's sleep feeling almost like myself.

Henn and I reach our hotel room and head straight to the bathroom to brush our teeth before sliding into bed. Henn doesn't have pajamas like me, so he strips to his underwear before crawling under the covers next to me. When he gets himself situated, he takes me into his arms, and I cuddle against his chest.

"You're safe now," he whispers. "Sleep as long as you can."

I yawn. "I really want to tell you some things—stuff I haven't had the courage to tell you before now. I want you to know everything about me. But I'm too tired to say it all now."

"Whenever you're ready."

"When I thought I was going to die, in that moment, I knew the only things that mattered to me in the whole world were you, Mom, and Maddy. That's what my whole life boils down to—my love for you three. And Kat, too. She's like a sister to me. I love more people than that, but when I thought I was going to die, those are the faces that flashed before my eyes."

Henn pulls me closer and kisses the top of my head. "When I thought you were going to die, I knew for a fact I wouldn't survive the loss." He kisses the top of my head again. "I've got some things to tell you, too—things I'll never tell anyone else. Literally. But I want you to know every-thing about me, too."

"I can't wait to hear all of it."

He kisses my head a third time. "Not now, though. Sleep. You've been through a lot. When we wake up, we'll order a huge breakfast and talk all day, if you want. All week."

"That sounds good. I'm gonna order blueberry pancakes for breakfast. Bacon, too."

Henn chuckles. "Sounds good."

I exhale, close my eyes, and snuggle closer. But sleep doesn't come. "Henny?" I whisper. "Are you awake?"

"Yes."

"How many departments of motor vehicles in how many states did you have to hack to make them think *all* those cars were registered in Greg Smith's name? That was brilliant of you."

"Yeah, brilliant, except for the part where it pushed a serial killer into having a full-blown psychotic breakdown and coming after you."

"Bah, no plan is perfect."

Henn chuckles. "It wasn't a hack. I bought a whole bunch of shitty used cars the old-fashioned way and registered them all in his name. Immediately after each purchase, I always made sure the car would get ticketed and/or impounded by ditching it in a high-profile red zone, usually at the nearest airport."

I lift my head, utterly floored. "You did *what?*"

Henn snickers. "I did it over and over again, in every possible city, even when I was only in a city for a short layover. And when I got too busy to keep doing it myself, I hired a hacker buddy who lives in a van to take over the job. And, man, did he come through for me. I think he's bought close to a hundred-fifty cars in twenty states under Greg's name. Oh, shit. I need to message him and tell him he can stop buying cars now. Ha!"

Henn slides out of bed, grabs his laptop, and clacks on his keyboard for a minute. When he crawls back next to me, his nearly naked body is cold as ice against mine.

"Oh, honey. Come here. Let me warm you up."

We cuddle while I rub Henn's arms and back to create friction, until, eventually, when he's all warmed up again, I settle against his chest.

"How was it possible to register all those cars in Greg Smith's name?" I ask. "Don't you need ID to buy a car and register it?"

"Sweetheart, I hate to tell you this, but fake IDs are exceedingly easy to create for people like me and my hacker buddy. That wasn't the slightest hurdle for either of us."

"Oh, wow. You really are Denver, aren't you?"

"In the flesh." He squeezes me. "But always for a good cause. I promise you that. I mean, except when it came to Greg Smith. I wanted to destroy that fucker for sheer vengeance. I've never done that before:

avenged someone I love. Normally, I go after horrible people who've never harmed me, personally—pedophiles, rapists, embezzlers, white-collar criminals— so it's easy for me to keep emotion from clouding my judgment."

"Maybe you went after Greg Smith so hard because you had a hunch what he did to me was only the tip of the iceberg."

"As much as I'd love to say that's the case, I can't. I went after him, simply to avenge you. That was my only motivation."

I pat his bare chest. "Thank you for doing that."

"I put you in harm's way."

"Meh. It all worked out in the end. Honestly, it makes me swoon to find out you were hell-bent on avenging me like that. I wouldn't have expected that of you. You're normally so chill."

"Not when it comes to you."

I nestle into him. "I love you so much."

"I love you, too. More than there are stars in the universe. Now, please, try to get some sleep, love. You've been through a lot. We'll talk tomorrow, for as long as you want."

"Okay. Goodnight." I close my eyes and command sleep to come. But it's not too long before I realize I'm still way too wired for my body to comply. "Henny? Are you still awake?"

"Yes, love."

"Will you tell me *one* of the secrets you're planning to tell me tomorrow? Try as I might, I can't fall asleep, and I'm dying to know what you're going to say."

"Do you want to take one of the sleeping pills the doctor gave you at the hospital?"

"No. I'll fall asleep eventually. In the meantime, pretty *please* tell me one of your secrets. Your biggest one."

Henn pauses. And then, "My hacker handle is Bluebird. I chose it way back in middle school because it's a symbol of happiness and prosperity, and that's what I was hoping to bring to the world with my online crusades."

"I love that."

"You're now the only person in the world, other than me and Deputy

Director Leach and her team, who knows Bluebird's real-world identity. Well, actually, a few top-level contacts in the international intelligence community know it, too. But that's it. I've never even told Josh and Reed my handle."

"Wow."

Henn squeezes me. "So, you see, my beloved, way back in middle school, it was my destiny to meet you—my perfect match—the perfect birdhouse for the little *bluebird* that is my soul."

Electricity courses through me. "You're the perfect birdhouse for my soul, too. But even so, let's never forget neither of us is perfect. Let's promise to work on revealing our imperfections to each other, from this moment forward."

"Well, I think we discovered one of my biggest imperfections over the past twenty-four hours: *arrogance*. I thought I could control everything in my real life, the same way I control my online world, and I couldn't have been more wrong about that."

"You're not arrogant. You're the humblest person I know. The fact that you've resisted bragging to me about whatever you did in DC is pretty damned impressive. Whatever it was, Deputy Director Leach made it sound like a really big deal." I'm shamelessly fishing—hoping that whole situation is one of the big secrets Henn is planning to reveal to me tomorrow.

"Real subtle, Hannah."

I laugh. "A girl can try."

Henn pauses a long time—much longer than right before he revealed his Bluebird handle to me a moment ago. Finally, he says, "Would you like me to tell you, confidentially, what I did in DC now, or save it for tomorrow?"

I jerk my head up. "Now!" I sit up and look down at his face in the moonlight. "*Please*. I'm dying to know."

"Really? I couldn't tell." He reaches up and gently touches the angry contusion on my cheek as he speaks. "The work I did there was top-secret. So, even though I'm only going to give you an overview and not reveal any micro-details to you, you still can't tell a single soul what I'm about to say."

"I promise."

"As far as I'm concerned, you're my wife. People who are married can say anything they want to each other, and nobody can ever make them spill it beyond the marriage. Did you know that?"

I nod to convey my prior knowledge of that fact. Also, my understanding and assent to his requirement of total confidentiality. And all the while, my heart is skipping a beat at the romantic analogy he's made. Henn and I haven't talked about that thing I said to him in Maui before our big fight last week—namely, that I was finally ready for Henn to propose to me back in LA. But I'm assuming, based on the comment he just now made about marital privilege, he feels confident we're back on track with that. To be honest, I'm not feeling in any rush to get married, or even engaged. Like Henn said, I'm suddenly realizing I already think of him as my husband, anyway.

Henn takes a moment to gather his thoughts, before patting his chest. "Snuggle up again," he says. "It's kind of a long story."

I lie back down and cuddle against his bare chest, and Henn launches into his tale. He says he met Deputy Director Leach in DC in connection with the Vegas job. Apparently, she was so impressed with the work he did in that context, she sang his praises to her boss—the bigwig, top-dog Director of the FBI—who then mentioned Henn to some heavy hitters in other federal departments, including people in the intelligence community, who then, in turn, told some of their international counterparts. Hence, Henn's eventual meeting in Munich, where members of the international intelligence community were converging for a summit about several critical matters of grave importance, including a global threat of terrorism that was becoming increasingly urgent. A staff of hackers had already been working on the problem for some time in DC, as paid employees of the US government. But to no avail. And so, when it was determined that the threat level had recently elevated sharply, the group recruited several freelance hackers, including Henn, and offered them the chance to win a huge reward if any of them could get the job done.

"Are you still awake down there, Milly Vanilli?" Henn asks softly.

"Wide awake."

"You're so quiet."

"I'm riveted. What was the terrorist threat you eventually thwarted?"

"A cyberattack on power grids. On a whole bunch of 'em, all at once.

Experts have long postulated that's going to be our country's next Pearl Harbor—a cataclysmic attack on power grids. When they recruited me and the others, they had reliable intel that a foreign power—one that would be happy to blow the US and all its allies right off the map—was in the final stages of developing a new technology that, if successful, would allow them to hack into numerous power grids, all at once—as many as a hundred at a time—"

"Jesus."

"—and destroy their internal technology."

I gasp. "You mean, shut them all down, all at once?"

"Exactly. There'd be no power for millions and millions of people—and none in sight. Not just in the US, but in other countries, too. We all use the same power grid technology, as well as the same smart encryption technology to protect them from hacking. This technology that was reportedly in the final stages of development—it was an encryption buster, basically—was unlike anything seen before. Nobody on their staff was having any luck breaking into it and dismantling it, so they brought in people like me from around the hacking world to try our luck."

"What's an encryption buster? Is that like cracking a code?"

"Yeah, in one fell swoop. You know how hotels have a universal key that unlocks every room? That's what this program was designed to be—a universal key to unlock the encryptions protecting every power grid using the same kind of technology. When I got to DC to start my work, every day felt like a race against time to hack into their 'key' and dismantle it before they could perfect it and use it to pull off the biggest and most calamitous cyberattack the world has ever seen."

"Oh my god, Henn," I whisper. "You're a genius. A hero. You literally saved the world."

"By the skin of my teeth and a whole lot of luck."

"No. When I get lucky, my phone screen doesn't crack when it hits the ground. Luck doesn't cause you to crack a code to keep the world safe from a hundred power grids being destroyed, all at once."

"Well, however we got here, we're safe now. For the time being, anyway. Who knows what will happen when they come up with their next thing."

"I have a stupid question. Even if you destroyed their key for now, wouldn't the bad guys have made a copy of it?"

"That's not a stupid question. But that's now how it works. Their key wasn't a physical thing. It was a program—a bunch of code that was designed to not only hack into power grids, but also to be inherently unhackable, in and of itself. Once I cracked into the program, the second part of its function was rendered obsolete. Which means, no matter how many times they might try to use that same key, we'll be able to get in and disable it again and again in record speed. Do you understand?"

"I think so."

"When something that's inherently designed to be unhackable gets hacked, then it's back to the drawing board on the whole technology, because you're now vulnerable to getting stymied at every future turn. There's no point in heading down that same path, ever again. The bad news is we only won the battle, not the war. I'm sure they're already hard at work on an entirely new version of it, in a new language that's never been seen before. Hopefully, it'll take 'em a while to come up with something, though. And in the meantime, maybe their staff hackers can learn from what I came up with and use that as a launching point for future work."

"If they don't, I'm sure they'll be calling you again, like Deputy Director Leach said."

"If that happens, I can only hope and pray I'll get lucky again, before it's too late. Or that one of the other gunslingers will. I'm telling you, Hannah, it was only by the grace of God or Steve Jobs' Ghost I figured the thing out. I don't have confidence I could do it, again and again, like clockwork."

"Well, I do. I have complete faith in you." I lift my head and kiss him. "I'm so proud of you. Thank you for telling me about all that. I promise I'll never tell a soul."

"I know you won't. I trust you completely."

"And I trust you. I love you so much."

"I love you too. Now, get some sleep, my brave and beautiful Banana. We'll talk some more tomorrow. I promise, I'll tell you anything you want to know."

"I've got some things to tell you, too."

"I'll be all ears. But now, it's time to sleep, my love."

"Goodnight." I close my eyes and relish Henn's body warmth. His gentle strokes across my back. And I'll be damned, in no time at all, I feel myself drifting. When sleep finally envelops me, I have one of the deepest and most refreshing slumbers of my life, thanks to the strong and loving arms holding me all night long.

47

HENN

There's a loud knock at Hannah's door that prompts Hannah to shriek, stop transferring cookies onto a cooling rack, and bound enthusiastically across her living room.

Laughing at Hannah's excited reaction, I amble behind her, figuring I'll hang back and give Hannah a private moment to welcome her new roomie to her new digs.

For the past few days, as Maddy's traversed the thousand-mile distance between Seattle and LA in her little hatchback, Hannah's been eagerly preparing for her sister's much-anticipated arrival. Hannah cleaned the apartment, top to bottom. Cooked several of Maddy's favorite meals and stored and labeled them neatly in the fridge. She went to Trader Joe's and stocked the pantry with all Maddy's favorite snacks and goodies. And if all that wasn't enough to welcome her little sister to LA in style, about an hour ago, right after Hannah received Maddy's most recent text with her ETA, Hannah started baking a batch of Maddy's all-time favorite cookies. "I want the apartment to smell like freshly baked cookies when Maddy first walks in," Hannah explained. "Maddy loves that."

When Hannah reaches her front door, she gleefully flings it open and hurls herself outside with a loud shriek. I can't see what's going on out there from my vantage point, but I can certainly hear Hannah screaming, "Welcome to your new home!" Also, a male voice chuckling.

Surely, the owner of that male voice is Keane Morgan. When Hannah expressed concern about her little sister making the multi-day drive from Seattle all by herself, Dax—who now lives across the hallway with his two bandmates, Fish and Colin—kindly enlisted his older brother to accompany Maddy. According to Dax, his big brother has been wanting to visit him in LA since his move a couple months ago, anyway. Plus, Dax said, Keane has some kind of "stripper showcase" in LA he's been invited to perform in—an audition to be represented by a big talent agency in Hollywood—so Dax said the ride-sharing arrangement would be a win-win-win: Maddy wouldn't have to make the drive alone; Hannah wouldn't have to worry quite as much about her little sister; and Keane would be killing two birds with one stone: visiting his rockstar little brother and performing in the showcase.

I lean against the doorjamb and smile when I see the joyful scene unfolding before me. As expected, the Milliken sisters are embracing and shrieking like it's been years, not months, since they last saw each other. The only surprise is that Keane Morgan has dyed his blonde hair an eye-popping shade of electric blue since I last saw him in Maui.

My heart skips a beat to see Hannah looking so happy. When she and I said goodbye to Maddy in Seattle, I wasn't sure if my beautiful girlfriend would fully bounce back from the nightmare she'd endured at the hands of Greg Smith. To my massive relief, though, she's not only accomplished that feat; she's better than ever. I've heard stories of people coming off near-death experiences with renewed purpose and a greater appreciation of life and love. But observing the phenomenon firsthand with Hannah has been inspiring. Electrifying. And a huge relief. As it's turned out, therapy, unwavering support from Hannah's loved ones, and an exciting new job she absolutely loves, have all laid the groundwork for her to not only heal, but to thrive.

When we found out Greg Smith had three more confirmed victims—two women he'd raped and another he'd raped and murdered—I worried the horrifying news would create a set-back for Hannah's mental health. But that wasn't the case. On the contrary, finding out about those additional atrocities only helped Hannah heal that much faster. According to

Hannah, knowing her trauma had helped even more women rest in peace and/or get some measure of justice or closure made her feel even more so like it had a higher purpose.

Keane's chuckle draws my attention to him, as the sisters continue hugging and talking excitedly. What's that I'm seeing on Keane's face? Is this notorious fuckboy stripper gazing at our sweet Madelyn with . . . *adoration*? Nah. I must be projecting because *I* adore the kid so damned much.

I still don't know Keane, personally, despite our time together in Maui. We mostly traveled in different sub-groups that week, and before that, he wasn't my contact on the hack I did for him. It was Josh. In fact, I don't think Keane knows to this day that Josh's nerdy groomsman at the wedding was the same guy who'd hacked that cougar and saved his horny, stupid ass.

I do know Keane's fuckboy *reputation,* however, from all the crazy stories I've heard about him, as well as from observing him hitting on cocktail waitresses and Kat's single friends at the wedding. And that's why, despite my lack of personal interactions with Keane, I'm nonetheless highly confident our sweet, shy, intelligent, sensitive, goofy, deep-thinking, tap-dancing, filmmaking feminist, Maddy, isn't his type. Not to mention, Keane's not Maddy's type, either. *At all.*

And yet . . .

There it is again. An expression of unmistakable affection on Keane's face, as he gazes at Maddy. Could it be this fuckboy stripper genuinely enjoyed his lengthy road trip with little Miss Maddy Milliken, against all odds?

"You're Keane, right?" Hannah says. "We met at the wedding."

Keane jerks his gaze from Maddy to Hannah and flashes a mega-watt smile. "Oh, yeah." He steps forward and extends his hand to Hannah. "Great to see you again."

Hannah disregards Keane's hand and pulls him into a warm embrace. "Thank you for taking such good care of my little sister."

"Oh, believe me, Hannah, it's been my . . ." Keane pulls out of their hug and looks at Maddy, his cheeks flushed. "I've loved every minute of hanging out with Mad Dog here."

Maddy bats her eyelashes at the compliment while flashing Keane a big, toothy smile, which he returns in kind—only bigger. *Well, I'll be damned.*

His cheeks flushed, Keane points at various nearby doors in the hallway. "Which one is my brother's apartment?"

Hannah indicates the apartment directly across from us, prompting Keane to chuckle and say, "Wow. You weren't kidding when you said Dax lives *right* across the hall." He leaps to his little brother's front door like his body is a motorized pogo stick and pounds away like he's administering a search warrant on a drug lord. "Hey, Rockstar! Open up! It's your favorite brother!"

In short order, the door swings open and Dax Morgan appears in all his handsome, charismatic glory, his long-ish, blonde hair hanging close to his shoulders and his blue eyes looking stoned as fuck. As the two brothers embrace and exchange a rapid-fire flurry of greetings, I hug Maddy and welcome her to LA. I'm thrilled she's here for Hannah's sake, of course— I know how much Hannah loves her little sister—but in this moment, I'm even more thrilled Maddy is here, safe and sound, for my own reasons.

First off, I love the kid and I like having her around. It's as simple as that. But second off, I know Maddy's arrival is setting off a countdown of sorts. From this day forward, it's only a matter of time until Maddy makes some friends in the film school and decides she'd rather live with one of them in the fall, rather than with her big sister. Or maybe, worst case, that fine day will come after Maddy's graduation in a couple years. But either way, Maddy's arrival today marks the beginning of a new era—the beginning of the unknown countdown until the day Hannah finally moves into the new house I recently bought in the Hollywood Hills.

I mustered the nerve to ask Hannah the timeline she's envisioning for her move-in date the other day, and she said exactly what I've been thinking—that she's expecting Maddy to want to move out at some point in the summer and room with fellow film students in the fall. But she also said, "We're in no rush, though, right? We both know we want to get married and be together forever, no matter what. Nothing is ever going to change that. So, if you think about it, it doesn't really matter when we start our forever, within reason—if it's in three months or six or a year or two."

That was the moment where my thinking about the situation parted ways from my girlfriend's. While Hannah was certainly right that nothing will ever change our love or the lifetime commitment we've both already made, I'm not nearly as patient about taking our relationship to the next level. In fact, knowing for certain I want to be with Hannah forever only makes me that much *more* excited—and impatient—to start our forever, as soon as possible, especially when the ring I bought for Hannah in Maui has been burning a hole in my pocket ever since.

The good news is that Hannah has recovered enough from the kidnapping for me to start thinking seriously about proposing again. Also, we've both agreed we don't need to live together at my new place to be engaged. The bad news, however, is that, for the past month or so, it's taken all my willpower not to spontaneously kneel and pop the question to Hannah every time I have so much as a couple beers. The only thing holding me back, each and every time, has been the voice memo left deep inside my brain by my sober self—the one that says, "When you finally pop the question, you have to do it right, Peter. You promised her that in Maui."

Hopefully, I'll be able to put together the perfect plan soon. Because now that Maddy is finally here, and Hannah is doing so great, and our relationship is going so fantastically well, and I've finally moved into our dream house, I've never felt more excited and impatient to turn my beloved girlfriend into my beloved fiancée and future wife.

48

HENN

I look around my crowded living room in drunken awe at the raucous party in front of me. Leaning into Hannah to be heard above the music, I say, "Thanks for ordering all that food. That was a stroke of brilliance."

"Door Dash, dude." She snaps her fingers. "Easy peasy lemon squeezy."

My heart skips a beat. To my knowledge, that's the first time Hannah's said lemon squeezy, instead of pumpkin. It's stupid, I know, but I can't help feeling like her conversion to lemon is a love letter to me.

Returning my huge smile, Hannah says, "The thing that should impress you far more than my uncanny ability to order from Door Dash is Reed's jaw-dropping ability to get a DJ here at the drop of a hat, plus all these fancy party people. How did he do this?"

"He's Reed Rivers, babe. Throwing the best parties in town, even at a moment's notice and at someone else's house, is one of his many super-powers. Thanks for saying *lemon* squeezy, by the way. Be still, my heart."

Hannah bats her eyelashes. "What can I say? You've rubbed off on me, kid."

We're at my new house in the Hollywood Hills in the midst of my *ad hoc* housewarming party—and it's quite the spontaneous shindig, thanks to the magical powers of one Reed fucking Rivers. When I texted Reed with the idea for a party mere hours ago from the club where Keane Morgan had performed in that stripper showcase tonight—Keane was surprisingly entertaining, by the way—Reed somehow managed to quickly wrangle not only a DJ, but also a bunch of artists from his label and some of their friends and entourages, too. And now, here we are, having a blast, other than the fact that I keep looking at the front door, hoping Maddy will get here soon. I want her to meet Reed and his artists for the sheer fun of it, but also in furtherance of her stated professional aspirations.

After Maddy and Keane's arrival last night, Hannah and I had a pizza-poker night with them and the three Goats across the hall, and that's when Maddy said she's hoping to break into directing music videos as a side gig to her documentaries. Well, if becoming a music video director is one of Maddy's career goals, then coming to this party and chatting up Reed and some of his artists would be a huge boon for her. So, why the fuck isn't she here yet?

When Hannah and I left the club after Keane's performance, Maddy said she, Keane, and Keane's buddy, Zander, who'd flown down to cheer on Keane's performance tonight, were all heading backstage to chat with some strippers from the show and they'd come to my house after that. But that was over two hours ago. How long does it take to chat up a few strippers about a possible documentary movie idea?

I lean into Hannah again. "Reed is playing Patron pong over there. Not beer pong. If Maddy wants to have a conversation with him that he actually remembers tomorrow, she'd better get here soon."

Hannah snickers. "Maddy will have to meet Reed another time, babe. She's not coming to the party."

"Is she okay?"

"She's fan-*fucking*-tastic. Emphasis on the *fucking*."

My jaw drops. "Maddy's fooling around with *Keane*?"

Hannah smiles and puts her finger to her lips, letting me know a) yes, and b) it's a secret. She winks and says, "After the club, they went back to the apartment."

"Well, I'll be damned." It's hard for me to think of Maddy as a sexual being at all, given the brotherly way I love that little cutie. But it's especially weird for me to think she's messing around with Keane, of all people. Yes, I noticed the pair exchanging googly eyes upon their arrival yesterday, and then, throughout our poker game last night. But I kept telling myself I was imagining things. Now that I've spent some quality time with Keane, I actually like the guy. He's funny and clever and surprisingly sweet. But even so, I'm still shocked our shy, intelligent Maddy is giving a fuckboy stripper like Keane the time of day. "Does Maddy want to keep it a secret because she's embarrassed to be messing around with someone like Keane?"

Hannah purses her lips. "I think she's keeping it on the downlow because it's nothing but a fun little fling, and she doesn't want everyone asking her about it after Keane goes back to Seattle."

"Yeah, that makes sense, given that Keane's brother lives across the hallway."

"Exactly. Maddy doesn't want everyone knowing her business. Speaking of which, I told Maddy I'd stay here tonight to give her and Keane some privacy at the apartment. I assume that's okay?"

I don't need to reply. Hannah knows she has a standing invitation to stay here every night for the rest of her life. She knows I consider this place hers, every bit as much as mine, especially because it was Hannah who walked through the front door and instantly fell in love with the place.

"I just hope Keane doesn't hurt Maddy's sensitive little heart," I say. "If you look in the dictionary under fuckboy, there's a photo of Keane Morgan."

To my surprise, considering how protective Hannah usually is of her little sister, she doesn't look concerned. "That's exactly why I'm not worried," Hannah says. "Whatever Maddy's doing with Keane, I'm sure she went in with eyes wide open. Plus, she knows he's only visiting LA for a few days."

"Unless he gets picked up by a talent agency and decides to move down here to chase his Hollywood dreams. He was damned good in that showcase tonight."

"Yeah, but still, what are the odds of all that happening? I'm sure Maddy isn't expecting an actual relationship with Keane. She's just having fun. Getting her groove back." Hannah smiles. "And I'm all for it. This is Maddy's first fling since Justin died. Hopefully, this means she's feeling ready to open her heart again when school starts next week."

"Hopefully, to someone who's actual boyfriend material."

Hannah nods. "Wouldn't it be amazing if Maddy fell in love with someone in film school?"

"Yeah, that'd be great." I'm rooting for Maddy to find happiness in whatever form, not only because I love Maddy like a sister, but also because I know in my bones the sooner Maddy is having a blast in her new life, the sooner Hannah will feel like the time is right to move in here with me.

"Don't let Maddy know I told you about her messing around with Keane, okay?" Hannah says. "And, please, don't tell anyone else."

I laugh. "Who would I tell? Reed doesn't give a shit and half the people here don't even know I'm the owner of this house."

"Dax, Colin, and Fish are here, remember? Don't get drunk and blab to any of them."

"My lips are sealed."

"Maddy specifically asked me not to say a word to *anyone,* not even to you, but I didn't want to lie to you when you asked where she was."

"I won't tell the boys of 22 Goats or anyone else. And thank you for not lying to me."

We share a smile.

"Are you Henn?" someone says. I turn my head and instantly recognize the source of the voice. He's the lead singer of Danger Doctor Jones, one of Reed's most popular bands.

"Yeah, hey. We met backstage once." I shake his hand. "I'm a big fan."

"Thanks. Reed's over there, in need of a new partner. I told him I'd let you know on my way to the kitchen."

I look across the room where Reed has been playing team Patron pong with his assistant, Owen, as his partner, and sure enough, he's beckoning to me with a commanding look on his face.

"Go on, Henny," Hannah says. "Nobody keeps Reed Rivers waiting."

"Maybe I could be the first."

She chuckles. "While you're playing, I'll check the food and booze in the kitchen and order more, if necessary."

"You're the best." I peck Hannah's cheek and then gallop off through

the crowd toward Reed. When I reach my destination, Reed's former partner, Owen, is gone, and Reed declares it's time for our "dynamic duo" to
crush the team comprised of brothers Kendrick and Kai Cook, the
drummer and bassist, respectively, of Fugitive Summer. That's the band
we flew to Chicago months ago to watch perform, and then proceeded to
party with them, way too hard, after Reed signed them that night. To my
surprise, both brothers instantly recognize me from our night of partying,
and they greet me warmly.

I ask the brothers how they and their other bandmates are enjoying
living in LA now, and they regale me with some funny stories involving
their unpredictable lead singer, Savage.

After a while, though, Reed abruptly ends the conversation with a curt
but playful, "Okay, stop fraternizing with the enemy, Peter. It's time for us
to show these two kiddies why we used to dominate at this game in
college."

He's having a false memory, apparently. Reed and I never dominated
together at this or any game. That was Reed and *Josh*. Those two were
unstoppable in everything they played, whether individually or as a team.
But, still, I'm drunk, and Reed's a powerful motivational speaker, so I
reply with a fist in the air and a resounding, "Fuck yeah. Let's do it!"

Forty-five minutes later . . .

Reed and I have not, in fact, shown the kiddies why we used to
dominate at this game in college. On the contrary, the Cook brothers have
crushed Reed and me to a bloody, Patron-infused pulp in three straight
games. In our defense, the Cook boys apparently grew up playing beer
pong with their older brother and his friends, whereas Reed and I used to
play, only now and again, over a decade ago in our fraternity house. But
whatever. The end result is that I've never downed so many tequila shots
in such a short timeframe in my life. Jesus God. *Help me.*

"You want to show us kiddies how it's done again?" Kendrick, the
jovial drummer, teases. He spreads his muscular arms toward Reed as if to

say, "Come at me, bro!" And, of course, his older brother, Kai, laughs his ass off.

"Fuck yeah, we do!" I shout. "Come on, Reed! Fourth time's the charm!"

Thank God, Reed grabs my shoulders and saves me from myself. "Rain check, little buddy. I need to get some food and water into you before we play again."

"I'm fine. Let's beat their cocky asses!"

"You're not fine. Thanks for the games, boys. And fuck you." As the Cook brothers laugh, Reed grabs my arm and pulls my listless body toward the kitchen. "Come on, Pietro."

"Thank you," I whisper to Reed. "So fucking much." As I salute the Cook brothers, Reed hurls my slack body onto his back and carries me into my kitchen like a human backpack. "How are you still sober?" I ask from my perch on Reed's back. "You downed as much tequila as I did."

"You mean, why have I not turned into a living Jell-o mold? Because I can hold my liquor, unlike you."

"Well, that explains it."

In the kitchen, Reed sets me down in a chair and pours me a huge cup of water. "Drink this," he commands. "I'll get you some food."

As I drink, I marvel at all the attractive and hip people crammed into my new kitchen, many of whom are serving themselves food from large, disposable takeout trays spread out across the island counter. Out of curiosity, I put down my water cup and pop up to peruse the food offerings. Wow. Thanks to Hannah, there's a virtual smorgasbord here: lobster macaroni 'n' cheese, cheeseburger sliders, sushi, tacos, and more. Plus, all kinds of booze with mixers. Cookies and cupcakes, too. It's damned impressive.

"Can you believe Hannah did all this?" I say to no one in particular, since Reed has gotten distracted and is now chatting with someone I don't know. "She's so amazing," I add with a happy sigh. "So nurturing and thoughtful." I jerk my head up. "You know what? I'm going to propose to her right fucking now!" I haphazardly pull out the ring box from my pocket—the one I've been carrying around with me for months now. "Hannah!" I shout. "Where are you, baby? I have something important to ask youuuuu!"

"What the fuck?" Reed shouts. In two seconds flat, he's at my side, snatching the ring box out of my drunken hand. "*No*, Peter," he chastises. "Bad boy."

I laugh.

"You can't drunkenly propose to her at a spontaneous house-warming party, dumbass! We've already talked about this. You're gonna do it in Paris, remember?"

My shoulders slump. "I said that when I thought I could take Hannah to Paris next month. Turns out, she doesn't have vacation time from work till early summer."

"Okay, then you'll do it then. The Paris Plan is perfect. Don't mess with it."

"But it's too long to wait. I'm dying to ask her."

"You'll survive. There's no better plan than proposing to her at the top of the Eiffel Tower, exactly like you said. Remember? Now, pull yourself together."

I flap my lips together. "I guess you're right."

Reed rolls his eyes. "Jesus. You're so impulsive when you get shit-faced—a goddamned loose cannon."

"That's because I have to be so fucking methodical and careful all the time for work. It feels good to let loose sometimes."

"Yeah, but not about this." Reed slips the ring box into his pocket. "When I get home, I'll put this in my safe, so you don't get drunk again and stupidly ask her before Paris." Reed motions to the island. "Did you get something to eat?"

"No. You said you were getting it for me."

"I did? Well, that hardly seems necessary. Fill a plate. Eat something to counteract all that tequila."

I slump over the island on my forearms. "I can't wait to propose. I love her so much."

"Yes, I know. Eat."

I lift my head. "Do you really think Paris is a good plan?"

"It's an amazing plan. Eat."

"I don't think simply taking her to the top of the Eiffel Tower is good enough, though. Not when any tourist could go there for any occasion or no occasion at all. How would that be special?"

"It'll be special. It's fucking Paris."

"When it comes to me giving Hannah gifts, I'm not allowed to rely on hacking anymore. Did I tell you I promised her that? So that means, when I ask her, she's gonna be surrounded by a bunch of strangers. Also, I won't be able to make sure my proposal is timed perfectly with the sparkles. I really want it to start sparkling when she says yes, you know? But how can I do that if I can't—"

"Okay, stop. I can't take it anymore." Reed exhales with exasperation. "I'll handle everything, okay? If only you'll promise to stop talking about this, for the love of fuck."

I slide my forearms out, until my chest is flush with the cool marble of my kitchen island, and then turn my head and lay my cheek onto the smooth, cool surface. "How could you possibly handle everything, when you can't hack the Eiffel Tower, either?"

"I've got a business partner with some connections in France. He's good friends with a couple French billionaires. If he can't help me, then I bet Josh's uncle can. One way or another, we'll figure out a way for you to get up there and have a little privacy and some well-timed sparkles. But listen, if I'm gonna go to all this trouble for you, then you've got to promise not to spontaneously propose to her before then, or I'm gonna fucking throttle you."

I straighten up excitedly. Even with all the tequila in my bloodstream, my heart is suddenly racing. "I promise. You really think you can hook all that up for me?"

"I'm pretty sure."

"Let's call Josh now to see if his uncle can help."

Reed laughs. "That's a great idea, actually. I'm sure Josh will get a kick out of seeing you like this. It's been a while since Shitfaced Henn has made an appearance."

I pull out my phone and place the FaceTime call, and a moment later, we're staring at Josh and Kat's smiling faces. They're in bed, their infant daughter snuggled between them.

After warm greetings all around, Reed says, "You're missing a great housewarming party featuring an appearance from Shitfaced Henn."

Josh looks down at his sleeping baby girl and says, "I wouldn't trade places with you for anything. Not even to see Shitfaced Henn. In fact, there's no place I'd rather be." He winks at me. "No offense, Henny. Congrats on the new place."

"No offense taken. I wish I could be doing exactly what you're doing, honestly. With my own wife and baby, though. Not with yours."

As Josh and Kat chuckle, Reed says, "I just now had to talk Henn out of drunkenly proposing to Hannah on the fly. I'm hoping we can all help him plan the perfect proposal for Paris, so he doesn't fuck things up by doing something half-assed before then."

I tell them my concerns, including the important part about me wanting to time my proposal with the Tower's famous sparkles. When Kat asks what I mean by that, I explain that the Eiffel Tower's highest point is programmed to glitter gloriously against the night sky for a full five minutes at the top of every hour.

"Oooh, I agree the proposal should be timed with the sparkles," Kat says. "How romantic."

"Okay, leave everything to me, Henny," Josh says. "You helped make my proposal to Kat perfect, so now I'll return the favor."

"Really? Wow. Thanks so much."

"*Hello, Hannah!*" Kat shouts at top volume, out of nowhere.

Everyone clamps their lips shut as Hannah appears at my shoulder, carrying a stack of large takeout containers. After placing her load onto the island, she says, "Oh, hey, Faradays! Are you giving us an update on Baby Gracie? What'd I miss?"

"Not much," Kat says. "Henn just wanted us to join the housewarming party via FaceTime for a few minutes."

"Aw, how sweet." Hannah leans forward and sticks her nose into my phone. "Let me see that baby up close. Put the phone right up to her sleeping face."

Kat complies, and for the next several minutes, the group talks about Baby Gracie: the fact that she adamantly refuses to fall asleep unless someone is holding her; the fact that she's already got her daddy wrapped firmly around her tiny finger; and, of course, the fact that she's the spitting image of her gorgeous mommy.

After a while, though, Reed says, "Henn and I have to go now. The Cook brothers beat us three straight times in Patron pong, so we need to find them and demand a rematch."

Kat scoffs. "You should have played with Hannah as your partner. Banana's an ace at beer pong."

Reed looks at Hannah, his eyebrows raised. "Is this true?"

Hannah shrugs. "Well, I'm not sure I'm an ace, *per se,* but, yeah, I'm pretty good."

"She's being humble," Kat calls out. "During my birthday pub crawl, Hannah beat every opponent in every bar we went into. She was a beer pong sniper. A can't-miss *assassin.*"

Reed turns from Hannah to me and thwaps me across the head in mock disgust. "You didn't think to tell me this little factoid about your girlfriend while we were getting our asses kicked *three* times?"

"I didn't know! I've never seen Hannah play beer pong."

"Well, watch and be amazed now," Kat says. "Really, the back of Hannah's jersey at the wedding should have said 'Hannah Banana *Beer-Pong* Milliken."

After shooting an icy glare at me, Reed gallantly offers his arm to Hannah. "Come on, partner. Let's go kick some Cook-brother ass together."

"I'll do my best," Hannah says.

"Oh, hang on," Reed says, stopping on a dime. "Hannah, would you mind going out there and reserving our spot for next game, while I talk to Josh about something, real quick? I'll be right there."

"You've got it, partner," Hannah chirps. And off she goes, practically skipping out of the kitchen.

When Hannah's gone, Reed slides his arm around my shoulders and returns to Josh and Kat on my phone. "Hey, Faradays, let's set up a time to brainstorm with Henn this week about his proposal in Paris." Reed rustles my hair. "If we put our heads together, I know we'll come up with something that'll be worth Henny's wait . . . and even more importantly, worthy of our sweet little Hannah Banana Beer-Pong Milliken."

49
HANNAH

oh la la!

Oh la la! I've finally fulfilled a lifelong dream and made it to Paris, bitches! And it's everything I dreamed it'd be and more. *Enchanté*! Henn brought me here to celebrate my twenty-eighth birthday today, but like I told him last night at our fancy hotel, I feel like we're celebrating so much more than the day of my birth. We're also celebrating the joys of being alive, healthy, and madly in love with the most perfectly imperfect person who ever lived.

As promised, Henn and I have made a conscious effort to reveal our imperfections and flaws to each other over the past several months, and as it's turned out, the exercise has only made our bond that much stronger. Our love and commitment that much more unbreakable. Which, in turn, has made our relationship even more . . . well, perfect.

Speaking of perfect things, Paris is already the best vacation of my life, and we haven't even been here a full day yet. We landed here yesterday afternoon after flying in on Reed's luxurious private jet—shout out to Reed for the amazing birthday gift!—and we spent our first evening wandering around the city, hand-in-hand, like wide-eyed, jetlagged, giddy zombies. Henn said we had to stay awake until it was a reasonable hour to crash, local time. And my seasoned traveler of a boyfriend was right.

Today, after a long sleep, I feel bright-eyed and bushy-tailed and ready to tourist my ass off.

After enjoying a delicious French pastry and *café au lait* for breakfast, we headed to The Louvre and spent our day exploring the masterpieces there, followed by enjoying a scrumptious late lunch at some famous restaurant Henn said I had to experience. I've already forgotten its name, but I'll look it up when I write about it in my travel journal tonight. All of that would have been plenty for our first full day. And yet, as dusk descends upon us now, we're standing in line at the freaking Eiffel Tower —the *real* one, not the fake one in Vegas—awaiting our turn to ride to the top in one of those big elevators over there.

I can't wait to check off one of the biggest bucket list items in my life: viewing Paris and the Seine below from the iconic viewing area at the top of the Tower. Thanks to Henn and the nifty VIP passes around our necks— which I'm afraid must have cost sweet Henny a fortune—we're going to get to take in the views in grand style—from a corner that's normally roped off to the general public. Which means our once-in-a-lifetime selfie will be extra, extra pretty. Oh, and also thanks to these special VIP passes, we're even going to get to take in the iconic views while sipping the finest French champagne. *Quelle belle vie!*

The attendant at the elevator signals to a large group from the other line, and they excitedly head over to him. The guy then looks at Henn and me pointedly, like he's going to wave us forward, too, but after glancing at the plastic passes around our necks, he instead holds up his palm, telling us to stay put. *Shoot.*

With an exhale, Henn looks at his watch, his body language conveying he's got the weight of the world on his shoulders. It's so unlike him. Normally, a long line doesn't bother him at all.

"It's fine," I say, patting Henn's arm. "Our time will come soon enough. And in the meantime, the people-watching is *elite*." To my surprise, when I smile at Henn, his return smile feels a bit stiff. Is there something going on with one of his jobs that's weighing on him? I know he sometimes deals with some really dark stuff. Is he tracking a particu- larly abhorrent human and hasn't told me about it because it's my birth- day? Or is he simply feeling anxious about our trip—wanting everything he's planned to go off without a hitch? He's the one who made every arrangement and reservation for all our travels, and now that we're here, I'm realizing what a big job that was.

"Everything is perfect," I say, this time squeezing Henn's arm. "Just being in this city with you, all my dreams have already come true. Everything else from this moment on will be icing on *le pâtisserie.*" I kiss his shoulder. "You want to play Who's European and Who's American again?" We played that funny game regarding passers-by while taking a break on a bench in The Louvre and it was endless fun.

"Yeah, sure, let's do it," Henn replies. But he's no sooner said the words than the Tower's lights turn on, illuminating the entire structure, top to bottom, which makes everyone in line, including Henn and me, collectively gasp and talk about the pretty sight.

"It's magic," I say. "*Le magie.*"

"Actually, the lights are linked to sensors and programmed to turn on automatically at dusk."

"Like I said, magic." I tilt my head back and gaze up the full length of the Tower again, mesmerized by the illuminated structure. "I hope we're up there when the top sparkles. I'd love to get a selfie with the sparkles going off behind us. Wouldn't that be a spectacular photo?" I'm referring to the fact that, at the top of each hour, the Tower's highest point glitters spectacularly against the Parisian night sky for a full five minutes. I'm sure Henn already knows I'm hoping to see the sparkles up close and personal, since he's caught me viewing YouTube videos of the phenomenon, more than once.

"We'll stay as long as needed to get that selfie for you, Birthday Girl."

"There's no time limit, once we get up there?"

"Nope. Once we're there, the Tower is yours as long as you like."

I squeal. "We should have brought snacks. I might want to stay till sunrise."

Henn chuckles. "I should have more accurately said the Tower is yours till closing time at midnight."

Henn still looks a bit stressed, so I put my cheek on his shoulder and say, "That's more than enough time. I was being silly."

He kisses the side of my head. "I know. We've actually got late-night dinner reservations, but I promise we'll have plenty of time at the top."

I lift my head and smile. "Thank you so much for everything. This trip has been incredible."

"It's only our first full day."

"I could leave tomorrow and gush about the best vacation ever."

"Nah. We're only just getting started, baby." Ain't that the truth. From here, Henn is taking me to Italy and Spain. But he knows me well enough to have taken me to Paris first for my actual birthday—the top destination on my bucket list.

My phone pings, and when I look down, I blurt, "Maddy sent a photo from the set!" I tilt my screen toward Henn to show it to him, and he laughs along with me at the funny image. In the shot, my gleeful sister is surrounded by a group of handsome, muscular, shirtless men—actors portraying male strippers in the movie she's currently observing being filmed in LA. One of the actors in the shot—the one standing immediately to Maddy's left—is a huge movie star who requires no introduction. A few others in the group are also vaguely recognizable to me, though I couldn't name them without peeking online. And last but not least, my sister's gorgeous, silly, sweet boyfriend, Keane Morgan, is in the shot, standing to Maddy's right with his arm around her shoulders and his dimpled cheek squashed against hers.

Keane's smile radiates pure joy, the same as Maddy's. And it's no wonder. After Keane moved to LA to pursue both his acting dreams and his relationship with Maddy, he landed this, his first movie role—"a *Magic Mike* rip-off," he keeps calling it—that's helmed by a big-name director. Keane's first-ever role is small, but he's got a few lines and several scenes where he'll be dancing in group numbers. Apparently, that's quite a coup for a new actor's first role in Hollywood.

The attendant at the elevator looks at Henn and me and waves us forward. It's finally our turn to board one of the big elevators! I nudge Henn's shoulder, since he's looking at his phone. "It's our turn to ride, *mon amour*!"

We bound onto the large elevator and scoot to the far back to allow the people waiting behind us in line to cram into the space. But when the doors close, we're the only people in the big box, other than the attendant.

"Why nobody else?" I ask. Countless times during our wait in line, I watched the attendant pack both elevators to the brim. So, what gives?

Henn shrugs, but the attendant points to the passes around our necks.

"Oh my gosh, Henny. Did you know these passes would get us a private elevator ride?"

"I had no idea." When I furrow my brow, Henn smirks and says, "No superpowers were activated, if that's what you're wondering. A promise is a promise." The day after my kidnapping, Henn and I talked for hours and hours in our hotel room. It was then that we set boundaries and expectations for our relationship going forward, including Henn's promise that he'd never secretly use his superpowers to impress or "help" me in any way, ever again, without first telling me and getting my explicit buy-in. Since then, that's translated to Henn using his superpowers only twice—both times to score tickets to a sold-out show I was dying to see.

As our elevator ascends, the views through its clear walls become more and more breathtaking. I begin chattering excitedly about everything I behold. The river. The bustling streets. The history I picked up from our guidebook. As I speak, Henn nods and makes all appropriate exclamations. And yet, I can't help feeling like he's not entirely present. A bit distracted, maybe. What's going on? Am I imagining the anxiety and nerves wafting off him?

Henn's phone pings, and when he looks down, he exhales and quickly shoves his phone into his pocket.

"Everything okay?" I ask.

He smiles. "Yes. Sorry. You've got my full attention now." He takes my hand and kisses the top of it, and then flexes his hand a la Mr. Darcy, making me giggle. "Happy birthday, my pretty *Plátana*."

My heart skips a beat. "This is the best birthday, ever."

"We haven't even made it to the top."

"It doesn't matter. Thank you for a magical birthday."

The elevator stops. The doors slide open. Henn takes my hand, and we bound out and head straight toward a far railing. As we walk toward our destination, I'm floored to discover there's nobody else in the immediate vicinity, other than a handful of staffers smiling at me. Yes, there's a packed crowd of tourists on the other side of the expansive viewing area, but that area has been kept separated from ours by a velvet rope. Holy crap, it feels like we've got our own private party up here.

I touch the pass around my neck. "I thought this gets us a selfie in a special little VIP corner and a glass of champagne. You didn't say anything about us having a quarter of the viewing area, all to ourselves."

Henn winks. "Happy birthday, baby."

I look around in shock. "You really, truly didn't use your superpowers to make this happen?"

"Not unless you consider having Josh Faraday as a best friend a superpower. His uncle's business partner is a French billionaire who kindly called in a favor to make this happen for us."

I gasp. "You mean this dish isn't even on the regular menu?"

"Nope. It's not even an option, normally."

"I can't believe this is my life."

We reach the railing and gasp at the view. In short order, a waiter appears bearing two sparkling flutes of champagne. We take his offering and continue marveling at the gorgeous view, this time, while enjoying the finest champagne I've ever tasted. It's even better than the amazing champagne we had earlier today at lunch!

"A toast," Henn says, raising his glass. "Happy birthday, my love. You're the great love of my life. The best thing that's ever happened to me. You're totally and completely *schmamazing,* Hannah Milliken."

I laugh. "So are you, Peter Hennessey."

His cheeks are blooming. "You're the only bee in my bonnet," he adds, which I'm assuming is a reference to the lyrics of "Birdhouse in Your Soul." In that song, the singer asks his listener to say those exact words. Henn and I have never discussed it, but I'm assuming Henn thinks of that song as ours, every bit as much as I do. So, of course, I return the favor by saying the line back to him.

Suddenly, I hear the dulcet sounds of a live violin behind me. I turn around and discover a woman dressed in black, lovingly playing her instrument. "How romantic," I gasp out. But after a beat, when I recognize the song, I gasp even louder and blurt, "She's playing 'Birdhouse in Your Soul!' Oh, Henny!"

Henn nods excitedly. "Our song."

I bring my hand to my heart, feeling like it's going to burst from joy. "I can't believe you arranged all this. Thank you!"

Henn kisses me, and we cuddle up and enjoy the view and the violinist's performance while sipping our glorious champagne. Midway through the song, however, Henn wordlessly takes my glass, places it on a nearby ledge, and guides me into a gentle twirl, which then leads to us dancing in a clinch throughout the remainder of the song.

When the violinist's performance ends, Henn dips me dramatically and kisses me while I'm hanging low. When he raises me up, he nuzzles his nose to mine and whispers, "Happy birthday, my love. You're the bird-house for the little blue birdie that is my soul."

"And you're mine. Thank you so much."

With a peck to my cheek, Henn releases me and reaches into his coat. A second later, he's holding up a little wrapped box—a cube shape that's wrapped in bright blue "Happy Birthday!" paper and tied with an elegant, golden bow.

My heart stops at the sight of Henn's gift.

Is that an engagement ring? Is he about to propose?

No. Calm down, Hannah. The wrapping reads "Happy Birthday!" and people don't wrap up engagement rings—they kneel with them on full display while popping the question.

But maybe Henn doesn't know that. Or maybe this birthday wrapping is a ruse to throw me off, so when I unwrap his gift and see the ring, I swoon even harder at the surprise of it all!

"Thank you," I whisper, taking the wrapped box from him. I unwrap it, slowly, with shaking hands, and what I ultimately find inside the box is so damned lovely and thoughtful and perfect, I forget all about hoping it's an engagement ring. Henn has gifted me with a necklace—a dainty one featuring a jeweled pendant: a sapphire birdie nestled inside a sparkling, diamond-encrusted birdhouse.

Teary-eyed, I hug him. "Thank you. I love it. Where on earth did you find it? It's perfect."

"I had it made for you. Apparently, little blue birdies sitting inside birdhouses aren't a hot commodity on the open jewelry market."

As I laugh, I suddenly realize there's a photographer snapping photos of the moment. "Did you hire her?" I ask, wiping tears. "Because if she's an Eiffel Tower staffer, I'm going to blow every dime of my savings purchasing every shot she takes."

Henn chuckles. "She's ours for as long as we want. I thought you might like some professional photos of your birthday celebration."

"Wow, you truly thought of everything. Thank you."

"I've got another birthday present for you. Come with me." As I protest the fact that Henn has already done too much, he takes my hand and guides me several feet away. "Thankfully, the weather cooperated," he murmurs excitedly. "The stars are out for us tonight in full force."

We stop at our apparent destination—a telescope—at which point, Henn pulls out a piece of paper from his coat pocket, studies it, and then bends over to peer into the telescope. He shifts its aim a few times, zeroing in on something specific, and when he's got the telescope pointed the way he wants, he gestures for me to take a peek. When I do, he asks, "Do you see those two stars in the middle of the framing? The ones that look closer together than any of the others, like they're holding hands?"

It takes me a few seconds, but soon, I see what he's describing. "I see them! *Aw*. Are those two stars you and me, Henny?"

"They are. Officially. According to the official registry of the International Space Registry."

I straighten up. "*What?*"

By way of explanation, Henn hands me the piece of paper in his hand —an official-looking certificate. With a huge smile, he says, "The star on the left is officially registered as *Dorkus Millikeningus*. The one on the right, as *Dorkus Hennessingus*."

I look down at the certificate he's handed me, and sure enough, it confirms everything he just said. I hug him, thank him profusely, and pepper his face with kisses. "What an amazing gift."

When we pull back, Henn's eyes are as moist as mine. He says, "I registered those two stars during my first visit to Seattle. All the way back then, I knew we were two of a kind—written in the stars. That one day, I'd show you those two stars and that certificate, and that I'd then . . ." As his sentence trails off, Henn looks down at his watch. He holds up an index finger, telling me to hold on. About ten awkward seconds pass, during which I can't help shifting my weight and making all manner of weird faces. What is he waiting for? What's the rest of his sentence? Finally, Henn lowers his finger and says, "And that I'd get down on my knee and beg you to marry me."

Before my brain has fully processed his words, Henn kneels before me and holds up a closed ring box.

"Henny!" I gasp out, throwing a palm to my mouth. "Oh my gosh."

With a beaming smile on his gorgeous face, Henn flips open the lid of the box, revealing a dazzling diamond ring that makes me gasp again. "Hannah Suzanna Montana *Plátana* Milliken," he says, "you're the great love of my life. The only other member of the *Dorkus* genus in existence, among an entire universe of stars. The minute I saw you, my flabber was gasted. My gob pummeled into a bloody pulp. You've inspired hand flexes since the moment I first touched you. I knew, from the moment I first saw you, literally, you'd one day become my wife." Henn looks down at his watch again, like he's waiting for something specific. Several awkward seconds pass, during which I feel like I'm going to explode if he doesn't ask the actual question. Finally, Henn looks up, grins adorably, and says the words I'm dying to hear: "Hannah Milliken, will you make me the happiest, luckiest *Dorkus* in the world and say yes to marrying me?"

"Yes!" I shout. Suddenly, as if on cue, the Tower's spire erupts above us in mesmerizing sparkles that provoke a whoop from every person in the viewing area, including Henn and me.

"It's like a giant bottle of champagne being popped in our honor!" I shriek happily, as Henn rises from his knee and takes me into his arms.

"All of Paris is celebrating with us, baby!" Henn shouts. He kisses me, and then leans back in order to slide the ring onto my finger as those glorious sparkles continue bathing us in golden, glittering light. As we kiss, the violinist from earlier starts playing our song again. And for the entirety of her performance, we can't stop giddily laughing, hugging, kissing, and cuddling.

When the song ends, I embrace Henn again, and then gaze joyfully at my ring glittering behind his neck. "This ring is stunning. God, I hope you didn't feel like you had to keep up with Josh." I'm pretty sure he did, since the ring's central diamond is nearly as big as Kat's, which she lovingly calls her "Rock of Gibraltar."

"Don't worry about that," he says. "All that matters is you love it. Do you?"

"How could I not? It's spectacular."

"Reed helped me pick it out in Maui. It's been burning a hole in my pocket since then." He chuckles. "I was going to propose to you at Josh and Kat's reception, after you caught Kat's bouquet. And then, like three different times since then, basically whenever I'd had more than one drink."

"You were planning to propose to me the night of our fight in Maui? Aw, Henny. You poor thing."

"Don't feel sorry for me. I had no business doing it then, before I'd been completely honest with you about everything. Plus, I can't believe I didn't realize then that I could only ever propose to you *here* and nowhere else. What was I thinking?"

I chuckle. "This has been perfect. I'm in awe of everything you've arranged."

Henn motions to a waiter, presumably to refill our flutes. But when the waiter arrives, he's got more than a champagne bottle. He's also got a tray of gorgeous *petit fours.*

"You really did think of everything!" I exclaim, before selecting a treat from the tray.

"This was Kat's suggestion," Henn admits. "She thought you'd appreciate a little post-engagement treat."

I laugh. "She knows me well." I take a bite. "Delicious."

"Mine too." Henn looks sheepish. "Kat helped me with the design of your pendant, too. I shudder to think how clunky it would have looked if I'd gone with my initial idea."

"You were a genius to get her input."

"I can't take credit for the violinist, either. That was Reed's idea. Although it was my idea for her to play our song."

"It makes it even sweeter to think this was such a team effort. Genius includes knowing when to delegate, babe." Laughing, I kiss him—and as our tongues swirl, I suddenly realize I'm more than ready to say something Henn has been waiting to hear for a while now. "When we get back, I'll tell Maddy to start looking for a new living situation," I declare. "I don't want to live apart from you anymore. I want to move into the house and live with you, forevermore."

Henn's entire body, not only his face, lights up. "Seriously?"

I nod. "I'm sure Maddy can live with Keane and Zander. Or, if she's not ready for that, then she knows plenty of film students she could live with. I think a group of them live together in a big house. Maybe there's room for her there."

"Are you sure?" Henn asks.

"I'm sure. Honestly, I can't wait. Maddy will be fine. Better than fine. She hasn't said it, but I think she's feeling ready to spread her wings and start a new chapter of her life, without feeling coddled by her big sister. I honestly think she'll be relieved and excited when I tell her I think it's time for a new beginning for us both."

Henn whoops and raises his flute to me. "To new beginnings."

"To new beginnings." I clink his glass. "And to love—a once in a life-time love that will never, ever end."

"Cheers to that," Henn murmurs.

We kiss and hug, and when we realize the photographer is furiously snapping away, we stop kissing and canoodling and pose for a few shots, with me quipping that this is our engagement photo shoot.

When the photographer says she's got everything she needs, she lets us swipe through the images she's captured on her digital camera, and we both "ooh" and "aah" at all of them.

"I can't wait to show these to everyone," I say, after we've reached the final photo.

"In the meantime, let's make some FaceTime calls," Henn suggests, and of course, I agree that's a splendid idea.

Our first call is to my sister, who's still on-set with Keane, and happy tears abound. Next up, we call both our mothers. And again, happy tears flow. Especially from Henn's mom, Carol, who seems so overjoyed by our news, I'm momentarily worried about the happy woman's health.

Next up, we call Reed, who's in the middle of a work meeting in New York when our FaceTime notification comes in. When he sees our smiling faces, he steps outside whatever conference room and booms, "Well, if it isn't my best friend looking happy in Paris . . . And look, she's with Peter!"

We all laugh. Reed has been calling me his best friend since he and I beat the Cook brothers in Patron pong at Henny's housewarming party months ago, and the joke never fails to land.

"Look, bestie!" I say, holding up my ringed hand to Henn's phone.

Henn shouts, "She said yesssss!"

Reed whoops and congratulates us, and we excitedly tell him the story of Henn's amazing proposal.

"Thanks for suggesting the violinist," Henn says. "She was perfect."

"Hey, I'm never going to propose to anyone," Reed says, "I might as well give all my best proposal ideas to you. Have you called Josh and Kat yet?"

"They're next on our list," Henn replies.

"Tell 'em Uncle Reed needs a new Gracie video. It's been over a week."

"We'll let them know."

After one last round of congratulations from Reed, we end the call and place one to Josh and Kat, who cheer and clap effusively at the sight of the bling on my finger. Kat demands we recount every detail of Henn's proposal, so I launch into the story with occasional, tag-team help from Henn. In the middle of our story, however, our call abruptly disconnects, mid-sentence.

"Shoot," I murmur. "The call dropped." I try to call them back, but the call is declined. Suddenly, there's a tap on my shoulder . . . and when I turn my head, I'm met with Kat's gorgeous face. In person. She's here. In Paris. With Josh right behind her.

Shrieking, I throw my arms around my best friend's neck and promptly burst into big, soggy tears. "I can't believe you're here," I say over and over again. "Thank you, thank you."

"Happy birthday, honey," Kat whispers into my hair. "And happy, happy engagement."

It takes a moment to gather myself enough to speak. When I finally do, I choke out, "I can't believe you and Josh came all this way to celebrate with us."

Kat exhales dramatically. "It was a tough sell. Henn really had to twist our arms to fly to a shithole like Paris on a private jet to join you two assholes for a celebratory dinner tonight. But that's the kind of friends we are, I guess."

I laugh, even as I'm wiping tears. "Seriously, though, it really is a big deal for you to travel now that you have Gracie. Who's watching her?"

"My parents—at our hotel. They were elated to get a free trip to Europe in exchange for some occasional babysitting here and there. After Paris, we're taking them to Italy. My mom has always dreamed of going there."

Josh steps forward. He's finished congratulating my fiancé, apparently, and he's now demanding a hug from me. While I embrace Josh, Kat flits over to Henn, and by the time we've finished with all permutations of embraces and greetings, a waiter appears with two more champagne flutes and refills for Henn and me.

Bubbly in hand, our foursome makes several toasts—the first to our engagement. Another to my birthday. A third, to Kat and Josh for joining us on our special night. And, finally, to Kat for serving as our beloved, and oh-so brilliant matchmaker.

"I knew you two would be perfect for each other," Kat says. "Matchmaking is in my blood."

Josh chuckles. "They're literally your only success story, babe."

"That's not true," Kat insists with a sniff. "Before Henn and Hannah, I brilliantly pushed two of my former co-workers together, and they're happily married now."

"That's true," I confirm. "She *Parent Trapped* them."

"I sure did. *Brilliantly*. But even if Henn and Hannah were my only success story, they'd be enough on their own to confirm my matchmaking genius. Talk about two people living the fairytale!"

"That's a very good point," Josh concedes. He raises his drink, once again. "To the fairytale!"

Everyone clinks and drinks to that happy toast, and then each couple cuddles up at the railing and beholds the glittering view while Josh identifies various landmarks beneath us, since he's been to Paris many times.

"Where's the restaurant we'll be dining at tonight?" Kat asks.

"Over there somewhere," Josh replies, indicating. "Trust me, this place is going to blow you away."

Henn nudges me. "Remember the fancy restaurant Josh took us to in Vegas? Apparently, that place is a truck-stop diner—a Wendy's—compared to the place we're going tonight."

"Wow." I look down at my outfit. "Am I dressed fancy enough for a place like that?"

"Actually, no," Henn says. "But never fear because our fairy godmother has brought both of us some dapper duds to change into."

Kat gestures like she's waving a magic wand. "Bibbity bobbity boo!"

I thank Kat and throw myself into Henn's waiting arms—and as we're in our latest clinch, another round of glorious sparkles erupts above our heads.

"Wow!" Kat gasps out, her blonde head tilted back in awe. "It looks like a giant champagne bottle being popped!"

"That's exactly what I said!"

Our trusty photographer appears and snaps several shots of our foursome. Until, finally, Josh says it's time to head to the hotel to change clothes before going back out to the fancy restaurant in time for our reservation.

Henn grabs my hand, and we head into an elevator with Josh and Kat and an attendant. As we descend, Kat and I gush over my ring. And then, my little-birdie-in-a-birdhouse necklace. When we reach the ground floor, we start walking across the bustling plaza toward the car and driver Josh and Kat have arranged for all of us. When we're far enough away that the Tower would fit in its entirety into the background of a photo, however, we stop to snap a group shot, after enlisting the help of a passing tourist.

Midway through our photo session, I turn to look at my new fiancé, my future husband, and discover he's already gazing at me like I'm the great love of his life. When our eyes meet, I smile and say, "I'm so happy. I love you so much, Henny."

"I love you, too," he whispers. "Man, I can't wait to be your husband."

50

HENN

"Go Hennah! Go Hennah!"

That's what everyone on the dance floor is chanting, as my new wife and I dance in the center of the circle like silverback gorillas, each of us enthusiastically defending our territory. We're deep into our rowdy wedding reception at Reed's sprawling mansion. Our traditional first dance, the one where Hannah and I looked picture perfect and photo ready, is long over now. At this point in the night, Hannah's meticulously applied makeup has mostly melted off and the up-do she started the festivities with has mostly fallen down. For my part, my tuxedo jacket is off, my bowtie untied, and my hair askew. We're celebrating *hard*. As my closing move in the center of the circle, I dip and kiss my new wife, soliciting a squeal from her and cheers from our dancing onlookers, before leading her to the perimeter of the circle to let another couple take center stage.

As Hannah and I merge with the gyrating crowd, Keane pulls Maddy into the center, where he proceeds to dance around his blushing fiancée like she's his own personal stripper pole. As odd a pairing as these two seemed at first, it's now clear to everyone they're perfect for each other. A few months ago, Hannah told Kat in my presence she couldn't have customized a better boyfriend for her sister, even if some kind of build-a-boyfriend service existed online, and Kat replied that her family feels the same way about Maddy. "In fact," Kat said to Hannah at the time, "if those two don't work out, I'm positive we'd all unanimously vote to keep Maddy in the Morgan family and kick Keane the hell out."

As Keane and Maddy depart the circle, Ryan and his wife enter and set the place on fire with their white-hot moves. In the end, Ryan not only found his Samantha; he married her, too. And then achieved a much-desired positive result on a pregnancy test in record time. The first of many, they hope, according to what Kat told Hannah on the downlow.

As Ryan and his wife leave the circle, they tag Colby and his wife, Lydia, but not surprisingly, Kat's quiet oldest brother shakes his head and refuses to take the spotlight. As I recall, it's the same thing Colby did in Maui during a luau, when, toward the end of the show, the performers invited audience members to join them onstage and shake their booties in grass skirts. A group of extroverts that included me bounded to the stage to perform a silly dance-off. But when I passed Colby on my way to the stage, he was practically gripping his chair with white knuckles, steeling himself against anyone who dared try to drag him up there.

When Colby and his wife make clear they're opting to remain on the outskirts of the circle, Josh and Kat shimmy their way into it, and then proceed to get everyone whooped up with their enthusiastic moves. As our best friends are dancing, the song ends and a new one begins, which causes the circle to disintegrate and turn into an amorphous swarm, once again.

As I shake my ass to the new song with Hannah, I suddenly wonder about the whereabouts of my mother. If she's dancing close by on the dance floor, I think I'll pull her over here to dance with Hannah and me. When I finally spot Mom's smiling face, she's not on the dance floor; she's sitting at a nearby table with Hannah's mom and Kat's parents, all of them laughing and looking happy as can be.

Another pang squeezes my heart and reverberates through my soul. It's the same ache I've felt countless times tonight, whenever my thoughts have drifted to my dad. I wish so badly he could have met Hannah and been here tonight. We left a chair open for him next to Mom during the ceremony. And I mentioned him in my toast before dinner, too. So, while he's up there watching me from his perch on a cloud, then Dad surely knows he's deeply loved and missed and always close to our hearts.

By the time I return my gaze to Hannah dancing next to me, we've been joined by Kat and Josh and Jonas and Sarah. Nearby, Maddy and Keane are dancing with Ryan and his wife, as well as Reed's little sister, Violet, and Kat's youngest brother, Dax, and Dax's two bandmates.

During the time Dax and his two bandmates, Fish and Colin, lived across the hallway from Hannah, I got to really like all three of those guys and genuinely root for their band, 22 Goats, to make a huge splash with their then-upcoming debut album. So, of course, when the album finally came out and the music video for their first single, "People Like Us," went mega-viral earlier this year—with no behind-the-scenes assistance from me, by the way—thereby rocketing the song to the top of several charts and catapulting 22 Goats to worldwide fame, I couldn't have been happier about it. Reed is known in the industry as The Man with the Midas Touch, and it's now abundantly clear he truly deserves that nickname. The dude can't miss. At least, when it comes to River Records and his other business dealings. When it comes to relationships, I'm still deeply unimpressed. But, hey, to each his own.

Speaking of Reed, where the hell is he? Now that I think of it, I haven't seen him for a while. I look around, but Reed's nowhere to be seen. He didn't bring a date tonight—he never brings dates to personal parties and events—so, he couldn't have slipped away to get laid. Is he smoking another joint in his backyard with Keane and the boys from 22 Goats? No, all those guys are dancing nearby. Plus, Reed has always been a one-joint-per-party sort of guy, and he's already enjoyed his allotment.

When the song ends, the dance floor erupts in applause, and a half-second later, Reed's voice booms through the sound system. "May I have your attention, please?"

I turn completely around to face the DJ and discover Reed standing next to him with a microphone in his hand. "Sorry to interrupt the dance party," Reed says with a dazzling smile, "but I'm told a gift I got for Mr. and Mrs. Hennessey has just arrived."

I put my hands on either side of my mouth and shout to Reed, "We said no presents!"

"It's my house, so I can break any rule I want," Reed quips. As the crowd chuckles, Reed continues, "I originally planned to give the happy couple this surprise earlier in the night. I'd planned to provide the accompaniment for their first dance, actually. But due to a flight delay, that wasn't possible. Better late than never, though." Reed motions to his trusty assistant, Owen, who opens a door, and a moment later, a man with a guitar waltzes into the room. As the man makes his way toward Reed, the latter says, "We all loved watching Henn and Hannah's first dance earlier. What a perfect song for them, right? Well, this gentleman here is the musical genius who wrote that song and performed it on the hit record."

As the crowd applauds, the guy waves to everyone. When he reaches Reed, the men shake hands and slap shoulders. Reed introduces the musician to the crowd by name and explains he's a founding member of They Might Be Giants, one of Reed's all-time favorites in the alt rock genre.

Of course, the crowd cheers and applauds again, even more wildly this time, but nobody more so than Hannah and me. Perhaps I should have suspected Reed would pull something like this, given how generous he is. Also, because he flew Josh and Kat's favorite troubadour to Maui for a private performance during their wedding reception. But somehow, the thought never even crossed my mind. Reed is hosting our entire wedding at his house, after all. He's already given us the best possible present.

"Henn and Hannah," Reed says with a grin. "We all love you so much. You two light up every room you enter. You're a joy to watch and an inspiration to us all. Congratulations from the bottom of my heart." He looks directly at Hannah. "To Hannah, specifically, thanks for being my best friend."

Not surprisingly, Hannah guffaws—that joke never misses—before blowing Reed an enthusiastic kiss.

A crowd has formed around Hannah and me again. Plainly, everyone thinks we're going to perform our choreographed routine again—this time, to the live version of the song. We wowed them earlier tonight during our first dance with our hilarious, synchronized, well-rehearsed moves, after all. But no. This time, as the talented musician begins his surprise acoustic performance, I take Hannah into my arms and simply sway with her to the quirky love song.

As the performer gets to his chorus, I lean down and softly kiss Hannah's cheek—and to my surprise, my lips come back salty and wet.

Aw, baby. I slide my fingertip underneath Hannah's chin and tilt her face toward mine, and that's when I'm treated to the world's most gloriously electrifying smile, topped off by two stunningly gorgeous blue eyes. She's got the face of an angel, my wife, especially when she's crying tears of unadulterated joy.

"I love you so much," she chokes out.

"I love you, too, Mrs. Hennessey. 459, baby. All day every day."

"What's 459?"

"I've never told you about that? Oh. I thought I did. On a cell phone dial pad, four is I. Five is L. Nine is Y—I. Love. You."

Hannah giggles. "Oh, Henny. That's so cute."

"If you like that, I've got more where that came from." I toss out a series of coding strings, all of them used to create infinite loops in various coding languages, and then take Hannah's face in my palms. "No matter how I say it, or code it, my feelings will always boil down to the same thing. I love you, Hannah Banana la *Plátana*, my birdhouse, my *wife*. You're the only bee in my bonnet. Function: *forever*."

EPILOGUE
HANNAH

My eyes shoot open.

Hazel.

Did I miss her waking up and crying out for me? It feels later than her usual wakeup time. Did I miss my alarm for work? No, it's Sunday. Henn must have gone to her.

I turn to see if my hubby is sleeping next to me, and his side of the bed is empty, save for a red envelope placed neatly on his pillow. I grab it and discover Henn's jagged handwriting on its face: "Sleep as long as you like, my love. Happy Mother's Day." Oh yeah. Today is my first Mother's Day!

"Well, hot damn," I murmur, before flopping back onto my pillow, pulling up the covers, and immediately falling back to sleep. When my eyes open again, I smile and sigh happily in the late-morning light streaming through the window. I don't know what time it is or how long I've slept. All I know is I feel more rested than I have in months. I sit up, grab the red envelope off Henn's pillow again, and open it this time. Inside, there are two handwritten notes. Dutifully, I open the one marked "Open first."

Dear Mommy,

Happy Mother's Day! I can't write yet, so I dictated this note to Daddy, who translated my babbles and expertly transcribed them all. You're da best mommy in da world and I love you so much! I can't wait to tell you "I love you, Mommy!" one day soon. But for now, I'll leave you with the tried-and-true sentiments many an infant has babbled to their beloved mommies before me throughout history: da-ga-goo-bee-doo-ma!

Love,
Hazel

Giggling, I unfold the second note and smile the whole time while reading it:

My Pretty, Precious Plátana,

Happy First Mother's Day! I decided to write a separate note from Hazel's because mine is bound to get a lil spicy, and I didn't want Hazel to read those parts later and get grossed out. I don't know if husbands normally get X-rated with their Mother's Day tributes to their wives, but the fact that I can't get enough of your hot body is a major contributing factor to Hazel being here in the first place, so I feel like a lil spice makes perfect sense under the circumstances.
I know how much you like surprises, so I've got several for you today, my love. Whenever you're ready, come out and join the other two members of the Hennessey Hoodlums for some fresh donuts, purchased this morning by Hazel and me from Allison's Bakery for this very special occasion.
This afternoon, you've got a massage appointment, and tonight,

I've arranged a babysitter so we can go out and feast till our stomachs' delight. When we get home from dinner, we'll kiss our sleeping baby and head into our bedroom where I'm going to make you my dessert, baby! Woohoo! Just thinking about what I'm going to do to your user interface tonight is making my floppy disk hard. Of course, I'll be sure to hit you with plenty of hot cum-puter-speak, since you love it so much. In fact, here's a little preview to get your Slip 'n' Slide slipping and sliding about tonight's late-night festivities:

Ooooh, baby, tonight, I'm gonna crash your hard drive. First off, I'm gonna diagram your touch points and make your power supply surge. From there, I'll byte your Back End and penetrate your fire-wall, making sure to give you plenty of RAM. Over and over again, I'll make your processor race and your central processing unit halt and catch fire. Why? Because you're my Endpoint, my love. My eternal Touchpad. 459, baby, on an infinite loop. Function: forever. You're my birdhouse, Hannah. And now, you're Hazel's, too. Thank you for being the best wife and mother, ever. Happy First Mother's Day.

Love,
Henny

With tears in my eyes, I kiss the letter and leave it on my nightstand, and then shuffle into the bathroom. After doing the basics of my morning routine, I amble into our family room, where I find my husband on the floor next to our beloved baby, Hazel Katherine Hennessey. At the moment, she's sitting like a big girl on a blanket with a little assist from a U-shaped pillow around her torso.

"Good morning!" Henn says as I enter the room. "Hazel's *this* close to sitting without the pillow."

I slide onto the couch. "Such a biggie wiggie girl."

Henn scoops up the baby and bounds to me on the couch. "Happy Mother's Day. Did you get our notes?"

"I did. Both were amazing. Thank you." I kiss his cheek. "All that *cum*-puter speak had its desired effect, by the way. I can't wait to hear more in person tonight."

"I'm at your service."

Hazel is reaching for me, so I take her from Henn and kiss her fat cheek. "Thank you for the note, Hazy Baby. Your sentiments, especially considering your tender age, were most impressive and appreciated."

"She's a genius. What can I say."

"Thank you for the extra sleep. I feel amazing."

"Good. Mission accomplished, then." Henn motions toward the kitchen. "Donuts and a fresh pot of coffee are in there. You want me to get you some?"

"I'd love it. Thank you."

As Henn bounds into the kitchen, I address Hazel in my arms. "Are you hungry, bubba?"

"She just ate," Henn calls from the kitchen.

"Wow. The service here is impeccable. Five stars."

Henn appears with a mug and a donut, as well as two wrapped presents, a big one and a small one, all of which he places on the coffee table. "A present from Hazel and me. And one from my mother."

"How sweet. Should I open them now?"

"Absolutely. Start with the big one. It's from my mother."

I open the one from Henn's mom and discover she's cross-stitched a pillow for me, its face bearing the message, "World's Best Mommy."

"Aw. This will be so cute next to the one she gave me for my birthday." That other pillow bears a cross-stitched message that reads, "The fun is in the trying, not the succeeding." It's the thing I said to Carol while teaching her to catch popcorn kernels in her mouth all those years ago.

"Okay, open mine and Hazel's now," Henn says, indicating the small box on the coffee table.

I open it and find a necklace with three jewels inlaid at the center—my birthstone, Henn's, and Hazel's. "I love it! Thank you so much. It's gorgeous." I kiss Henn and thank him profusely and then make a big show of thanking Hazel, too, who giggles and smiles like she understands every word I say. "You're both so generous."

"We're lucky to have you."

All of a sudden, Hazel on my lap makes a silly noise that sounds an awful lot like a dog barking.

I gently clap Hazel's fat little palms together and squeal. "Yes, baby! That's what the doggie says!" Logically, I know Hazel's far too young to be able to mimic animal sounds—and yet, we read a book about animals every night to her, and she's awfully smart, so on the off chance she's made that sound on purpose, I'm not going to miss the chance to praise her.

Henn says, "We met a fluffy dog outside the bakery today who licked Hazel's face. She giggled so hard, she pooped."

I gasp. "My baby *giggle-pooped*?"

"She did. Like a pro."

"Finally, some evidence my genes are in there somewhere."

Henn howls with laughter. I'm always joking there's no evidence of my genes actually existing inside our daughter. Hazel looks exactly like Henn, she's smart as hell, and clearly has her daddy's easy-going disposition, too. That was probably the best joke I've ever made along those lines, though. I'm actually pretty impressed with myself.

"Hey, would you be upset if I reschedule the massage?" I ask, as Henn takes the baby from me so I can eat and drink. "Thank you for the thoughtful gift, but I think I'd rather spend my first Mother's Day with you and Hazel."

"It's your day. We can do whatever you want."

"Do we have enough time to take her to the zoo before the babysitter comes tonight?"

Henn's dark eyes twinkle with his smile. "We do. You're sure you don't want to be pampered, though?"

"I'm sure." I hold up the half-eaten donut in my hand. "This is pampering enough. Plus, all that extra sleep and presents and dinner tonight."

We have ourselves a little family hug. "I love you both so much," Henn whispers. "Whatever we do today, the most important thing is you both know you're loved beyond all measure. Infinite loop. 459. Indubitably. *Forever.*"

THE END

Thank you for reading Hacker In Love, I hope you loved this story as much as I do. Keep reading for a ***bonus pregnancy reveal scene with all the spice that got them there***!

Want more?
Why not start reading the Josh & Kat Trilogy and read all about how billionaire, playboy Josh Faraday captured the brilliant Party Girl Kat Morgan. Start reading their steamy love story today with *Infatuation*.

Or, if you prefer, feel free to check out any of the romance titles in Lauren's catalogue including stories for **Reed Rivers and The Morgan Brothers**, keep reading for descriptions to all.
All books by Lauren Rowe are available in ebook, paperback, and audiobook formats.

BONUS PREGNANCY REVEAL
SCENE WITH EXTRA SPICE
HENN

I t's a Sunday afternoon. Hannah's out with Maddy for the day, while I'm sitting at our kitchen table working on a job for a regular client. When my phone on the table buzzes, I glance at my screen, expecting to ignore the call and let it go to voicemail. There are only a few people in this world I'd stop working for when I'm in the zone, and, to my surprise, this particular caller is one 'em. It's Jonas Faraday calling me. That dude never calls me. In fact, he rarely even makes a peep in the group chat we have with Hannah, Sarah, Josh, and Kat. My interest soundly piqued, I quickly connect the call.

"Hey, Jonas."

"I need you to find someone for me as soon as possible."

Ha. That's so Jonas. No greeting. No pleasantries. Straight to the point. Clearly, he's in the midst of some sort of fixation, which is so on-brand, I can't help chuckling. "Why, hello, Jonas," I say pleasantly. "I'm doing great. Thanks for asking. How are you?"

"It's this guy on YouTube," he says. Plainly, he's a man on a mission. "I'll send you the link. His video is pay-per-view, but I'll buy it for you."

"A pay-per-view video?" There's really no point in trying to make Jonas Faraday act like a normal human. Only Sarah knows how to do that. Sometimes, Josh. But mostly, Sarah. So, if you can't beat 'em, join 'em, right? "Is this video *porn*, by any chance?" It's a joke, of course. Jonas has talked my ear off several times about the modern plague of easy-to-access porn—the fact that easy porn has turned an entire generation of men into lazy lovers who don't understand what actually turns women on and who can't get it up without digital stimulation.

"I emailed you the link," Jonas says, not bothering to acknowledge my joke. "Watch the video and find me the guy. I need to talk to him." I'm well aware Jonas can be obsessive at times, so his tone doesn't surprise me. Clearly, he's a dog with a bone.

"Hang on," I say. "Let me open your email." I click the link, and to my shock, the name of the video is "How to Make a Woman Squirt Every Single Time." "Holy shit!" I choke out. "I was joking about the video being porn."

"Can you find him for me?"

"I can do anything. I'm a fucking genius. Hang on." I press play on the video and an average-looking dude—a guy who basically looks like me—appears as the host of the "how to" squirting video.

"Hey, guys," our host says. "Do you want to make your woman squirt? Do you want to do it every single time, like clockwork? Well, through years of practice and experimentation, I've figured out a method for making any woman squirt, every time, without fail . . ."

"This guy is showing his face, Jonas. Dig around a little bit, and I'm sure you'll find him without me."

"I don't have time to hunt this guy down and figure this shit out. I'd rather pay you to do it for me."

"Well, I'm not going to take your money to find him. I should be paying *you* for buying me this video. You've made my day." I snicker. "And Hannah's night."

I return to the video, where an extremely attractive woman is now walking into frame and standing next to our host. "Oh, hello," I murmur, as our video host introduces her as Carla. "You want me to find this woman, too?"

"Of course, not," Jonas snaps. "Just the guy."

"Just wondering."

As the woman begins undressing onscreen, Jonas says, "I'll never ask you to find me another girl as long as I live, Henn. I'm *married.*"

"Well, obviously, Jonas. I was only asking because I thought maybe this is a business matter for you. Maybe these two embezzled funds from one of your companies, for all I know. How was I supposed to know you're asking me to hunt down a squirt-master for personal reasons?"

"I need this guy's phone number. I want to ask him a few questions."

"So do I. *Damn.*" The woman is naked now, and the dude is kissing her while both are seated on the edge of a bed. Is he priming her for the Big Squirt? I sure hope so.

"Just find him for me," Jonas murmurs.

"Only if you pass along anything really good you find out."

"Deal."

"Damn. I feel like such a pimp right now." I continue watching the video for half a minute. He's stopped kissing naked Carla now. He's sliding his hand between her legs. "So, how's—" I'm intending to ask Jonas about Sarah and their twin preemies. But I stop talking when, all of a sudden, so much cum shoots out of the naked woman on my screen, it's like she's a broken fire hydrant. "Whoa! Carla just blew her load all over the bed! Now *that's* what I call entertainment. Hot diggity damn."

Jonas can't help chuckling with me. "So, you're on it?"

It takes me a second to reorient myself, but I quickly surmise he's asking if I'm down to find the squirt master for him. "Like purple on Barney. This is definitely a white-hat job. Absolutely free of charge."

"Thanks."

"Is this a thanks-for-having-my-babies surprise for Sarah? Most guys give their woman jewelry for that occasion, but Jonas Faraday makes his wife squirt."

"Most guys give their wife jewelry after she gives birth?"

Aw, poor Jonas. As Josh always says, he's the dumbest genius who ever lived. "Yeah, from what I've seen." Granted, I've only ever personally observed the jewelry-for-a-baby phenomenon twice: when Josh showered Kat with jewels after she gave birth to Gracie and Ryan gave his wife diamond earrings after the birth of their son, Zachary. But I have to believe they're not the only husbands who've given their wives jewels to celebrate a birth. If Hannah and I are lucky enough to get pregnant one day—we've certainly been working hard at it—then I'll one hundred percent give Hannah some sort of jewelry to commemorate the occasion.

Jonas is silent on the other end of the line, so I pipe in to narrate what I'm seeing on my screen, where the first woman has left and a second one arrived. "Ooh. Enter woman number two."

"Okay, thanks," Jonas mumbles. "Gotta go."

Ha. If I know Jonas, he's freaking out about my jewelry comment. Maybe even planning to hang up and dart out of his house to remedy his oversight.

"Hang on," I say. "How are Sarah and the babies doing?"

"Good. Sarah's still not feeling great, but—"

"But she's about to start feeling a whole lot better! Ka-*bam*!" I'm referring to the squirting video, of course. Making one hell of a funny joke, if you ask me. But Jonas isn't laughing.

"Shut the fuck up, Henn," Jonas says. Thankfully, there's no venom in his tone. Only playfulness. "You're talking about my wife."

"Sorry."

Jonas joins me in chuckling. "It'd be hard to get pissed at a comment like that when we're watching a squirting video together."

"True. So, how are the babies?"

"The girls are great. They should be coming home in about three weeks. They have to get to the point where their lungs are fully developed. Pretty normal with preemies, I guess."

Hannah and I saw the teeny-tiny twins in the NICU in Seattle about three weeks ago, right after they were born. There were some complications—some really scary days for poor Jonas and Sarah—so Hannah and I quickly hopped a flight to be there for our friends. For Josh and Kat, too, given how distraught and worried they both were. Ultimately, mother and babies were fine, thank God, so Hannah and I returned home. But not before holding those tiny twins in the NICU and marveling at their miniscule body parts.

"Send me a pic," I say.

"Hang on."

As I await Jonas's photo, I return to the video on my laptop, where our host has his hand inside the second woman. "Whoa! Woman number two just wet the bed!" I announce gleefully. "Oh my God. This is my favorite thing."

Ping.

"Just sent you a pic."

I look down to find two tiny, adorable humans staring at me. "Aw, they're so cute. They've filled out a ton since I saw them. They look like actual humans now instead of raisins. I can't wait to see them again. Hannah and I are planning to come to Seattle when Josh and Kat have baby number two."

"Did you hear it's a boy?" Jonas says.

"Yeah. They FaceTimed Hannah and me with the news. Kat was freaking out about having a penis inside her at all times, and Josh was like, 'What's new about that?'"

We both crack up as a third woman appears on-screen.

"Oh, here we goooo!" I bellow. "Woman number three, step right up."

"You and Hannah should stay here when you come to Seattle."

"Cool. I'll tell Hannah to calendar it—right after I make her squirt."

"Okay, that's it. I'm hanging up. Sarah will be home soon."

"And you've got some more porn to watch?"

"Nah, I've got actual work to do. I'm a respectable member of society, if you haven't heard."

"I read that article about you guys in whatever magazine. The one about Peru? So impressive. You looked like Thor. I told Josh they made you look way cooler than him and he almost punched me in the face."

"Poor Josh. He's so used to Kat lying to him about his good looks. He's not equipped to handle the truth."

"I'll tell him you said so."

"Please do."

We share another chuckle.

"Talk to you later," Jonas says. "Thanks for the favor."

"You're not going to ask me if I've got any news about The Club before we hang up?" Every time we talk, Jonas asks me if I'm one hundred percent positive the fire we put out together in Vegas is one hundred percent ice-cold, or if there could possibly be any embers among the ashes.

"Do you?"

"Nope. Nothing at all. I'm just shocked you didn't ask me about it. I think that's what the psychologists call *progress*."

"You'll tell me if something comes up, right?"

"Indubitably."

"Then, I trust you."

Well, that's new. Is our beloved master of obsession turning over a new leaf? "Cool," I say. "Talk to you soon, Jonas."

"Talk to you later, Henn."

"Happy squirt-questing!" I call out.

"You, too."

"Oh, Jonas? Get Sarah a whole mess of diamonds. She's been through a lot."

"I'll do exactly that. Thanks for looking out."

"You bet, brother."

We say our goodbyes, and the minute we hang up, I cue up the squirting video and watch the entire thing again. And then a third time to make sure I didn't miss a single detail of the guy's instructions. I've already read the amazing book Jonas gave me years ago, as well as a couple videos suggested by Reed. And it goes without saying I've watched all Keane's "Ball Peen Hammer" videos, too, the ones he used to make with "Maddy Behind the Camera." Of course, I paid closest attention to Keane's video about "The Sure Thing"—the technique Ryan told me and others about in Maui, years ago. But it seems like this squirt-master's technique is something slightly different than all the rest. Even if it's not, it's awfully hard to beat a video featuring a dude actually performing the technique before my eyes, as opposed to me simply reading about it or watching Keane talk about it. To be fair, Keane's a million times more entertaining than this milk-toast dude. There's no contest there. But, still, I'm grateful for the step-by-step instructions, coupled with visual demonstration.

For a while now, I've been looking for something new to shake things up in the bedroom with Hannah. Specifically, something to get her mind off the baby-making aspect of our lovemaking. In the very beginning, when we first decided we felt ready to try for a baby, we simply started having unprotected sex. "Let's not do all that counting and tracking," Hannah suggested. "Let's simply have fun and let fate decide." Of course, I agreed.

But at some point, it seemed like "fate" was either permanently out to lunch or had affirmatively decided a baby wasn't in our future. Hannah became visibly frustrated, and I had to admit I was feeling at a loss myself. When we finally went to a doctor to find out if either or both of us had some kind of issue, we both got clean bills of health. "All pipes are in perfect working order for both of you," the doc said. "It'll happen when it's meant to happen. Just keep having fun and remain relaxed about it."

Easier said than done.

We're still thoroughly enjoying our sex life, of course. How could we not? I'm totally obsessed with Hannah, and she continues to find me barely tolerable. But even so, there's no denying we're at the point now where we both *really* want a baby. And I can't help wondering, after every time we have sex, if a piece of Hannah is wondering, "Did *that* time do the trick?" If I'm being completely honest, that's what I'm usually wondering afterwards, too. So, maybe, this new squirting technique will be just the thing to get our minds off all that stuff and help both of us have nothing but fun again—this time, on Hannah's extra-extra-wet Slip 'n' Slide.

Later that night

I stroke Hannah's slit and she shudders with anticipation and lies back onto our bed.

My cock straining and wet, I open her thighs and lick her gently. When she's trembling and breathing hard, I move on to massaging her clit, manipulating it firmly in circles, and Hannah lets out a soft whimper.

"Take deep breaths," I instruct. "That's it. You look so hot in the moonlight. Gorgeous."

I slide my fingers inside her and get to work with both my tongue and fingers, and in short order, her inner muscles begin rippling against my fingers with a powerful orgasm.

Even before Hannah's body stops warping, I plunge myself inside her, all the way, and she growls ravenously at my invasion. With my hands gripping her hips, I move in and out, decidedly, over and over, my tip ramming against her farthest reaches. Over and over again, I pound her, as my palms explore her gyrating, naked torso. And all the while, I tell her that she's hot. Beautiful. Turning me on. I tell her she's a drug to me. The sexiest woman alive. And hottest of all, at least for me, I say, over and over again, "This gorgeous woman here is my *wife*."

When I find the angle and speed that make her groan the loudest, I stay the course—pounding her the same way, without variation, until she's screaming at me not to stop. Her eyes roll back, but I don't stop. She emits a long, animalistic, desperate growl. But still, I don't stop. I fuck her until each thrust elicits a delicious kind of sloshing noise—a sound that tells me my wife is losing her fucking mind.

When it's clear she's on the bitter cusp of ecstasy, I pull out, reach inside her, and touch a specific spot inside her—the one the dude in the video called a "trip cord." And then plunge myself back inside just in time to feel her innermost muscles tighten sharply around my cock and warm liquid squirt from her body all over mine. The pleasure is so fucking intense, I'm in danger of blacking out. My eyes roll back, and I come inside her with the force of a missile.

When I'm able to command my body again, I find myself collapsed and shaking on top of her. I lift my head to look into her eyes, and she grips my cheeks and kisses me passionately.

"Oh my god, Henny!" she shouts. "What did you do to me? That was fucking amazing!"

I roll onto my back and try to corral my ragged breathing. "You think?"

"*You don't?*"

"Meh." I turn my head and beam a huge smile at her. "It was barely tolerable, if you ask me."

Hannah laughs and swats my shoulder. "Peter the Great rides again! Wooh!" She rests her head on my chest for a long moment, before raising her head and beaming a smile at me. "I know we said we'd ditch the ovulation tracker and not stress or worry, but I was bad, and I used an ovulation tracker this morning and I'm right in the zone. Like, smack in the middle of optimal fertility. And, damn, you just felt like a freaking firehose inside me, babe." She laughs. "I'm telling you, that time worked. I can feel it in my bones. I know it."

I stroke her hair. "And if not, then we'll keep going and have fun. If a baby isn't in the cards for us, for some reason, then that's okay, too, right? We'll always have each other. Or we can adopt."

Hannah nods and smiles. "Don't worry, love. No matter what happens, I promise I'll always be happy, as long as I'm with you."

A month later

"Babe!" Hannah calls from our bedroom. "I'm running late. Can you pull the lasagnas out of the oven and the cake out of the fridge? I want the cake to be room temperature when I serve it. It'll taste better that way."

"Doing it now." I get up from the couch and walk toward the kitchen. "How soon will they be here?"

"Any minute now. They're coming straight from the taping."

Keane and Maddy are coming over to celebrate three exciting accomplishments tonight. One, Maddy's first full-length documentary—the one she made at U Dub about college basketball that won several awards way back when—was recently picked up by a major distributor and is now going to be available for streaming on a major platform. Two, Maddy's landed a deal with a production company that will finance her next two projects. And three, Keane's been cast in his biggest role yet—a plum part as a series regular on a popular show with a huge following. Keane and Maddy just returned from Seattle, where they celebrated all of their various accomplishments with the Seattle branch of the Morgan clan. But now, it's our turn to celebrate with them, too, albeit on a much smaller scale—with a little dinner party for four.

When I open the oven, I'm surprised to find *two* massive lasagnas, even though there's only going to be the four of us tonight. "Babe, you made enough food for an army," I shout to Hannah in the bedroom. "I'm not complaining. I love having leftovers."

"I know how much you love leftovers!" Hannah calls back. Plainly, she didn't catch my second comment. She adds, "Plus, I can take some to work for lunch!"

Makes sense. Hannah works hard at her job. So hard, she often doesn't leave her desk for lunch. That is, unless I whisk her away from her desk for a surprise picnic or lunch at whatever nearby favorite restaurant. I do that kind of thing often, actually, since I can work whenever the fuck I want on whatever the fuck I want, if at all.

The lasagnas out and cooling on the counter, I open the fridge to collect the cake and pause in confusion when I read the lettering on its frosted face. *Congratulations, Daddy!* All of a sudden, blood whooshes into my ears. My heart rate skyrockets. My breathing halts. *Does this mean . . .?*

"Henny."

The refrigerator door still open and blasting cool air onto my hot face, I spin around and discover my gorgeous wife standing before me with her hands on her hips and her chest jutting out. She's wearing a black T-shirt, jeans, and a wide, beaming smile. It takes me a half-second to process the meaning of her pose, but when my eyes finally drift down to the message on her T-shirt, all is clear. My hopes are confirmed. The shirt reads "*Pregnant AF.*"

"Oh my god," I choke out, as tears well in my eyes. But that's all I can manage. I'm too overwhelmed, too ecstatic, to say more. *We finally did it?*

"You're going to be a daddy," Hannah whispers, her blue eyes watering like mine.

I fold her into my arms, and she crushes her body against mine and breaks down in happy sobs. Finally, I regain my voice. "I love you so, so much."

"I love you, too."

I lead Hannah's weeping frame to the couch, and when she pulls herself together, she tells me everything. How she took a test yesterday morning and lost her damned mind, yet somehow managed to keep the amazing news a secret until she could take ten more tests, and then quickly get this T-shirt created with iron-on letters she bought at a craft store.

"You haven't even told Maddy yet?" I ask.

"Of course not. You're the daddy. You get to be the first to know."

I'm buzzing. "Should we tell Maddy and Keane when they get here, or wait till the first trimester is over?" Without waiting for her reply, I quickly say, "Fuck it. Let's tell them. And let's call our moms tonight, too. And Josh and Kat. But that's it. Oh, and Reed, of course. Shit. He's in London, I think. What time is it there? Oh, let's tell Ryan, too."

Before Hannah replies, our doorbell rings. With a little waggle of her eyebrows, Hannah says, "Looks like Keane and Maddy are about to find out our awesome news, thanks to my T-shirt. Unless you want me to change while you answer the door?"

"Fuck no. Answer the door like that. Let's tell the whole world!"

I get up and excitedly follow Hannah to our front door, dying to witness Keane and Maddy's reactions to Hannah's T-shirt. But to my surprise, when Hannah opens the door, I get a whole lot more reactions than I bargained for. Not only are Keane and Maddy standing on our doorstep, as expected, but also Josh and Kat, Jonas and Sarah, and Ryan and his wife, along with a whole mess of babies and toddlers that belong to all of them.

"Hellooooo!" Hannah bellows gleefully to the group in our doorway. With a loud squeal, she gestures to the message scrawled across her ample chest, and the group simultaneously bursts into enthusiastic cheers and exclamations of well wishes.

In short order, our friends and family members swarm Hannah in the doorway, and then me inside, and then both of us together, before finally being led into the heart of the living room. When we all settle into seats, I tell our rapt audience the story of the cake and Hannah surprising me with that T-shirt, and everyone is thrilled.

When the initial shock tamps down a bit, Sarah explains she and all our Seattle friends came down to LA for the weekend to take their kiddos to Disneyland, not realizing Hannah's last-minute dinner invitation would turn out to be such a momentous occasion.

"It was pure luck," Hannah says. "I only took the pregnancy test yesterday, well after I'd already invited you all to join us tonight as a surprise for Henn." She smiles at me. "Until yesterday, I thought the big surprise I'd be giving you tonight was having all our best friends show up for dinner, unexpectedly. I had no idea tonight would be *this* big a surprise."

I lean in and kiss Hannah. "It's fate. A sign everything's happened exactly as it was meant to be."

"I think so, too."

Josh reveals he's brought a cooler full of the finest champagne, as well as a bottle of sparkling apple cider for Kat, who's pregnant with baby number two. And soon, the bottles are opened, and everyone is raising a glass.

"Congrats to *Hennah*," Josh says. "I can't think of two people who should reproduce more than you two—myself and Kat, included." As Kat agrees, and the whole group laughs, Josh says, "Good lord, that's gonna be one smart, kind, adorable kid!"

"Here, here!"

"Congrats to both Keane and Maddy, too," I interject. I count off all the reasons the pair deserves our well wishes, and everyone clinks and drinks to them.

Hannah falls into a hug with Maddy, and the sisters embrace for what seems like an eternity. When Hannah's finally free, I pull my wife into me and kiss her lips. "I love you so much," I whisper.

"I love you, too," Hannah whispers back. "I can't wait to see what happens next—as long as, whatever it is, I'm doing all of it with you."

ACKNOWLEDGMENTS

Huge thanks to Sophie Broughton for all you do.

Also, to Letitia Hasser of RBA Designs for your wonderful cover designs (you truly outdid yourself this time, woman!).

Thank you to my amazing and generous beta readers, Lizette Baez, Sarah Kirk, and Selina Washington.

Thank you to some hackers I met at a hacker convention in Las Vegas who gave me fantastic information and insight into my beloved Henny and his world.

Thank you to Madonna Blackburn and Amy Bourne for all your support and help, and to Alison Evans-Maxwell for proofing.

Thank you, to The Training Room, the physical therapy facility in Poway that helped me rehab a severely broken ankle for so many months while working on this book. You brought me back to life and made me feel like me again, which therefore allowed me to write again, thankfully. For that, and your friendship, I'm forever grateful to you all. Special shout-out to the wonderful Rick Stauffer, Alexandra Blits, Eric Julienne, and Leonardo Mendoza. To Leo, specifically, you let me bounce specific ideas off you and also gave me a few fun ideas of your own. Thank you.

Last but not least, thank you to my readers for begging me to write Henn's book for so many years. Each and every time you asked, I said it wouldn't happen. When I told you never, I honestly meant it. But "never say never" certainly applies here, because you were absolutely right: there *was* a story to tell, after all. An exciting one! One I'm sure I wouldn't have stayed put to tell, if I hadn't been rehabbing for so long from an injury. So, there's a silver lining in everything.

Thank you, readers, for reading and loving these characters, and this whole world, as much as I do! If you're a newbie to me reading this note, if *Hacker in Love* was your first book in my sprawling Faraday-Morgan-Reed Rivers universe, then you'll be happy to learn that every single major side character in this book already as their own full-length story for you to devour, most of them with cross-over timelines and a whole bunch of cross-over scenes. Even when those books include scenes you've already read here from Henn's or Hannah's point of view, there will be many surprises and twists you didn't see coming while reading this story. That's life in a nutshell, right? We might all be at the same party, but we'll surely experience it differently, because we're *all* the main characters in our own stories! *Enjoy*!

BOOKS BY LAUREN ROWE

Dive into Lauren's universe of interconnected trilogies and duets, all books available individually and as a bundle, in any order.

A full suggested reading order can be found here!

The Josh & Kat Trilogy

It's a war of wills between stubborn and sexy Josh Faraday and Kat Morgan. A fight to the bed. Arrogant, wealthy playboy Josh is used to getting what he wants. And what he wants is Kat Morgan. The books are to be read in order:

Infatuation

Revelation

Consummation

The Club Trilogy

When wealthy playboy Jonas Faraday receives an anonymous note from Sarah Cruz, a law student working part-time processing online applications for an exclusive club, he becomes obsessed with hunting her down and giving her the satisfaction she claims has always eluded her. Thus begins a sweeping tale of obsession, passion, desperation, and ultimately, everlasting love and individual redemption. Find out why scores of readers all over the world, in multiple languages, call The Club Trilogy "my favorite trilogy ever" and "the greatest love story I've ever read." As Jonas Faraday says to Sarah Cruz: "There's never been a love like ours and there never will be again… Our love is so pure and true, we're the amazement of the gods."

The Club: Obsession

The Club: Reclamation

The Club: Redemption

The fourth book for Jonas and Sarah is a full-length epilogue with incredible heart-stopping twists and turns and feels. Read The Club: Culmination (A Full-Length Epilogue Novel) after finishing The Club Trilogy or, if you prefer, after reading The Josh and Kat Trilogy.

The Reed Rivers Trilogy

Reed Rivers has met his match in the most unlikely of women—aspiring journalist and spitfire, Georgina Ricci. She's much younger than the women Reed normally pursues, but he can't resist her fiery personality and drop-dead gorgeous looks. But in this game of cat and mouse, who's chasing whom? With each passing day of this wild ride, Reed's not so sure. The books of this trilogy are to be read in order:

Bad Liar

Beautiful Liar

Beloved Liar

The Hate Love Duet

An addicting, enemies-to-lovers romance with humor, heat, angst, and banter. Music artists Savage of Fugitive Summer and Laila Fitzgerald are stuck together on tour. And convinced they can't stand each other. What they don't know is that they're absolutely made for each other, whether they realize it or not. The books of this duet are to be read in order:

Falling Out of Hate with You

Falling Into Love with You

Interconnected Standalones within the same universe

Hacker in Love

When world-class hacker Peter "Henn" Hennessey meets Hannah Milliken, he moves heaven and earth, including doing some questionable things, to win his dream girl over. But when catastrophe strikes, will Henn lose Hannah forever, or is there still a chance for him to chase their happily ever after? *Hacker in Love* is a steamy, funny, heart-pounding, **standalone** contemporary romance with a whole lot of feels, laughs, spice, and swoons.

Smitten

When aspiring singer-songwriter, Alessandra, meets Fish, the funny, adorable bass player of 22 Goats, sparks fly between the awkward pair. Fish tells Alessandra he's a "Goat called Fish who's hung like a bull. But not really. I'm actually really average." And Alessandra tells Fish, "There's nothing like a girl's first love." Alessandra thinks she's talking about a song when she makes her comment to Fish

—the first song she'd ever heard by 22 Goats, in fact. As she'll later find out, though, her "first love" was actually Fish. The Goat called Fish who, after that night, vowed to do anything to win her heart. SMITTEN is a true standalone romance.

Swoon

When Colin Beretta, the drummer of 22 Goats, is a groomsman at the wedding of his childhood best friend, Logan, he discovers Logan's kid sister, Amy, is all grown up. Colin tries to resist his attraction to Amy, but after a drunken kiss at the wedding reception, that's easier said than done. Swoon is a true standalone romance.

The Morgan Brothers

Read these standalones in any order about the brothers of Kat Morgan. Chronological reading order is below, but they are all complete stories. Note: you do not need to read any other books or series before jumping straight into reading about the Morgan boys.

Hero

The story of heroic firefighter, Colby Morgan. When catastrophe strikes Colby Morgan, will physical therapist Lydia save him . . . or will he save her?

Captain

The insta-love-to-enemies-to-lovers story of tattooed sex god, Ryan Morgan, and the woman he'd move heaven and earth to claim.

Ball Peen Hammer

A steamy, hilarious, friends-to-lovers romantic comedy about cocky-as-hell male stripper, Keane Morgan, and the sassy, smart young woman who brings him to his knees during a road trip.

Mister Bodyguard

The Morgans' beloved honorary brother, Zander Shaw, meets his match in the feisty pop star he's assigned to protect on tour.

ROCKSTAR

When the youngest Morgan brother, Dax Morgan, meets a mysterious woman who rocks his world, he must decide if pursuing her is worth risking it all. Be sure to check out four of Dax's original songs from ROCKSTAR, written and produced by Lauren, along with full music videos for the songs, on her website (www. laurenrowebooks.com) under the tab MUSIC FROM ROCKSTAR.

STANDALONE Rom Com Series

The Secret Note

Looking for a quickie?

He's a hot Aussie. I'm a girl who isn't shy about getting what she wants. The problem? Ben is my little brother's best friend. An exchange student who's heading back Down Under any day now. But I can't help myself. He's too hot to resist.

AND MANY MORE TO COME! STAY TUNED!

Misadventures Standalones **(unrelated standalones not within the above universe):**

- *Misadventures on the Night Shift* –A hotel night shift clerk encounters her teenage fantasy: rock star Lucas Ford. And combustion ensues.

- *Misadventures of a College Girl*—A spunky, virginal theater major meets a cocky football player at her first college party . . . and absolutely nothing goes according to plan for either of them.

- *Misadventures on the Rebound*—A spunky woman on the rebound meets a hot, mysterious stranger in a bar on her way to her five-year high school reunion in Las Vegas and what follows is a misadventure neither of them ever imagined.

Lauren's Dark Comedy/Psych Thriller Standalone

Countdown to Killing Kurtis

A young woman with big dreams and skeletons in her closet decides her porno-king husband must die in exactly a year. This is not a traditional romance, but it will most definitely keep you turning the pages and saying "WTF?" If you're looking for something a bit outside the box, with twists and turns, suspense, and dark humor, this is the book for you: a standalone psychological thriller/dark comedy with romantic elements.

AUTHOR BIOGRAPHY

Once you enter interconnected standalone romances of USA Today and internationally bestselling author Lauren Rowe's beloved and page-turning "Rowe-verse," you'll never want to leave. Find out why readers around the globe have fallen in love with all the characters in this world, including the Faradays, the Morgans and their besties, alpha mogul Reed Rivers and the artists signed to his record label, River Records.

Be sure to explore all the incredible spoiler-free bonus materials, including original music from the books, music videos, magazine covers and interviews, plus exclusive bonus scenes, all featured on Lauren's website at www.laurenrowebooks.com

To find out about Lauren's upcoming releases and giveaways, sign up for Lauren's emails here!

Lauren loves to hear from readers! Send Lauren an email from her website, say hi on Twitter, Instagram, or Facebook.

Made in the USA
Middletown, DE
23 May 2023